The Rapture has begun . . .

Several have already left. I am told this by their own families and friends. Some believe it so fervently and with such devotion that I am convinced something is certainly happening. The believers who keep vigil are locked in a room for the night. In the morning they are gone. I have examined the Vigil Room and there is no way in or out except for the one door. It is a small room without windows and with a floor that is a solid slab of cement. There is no way for these people to leave. And yet they do.

Brother Gabriel claims they have been lifted up into the Rapture.

Other Father Mark Townsend Mysteries by
Father Brad Reynolds, S.J.
from Avon Twilight

THE STORY KNIFE
A RITUAL DEATH
CRUEL SANCTUARY

DEADLY HARVEST

A FATHER MARK TOWNSEND MYSTERY

FATHER BRAD REYNOLDS, S. J.

AVON

TWILIGHT

AVON BOOKS, INC.
1350 Avenue of the Americas
New York, New York 10019

Copyright © 1999 by Father Brad Reynolds, S.J.
Published by arrangement with the author
Library of Congress Catalog Card Number: 99-94814
ISBN: 0-380-79844-1
www.avonbooks.com/twilight

First Avon Twilight Printing: October 1999

AVON TWILIGHT TRADEMARK REG. U.S. PAT. OFF. AND IN OTHER COUNTRIES, MARCA REGISTRADA, HECHO EN U.S.A.

Printed in the U.S.A.

WCD   10 9 8 7 6 5 4 3 2 1

A.M.D.G.

And for Pat Lee, S.J.,
who listens with his heart

ACKNOWLEDGMENTS

I am indebted to several people for the time and expertise they gave to this book. Those qualities that help move the story forward are largely due to them. Whatever mistakes appear are (unfortunately) largely due to me.

Thanks to Diana Guzman for pointing me in right directions, and Marvin Record, who taught me more about apple-growing than I could have learned from a dozen books. Mike Chamness, yet again, provided helpful background on police procedures.

For support, encouragement, and sage counsel I'm indebted to my agent at Curtis Brown, Ellen Geiger, and to my editor at Avon Books, Jennifer Sawyer Fisher.

I am especially grateful to Matt Miller. Not only did he offer helpful changes and additions to the story, but he provided more support and hope than he knows. I'm not sure this book would have been finished without him.

I'm also grateful for my Jesuit companions who continue to support this work. As always, my Provincial, Bob Grimm, gave me the time and encouragement needed. Ed Lopez assisted very early on and Mike Tyrrell and Roger Gillis helped as the end drew near. The real Jesuits working at St. Joseph's Church in Yakima were invaluable— particularly Neill Meany and Chuck Schmitz.

ONE

Quality control. What this virgin needs is a little quality control.

Angelina Sandoval Ybarra had a way with words. For the umpteenth time, Father Mark Townsend unfolded the woman's letter and read her strange, engaging message. *Mother Mary is making more appearances in the Yakima Valley than the Rolling Stones made on their last tour. And drawing crowds almost as big. She has appeared throughout the valley, from Selah down to Grandview. Each apparition is dramatic, unique and arresting, with only one thing lacking. Quality control. What this virgin needs is a little quality control.*

The priest shifted uncomfortably in his car seat and glanced out the side window. They were passing Issaquah, just beginning the climb toward Snoqualmie Pass. He wondered if Emily would make it. As if he could read the priest's thoughts, the car's driver cleared his throat.

"She loves a good challenge." Tim Connell patted the steering wheel. "Emily may have a lot of miles, but she's still good for the long haul."

Mark smiled kindly, but he had his doubts. The Volkswagen's engine sounded like it was about to fall out on the pavement behind them. And with the weight of both men and their luggage, he did wonder if the old car could make it up and over the high mountains in front of them. The Cascades held no danger of snow in August, but the climb was still steep and Connell's 1965 Volkswagen Beetle was already sucking air.

"Why'd you name it Emily?" Father Townsend asked.

"Dickinson." Connell offered the Jesuit a sly grin. "When I bought this beauty I was getting my master's at Seattle U., writing my thesis on Emily Dickinson. I thought it fit."

Mark glanced around at the car's shabby interior. There were tears in the fabric and a large diagonal dent in the dashboard. A nasty crack jogged like a secondary highway across the windshield. The broken backseat was littered with books, magazines, and old newspapers. The Beetle's exterior looked no better. The car's paint job, once a bright orange, was now faded and splotched with rust. There were more dings, scrapes, and dents than Mark could count.

" 'How frugal is the chariot that bears the human soul,' " Mark recited.

"You Jesuits!" Tim Connell's grin grew wide in appreciation. "Where'd you learn Dickinson?"

Connell was a handsome enough man, with a square jaw and bright blue eyes. His red hair was thinning and he wore it overly long in a vain attempt to cover the damage. In another year or two it would probably start looking silly, but for now Father Townsend thought it was okay. Tim's small frame fit inside the Beetle a lot better than his own. He had a disarming smile that made him look several years younger than his actual age, which the priest figured was about twenty-eight. Tim Connell taught English at a middle school in north Seattle and Mark imagined he was a popular teacher. According to his wife, Angelina, he had a weakness for beer. But Father Townsend had not been around the man enough to notice.

Tim and Angelina had joined St. Joseph parish four years ago, shortly before their marriage. They seemed like a nice enough couple, and Father Townsend had done what he could to introduce them and make them feel welcome. But the relationship between the couple and the parish had never quite clicked, at least to Father Townsend's thinking. There was always just a slight awkwardness to them, as if their Irish and Mexican backgrounds had never quite melded. They both went by their own last name, and as much as he tried, Father Townsend could never find a comfortable way of introducing the two. At their wedding he remembered asking the congregation to applaud the newlyweds, Timothy Connell and Angelina Sandoval Ybarra. Too many names with too many dissonant sounds. Even for a wordsmith as gifted as Emily Dickinson.

"How long has Angelina been in Yakima?"

Connell rolled his eyes. "Forever!" He squinted at the road rising up in front of them. Emily coughed daintily and Tim eased her over into the right lane. "That might be a slight exaggeration," he admitted. "She left Seattle on June eighth, the last week of school."

"That seems like a long time for just one article," the priest observed.

"Yeah, but it's a big one," Tim answered. "She thinks this might be the one to put her over the top."

"Meaning?"

"Make her career."

Father Townsend thought he detected a slight sour note in the man's reply. If so, it was not too surprising. Wedding rings do not prevent envy. He knew Tim Connell was a frustrated writer himself. The man had his master's degree, but was teaching English to seventh- and eighth-grade children while his glamorous wife got to travel the world as a freelance journalist, publishing articles in magazines and newspapers like *Atlantic Monthly*, *Harper's*, and the *New York Times*. To the Jesuit, that sounded pretty over the top already.

"Does she know where she'll publish the story?" Mark asked.

Tim shrugged his shoulders. "*New Yorker*, maybe. *Vanity Fair*. *Atlantic*. Depends on how she writes it. Her agent says the editors are already drooling." He leaned forward over the steering wheel, as if urging Emily to move faster. "It's got all the right stuff: mystery, suspense, religion, money, and the millennium. All that's missing is sex."

Mark heard a definite sour note that time, no doubt about it.

They were past North Bend and Emily was laboring. Tim kept her to the right as traffic streaked past them on the way to Snoqualmie's summit.

Father Townsend continued holding Angelina's letter in his hands, absentmindedly turning the folded pages over and over, staring out the car window as they rolled past dense forests of evergreens. Tim Connell was right. Her story did have the right stuff. The letter she wrote did not describe everything, but it contained enough to capture his interest. And not only capture it, but draw him out of Seattle, over the Cascades, and into the Yakima Valley. There was no doubt about it, Angelina Sandoval Ybarra had a way with words.

Father, I need your help. An opening line like that would grab any priest's attention. *There is much evil here, and I feel my life is in danger. Not only my life, but all that I hold dear and true. That includes my faith. I realize that I am asking a great deal, but I need to have you here.*

The Jesuits were once called the pope's storm troopers. Father Townsend did not have much use for labels, but it still managed to capture some of the Society's sense of purpose. If Ignatius Loyola, founder of the Jesuits, was willing to travel to Jerusalem for the sake of the faith, the least Mark Townsend could do was scrunch inside Emily for a three-hour ride to the Yakima Valley. Besides, a good friend was working there whom he had not seen in over a year. And in late August, St. Joseph was comatose. Most of the families at the parish were on vacation, as was most of the staff. The summer's wedding season was finally through and the school year had yet to start. Late August was the perfect time to escape the confines of his Capital Hill church for a couple of days of distraction. Especially if it could include helping a *dama* in distress.

Tim Connell's voice broke into Townsend's reverie.

"I'm sorry," the priest said, "I wasn't listening."

Connell nodded at the letter in Mark's hands. "I asked if you believe all that."

Mark lifted the letter. "Shouldn't I?"

"It's pretty dramatic, don't you think?"

Dramatic was an understatement. Angelina's letter was apocalyptic.

"Yes, it's dramatic. I don't see how the end of the world could sound anything but dramatic," Father Townsend replied. He stopped, as if waiting for Connell to disagree, then continued. "There's all sorts of predictions about the world ending. Especially now that we're getting closer to next year. Everyone knew the millennium would be like this. Just about every day there's a new prediction in the newspaper. Either a giant meteor is going to wipe us out or a spaceship is going to beam everyone aboard. I read a story the other day that said Noah's ark had mysteriously appeared floating in the Atlantic. The papers are full of this kind of stuff all the time."

"So why should this one be any different?"

"That's a good question," Mark conceded, looking down at the letter in his hand, turning it over once again. "Why should it?" he murmured.

There are moments when I feel my story is writing itself. I have no control. I do not know if anybody does. And Father, I fear the ending of it.

Angelina's letter described the article she was writing, a profile on a man who called himself Brother Gabriel. Although it was unclear what kind of a minister he was, there was no doubting his popularity. Since arriving in the valley a little over a year ago, Brother Gabriel had attracted a huge following, mostly Hispanics, but some Anglos, too. He refused to work in churches. All his preaching was under large tents in open fields or on the street in front of the established churches. Crowds of people swarmed around him as he warned of the End

Time and the coming of the Rapture. Angelina wrote that Brother Gabriel referred almost exclusively to the Bible's final chapter, the Book of Revelation, although he also spoke of private revelations.

The most disturbing part of her letter described two phenomena that were occurring in the valley. Apparitions of the Virgin Mary, particularly of the Lady of Guadalupe, were being reported up and down the valley. Wherever her image appeared, huge crowds assembled, followed closely by Brother Gabriel, who kept insisting she was there to help prepare the people for her Son's second coming. And according to Angelina, at the north end of the valley, outside of a small town called Cowiche, the Rapture had already begun.

Several have already departed. I am told this by their own families and friends. Some believe it so fervently and with such devotion that I am convinced something is certainly happening. The believers who keep vigil are locked in a room for the night and in the morning they are gone. Brother Gabriel's believers claim they have been lifted into the Rapture.

Father, I do not believe this for a minute. But I have examined the Vigil Room myself and there is no way in or out except through the one door. I have gone over every inch of the space. There is no other way for these people to leave. And yet they do.

The small car veered sharply and Father Townsend was thrown suddenly against the side door.

"Son of a bitch!" Tim exploded. A large semi was only a couple of yards in front of Emily, but pulling away fast. "That bastard pulled right in front of us!"

Mark had been looking down, intent on the letter, and never noticed the truck. Apparently, neither had Connell until it swerved into their lane. The Volkswagen was slowly creeping up a particularly steep grade of I-90, Washington state's main east-west highway. Fortunately, they were nearing the summit. Emily did not appear to have much energy left for the difficult climb and her forward progress had slowed to a poky forty miles per hour. Tim was hugging the far right lane as the rest of

the traffic zoomed past on their left. The passing truck
had cut back in too close.

Connell's face was a violent red and contorted in rage,
but the danger had passed and he was no longer cursing.
He looked over at the priest and tried to smile, but it
came off looking more like a grimace.

"I hate those things," he said. "They're so damn big
and they think they own the road. They could roll over
cars like Emily and leave nothing but a grease spot.
Pisses me off."

"I can tell," said Mark. Tim's sudden, intense fury
was startling. Father Townsend had seldom seen anyone's demeanor change as quickly and as dramatically.
He folded up the letter and put it in his shirt pocket,
studying his parishioner as if seeing him for the first
time. "Would you like me to drive for awhile?"

Tim shook his head, his attention still focused on the
truck disappearing around a curve in front of them. He
was biting on his lower lip. Father Townsend decided to
change the subject.

"I'm still not sure why your wife invited me along,"
he said, "although I don't mind coming. The priests at
the Jesuit parish in Yakima would give her any help she
needs. It's even called St. Joseph, just like home."

"And is there a Father Townsend at this St. Joseph?"
Connell did not wait for a reply. "Ange isn't a great
one for trust, Father. Maybe it's the reporter in her, but
she tends to confide in only a few select people. Ever
since we've joined the parish you've gone out of your
way to make us feel welcome. I guess we haven't said
it explicitly, but that's meant a lot. Ange and I don't
have a lot of friends. We stick to ourselves most of the
time."

The young man stopped and the silence felt awkward.

Mark tried feeding the conversation. "I thought you
are from Seattle?"

"I am. Angie was born in San Diego, although her
folks are Mexican. They crossed the border so she'd be
a U.S. citizen."

Mark remembered meeting the quiet, elderly couple

at the wedding. Angelina's parents spoke about as little English as Mark did Spanish, so their conversation together had been short and formal.

"What part of Seattle did you grow up in?" the priest asked.

"Edmonds, actually," Tim answered. "My mom taught at my grade school and my father taught at the high school. Which might help explain my lack of friends. When your parents are teachers at your own school, other kids don't hang around you too much. I guess coming over to our house felt too much like being at school. Anyway, I didn't make a lot of friends. And Angelina . . ." Tim paused and again the silence hung awkwardly. "Well, I guess . . . maybe her race is more of an obstacle than we'd like to think. But she hasn't made many friends either."

Angelina Sandoval Ybarra was a tall, slender, and strikingly handsome Chicana; bright, articulate and talented. Connell's accusation took the Jesuit by surprise.

"Do you really find that her race is an issue with people?"

The young man vigorously nodded his head. "Definitely." He pumped the gas and Emily gave a little shimmy. "For instance, last Sunday I was talking to someone after Mass and it felt really comfortable. Then Angie walked up and I introduced her. About a minute later the guy walked off. It was like he didn't know what to say to her."

"I'm sorry, Tim. That's disappointing to hear."

"Yeah. Well, it's not just at church, it happens all the time. We've talked about it and both of us can live with it. It's funny, but if there's just one of us, it doesn't seem as big a deal. Ange says she doesn't experience the same coldness from people as when we're together. I guess an Hispanic woman is easier to take if she's alone. But being married to an Anglo . . . that's something else."

"That's too bad," Mark said. "I imagine it puts a strain on both of you at times."

The young man nodded his head but added nothing. Another silence settled inside the car and both men became attentive to the labored wheezes of poor Emily, struggling the last half mile to the summit. Mountain peaks rose up all around them, and in the thin air the bright sunlight was startling in its brilliance. A steep mountain slope, covered by snow in the winter, was now blanketed with green grass and alpine flowers. Highway signs, pointing to ski slopes, announced the coming exits.

Tim Connell glanced at his watch. "It's nearly noon," he announced. "Should we pull off here for a bite or do you want to go on? We can stop at Cle Elum or go on into Ellensburg."

"It makes no difference to me," Father Townsend replied. "I'm not hungry yet."

"We'll go on," Tim decided, pushing harder on the gas, urging his small car ahead.

They reached the summit and the highway leveled momentarily. To their right they could see steep-roofed ski chalets among tall evergreens at the base of a ski slope that soared hundreds of feet above them. The skeletal frames of the chair lifts, now immobile and empty, traced their way up the mountainside from a central lodge just off the highway.

Tim's eyes were shining brightly with success. "We made it!" he crowed triumphantly, patting Emily's battered dashboard as if she were a trusty steed. "From now on," he happily proclaimed, "it's all downhill."

If he meant that as a prophecy, Father Townsend would have preferred they turn around and head back for Seattle. And if he had known what awaited them in Yakima, he might have insisted.

TWO

They were not through with the steep hills. After a quick stop for lunch in Ellensburg, they veered south and were immediately climbing the steep grades toward Umtanium Ridge. Once on the east side of the Cascade Mountains, the environment shifted dramatically. Cut off from the cold waters of the Pacific, the air was dry and hot; there was none of the lush greenery of the west side. Vast forests of fir trees gave way to open ranges of prairie grass and scrub pine. The terrain was hard, with none of the moist softness that so defines the land around Puget Sound. West of the Cascades was soft moss, mud, and green fern. On the east was rock, dirt, and sage. Westside, banana slugs; eastside, rattlesnakes.

The U.S. Army maintains a military reservation in the high hills of Umtanium Ridge. And the highway connecting Ellensburg and Yakima cuts through the western edge of their Yakima Firing Range. There is nothing to see from the highway. Any testing, training, or firing takes place well out of sight behind the dry, rolling hills.

The afternoon heat, coupled with Emily's sonorous whine and the double cheeseburger he had for lunch, lulled Mark to sleep. Volkswagens were not designed for napping, and the Jesuit had to scrunch his long legs tightly together, flattening his bushy brown hair against the side window as he leaned back and closed his eyes. Not yet forty, Father Townsend was only just beginning to show some of the strains of his work at St. Joseph parish. Small, shallow creases were starting to spread out from the corners of his gray eyes. His droopy, sandy brown mustache still showed no signs of graying, although a few early strands had appeared at his temples. He was still a handsome man, as evidenced by the attention paid him by some of his female parishioners.

He stirred in his sleep as Emily coughed. The battered Volkswagen lurched to the top of another dry hill and Father Townsend slowly awakened. Tim Connell's eyes were fixed on the road in front of them and Mark drowsily kept his own nearly closed. The highway was dipping back down, following a long, winding curve. In the hazy distance the priest could see another range of mountains, the snowy cap of Mount Adams poking over their tops. His eyes closed completely as Mark relaxed and let his thoughts drift.

He knew Tim had mixed feelings about his traveling to Yakima. He acted happy to have company on the drive over, although exactly why the priest was coming seemed as mystifying to Tim as it did to Mark. The summer's separation could not have been easy for the couple. Connell had already confessed that he was feeling nervous about reconnecting with his wife. While he was obviously deeply in love with her, he did not seem too secure in their relationship. Angelina was an independent woman, used to calling her own shots, and Father Townsend wondered how Connell dealt with that. During their lunch stop, Tim had talked about her frequent trips and how they left him feeling anxious. Although he did not address it directly, Mark had the impression Tim Connell did not consider himself as his wife's equal.

Connell had quietly admitted that their Capital Hill apartment was turning into a prison for him. More and more, he found himself seeking refuge in the microbrew pubs springing up around Seattle. He said he would wander around the empty rooms of their apartment until

noon, then bundle up a couple of notebooks and pens
and head out to "write." Father Townsend suspected
that meant there was usually a pint of porter, ale, or stout
in front of him. Tim Connell was spending Seattle's
summer searching for his inspiration in brewpubs while
all along she was a hundred and fifty miles and a mountain range away. If their marriage was indeed precarious,
then Angelina's invitation for Tim to join her in Yakima
was a hopeful sign for the couple. So Mark had no difficulty understanding why Tim had jumped at the opportunity, especially when she told him that she might
be in danger. Connell must have seen the trip as the
perfect opportunity to reunite with his wife.

About the only thing in their way, it seemed to Mark,
was himself. Why did Angelina feel she needed him in
Yakima too? Even when he pointed out to her that there
were perfectly good Jesuits already there, she continued
pressing him to accompany her husband. Eventually Father Townsend caved in. Angelina Sandoval Ybarra
could be most persuasive, especially when pursuing a
hot story. She was the type who let nothing stand in her
way, and would marshall every resource available if it
meant getting the story she wanted. Being talked into a
trip over to Yakima did not bother Mark too much. But
getting caught between Tim Connell and his wife was
something he did not want to do. Definitely not.

Mark stirred, opened his eyes, blinked and sat up,
groaning softly.

"You okay?"

"A cramp," the priest admitted, massaging his right
calf.

"Do you want to get out and stretch a minute?"

"Could we?"

Tim eased Emily onto the shoulder of the highway,
coasting to a stop and turning off the engine. There were
no other cars that they could see and it was eerily quiet.
Both men climbed out and stood at the side of the road.
The air was still and hot. At least when they were moving there was a breeze.

"Gotta be close to ninety degrees," Tim guessed.

"I think it's more than that," Mark told him. He was pacing back and forth along the side of the car. "I don't know how people can stand to live over here."

Tim agreed. "Pretty desolate country."

"It'll be a little better down below," Mark predicted, still pacing. "When we get into the valley we'll be in orchard country. It's kind of pretty, but still plenty hot."

They climbed back inside Emily and continued on their way. With Townsend now awake, Tim felt free to turn on the radio. He flipped the dial and immediately the car was pulsing with hot Latin music, trumpets and guitars competing for attention. Connell flipped again and a woeful Randy Travis filled the air.

"Your choice," he offered the priest, "salsa or CW."

The highway drops quickly out of the hills and into the upper end of Yakima Valley. From the top of the last high rise the two of them looked out over vast tracts of orchards quilting the valley floor in front of them.

Once in the valley, the highway caught up with the Yakima River and began following its twisted route as it snaked through the valley. The road skirted the town of Selah and, just before the Naches River joined the Yakima, squeezed through a narrow gap between two high hills, following a gentle curve that finished at the north end of Yakima itself. A railroad line ran along the opposite side of the river, heading toward the heart of downtown Yakima, which came into its own when the trains arrived. Long before Emily was even a gleam in her creator's eye, the Pacific Northern Railroad was supplying cattlemen and ranchers with easy access in and out of the valley.

Father Mark Townsend had not visited Yakima in years, so he was a little uncertain with his directions. He knew the Jesuit parish was near the center of the city and he pointed out the few tall buildings they could see from the highway. Finding St. Joseph Church was actually quite easy once they reached downtown. The church's tallest spire drew the Jesuit like lightning. Tim Connell nosed Emily up to the curb directly in front of the church. A sign next to a walkway pointed them toward the parish offices. The sign was in two languages, and the Spanish came first: *Bienvenido a San José*— Welcome to St. Joseph.

The young Chicana at the front desk offered a tentative smile as the two men approached. Tim and Mark were dressed for the road. Both wore blue jeans; Tim had on a T-shirt, and Mark was in a short-sleeved cotton shirt that was now sticking to his back. The girl's smile grew genuine when he identified himself as Father Townsend.

"Oh yes, Father," she spoke English with a heavy Mexican accent, "Father José said you were coming. I am very pleased to meet you, Father." She turned her attention to Tim next, but her voice was much more reserved. "Are you a Father also? They only told me there was one."

Connell shook his head. "No, I'm here to see my wife. Father Townsend rode over with me."

Relieved, she turned her attention back to the priest. "Let me tell Father José you are here." With that, she hurried down the hall. Moments later a loud voice cried out, "Hey, Mark! Come on back."

Townsend and Connell threaded their way past the desk and down the hall as the receptionist emerged from an office. "Please go in, Father," she said as she passed them.

Father Joe LaBelle was just standing up behind a cluttered desk when the two men entered. He greeted Mark Townsend with a bearhug and politely shook Tim Connell's hand.

"Have a seat," he urged them, gesturing to a couple of wingback chairs in front of a small coffee table. He dropped into a straightback chair that faced them. "Do you want anything to drink? A pop? Ice tea?" Both men declined.

Father LaBelle was six feet, seven inches tall, plus three more whenever he wore his cowboy boots, which was always. The man loomed over people and was so skinny he looked emaciated. His tanned hide was stretched tight over a framework of bones that looked devoid of even a pound of meat. His fellow Jesuits called him Bones. What hair he had left was cut down to white bristles that ran in a half crown around the sides of his head. His eyes shone brightly from behind thick rimless bifocals and he had a smile that stretched the length of the valley. Joe Bones had worked at St. Joe in Yakima his entire priestly life, which was fast approaching the forty-year mark. The fact that he spoke flawless Spanish practically guaranteed that the genial priest would finish out his career in the same place where he started. Whenever the possibility of a new assignment was raised, he always offered the same response. "Now why would you want to tinker with what ain't broke?" To date, no provincial superior had found an answer good enough to transfer him.

"So you're moving over here to join us, huh, Mark?" Bones thought the Vatican should relocate to Yakima. "You're making a wise choice, my friend."

"Don't I wish," Townsend sparred back. "But if I did, it would mean you moving over to Seattle."

Father LaBelle frowned deeply. "Seattle? That's over near Japan, isn't it?"

"Close, Bones, close. When was the last time you were in Seattle?"

"When was the World's Fair?" the older priest fired back, his mouth hanging open as if anxious to hear Mark's reply.

Townsend broke up. There was no way he would ever get the best of Joe Bones. Better men had tried.

"Actually, Joe, I'm here with Tim to visit his wife for just a couple of days."

LaBelle arched his eyebrows and looked askance. "And you're okay with this, young man? Do you know the kind of reputation this priest has? Is your wife pretty?"

"Don't listen to him, Tim. There's a good reason why Father LaBelle wears cowboy boots. Most of the people around him have to also." LaBelle was grinning, delighted to taste his own medicine. Mark continued,

"Tim's wife is a writer, Joe. You might have met her—Angelina Sandoval Ybarra? She's a niece of . . ."

"Luis and Rosa Castillo," LaBelle interrupted. "She comes to Mass with them on Sundays. Yes, I've met her." Turning to Tim once more, LaBelle waggled his head, "Your wife is not only pretty, but smart. And I would still suggest that you drive this man up into the Rattlesnake Hills and dump him on the side of the road."

A look of concern passed over Connell's face and LaBelle laughed out loud, delighted to get the response he wanted.

"Tim, ignore him," Father Townsend counseled. "It's the only way." Connell smiled weakly and Mark turned his attention back to his fellow Jesuit. "Angelina is writing a story about someone named Brother Gabriel. Do you know anything about him?"

"Plenty," LaBelle replied, tipping his head in the direction of the street. "He's been out there in front of the church about every weekend this summer, working the crowds as they leave Mass. He's got some idea that the end of the world is coming. Personally, I think Brother Gabriel is two cents shy of a nickel. But he's getting converts, that's for sure. Some of the folks are buying what he's selling and there hasn't been a thing I can say to change their minds."

"So you're losing parishioners?"

"Faster than a drowning dog sheds fleas," LaBelle rejoined. "And these so-called apparitions aren't helping things."

Tim Connell entered the conversation. "You're talking about the appearances by Our Lady of Guadalupe?"

"That's right."

"But I always thought that was a Catholic devotion, Father."

"You can call me Joe if you want to, Tim. And yes, Guadalupe is a Catholic tradition. But Bro Gabe has signed on to her big time. He wears a white alb and this big old cape with her picture on it. The guy's cagey. If you want to attract a lot of Hispanic Catholics to your cause, all you've got to do is start yelling Guadalupe. I don't know how he does it, but there've been sightings of her everywhere around here. Of course that always draws a big crowd, and then Brother Gabriel is right there to tell 'em what it means. The theological sophistication of some of our believers being what it is, they sign up with Gabriel and go off to wait for the Rapture. It's driving our poor bishop crazy.''

''There's nothing you can do about him?'' Townsend asked.

''Well,'' LaBelle drawled, a small smile edging onto his face, ''if the Rapture does come, we're all praying the good Lord takes Bro Gabe first. Or else he convinces his holy mother to go visit someplace else for awhile. Fatima or Lourdes would be just great—anywhere but the Yakima Valley.''

Despite his joking, it was apparent to Father Townsend that LaBelle was truly worried about the effect the evangelist was having on parishioners. Bones was not the kind of man to let too much bother him, but this obviously was.

''What kind of numbers are you talking, Joe?''

''Parishioners?'' His face grew somber. ''I'd guess that in the last three months we've probably lost ten or fifteen families. It's hard to say exactly, because there are so many migrants that come through for the harvests. But among our regulars there's been a definite decline. Old Father Stanley is beside himself.''

Father Paul Stanley was the assistant pastor at St. Joseph and had lived in Yakima even longer than LaBelle. Although in his eighties, the old priest still celebrated Masses and assisted with some of the parish duties. Nearly blind, he performed most of the church rituals from memory. Whenever he thought he could get away with it, he conveniently forgot any of the changes introduced by the Catholic Church in the past forty years. Then when he was reminded and asked to observe them, Father Stanley complained that ''the print's too small.'' He would have little tolerance for a Brother Gabriel, with or without the Virgin's accompaniment.

"How is Paul's health?" Mark asked.

"He's like a piece of old leather," LaBelle complained. "He's stiff and unbending and he smells, but you can't quite bring yourself to get rid of him. I appointed Brother Dennis to be his keeper and he's doing his best to steer Paul around and stop him from getting into too much trouble."

Brother Dennis Grib was in his first year at Yakima, a young Jesuit still in training, just turned twenty-four. Because he had expressed an interest in working with Hispanics, his superiors assigned the young religious to Yakima. Doubtless, Brother Grib had not expected his job description would include watching over the tenacious Father Stanley. Townsend wondered how long it would last.

"They're both over at the house," Joe Bones said, "if you want to get settled in." He stood slowly, stretching to his full height above his two visitors. "Tim, if you haven't seen your wife in awhile, I don't imagine I should be offering you a room in a house full of celibates. But you're welcome to stay with us if you like."

"Thank you, Father . . . Joe, but I think Ange is expecting me. In fact, if you don't mind, I'll give her a call and let her know we're here."

Father LaBelle showed him the phone and how to dial an outside line, then the two priests left him to make his call. LaBelle led the way outside and they stopped to wait in front of the church.

"You figured out why she wants you over here yet?"

Townsend shook his head. "Tim says it's because she trusts me. But all she told me was that she needed help with the religious side of her story."

The gentle giant next to him laid a long, heavy arm across his shoulder. His voice grew soft and low. "You be careful, Mark. There's something about this business that smells worse than Friday's fish on Sunday. Gabriel has a lot of folks behind him, and some of them are pretty powerful. I've heard that when you join his flock you make an offering of everything you own as a kind of testimony of your good will and freedom from earthly possessions. That's a great idea, but I haven't seen Gabe sharing the goodies. I don't know what he's planning to do with all that money when the Rapture comes. It makes you kind of wonder.''

The afternoon sun was beating down on them and Mark Townsend could feel himself beginning to sweat. He shifted uncomfortably. Bones stood at ease, apparently unaffected by the heat.

''I don't plan on being here long enough to get involved,'' Mark told him. ''This was just an excuse to get out of Seattle for a couple of days. I'll do what I can to help Angelina with her story, but then I'm going home. If there's going to be a Rapture, I want to be in Seattle when it comes. It's too hot over here.''

''Think of it as getting your time in purgatory out of the way,'' Bones suggested. ''That won't make you feel any cooler, but it gives you a little more reason to stay.''

''Maybe for you,'' Mark rejoined, ''but I'd just as soon put off purgatory until later. Besides, this feels hotter than that.''

The tall priest chuckled. ''That it is, Father. That it is.''

His phone call completed, Tim Connell joined them in front of the church. His face looked a bit more relaxed than when the priests left him. Obviously, he had gotten through to his wife.

''Angie says hi,'' he told Father Townsend, ''and she's looking forward to seeing you. I'm going to drive out to her uncle's place now. They've invited you for dinner if you want. You too, Father Joe.''

Both priests declined. Joe LaBelle had a prior engagement and Mark begged off, saying he wanted to visit with the other Jesuits. What he really wanted was to find an air-conditioned room and take a nap, but he let that go unsaid. Instead, he promised to meet the couple later in the evening, after dinner. With that decided, LaBelle dismissed the two of them with a casual wave and sauntered back into the parish office. They climbed back into Emily for the short ride to the Jesuit residence. Although the house was only a block away, Mark had no desire to haul his suitcase in the heat when a ride was at hand. At Mark's direction, Tim pulled into the drive next to the back door.

"I'd invite you in for a cold drink," Mark said as he got out, "but I'm guessing you'd rather take off."

Tim handed him his suitcase out of the front trunk. "If you don't mind," he agreed. "I'm kind of anxious to get out there."

"I understand perfectly," Mark replied. An air conditioner's hum would lull him to sleep before Tim reached the highway.

"Father." Connell halted before climbing back in his car. "Ange asked me to tell you that you should watch who you talk to." He paused, obviously uncomfortable. "She sounded kind of worried."

Now it was the priest's turn to hesitate. "Do you think I ought to go with you?"

"No, that's not necessary," Tim said, reassuringly. "She just said to be careful."

"I don't plan on going anywhere or seeing anyone," Mark told him. "Just the guys here at the house. And what could happen in a Jesuit house?"

THREE

"Satan's fire is licking at the doors of St. Peter's and no one is doing a blessed thing about it!"

Fortunately, dinner was nearly finished. Unfortunately, Father Stanley was not.

"Who is going to expel the demons? Answer me that!" There was no time to draw a breath, let alone answer, before he was off again. "Satan has penetrated the Vatican, including the pontifical palace itself. The secretariats, the congregations, the nunicatures, and those so-called bishops conferences are firmly in his grasp."

Father Stanley leaned across the dining table to shake a bony finger in their visitor's face. His own was bright red.

"I tell you, Father, from the sanctuaries and basilicas to every government power, including that most pagan of institutions, the U.N., there is not one place that is not possessed. Our Blessed Lady is making it abundantly clear that unless we are willing to exorcise Satan from our midst—and yes, that includes the Vatican—this world will suffer a fiery and tormented end. On that one point, Brother Gabriel is right. But on everything else, the man is Satan's spawn."

Brother Dennis Grib choked, then gasped for breath

and grabbed for his glass of milk. Mark could not tell
if the young religious was choking from laughter or
alarm, but he reached over and patted him on the back.
Dennis smiled appreciatively at him with tears in his
eyes. "Thanks," he managed.

Mark could see that Father Stanley had failed to notice Brother Grib's crisis, but he broke off his diatribe
long enough to scoop another spoonful of peas into his
mouth. The pork chop on his plate was untouched, as
were the mashed potatoes. While both the priest and the
brother were filling their mouths, Father Stanley was
taking the opportunity to educate them.

"The powers of hell will never bring down the
Church! On that you can stake your life, Father. Nevertheless, Mary has predicted the loss of faith and the
lack of charity we are seeing in our churches today.
Even here in Yakima. If more priests were only willing
to preach about the vision of hell, that would shake these
naive people's belief in universal salvation."

Mark was trying his best to follow the old priest's
arguments. But he had missed out on the nap he had so
deliciously imagined and instead, for the past two and a
half hours, had endured Stanley's ravings. Brother Dennis tried his best to derail the old cleric, especially at the
start, before he had gained a full head of steam, but to
no avail. This train was bound for glory and anything in
its way was doomed to hell.

Mark waited for the next spoonful of peas.

"You still haven't said whether you believe these appearances by our Lady of Guadalupe are real or not. The
ones here in the valley?"

Father Stanley chomped his peas, then lifted his water
glass for a drink. His sight might be going, but Mark
knew that he could hear just fine.

"Father Stanley?" he nudged.

The old priest shrank back in his seat and glared. "By
their gifts you shall know them," he snarled. "You look
at Fatima, Lourdes, Medjugorje—wherever our blessed
mother sanctifies with her presence there is peace and
there are conversions back to the Church. If she is here

in the valley, then we should expect those same wondrous gifts. To date, I have yet to see them.''

"So you think they're a hoax?''

Father Stanley squirmed in his chair and blinked my-
opically at Mark's face. "I'm ready for my dessert,'' he
demanded.

Brother Grib obediently pushed back his chair and
began to clear the table. Mark stood to help.

"Please, sit down, Father. You're our guest. *Hospes
venit, Christus venit.* Brother can get the dishes. Tell me
about your parish in Seattle.''

Dennis Grib whispered as he bent over to clear his
place, "It's okay, Mark, don't worry about it.''

Mark leaned back in his chair. "What would you like
to know, Father? St. Joe's is doing fine. We've got a lot
of young families moving into the parish, and that's giving us a lot of life.''

Father Stanley nodded his head in approval. "Young
families are the hope of the church,'' he intoned, "as
long as they are taught to remain faithful to its teachings.
But there is so much evil placed in front of them as
obstacles: birth control, abortion, divorce—these tear at
the very seams of family life, Father.''

There was a loud crash in the kitchen and the sound
of breaking plates. Mark jumped up.

"I'd better see if Brother needs help,'' he said over
his shoulder.

Dennis Grib was scraping gravy and mashed potatoes
off the floor and smiled apologetically as Mark knelt
down to help.

"Sorry about this.''

"It'll clean right up,'' Mark assured him.

"No, I mean about Paul. He's on a roll tonight and
I'm sorry that you're getting the brunt of it. Some days
he's fine and then something sets him off and there's
nothing you can do. I'm sorry.''

"It's all right, Dennis.'' Mark helped him stack the
rest of the dishes in the sink. "I'm just here for a couple
of days; you've got to live with him. Are you doing
okay?''

"Yeah," he nodded, "most of the time. This first year started out a little lonely, but I'm meeting people and getting out more. Paul is a good man but hung up about some things. I guess that comes with getting old, huh?"

Father Townsend could not tell if he was being lumped as a contemporary of Stanley's or if the kid was just looking for agreement. He answered with a noncommittal nod.

"Anyway, I think the provincial is getting ready to move him. When he started writing letters to bishops and cardinals about exorcising the Vatican, the prov got some phone calls about him. I keep warning Paul that they're going to yank him out of here, but he doesn't listen."

For all the abuse the young Brother seemed to be taking, he appeared genuinely concerned about the old priest. Perhaps there was even some affection. Mark was impressed.

"I'll bet you never thought you'd be assigned as a lion tamer, did you?"

Dennis shook his head. "He's usually not that difficult. Most days I spend ninety percent of my time with the Hispanics and ten percent with Paul. It's only on these off days that he demands a hundred and twenty percent."

Father Townsend was meeting Angelina and Tim in the lounge of a downtown hotel at eight o'clock. Brother Grib offered to drop him off, but the priest decided to walk the half mile. There had been no time for himself during the day and he wanted a little quiet to think. The sky was still bright when he left the house and the temperature had not dropped more than a few degrees. He could feel the heat radiating off the brick buildings as he strolled through town. There were still plenty of shoppers and people wandering the streets. By the time Mark found his way into the dark hotel lounge, he was fifteen minutes late. He was hot and sweaty and the coolness of the air-conditioned room hit him like an arctic blast. He would be lucky not to catch a cold. Tim and Angelina were sitting in a back corner and Connell waved when he spotted the priest. Both stood to greet him.

"Angelina, it's good to see you." Mark gave her a light hug, which she returned.

"Father, I can't tell you how good it is to see you!"

Angelina Sandoval Ybarra was tall and slender and the top of her black hair brushed against the bottom of Mark's nose. He caught the scent of wild flowers and honey, either her perfume or her shampoo. Despite the coolness of the room, her skin was warm as he held her. She was dressed in light tan slacks and a white cotton blouse that drew out her coloring. Angelina used clothes like she did words, simply but with a beguiling elegance. She was a beautiful lady, as every man in the room was quick to notice, and Tim stood close to her side, an expression of unadulterated pride on his face. Connell appeared quite content, as if he had gotten the nap that Mark had wanted.

Sensing that his thoughts might be headed for a minefield, Father Townsend plopped into a chair while the couple settled across from him. A waitress appeared at their table and, seeing the schooners in front of Tim and Angelina, Mark asked for something local. She suggested a Grant's, which sounded fine. As she took his order, Tim Connell drained the remainder of his glass and ordered another, too. She returned with their drinks in amazingly short order.

"So, tell me how you've been," Mark said to Angelina when the waitress left.

She gave him a small smile. "I am better for having you two here." She wrapped her arms around one of her husband's and clasped his hand. "But it has been difficult, especially these last two weeks."

Mark tentatively sipped his beer; definitely a good choice. "How so?"

The Chicana shook her long hair back and raised her chin. "I think Brother Gabriel has started taking an interest in me," she told the priest. "And I am not sure what it means."

Father Townsend watched as Tim Connell released

his wife's hand and reached for his schooner of beer. His face was an open book and consternation was written all over it.

"Does Brother Gabriel know you are doing a story on him?"

"Oh, yes," Angelina replied. "The first time I met him I said that I was interested in his ministry and his message and that I wanted to write a story on his impact in the valley. He has known that from the beginning."

"And that's okay?"

"Not at first, no. He stayed very distant and would not talk directly to me. He refused to give me an interview. But when he saw I was not going to go away, he began to change a little bit and then to smile when I would come around. Actually, I think he is quite a shy man and is not so used to attention. But now"—she paused long enough to sip her beer—"he is never left alone. He is like Jesus."

"Ange!" Tim protested. "Don't you think that's just a slight exaggeration?"

She dipped her head prettily and looked thoughtfully at her husband. "Perhaps," she admitted, "but wherever he goes, crowds follow him. And there are some who claim he is curing sickness. I have not seen that myself, but I have heard it mentioned."

From the other side of the room someone began to play a piano, a melody light and dreamy. The sound distracted Townsend as he strained to recognize the tune. Finally he remembered Jimmy Durante's version: "As Time Goes By." There was some movie that had used it. Mark took another swallow of his beer.

"And then there are the raptures," Angelina continued, lightly shrugging her shoulders. "How can you explain those?"

"Those raptures!" There was a new note of belligerence in Tim's voice.

His wife caught it and stared at her husband before answering. "There are people who have left. Just disappeared. Brother says they were raptured."

"That's ridiculous!" Connell protested, draining the last of his schooner. He raised an arm high over his head and waved into the darkness until a waitress appeared.

Mark waited until she had left with Tim's empty glass. "What does that mean, Angelina?"

She leaned across the small table, giving the priest her full attention, ignoring Tim's presence at her side.

"They disappear," she said simply. "At night they keep vigil and in the morning they are gone. There is a place in Cowiche, west of here, that some of Gabriel's supporters gave to him. They added a building they call the Vigil Room." Connell snorted. His wife glanced over at him, then continued, but still speaking directly to Father Townsend. "I have been inside several times," she said. "Once, for a night with some of the vigil keepers. Nothing happened then, but on other nights the vigil keepers are raptured. They just disappear." Her eyes widened and she released a small, embarrassed laugh.

"There's no way in hell," Tim Connell proclaimed. He was already halfway through the new schooner. "That's a bunch of . . ."

"Tim!" Angelina scolded her husband. "I have been in there and you haven't. These people are gone. I have interviewed their families and friends and no one has seen them. Don't tell me what I know to be true!"

"It's a trick, Angie!"

"You tell me how, then." Her dark eyes flashed angrily. "Tell me how! The Vigil Room is a separate building, made of concrete block, and the floor is solid cement. There are no windows, only small air vents up on top. And just one door that they lock from the outside. Now you tell me how it is a trick. Where do they go?"

"To hell," her husband grumped, looking into the bottom of his empty glass. "They go to hell!"

Mark was listening intently as the couple argued, pulling at the sides of his mustache as he tried imagining the room Angelina described. "What about the roof," he asked. "Could there be a trap door?"

"Father, I have looked over every inch for one. *Hay nada.* There is nothing that I could find."

"And this Brother Gabriel, he says the people, these 'vigil keepers,' are raptured?"

She nodded. "In the morning they unlock the door and inside there is no one. Only their shoes are left."

"Their shoes?"

"*Sí.* There are benches, and on the floor in front of them, pairs of shoes. But no sign of the people who wore them."

"Raptured right outta their shoes!" Connell's voice was growing loud and brash and he was signalling for the waitress again.

"Sssshhhh," his wife hissed, "you are sounding foolish."

Tim swallowed a belch as he handed his glass to a young woman who looked like she was shivering in her short skirt and thin blouse. "Not as foolish as your story."

"Every word is true. I know there must be some rational explanation, but I have not found it. And the people up there, as much as I can tell, seem devoted and sincere. They are true believers, of that I am certain."

"How does Brother Gabriel fit in with these apparitions of Mary?" Father Townsend asked her. "The way you described it in your letter sounded bizarre. *This virgin needs a little quality control.*"

Hearing her letter quoted was flattering, and a look of pleasure passed across her face.

"It is true," she told the priest. "She is appearing everywhere, and in most unusual circumstances. First it was on the back of a highway sign. Engineers for the state said it was just some sort of coating sprayed on as protection against the weather. I have seen pictures of the sign, and there was the definite outline of the Lady of Guadalupe, with all the right colors. If it was just a spray, then it was an incredible coincidence. It would be like somebody spattering paint and reproducing a Mona Lisa by accident.

"So many people began going onto the highway to

see her that the police had to direct traffic. The sign post was surrounded by flowers and candles, *veladoras*, and there were people always there to pray and say rosaries. This went on for several weeks.''

"Then what happened?''

"It went away,'' she told Mark. ''One day the image was just gone. Some believed that highway workers washed the sign. But if they did, no one saw them do it.''

"And Brother Gabriel? Where does he fit in?''

"Ah, *sí*,'' she took a small sip from her beer. ''Brother Gabriel believes our Lady is here to warn us that the end is coming. He is convinced this is true and he is telling his followers not to think Mary is only a mother for Catholics. If her Son is for everyone, he says, then so is she. He is quite insistent on this, even though some of his people have a hard time with that belief. They are not used to thinking about Mary.''

Mark was still confused. ''But what's his basis for saying this?''

"*Con permiso*,'' Angelina said, picking up her purse. She pulled out a long, narrow reporter's notebook. ''I need my notes, so I can explain to you.'' Quickly, she rifled through pages filled with her small handwriting. ''I know it is here,'' she murmured softly, ''I asked him this only the other day.''

Tim Connell had fallen silent, leaning far back in his chair, looking disdainfully at Mark and his wife. The schooner never left his hand and was never far from his lips. He was well on his way to visions of his own.

"Yes,'' his wife said, ''here it is.'' Her lips moved silently for a few moments, then she began to read aloud to Mark. ''He says it is in Revelation, in chapter twelve.'' Angelina's eyes scanned her notes. ''The sign of a woman clothed with the sun . . . moon under her feet, with a crown of stars . . . Ah, yes, this is it. Brother says there is a prediction that she will flee into the desert, to a place prepared for her by God, where she will remain for twelve hundred and sixty days.''

Father Townsend was nodding as he listened. The

opening verses of that chapter were familiar to him. They were filled with graphic images of a dramatic battle between heaven's angels and a huge serpent identified as Satan. The serpent tries to drown the woman hiding in the desert by spewing water from its mouth, but when that fails, a wild beast rises out of the water to wreak havoc on the world.

Angelina was still consulting her notes. "According to Brother Gabriel, Mary's appearances here mean that this is the desert place where she is hiding. He says when the twelve hundred and sixty days are over that the world will end."

"That's three and a half years," Townsend remarked. "But starting from when?"

The woman shrugged. "That is what Brother is trying to discover. He told me he came to Yakima Valley after this truth was revealed to him, but that the Virgin was already here. So maybe a year has already gone by. Maybe more."

"And Mary keeps appearing?"

"*Sí.*" She nodded decisively. "First it was on that sign, as I said. But now people see her everywhere. In Cowiche, they cut an apple tree in an orchard, and in the trunk where they cut, there was a perfect image of our Lady's head, with her hands folded in front of her. I have seen this one, too. Then in Sunnyside, her image was found on a tortilla."

She caught Mark's widening smile and answered with one of her own. "I know," she said defensively, "but I am telling you what has happened. Then there was the peach found by a picker, very small but shaped exactly like a statue of Mary. A baby was born in Grandview with a birthmark on her back in the shape of the Lady of Guadalupe. And in Toppenish, on a mural of Indians fishing, Mary was in the mist rising from the river. With that one, hundreds of people stayed in a park across the street. Brother Gabriel said this was from the Scriptures, the part where the devil tried to drown the woman. This was also before I came, but I have interviewed people who saw it. That was the appearance when Brother got most of his followers. He stayed in the park and read them the Bible passages and convinced many of the truth of his words.''

"Sounds like you're buying his shit, too, honey." Tim Connell's voice was slurred and rude. Angelina glanced over at her husband and then pointedly shifted in her chair, blocking him from her sight. If he felt slighted, Tim gave no sign of it but continued sipping his beer, lapsing back into silence. His wife rolled her eyes at Father Townsend but said nothing.

"From the way you're describing it," Mark said, "there's no way this man could be causing all those things."

Angelina nodded.

"I mean, the tree trunk and the baby's birthmark . . . those things can't be faked. At least not that I can figure." Father Townsend was pulling hard on his mustache, his features knotted in thought. "So it sounds like Brother Gabriel is capitalizing on some natural phenomena."

"What about shupernatural?" chirped Tim. The other two ignored him.

"What surprises me," continued Mark, "is that people are willing to believe him."

Angelina closed her notebook and tucked it back in her purse. "You have to realize, Father, most of his followers are Mexican laborers—*campesinos*. Yes, he does have some Anglos who believe him, but for the most part they are people working in the orchards or warehouses. Many are migrants and most are not well educated. What Brother Gabriel is saying is not so hard for them to believe."

Father Townsend was listening intently. He recognized the truth in what the young woman was telling him. When you are working hard, living a difficult life and gaining very little, the promise of happiness in a newer life must sound alluring. Karl Marx called religion the opiate of the masses, and to the degree that it eases pain, Mark had to agree that he was probably right.

"Angelina, why did you ask me to come here? You

seem to be getting what you need for your story. It's nice to get a little break from the parish, but why did you want me here?''

"Father Mark, do you believe God can send certain people just so they can communicate something to someone else? Maybe you do not understand, but I feel God sends us messages in our lives and sometimes that is through other people. Before she died, my grandmother gave me such a message about loving Tim." Angelina turned briefly to gaze at her dozing husband. "Well, I believe Brother Gabriel was sent to communicate such a message to me. I do not know what, but that is why I wanted you here. Because, Father, I am afraid of Gabriel's message for me."

The lounge was cold anyway, so the chill Mark felt could just have easily come from the air conditioning, but the fear in his parishioner's eyes was unmistakable. Whatever this woman was expecting to happen had her terrified. Mark reached over and laid a reassuring hand on her arm. He felt and saw a shiver course through her body.

"Okay, I'm here," he said. "So now tell me more about Brother Gabriel. Is he Hispanic himself?"

Angelina Sandoval Ybarra's eyes grew wide with disbelief and she laid one hand across her breast.

"You do not know? No, Father, he is white. Only more so."

"Meaning?"

"My pardon, but I thought you knew. Brother Gabriel is albino."

FOUR

The Jesuit residence was quiet when Mark returned. Someone had left the porch light on for him, but inside the house it was as dark as the night outside. Father Townsend eased the latch into place and heard the soft click of the lock. From one of the bedrooms up the stairs he could hear snoring. The red glow of a digital clock read 12:18. He had left the lounge about an hour earlier, once Angelina ran out of things she wanted to tell him. But his clothes reeked of cigarette smoke and his head was aching from all that she had told him, so Mark Townsend wandered up and down the streets of Yakima, trying to air both his clothes and his head.

The temperature had finally dropped. But the air was dry, so much different than Seattle's. On the other side of the mountains, the air seemed to penetrate inside you, grabbing at your muscles. But in Yakima, it stayed on the surface of your skin, and the light breeze felt like cool silk sheets brushing against you. There was a sensual, intoxicating feel to this air that bespoke of green grasses and ripe orchards and full moons. Mark was in no hurry to go back to his room and so he wandered.

Angelina was clearly afraid, but no matter what he asked her, she was unable to come up with any solid answer as to why or what. Her fear was the kind that replaces your heart, leaving you with something inside your chest that feels vague and worried. She told him she was not sleeping well, that her thoughts were becoming confused.

"I am afraid Brother Gabriel may have gotten inside my soul," she whispered to the priest.

Tim Connell slept through the last part of their conversation, his chair pushed back into the corner, legs extended, and head slumped onto his chest. At one point his wife apologized to Mark for her husband's behavior. She was concerned by how much he was drinking, she told Father Townsend. Even before coming to the lounge, he had drunk four or five beers with her uncle Luis. But with Tim asleep, Angelina seemed much freer to talk.

She tried to describe her feelings for the strange evangelist she was profiling. Hers was an odd mix of revulsion and attraction. So much about the man seemed abnormal. And yet, she explained, there was a gentleness to him. Angelina was convinced that Brother Gabriel truly believed in what he was saying.

His heart is pure, she told the priest, and he is sincere. I know that what he saying is not true, but I am convinced that he believes it is. Father Townsend wondered if she was talking about self-delusion.

"No, that is not it."

But she seemed unable to come up with the words to describe exactly what she meant. She tried "misguided faith," saying it over and over several times before finally rejecting it. That was not exactly it, either. She told Father Townsend she would keep trying.

Her description of Brother Gabriel bothered the priest, and much of his wandering around Yakima was taken up with trying to visualize the evangelist's strange appearance. Angelina told him that Brother Gabriel was only thirty-two, although his long white hair and pale soft skin made him look like a man much, much older. His skin, she said, was almost translucent, like white parchment. And she described his clothes much the same way Joe Bones had. He wore a long white robe that he cinched at his waist with a knotted cord of rope. When he went out in public, he put on a long cape made of pale blue silk. Across the back, in colored threads, was stitched a replica of Our Lady of Guadalupe; the image of Mary with the olive-complected features of a young Mexican woman, draped in a long blue-green mantle studded with golden stars, and standing on top of a quarter-moon, supported on the arms of an angel. From behind her emanated the sun's luminous rays. No matter where Brother Gabriel appeared, dressed in garb like that he was guaranteed to become the focus of attention.

Mark Townsend moved quietly through the darkened living room, cautiously avoiding the furniture, and then into a smaller room used by the Jesuits to house their television and sparse library. He clicked on a floor lamp and began searching the bookshelves. He found several translations of the Bible, including some in Spanish, on a shelf at waist level. Mark chose the New American and perched onto the edge of the couch in front of the TV, opening the Bible on the coffee table in front of him. Quickly flipping to the back of the book, he found Revelation and the passage he was searching for.

> *I saw seven lampstands of gold, and among the lampstands One like a son of Man wearing an ankle-length robe, with a sash of gold about his breast. The hair of his head was as white as snow-white wool and his eyes blazed like fire.*

Brother Gabriel might be suffering from self-delusion or misguided faith, but one thing was certainly clear; he had his role down pat. Mark closed the book and leaned back against the couch. Bones thought the man was two cents shy of a nickel, and Angelina believed he was a messenger sent specifically for her. No matter what he turned out to be, Father Townsend was increasingly anxious to meet this most unusual man.

He glanced at his watch. If things went as Angelina predicted, that would happen in less than twelve hours. Luis and Rosa Castillo, Angelina's aunt and uncle, were the *padrinos* for a young girl celebrating her *quince-añera* at ten in the morning. The ceremony was unfa-miliar in his own St. Joseph parish back in Seattle, but Father Townsend knew that a *quinceañera* was a tradi-tion for young Hispanic girls turning fifteen—a type of coming-out celebration that was partly religious and partly social. With many of the same trappings as a wed-ding, it was nearly as significant, at least for the young girl and her family. As the honored godparents, or *pad-rinos*, Luis and Rosa Castillo were intimately involved in the celebration, not only by their presence, but by their financial assistance. Mark was to meet Angelina, Tim, and the Castillos in front of St. Joseph Church at nine-thirty in the morning. For an event of such impor-tance, Brother Gabriel was almost certain to be in po-sition on the sidewalk across the street from the church. And if he was, Angelina promised to find some way of introducing Father Townsend to Brother Gabriel.

"It is important to me that you meet him, Father. I need you to understand." And with that last enigmatic comment, she stood, lightly brushed his cheek with her lips, then roused her sleeping husband. Together they guided a sloppy Tim Connell to Angelina's Chevy Blazer. Mark declined her offer of a lift back to St. Jo-seph and instead, waited until they drove off and then began his wandering through the nearly deserted streets of downtown Yakima.

Jesuits call themselves contemplatives in action. There was one industrious member who claimed they had only two speeds: fast forward and stop. The trick for most of the men is learning to balance the two; to remain ac-tively engaged in the work, yet with enough personal composure and spiritual savvy to stay attentive to inte-rior movements. It is sort of like riding a bicycle through traffic, keeping alert to what you are doing and to what is going on around you while still enjoying the ride. There was not much traffic to worry about on Yakima's streets at midnight, but Mark had plenty to contemplate.

If Brother Gabriel truly did see himself as some sort of prophetic figure sent to herald the end of the world, then his actions were in keeping with his role. Pointing to signs and wonders and interpreting them for the masses are part of a prophet's charism. But unfortunately, in the hands of religious charlatans and hustlers, the same charism becomes a ruse. Angelina assured Mark that Brother Gabriel did not seem overly concerned with what his followers did with their material goods, as long as he felt they were prepared for the coming Rapture. Most of his flock did not own much of real value anyway, she reminded him. But it did not seem to matter to the evangelist if they gave it away, left it to family and friends, or donated it to Brother Gabriel's movement. The important thing, he told his followers, was to possess an interior freedom from anything on earth that might become an anchor. If you feel weighed down or possessed by your belongings then it is nearly impossible to be lifted up, he warned them. People can get entangled with what they own, with relationships, with their reputations, and those entanglements are like strong ropes attached to heavy anchors. And they will weigh you down just as surely.

With a message like that, Mark had no doubts Brother Gabriel was quite persuasive, especially if he had someone like the Lady of Guadalupe backing him up. He closed the Bible and wearily lifted himself off the couch. The day was going to be another long one; first with the ceremonies in the church, and then the fiesta at Luis and Rosa's. Angelina had already warned him that a *quinceañera* celebration could run into the wee hours of the morning. Father Townsend's little three-day vacation was looking more exhausting than if he had just stayed on the job in Seattle. But one thing was already clear, things were a lot more intriguing on this side of the mountains.

FIVE

Paul Stanley's loud voice woke him. Mark rolled onto his back and lay staring at the ceiling. His small room was bright with sunlight and he could hear the old priest's angry voice rising through the floor from the kitchen below. His words were not clear, but the tone certainly was. Mark could also make out Father La-Belle's laconic response, followed by Brother Grib's placating voice. Judging by the sound of things, the rest of the community was already wide awake. He rolled over, checked his watch, and groaned. Six forty-five is too early when you are on vacation. But still, when in Rome you do as the Romans, and he supposed the same was true in Yakima. Mark flung back the sheet and forced himself up.

Twenty-five minutes later, showered and shaved, he descended into the kitchen to find all three Jesuits still at the kitchen table. Each was engrossed in a section of newspaper, their empty glasses, cups, and dishes pushed aside, as well as their earlier discussion.

"So look what's finally up!" Bones proclaimed. "Good morning, Father!"

Dennis Grib pushed himself back from the table and began clearing a spot. "Can I get you some coffee?"

"Don't worry, Dennis, I'm a big boy. Just point me to the cups and I'll get my own."

Father Stanley said nothing, his attention and eyes riveted on the paper he held about two inches in front of his face.

"So how was your evening with the fair Angelina?" Joe Bones asked. "Did she catch you up to date?"

Mark told him about their conversation in the lounge as he fixed himself a bowl of cereal. He left out Tim Connell's gradual but steady deterioration but wondered to himself how the man would feel this morning. He would find out soon enough.

"Which of you is doing the *quinceañera*?" he asked, addressing the two priests.

Father Stanley rustled his newspaper and, after waiting a moment to see if he was going to speak, Bones replied.

"Both of us," he said firmly. "We were discussing that just before you came down. Paul and I will concelebrate the Mass."

Whatever their disagreement, Mark did not want to get into the middle of it.

"Maybe Father Townsend wants to join me, too," Father Stanley snarled. "Perhaps one supervisor won't be enough."

Whether he wanted to be or not, it appeared Mark was already in the fray. Joe LaBelle opened his mouth, considered a moment, then closed it. He refused to take the bait.

"My Spanish isn't that good, I'm afraid," Mark replied before the pastor had time to reconsider. "If you don't mind, I'll sit this one out."

Father Stanley lowered his paper and smiled sweetly at their visitor. "Oh, I don't mind at all, Father. In fact, I think that's rather sensible. We don't need to clutter up the sanctuary with any more clergy."

Dennis Grib gave Mark a broad grin. "The fathers are a bit feisty this morning," he explained. "Both want to celebrate Yolanda's *quinceañera,* but not together. It's what we here in Yakima call a Mexican standoff."

"Silence, impertinent pup!" Bones bellowed. "We don't air our dirty laundry in front of Seattle mossy-backs."

"Gosh, Father LaBelle," Mark was playing the innocent, "I thought this was Peaceful Valley over here. But when I woke up this morning I thought Mount St. Helen's was erupting again."

Father Stanley shook his paper and buried his nose even further inside it. None of this was the least bit funny. Bones raised his eyebrows in warning. Unless they wanted another eruption, it was time to play down the humor.

"You're going out to the Castillo's ranch afterward, aren't you?" he asked Mark.

Townsend nodded. "I'll catch a ride with Tim and Angelina, but maybe I can come back with one of you."

"We'll have two cars," Joe said. "Dennis and Paul will ride out together and I'll bring mine, too. Just let one of us know."

"What's proper attire? Clericals?"

"They're fine," Bones replied. "Or slacks and a sportshirt at the party. A lot of people will still be dressed up, but some of them change before the real party begins. So your blacks or mufti, it doesn't matter."

"Last night, Angelina said she thought Brother Gabriel would show up."

"Not into the church!" Father Stanley tossed his newspaper on the table. "Not into St. Joseph's!"

"I don't think that's what she meant, Father. She meant that he'd show up out in front somewhere, but no, not in the church."

Dennis chimed in. "He usually stands across the street from the front entrance. If he's there you won't have any problem spotting him. He sticks out like the pope in all that white clothing."

Father Stanley opened his mouth to object. Mark could see him preparing to argue, but after he thought a moment, the old priest shrugged and went back to his paper.

*   *   *

The Jesuits' breakfast club adjourned soon afterward. Dennis went over to the parish to assist with last-minute decorating and Bones wandered back upstairs to work on his homily for the Mass. Father Stanley, carrying his breviary, headed out the door. In good weather he liked to circle the block while he prayed. The neighbors had grown quite used to the sight of the old cleric hunched over his prayerbook, mumbling to himself as he wandered along the familiar sidewalk. Father Stanley was part of living under the shadow of Yakima's oldest church, just like church bells tolling the hour and heavy traffic on Sunday morning.

With no pastoral duties, Mark Townsend also headed out the door. The morning was still cool enough to walk and he set off in the opposite direction of downtown. Before he was ordained, and while still in studies, he had enrolled in an homiletics class taught by a popular Jesuit professor known equally for his brilliant lectures and the garish outfits he wore in the classroom. He used to lecture to the Jesuit scholastics while wearing a baseball cap with wings that sprouted from both sides. When he squeezed a bulb hidden in his pocket the wings would flap back and forth. Someone once asked the venerable old sage why he wore the stupid hat.

"For attention," he answered. "If you believe that your message is important enough that your listeners cannot afford to miss it, then you must do whatever is necessary first to capture and then to keep their attention. My hat is purely for attention." But then, eyes twinkling, he added, "Besides, I like the wings."

As part of his course each semester, the Jesuit professor took his students on a field trip to one of the city's Catholic churches. They never drove directly to the church. When they were still six or seven blocks away, the priest made the bus driver stop and let everybody off to walk the rest of the way. He waited until he had his class assembled in the back pews of the empty church before he explained his reason.

"Whenever you arrive to preach at a parish where you have never been, do not dare presume to step into their pulpit without knowing something about the people to whom you will be preaching. That is the height of clerical arrogance, gentlemen. The least you can do is arrive a few minutes early and spend some time becoming acquainted with your surroundings. Walk past their houses and look into their yards. Greet anyone you see and ask them how they are doing. Listen to their voices and observe how they are dressed. If there are billboards or signs about, read them. Learn five things about the people in that church before you dare say one word about how they should live their lives or love their God.''

Then, by way of example, he grilled the young Jesuits for the next fifteen minutes, asking them to describe what they had learned on their walk to the church. Was the neighborhood old or new? What kind of vehicles were parked in the street? Did you see many young children? How many old people were there? If you heard any music, what kind was it? What nationalities did you notice? How were the people dressed?

That professor's course was the most popular one at the school. And that field trip was the single most useful and practical experience of all Mark's years of studies.

The neighborhood he wandered through that morning in Yakima was a mix of older wooden homes, solidly built but modest in size. Mixed among them were newer, cheaply constructed apartment houses. The few cars that he could see were mostly older, almost all of them American-made. There was an occasional van and some battered pickups parked in driveways or along the street. The yards were neat enough, often with young children's toys strewn about. Despite Yakima's heat, there were very few air conditioners that Mark could see, and through the windows that were left open, he heard the music and voices of the people inside. The sounds were almost all Spanish; Latin music and loud, lilting voices speaking so rapidly that he could only catch an occasional word or two of what was being said.

Eight out of every ten faces he saw were brown. They were either very young or very old. Mark saw very few men. When he passed the children playing near the sidewalk, they stopped what they were doing and solemnly watched the tall stranger as he strolled past. Old women, sitting in the shade of their porches, studied him closely as he approached. Occasionally they nodded as he passed and some would even offer a shy, hesitant smile. Neither Mark nor they spoke any words of greeting, merely nodding instead.

"All right, gentlemen, that's enough. Time for a little quiz. Five things that you have learned, please. Mr. Townsend?"

Most of the neighborhood is Mexican. "Rather obvious, but please continue." The neighborhood is in transition and the population is shifting from white to brown. The people living around here are a mixture of field laborers and lower middle class. There is pride in what they have already accomplished by getting this far, but many are living here in fear. "And why would that be, Mr. Townsend?" Because they are here illegally.

"So now tell me, what message do you have for these people?"

It was also the most difficult class Mark had ever attended.

His walk and memories had carried him much further than he had intended. And once back at the house, Father Townsend had no time to waste. He was due to meet Tim and Angelina in half an hour. No one else seemed to be around as he dashed up the stairs to change in his room. The sun had grown hotter as he walked and he would have liked to take another shower before putting on his black pants and shirt. But wearing black clothes in a hot church would make it an exercise in futility and there was no time anyway. Mark slipped the white plastic collar into his shirt and sat on the bed to tie his black shoes. Reluctantly, he donned his suit coat. He would have preferred to leave it off in this heat, but Angelina had explained that most of the guests would dress as if attending a wedding. The priest stopped in front of the mirror and gazed at himself. The hair could use trimming, as could the mustache. And there was a spot on his right sleeve. He brushed at it impatiently. He could hear the clock downstairs as it began to chime. He was out of time and he stepped away from the mirror. Like it or not, this would have to do.

SIX

St. Joseph Church was lifted from the volcanic rock
that shapes the heights overlooking Yakima Valley. The
dark, dense basalt, carved into blocks for the tall church
walls, was quarried around the high bluffs near Cowiche.
The valley's Catholic ranchers and business leaders were
determined to raise an edifice as solid and firm as their
own futures. By 1900, Yakima firmly dominated as the
valley's hub, a position that was secured with the arrival
of the railroad. Cattlemen could now drive their herds
to Yakima and ship their livestock out of the valley with
ease. But a few who could read the signs of the times
were already selling off their herds and converting pas-
tures into orchards.

The generation of early pioneers was past, and what
were once dreams of a tamed and settled valley were
now real and solid as rock. These people wanted their
church just as solid, one that neither the forces of hell
nor anything else could ever prevail against. The dark
gray stone church that loomed in front of Father Townsend was a monument, a witness, and a silent challenge
to all those who approached it.

The ceremony was not due to begin for another
twenty-five minutes, but already cars and pickups were
angling into the curb in front of the church, people in

their Sunday best climbing out and heading toward St. Joseph's wide wooden doors. Many were stopping on the steps to greet friends and to visit, sharing a last cigarette before going inside. Their voices drifted across the street on the clear morning air as Mark approached. The only language he could hear spoken was Spanish. Suddenly, he felt woefully unprepared. He knew that the very first word out of his mouth would betray him as a gringo who did not belong there. Mark was walking into a cultural and social occasion where he had no business being. For a Jesuit priest, dressed like one and walking toward a Jesuit parish, it was an unsettling experience. And for a moment, he considered turning back.

"Padre! Padre Mark!"

He lifted his head and saw Angelina waving to him from the church's top step. Heads turned and looked his way. Mark's white skin began to itch, but he kept his eyes fixed on Angelina's smile and bravely crossed the street. That smile and her voice rising over the crowd's meant that he was welcome. He continued toward her as people stepped aside, nodding respectfully to the priest. He heard murmurs of welcome as he passed. *Hola, Padre. Buenos días. ¿Como se va?* Father Townsend did not trust himself to reply, but merely smiled. What Spanish he knew fit into one summer of an intensive language school and an intermediate class the following semester. Both were over fifteen years ago and he had done nothing to retain, let alone expand, what limited skills he once had. Despite the mandate that all Jesuits learn a second language, Mark had found plenty of excuses to avoid doing so. For that omission, he was about to pay.

A short, squat woman in a dark blue silk dress blocked his path. Her eyes and smiles were wide as she grabbed his hand and clasped it in both of hers.

"Padre, está bien verte aquí con nosotros esta mañana. Qué bueno que hayas venido para acompañarnos."

He had no clue what the woman was saying. Father Townsend was fumbling for a response when he felt another presence at his side.

Angelina intervened, gently laying her hands on the short woman's arms. *"Tía Rosa, el padre no comprende el español. Necesitas hablar con el en inglés."* She turned to Mark. "Father Townsend, this is my Aunt Rosa. She wants you to know how happy she is to have you here. She is so happy that she forgets which language she is speaking."

"Sí," Rosa said, still beaming. "Yes, it is true. But you are most welcome, Father. We are honored that you have come." She squeezed and pumped his hand and continued smiling.

"Gracias, Rosa. Muchas gracias." As responses go, it was about as mundane as you could get. But judging by Rosa's gasp of appreciation, you would have thought the Jesuit was quoting Octavio Paz.

"Come and meet my husband," she entreated the priest. She was still grasping his hand and now began tugging him toward a knot of people closer to the door. Rosa pulled him next to a man dressed in a black tuxedo and stopped.

"Luis," she commanded, *"pon atención."* Then, switching to English, "This is Padre Mark, Angelina's priest from Seattle. Padre, this is my husband, Luis Castillo."

The two men shook hands. Castillo was a powerful-looking man and he had a handshake to match his looks. He stood almost six feet tall, with a barrel chest and solid build. His upper arms strained against the material of his tuxedo's jacket and he seemed uncomfortable to find himself dressed in such an outfit. Both Luis and Rosa appeared to be in their early sixties. The man had short gray hair and a full gray mustache that was even more bristly than Father Townsend's. His glossy black cowboy boots were studded with silver toe guards and in his lapel he wore a tiny pink rosebud.

"It is a pleasure to meet you, Father. Angelina has told us much about you. You are very kind to come to Yolanda's *quinceañera.*"

The girl celebrating her fifteenth year was named Yolanda Flores. Angelina had explained a complicated fa-

milial relationship between the Flores and Castillos in
the lounge last night, but Mark had failed to retain most
of it. He did recall that Luis and Rosa Castillo were the
wealthy side of the family, which was why they were
invited to become Yolanda's primary godparents, what
Angelina called *los padrinos de velación*.

Luis Castillo had started out as a *bracero*—a farm
laborer—emigrating with his young wife from Mexico
in the late 1940s. For their first ten years they moved
around the valley, living mostly in the shabby camps
established for Mexican migrants. Eventually Luis found
permanent employment with a hop grower near a small
community called Moxee. By living simply and saving
every dime they could, the Castillos were finally able to
purchase ten acres near the highway. When their parcel
of land was chosen as the site for a large discount store,
Luis and Rosa gleefully sold it. And with the money
from that sale, they were able to buy fifteen acres in the
hills overlooking Moxee where they planted grape vineyards and settled into a comfortable life. Within the Hispanic community, Luis and Rosa Castillo were respected
as one of the early successes. There were many young
couples living in shanty camps on the valley floor who
knew the marvelous story of *Señor y Señora Castillo*.
Their fortunate lives fed the dreams of many young campesinos still climbing orchard ladders.

With introductions now completed, Angelina guided
Father Townsend toward the church's front door. Tim
was on his way, she explained. Her husband was a little
slow getting up this morning, she said, arching one of
her painted eyebrows. There was no need for either of
them to comment further. Mark followed the young
woman into the dark church. She was dressed simply
yet elegantly. For the occasion, Angelina had chosen a
rather severe suit of black crepe that was cut tight
against her slim body. The effect though, was voluptu-
ous. Her shiny black hair was pulled back into a tight
bun and around her neck she wore a chain of silver. Her
earrings were made of black onyx, surrounded by small
white diamonds, and on the velvet lapel of her jacket

she wore a matching pin. She had lightly dusted her cheeks with blush and wore dark lipstick the color of a rich and plummy merlot. Angelina Sandoval Ybarra was easily the most beautiful woman inside St. Joseph Church that morning.

Decorations for the *quinceañera* began at the doorway leading from the vestibule into the church. An archway of white and pink roses, with tidy clusters of baby's breath, was tied with white and pink ribbons that cascaded down to the floor.

"Yolanda's parents will escort her through the *arco* during the procession," explained Angelina as they passed beneath it. They paused to dip their fingers in the font of water and to sign themselves, the woman repeating the sign of the cross onto her head and shoulders three times before kissing her fingertips. She led him up the main aisle, about two-thirds of the way, then genuflected and slipped into a pew. "Tim will just have to look for us," she said in a half-whisper.

The church was filling quickly as couples and families of all ages filed into the pews. As they entered, practically everyone made the same multiple signs of the cross as Angelina, touching their fingers to their lips at the end. There was a hushed tone of reverence in the church, although that did not prevent people from pausing to hug and greet friends and relations. They moved about the pews, talking among themselves in quiet voices. Father Townsend settled back against the hard wood of the bench, took two deep breaths to relax, and watched the pageantry unfold.

As the young woman at his side predicted, most of the people had come as if dressed for a wedding. Many of the older women wore long black skirts and white blouses. The younger ones teetered into church on high spike heels, looking lovely in tight dresses bright with color. The men looked handsome and uncomfortable. Almost all of them wore something similar, tan slacks or pressed black jeans held up with wide belts and silver buckles the size of playing cards. They wore starched white cowboy shirts and stringy bolero ties with ornate clasps, often made of silver or turquoise. The smallest children were the most fancily dressed of all. Baby girls clung to their mother's hands in stiff, ruffled dresses and small straw hats festooned with ribbons and flowers. On their feet they had lacy stockings inside black patent shoes. Small boys twitched and squirmed inside scratchy black slacks and long-sleeved white shirts. Their hair was slicked back and the cowboy boots they wore were miniature versions of their father's, right down to the silver tips on the toes.

There was a general hum of excitement as six members of a mariachi band began warming up at the right side of the sanctuary. They self-consciously tuned their guitars as one of the trumpet players nervously tootled a few trial notes. Dressed as classic mariachis, they had on tight black pants and matching jackets trimmed in silver braid. The fronts of their shirts were nearly hidden by billowy silver *corbatas*. There were two trumpets, three guitars, and one violin. An old man, his white hair pulled back into a ponytail, was the leader and clutched the violin. He stood in the center as the others arranged themselves in a half-circle around him. They poised expectantly, holding their instruments. Mark glanced at his watch and saw it was five after ten. Bones had predicted they would not start on time.

People were still streaming into the church and down the aisles. The long wooden pews were almost filled. Angelina squirmed and turned nervously in her seat to scan the back of the church. "Timeo," she murmured, "where are you?"

Compared to his own St. Joseph back in Seattle, Mark found the sanctuary of this one cramped and cluttered with altars and statuary. The main and two side altars were ornately carved affairs, white and gold-leafed, with pointy spires soaring up to the church's vaulted ceiling. Frescoes covered the upper portion of the sanctuary. On one side, Jesus was calming angry seas while on the other, he missioned his disciples. A third image, in the exact center, had the Lord seated in triumph with one hand raised. But the tallest cross atop the high altar loomed directly in front, partially hiding the figure of Jesus. So the hand raised in benign benediction actually looked more like he was waving for attention from behind the altar's cross. "Here I am. Up here!"

"Sorry I'm late." A disheveled Tim Connell squeezed past Mark's long legs and flopped down on the opposite side of his wife. He offered her a sheepish and apologetic grin just as the music began with a blast from the trumpets. Angelina distractedly reached up to straighten his tie. She kissed him lightly as they stood and turned to watch the procession.

First down the aisle were fourteen young men, most of them no more than fifteen or sixteen years old. Each one looked like a groom, dressed in a tuxedo with a tiny pink rosebud in the lapel. They marched proudly to the front in two lines, their eyes fixed straight ahead, chins out. Once in position, they turned inward, facing each other across the aisle.

Angelina leaned into Mark. "Those are the *chambelánes*," she informed him. "Like best men. The girls are called *las damas*."

As she spoke, the fourteen young girls processed past them, their pale pink dresses brushing the floor. The bouquets they clasped were made of pink roses.

They were followed by the five couples Yolanda had chosen as her *padrinos*. The last in line were Rosa and Luis. Then came the girl herself, flanked by her mother and father. Yolanda was small for her age and looked quite timid, almost frightened of all the attention. She wore a white gown of lace and silk with a belt of pink ribbon that was tied in back with a bow that trailed down to the floor. White and pink ribbons were threaded among the long black curls cascading over her shoulders. She wore white gloves that tightly clutched her bouquet of fifteen roses, and her large eyes peered shyly through long dark lashes as she walked hesitantly but steadily down the long aisle with her proud parents. The people on both sides smiled approvingly as she passed.

The two Jesuit priests processed in behind them, both wearing white chasubles. Bones stood tall and erect,

beaming in delight, nodding to familiar faces and sometimes reaching out to grasp a hand or pat a back. Father
Stanley marched beside him, slightly stooped, with
hands tightly clasped and eyes firmly fixed on the
ground in front of him, wearing a scowl he intended to
look reverential. Mark Townsend swept his eyes over
the crowded church, searching for Brother Grib. He
caught sight of the young Jesuit standing on the far side
near the front, a happy smile illuminating his face.

Members of the procession filed into the pews reserved for them and the two priests mounted the steps
into the sanctuary, bowing first, kissing the altar, then
turning to face the congregation just as the mariachis
blasted a loud, final chord and quit. After the loud, tu-
multuous music, the silence in the church sounded deaf-
ening. Bones paused a brief moment and smiled at the
crowd before loudly signing himself: *"En el nombre del
Padre, y del Hijo, y del Espíritu Santo."*

There remain holdouts in the Catholic Church who
bemoan the loss of Latin, the language universal. One
of their top ten laments is that no matter where you were
in the world, you could attend a Mass and feel immediately at home. The ritual celebration used to be the
same in language, hymns, and gestures, no matter where
you traveled. But for Father Townsend, hearing the Mass
in different languages seemed like an incredible experience of universality itself. Whether it was standing
bundled inside a fur parka in a frozen church in an Alas-
kan Eskimo village while listening to the gospel read in
Yup'ik, or sweltering inside this one for the *quinceañera*
of a teenage girl he had never met, Mark experienced
the availability of the faith to all cultures.

The founder of the Jesuit order, Ignatius Loyola, no
stranger to foreign cultures himself, urged his men to
stay adaptable. In Jesuit terms it was referred to as inculturation. Instead of working to convert cultural values
and traditions to align with Christianity's, inculturation
meant entering into a people's traditions to discover and
proclaim the universal values that were harmonious with
Christianity's. Straddling someone else's culture while

remaining true to your own at the same time can be a high-wire act. Keeping your balance is never easy, and not everyone makes it. Jesuit history is spattered with the remains of well-intentioned men who lost their balance and slipped off one side or the other.

Joe Bones had already explained to Mark that the *quinceañera* itself was a good example of the church adapting values from other cultural traditions. The tradition of initiating girls who reached *quince años,* fifteen years, was traced back to Aztec and Mayan religious ceremonies.

"Four hundred years ago, they were puberty rites," LaBelle bluntly informed him. "Back then, Paul and I would be wearing feathers instead of chasubles and we'd be waving bones and shells over the girl. It was powerful medicine back then, and a way of alerting the community that this girl was ripe for making baby warriors." Father LaBelle's exegesis left little to the imagination. "You don't just do away with stuff like that," he told Townsend, "you adapt. That's what this whole wingding is about."

Father Townsend watched as the small, nervous Yolanda Flores knelt down on a silk pillow placed on the kneeler in front of the altar. Times and traditions change. This fifteen-year-old girl was no more prepared to bear a child than her ancient Aztec sisters could have worked a computer. Yet there were universal truths that spanned across the centuries. Mark studied the girl's parents, their loving eyes riveted on their young daughter, their faces glowing with pride. Some things never change.

The *padrinos* presented the girl with her symbolic gifts, each couple stepping forward in turn, offering their gift for the priests' blessing before bending over the teenage girl to make the presentation. The first couple placed a medal of the Lady of Guadalupe around Yolanda's neck. The second put a rosary in her hands. A younger couple, the mother holding a newborn baby in her arms, came forward to present Yolanda with a prayer book. The next ones slipped a ring onto her finger. Finally, the Castillos came up and placed a silver crown on the young girl's head. Luis stood awkwardly to one side as Rosa fussed, making sure the crown was anchored to Yolanda's thick curls.

Most of the people in the pews were attentive to the ceremony in front, with the exception of the children. Bored by too much sitting and unable to see over the heads of the adults, they waited for a chance to make their escape. All through the service half a dozen youngsters roamed the aisles, finding the people in other pews a lot more intriguing than the ones they had left. Parents followed the liturgy with one eye while keeping the other fixed on their child. If the youngster strayed too far away he was dragged back to his own pew, usually shrieking in protest. Some were still arriving at the church, wandering through the aisles, looking for an empty space. The constant noise and movement was so different from the quiet stillness at Seattle's St. Joseph, and during a lull in the liturgy Father Townsend caught himself wondering what the reaction would be if he were to transfer this kind of event back into his Capital Hill parish.

But he knew the setting would be wrong. The church in Yakima was thick with saints. In the front stood a large statue of Jesus, flanked by two smaller ones of St. Ignatius and St. Francis Xavier. Just those three were already more than his church in Seattle held. And then there was a tall statue of Mary, flanked by smaller ones of St. Theresa and St. Martin de Porres, and off to the side was a nearly life-size Pieta, racks of vigil candles flickering in front of it. While overhead, a choir of frescoed angels, hands clasped piously to their chests, gazed down from their clouds onto Yolanda Flores kneeling in front of the altar, the children running in the aisles, the parents pursuing them, the late-comers, the mariachi band, the priests and the people in the crowded pews. Mark caught himself grinning. Seattle was not quite ready for this, he decided.

The ceremony ended after Yolanda laid her bouquet of roses at the feet of the Lady of Guadalupe. She knelt in prayer for a few moments, then returned to her place in front of Father LaBelle and Father Stanley. The pony-tailed grandfather tapped a four-count with his boot and the mariachis blasted into their recessional song. Yolanda, trailed by her proud parents, led the procession out of church.

The aisles quickly filled with people as they pressed toward the doors and Mark, Angelina and Tim stood waiting their turn.

Angelina turned to the priest. "So, Father, what did you think?"

"If I were a fifteen-year-old girl," Mark began, "that would probably be one of the biggest things to ever happen to me. Certainly it's something I'd never forget."

"No, you never do," the woman admitted. She glanced over at her husband. "It is like your wedding."

"So what happens now?" asked Tim.

"Now we go back to the farm."

"This is for the party, right?" Obviously, Tim knew as little about *quinceañera* celebrations as Mark.

"What about Brother Gabriel?" Father Townsend asked Tim. "Did you see him?"

"Not when I came in," replied Tim. "There was a bunch of guys standing across the street, but no one like Angie described. I think I would have noticed him if he was there."

"*Sí*," his wife agreed. "If he was there, you would have seen him."

They were edging toward the front door, nearing the arch of flowers stretched over the entrance. Mark raised his head, trying to see above the crowd. But there were too many in front of them and they were still too far back in the church. They continued inching ahead. With the liturgy ended, voices were raised and the church was filled with the loud sounds of laughter and friends calling to one another. Mark had a hard time hearing Angelina over the din.

"What? Did you say something?"

"I said if Brother is out there, do you want to meet him?"

He hesitated. There was a natural curiosity to see this

personality everyone was talking about. But did it extend far enough that Mark wanted to shake the man's hand and make conversation? What do you say to someone who believes the end of the world is around the corner? About the last thing Father Townsend needed was a prolonged or heated theological exchange. He was ready for a party, not a debate. And the idea of standing in the hot sun, listening to someone in white robes describing the Rapture was not high on his list. At times, wearing the Roman collar can be a real hazard. That square inch of white plastic just below the chin acts like some sort of supernatural beacon that transmits signals indecipherable to normal ears. But every zealot with tinfoil in his hat or messages from archangels hears it loud and clear. They hone in like bees to honey. Mark had been stung more times than he could count. And usually it was at events like this, when all he wanted to do was relax and have some fun.

Angelina was still waiting for his response.

"I think I'd like to change my clothes first," he finally told her, pulling his black shirt away from his skin. "This suit is already sticking to me."

Angelina nodded sympathetically. "I know," she said, looking down at her black crepe dress. "Me, too. But maybe you could first say hello and then go change your clothes. If he is outside, this would be convenient."

Father Townsend acquiesced. After all, he had come to Yakima to support Angelina. And besides, he would have to pass right by the man to return to his house.

They were near the front entrance and bright sunlight spilled through the open doors, nearly blinding those approaching from inside the dark church. Father Townsend turned his head and squinted as they neared the doors. The heat from outside was pushing against him like an invisible wall. If it were not for the horde of people pressing from behind, he would have been tempted to turn back toward the dark coolness inside.

Just outside the entrance stood Yolanda with her parents and godparents. Most of the guests were filing past to congratulate them, shaking their hands and exchanging a few words. Which helped explain why people were backed up inside the church. Once in the vestibule, Angelina took charge. "Come with me," she said over her shoulder, veering away from the main entrance toward a side door. Others who decided to bypass the receiving line were also slipping out the sides and the three of them followed their lead.

The sunlight was blinding when he stepped out the door, and Father Townsend put his hand up to shield his eyes from the bright glare. As he did, he caught sight of a white brilliance across the street. Brother Gabriel's radiant clothing and his mane of white hair caught the sunlight and seemed to pull it in to himself. The man was shimmering with the energy of the sun. People's eyes were naturally drawn toward the light emanating from him. On the church steps, Yolanda Flores's white dress was a pale moon compared to Brother Gabriel's sun across the way. Even those pausing to speak to the teenage girl were turning their head to gaze on the man. Fortunately, the young girl was too caught up in her own excitement to notice she was losing to the competition.

About three dozen followers were clustered behind and to the sides of Brother Gabriel. Almost all were Hispanic. They stretched out in a loose line facing the church, standing in vigil. Their eyes were fixed on the people leaving the church and they were smiling. A few were engaged in conversations with some of the people coming from the *quinceañera*. They looked relaxed and seemed attentive to what was being said. Brother Gabriel kept his own eyes fixed on the church front, watching the people intently. Only his head and hands were exposed, and his skin looked translucent.

Father Townsend heard Tim Connell mutter behind him, "Christ, would you look at him! You weren't kidding, Ange."

From across the road, Brother Gabriel's eyes swept the crowded church steps. His head stopped moving and his eyes appeared to lock onto Mark's. Or maybe it was the collar. But he clearly and definitely gave a slow and solemn nod toward the priest. Or so it seemed. In the

heat, the crowd, and the noise, Father Townsend was
having a difficult time. He felt light-headed and disoriented. The voices all around him were loud but he was
unable to understand anything anyone was saying. Confused, he turned around, as if to head back into the dark
church. But Angelina grasped his hand. Her grip felt
cool and dry and Mark held her hand tightly, almost
afraid to let go.

"Come on, Father," she urged, leading him down the
steps, "I want you to meet Brother Gabriel."

SEVEN

The evangelist was smiling as the three of them approached. Angelina led the way, her hand still tightly holding Mark's. Her husband followed behind.

Father Townsend could feel himself pulled forward, as if drawn by some force toward the strange man. In large part it was because of his appearance. Never had he seen anyone who projected such radiance. His clothing was immaculately white. He was wearing a long white cotton robe that was tied at the waist by slim bright yellow cord. Mark recognized the man's costume right away. He had on an alb and cincture, the same vestments a priest wears at Mass. And over his alb, Brother Gabriel had draped what looked like a cope—the cape worn during Benediction. This one, however, was handmade and simpler. The material was shaped to drape over the shoulders and hang loosely along the sides of the body. At the neck, a simple gold clasp held it in place. Mark could not see the back, but he knew it displayed the image of Guadalupe that Angelina had described. Brother Gabriel stood no more than five foot six and appeared quite thin. His age was impossible to guess, although Angelina had told Mark he was in his early thirties. But with the white hair that hung nearly to his shoulders, he looked considerably older. He made no movement toward them as they approached, but continued smiling warmly, his eyes never leaving their faces. As they drew closer, Mark was arrested by his eyes. They seemed in constant motion, not moving so much as twitching. The sunlight must have been painful to him. He looked through half-closed eyelids that continuously fluttered, as if trying to close once and for all. Brother Gabriel waited until they were standing directly in front of him before speaking.

"Angie, it is nice to see you." He spoke with a soft lisp and his voice was surprisingly high. Mark had expected something deep and resonant. The preacher's eyes looked into the priest's. "Your friend is here, I see."

"And this is my husband, Tim." She stepped to one side, revealing the man standing behind her.

"Yes." Brother Gabriel extended his right hand and held Tim's for a brief moment before turning his attention back to Father Townsend. They shook hands. Gabriel's grip was firm and, unlike with Tim, he held the priest's hand in his for several seconds.

"I am pleased to know you, Father Townsend. Angie has told me that you are a holy man." He closed his eyes and nodded his head as if agreeing with his own statement.

Mark did not know how to respond to his strange greeting. But apparently a response was not expected. Brother Gabriel opened his eyes and smiled happily at the priest.

"You have come here with many questions," the man continued. "And not without some doubts. Angie has already described my ministry to you. But as you suspect, it is nearly futile." Brother Gabriel lifted his shoulders slightly, then let them drop. "A voice in the wilderness," he said.

"It's a hard message," Mark said bluntly. He was surprised by his own rudeness. "What I mean is . . ."

Gabriel raised one pale hand.

"No explanation is necessary. Yes, it is a hard message and a frightening one. And there are so many forces at work here. I am afraid that what I was sent for is already endangered.''

Angelina's voice interrupted. ''What do you mean, Brother?''

''Angie.'' His voice was soft and tender toward the woman. ''Patience. In good time.'' Then he turned his pale eyes back onto the Jesuit. ''Do you know how things are meant to end, Father?''

''Are you talking about for us or the Second Coming?''

''I am speaking about the end. 'All these things happened unto them for examples. And they are written for our admonition, upon whom the ends of the ages are to come.' Your Second Advent will come after that.''

Father Townsend listened intently, trying to comprehend the strange man's words. But he was already feeling lost.

''Where does the Rapture fit in?'' he asked.

Brother Gabriel gave him a sad smile. ''There is a first day and a last,'' he replied. ''The Translation of the Tribulation Saints is not until later. First there is the wedding and only afterward comes the reception. The Tribulation Saints will be invited then. But now . . . now we are already in the preview.'' Then a look of doubt swept across the evangelist's face and for the briefest of moments, his voice caught. ''At least, I thought we were.'' He turned his attention back to the woman standing at Mark's side. ''But Angie has to know this first.''

He took a small step closer to the woman, as if he wanted to touch her. Suddenly, one of Gabriel's followers, standing close by, laid a hand on the preacher's white sleeve. He was about the same size as Brother Gabriel, but balding, wearing a dark blue T-shirt and jeans. The man leaned forward and whispered in the evangelist's ear and Brother Gabriel stepped back to his original position. He smiled sadly.

''What are your plans?'' he asked them.

Disconcerted, neither Mark nor Angelina replied. They looked at each other instead, as if trying to decide on the spot what plans they might have. From over their shoulders, Tim Connell took charge.

"We're going back to the Castillo place," he told Brother Gabriel, "and party." There was a defiant edge to his voice, as if daring the preacher to disapprove. Tim had also caught the man's movement toward his wife, and he was interpreting it none too kindly.

"Of course," replied Brother Gabriel, acknowledging Tim with a dip of his head, "the *quinceañera.* I believe we are keeping vigil right down the hill from there." He turned back to the bald man, still lingering at his side. "Aren't we?"

The man did not reply but nervously licked his lips and nodded.

"Yes," Brother Gabriel said, "we'll be there, too."

"What? You're going to picket the Castillos?" Tim's voice was loud, clearly challenging.

"They don't picket, they vigil." Angelina spoke over her shoulder, answering her husband's question without taking her eyes off Brother Gabriel. "When there are large gatherings of people, they keep watch and pray." She leaned toward him. "You pray for the people's safety, don't you? That's what you do in vigil?"

Gabriel gently closed his eyes. There was a look of relief. And one of gratitude—as if he had finally found someone who understood. When he opened his eyes again, he was blinking furiously. The harsh sunlight was definitely painful for him.

"Perhaps we will have an opportunity to talk further then." Turning back to Mark, he said, "There is much more I could explain to you. And I would like to hear your own impressions of the Virgin's apparitions. You know she is making her presence felt in this valley?"

"Angelina told me about it, yes."

"But you have your doubts." Again, there was that sad smile. "That part of being Catholic has always puzzled me," Brother Gabriel told the priest. "Your church has almost claimed exclusive rights to the virgin mother. And yet, when she responds you become so suspicious and mistrusting."

"You'll have to admit, Brother, appearing on tortillas and the sides of walls is a little unusual," Mark argued.

"Why is that stranger than believing she conceived a child yet remained a virgin? Or that her body was raptured up to heaven?" Brother Gabriel did not appear to be arguing with the Jesuit, but asking questions he seriously wondered about. "I find those mysteries equally wondrous," he continued, "and as unnecessary to question."

From the look on Mark Townsend's face, he could see that the priest was taken aback. "You Catholics seem to think you have a patent on Mary. But there is no record that she was ever even baptized." Gabriel raised a white finger and waggled it gently, a playful smile on his lips. "And from her recorded behavior, it appears she remained faithful to her Jewish religious traditions."

Father Townsend knew he was being baited. He could feel himself growing warmer, but he blamed it on the sun. He was about to reply when Tim Connell interrupted again.

"If that's true," the young man argued in a loud, daunting voice, "then why does Mary only talk to Catholics? Answer that!"

His assertion was so outrageous that everyone who heard it burst out laughing, even Father Townsend and Brother Gabriel. The only one not laughing was Tim. He glowered at the others, his face flushed and his hands in fists at his sides. As the laughter continued, he spun around and stalked back toward the church.

"Timeo," his wife called out, "come back, sweetheart." But he continued on. Angelina turned back to them, a stricken look on her face. "Forgive me, but I should go with him. We'll catch up with you at the house, Father?"

Mark nodded.

"Angie." This time Gabriel stepped forward before anyone could restrain him. He moved very close to her, his white robe brushing against her black dress. "We do need to talk," he insisted. "There are things you need to know before you write your story.'' He was clearly agitated and Angelina stopped herself from stepping backwards.

''Of course, Brother. I can come to your place tomorrow, if you like. I wanted to show Father Townsend . . .''

''Before then,'' the albino hissed. ''Before then!'' He stepped back as quickly as he had moved forward. ''I will see you at Moxee, Father. Please come talk to me there.''

With that he turned toward the man standing at his side. He seemed to exhale a deep breath as if all his energy was leaving him. The one in the T-shirt held onto his arm and began leading him quickly through the crowd. His supporters parted like the Red Sea when they saw their leader coming.

''Is he all right?'' Mark murmured to Angelina.

''I don't know. I've never seen him like this.''

''Who is the man with him?''

''His first name is Tony,'' she answered. ''He is one of Brother's assistants. He drives him around and takes care of him.'' She looked back to the church. ''I am worried about Tim, I better go find him.''

They agreed to meet back at the house after Mark had time to change his clothes. There were still people clustered on the church steps and along the sidewalk, but the crowd was starting to thin. Mark searched for some sign of Bones and Paul Stanley, but both priests had apparently gone back inside. He spotted Dennis Grib across the street, looking over at him. The young Brother waved to the priest, then turned back to the people he was standing beside. There was no sign of the evangelist dressed all in white. Wherever he had gone, he had left quickly. His vigil in front of St. Joseph's was ended.

Mark let himself into the priests' residence through the front door. As he started up the stairs to his room he heard a noise coming from the kitchen. Someone else was in the house. Quietly, he moved through the dining room and around the corner. At the kitchen table, old

Father Stanley was bent over a magazine, slurping corn flakes out of a bowl.

"Oh, it's you," Mark said. The priest looked up at him. "I heard a noise and wondered who was in here."

"Just an old church mouse," Paul answered, his spoon raised halfway to his chin. He lifted it the rest of the way and chewed slowly. He swallowed and asked, "What were you and that woman talking to that character about?"

Father Stanley was able to put just the right emphasis on *you*, *woman*, and *character*, making each word sound slightly more despicable than the one before. It was really quite remarkable.

"That *woman*," Mark attempted to imitate his emphasis, "was Angelina Sandoval Ybarra, the parishioner I came here to visit. Her husband was right behind us." Trying to imply that Father Stanley saw only what he chose to see. "Angelina wanted to introduce me to Brother Gabriel."

"Hmmppff." Father Stanley turned back to his magazine as if their conversation was ended. But then he added, "There was a time when priests were more discreet about whom they saw in public."

Mark could feel his temperature rising. "Who are you referring to, Paul? The woman or the preacher?"

Father Stanley pushed his cereal bowl away from him and turned in his chair to face the younger Jesuit directly. "That man is making a mockery of the Catholic Church. He stands out there in front, taunting us by wearing our vestments. The only reason he comes around is to steal away our people. He prowls around like a wolf, waiting to spot the weakest ones in our flock. Then he snatches them away."

This was far different from what Mark had heard just minutes before.

"I was told that he keeps vigil and prays for the welfare of the people."

"And you believe that?" Stanley's voice sounded incredulous. "Don't be naive, Father! That man is a false prophet if ever there was one. His vestments are a disguise and his message is hogwash. The man is pure evil and ought to be driven out of our sight. Certainly he should not be encouraged by talking to him.''

Paul Stanley's voice was strong and passionate. He was speaking out of religious conviction, obviously committed to what he was saying. ''Make no mistake about it, Mark. We are living in an age of darkness. The power of God is in open conflict with Satan's dominions. Most of our culture is already under his control. We must fight back. Either the false prophets are done away with or we are pissing in the wind.''

His mouth was clamped tight and his eyes blazed. Mark stared at the old Jesuit for several long moments, trying to decide how to respond. Trying to decide if he even should.

When he finally spoke, it was in a calm, quiet voice. ''That's your opinion, Paul. I don't have time to argue with you, but I will say this. Language like that drives more people out of our church than anything a Brother Gabriel can say or do.''

Mark turned on his heels and stormed out of the kitchen and up the stairs to his room. He could feel himself weak with anger. He was upset with Paul Stanley, but even more with himself for letting the old guy get to him. When he was a young scholastic, not yet ordained, Mark used to listen to the grumblings of the older Jesuits and bite his tongue. He instinctively knew his opinions would be neither appreciated nor considered. Until he joined the presbyterial ranks he was expected to keep his mouth closed. Challenging a priest's attitudes would not only be considered a lapse in decorum, but would raise serious concerns about his aptitude for religious life.

Just as with any family, religious communities are generational. And when young and old are made to live together, rules for engaging the other need to be observed. Whether made explicit or left unsaid, the rules enable generations to coexist. And as with most families, there are certain topics best avoided. Politics and religion head the list. There is probably no Jesuit rec room anywhere on earth that has not turned into a battleground over politics or religion. And these are no small border skirmishes. If the priest across from you is turning into a braying ass, you nuke him.

Roughly, Mark Townsend changed out of his clericals. He expected Angelina and Tim to show up at any moment and he did not want to keep them waiting. Nor did he want Father Stanley greeting his guests. He quickly yanked on a pair of khakis and a blue polo shirt. The Castillos had urged him to dress informally and Mark was taking them at their word. He slipped on a pair of loafers and was headed back down the stairs just as the doorbell rang.

EIGHT

The ride to Moxee took twenty minutes. A long twenty minutes. Tim Connell was still steamed about Brother Gabriel's attentions to his wife and was making that evident by his silent brooding. Angelina carried the conversation along for Father Townsend's sake, keeping up a steady patter about the *quinceañera,* the Castillo's farm, and the valley they were passing through.

"That was where Luis and Rosa had their farm." Angelina was pointing toward the huge parking lot of the discount store crowded with Saturday shoppers. "They had a tiny little house that was over where that long truck is parked. And there was a pasture over on that side and Uncle Luis kept his old horse in there. Montezuma, he called him. He was big and fat, I remember, and if you did not watch out, he would bite you. My uncle used to call it Montezuma's revenge." She laughed. "I never knew what that meant until later."

Like all of the small towns in the Yakima Valley, Moxee was devoted to farming. When they reached the town, Tim began following a smaller road toward a line of low hills in front of them. Houses edged both sides of the road but behind them were orchards and hop fields.

The sun was high and the heat shimmered in waves

off the asphalt road. The three of them were comfortable enough in Angelina's air conditioned Blazer, but Mark felt sorry for the people working in the heat. He could see the laborers moving slowly through the trees or standing high atop the ladders stretched through the limbs.

"Those are specially designed," Angelina informed him. "See how there is only one leg on the other side of the rungs? That one fits between the tree limbs, so that the ladder can be set right into the middle of the tree. They call them orchard ladders."

"Angelina, when you were growing up did you work in orchards?"

"Of course! Everyone did." Her husband snorted. "I did!" she insisted.

"It was a summer job," Tim argued, "for spending money. It wasn't like you were earning your living. Not like those poor folks."

Angelina shook her head. "I don't know why you are being contrary, Timeo. Yes, I was in school during the year. But my whole family worked the orchards. You know that."

Connell concentrated on his driving, refusing to answer.

They turned right again as they drew closer to the hills, and once the road wound to their base it began following their contours. They drove about seven-tenths of a mile before Tim began slowing down. There was a knot of cars on the roadway in front of them.

"Looks like an accident," Tim said.

"No, they are off to the side, I think." Angelina leaned forward in her seat, craning for a better look. "That is right where we turn in."

As they approached the traffic, Connell slowed down further. About a dozen people were standing to the right of the road, their vehicles pulled off onto the shoulder. Three others faced them from the opposite side. In the midst of the larger crowd, Mark saw a flash of white. Angelina saw it at the same time.

"I think it's Brother Gabriel," she said. "He's here already."

"And that's your uncle Luis on the other side," Tim observed.

"Slow down, Timeo. Unroll your window."

Luis Castillo was shouting across the road at the evangelist, punching the air with his fist.

". . . stay the hell away!" His angry words came through the open window over the motor's noise. "If you put one foot on my land, I call the cops! You hear me?"

Brother Gabriel stood placidly on his side of the road. A couple of men hovered protectively on either side of the preacher, their eyes fixed on Luis. The others hung further back, alarmed by the farmer's vehemence but not wanting to abandon their leader entirely. Apparently the evangelist had decided to bring some of his flock to help keep vigil at the fiesta Luis and Rosa were throwing for their goddaughter; a gesture largely unappreciated by the *padrino*, who remained standing on his side of the road, gesturing and threatening. Two other Latinos backed him up, their faces dark with angry determination. One of them held a baseball bat tightly against his leg. Tim Connell drove directly between the two factions and stopped the car.

Angelina leaned across her husband and yelled out the open window. *"Luis, que pasa?"*

His line of vision blocked by the oversized vehicle, Luis muttered and stalked up to its side.

"Go on up," he ordered gruffly. "This I will handle myself."

"No, uncle, get in with us. We will drive you back up."

"I'm not going to allow him to ruin my fiesta," groused Luis.

"He will not," Angelina assured him. "Father Townsend, open your door please. Uncle, get in. Brother Gabriel is only here to vigil, he will not come onto your property. Now get in."

Luis glared through the windows at the crowd on the

other side. He was still unconvinced, but two other cars were now behind Tim, waiting patiently to turn into the drive leading up to the Castillo farm. Luis wavered, then stepped back.

"You go on," he ordered Tim. "I'll walk up with my friends. Go on, you're blocking traffic."

"You will not stay down here?" Angelina was still leaning across.

"I'm on my way," Luis promised.

"*Bueno*. Drive along then, Tim."

He rolled the window up before turning onto the dusty drive leading up to the Castillo's. The other cars followed. Luis and his friends, after staring across the road while the dust settled, turned and headed up the drive.

The Castillo home was surrounded by fields of grapes. Long rows of vines hung suspended chest high, thick with leaves and redolent with the smell of the fruit growing ripe beneath the hot sun. Luis and Rosa owned fifteen acres and all of it was devoted to grapes with the exception of one acre in the center. There they had leveled the ground and built their home, a solid affair of brick and adobe, with thick walls and high beamed ceilings. Large picture windows looked out over the valley floor. In the back, a high adobe wall encircled a huge expanse of lawn rimmed by Rosa's flower gardens. Today most of it was shaded by awnings put up for Yolanda's fiesta. A bricked patio near the house and the swimming pool in the center were left open to the sky. But with the exception of a couple of dozen children playing at the pool, most of the guests were choosing the cooler shade under the awnings.

Angelina led Father Townsend through wide wooden gates opening in the middle of the high garden wall. Inside, the lawn was crowded with guests, the hum of their voices filling the air. In the background, salsa music was being piped through loudspeakers set up around the patio, barely discernible over the loud shrieks and laughter of the children in the pool.

"*Hola, cara mia!*" Angelina's Aunt Rosa hurried up to them, her hands extended in greeting, her eyes large with delight and her mouth curled in a wide smile. In Spanish she said, *"Where have you been keeping your-selves? The fiesta, you can see, is already started."* Reaching high above her, she wrapped both short arms around Father Townsend's neck, pulling him down and planting a sloppy kiss on his cheek. "Welcome, Padre!"

"Did you know your Luis was down the hill, fighting with Brother Gabriel?" Angelina asked her aunt.

"Ah, no! Don't tell me this!" Rosa lamented. Remembering herself, she switched into English for Mark's sake. "Padre, you tell my Luis to leave that man alone, *sí*? He goes crazy whenever he is around."

"I think he's concerned that Brother Gabriel might crash your party," Mark told her.

"Which is craziness," Angelina cut in. "Brother Gabriel never intrudes like that. Luis should know better."

"We don't know him as well as you do, *cara*," Rosa replied. "To us he is a strange man. But you know him better."

Tim Connell emerged from the house with the long necks of two beer bottles clutched in his fingers. He extended one to Father Townsend. "Corona?" he asked. Small flecks of ice slid slowly down the glistening bottle. Mark gratefully accepted.

"What about your wife?" Rosa scolded. "Give her that one you have!"

"It is all right, Rosa." Her eyes never left her husband. "I can get one for myself."

If Tim heard what she was saying he paid it no heed, but moved off into the crowd.

Angelina watched as he strolled away, then turned to the priest. "Father, come inside, let me show you the house." The two of them moved inside through the patio doors.

Yolanda Flores's *padrinos* had spared no expense to honor the young woman on her *quinceañera*. The Castillos hired caterers to prepare traditional foods for the fiesta. Platters of tapas were being prepared in the kitchen. A barbecue was already glowing in one corner of the patio and soon marinated beef for *carne asada* and halves of chicken would be laid on the grills. The mariachis from the church were arriving, preparing to replace the recorded music. As Angelina showed Mark through the large rambling house, she described the fireworks planned for later in the night. Luis was promising to light up the sky over the entire Yakima Valley, she informed the Jesuit. It would be so bright that all of the apples would ripen at once, she laughed.

While Mark and Angelina were inside the house, Luis Castillo and his two companions returned to the party. And Tim Connell started on his second Corona. When they emerged, Mark spotted Tim huddled with Luis, gesturing broadly while he talked to the old man. One of the others from the roadside was standing beside them. He had put away his baseball bat, substituting it for a bottle of beer. Angelina excused herself and Father Townsend wandered over to the men.

"Welcome, Father!" Luis Castillo was calm, all traces of anger now disappeared. "Please meet my friend, José Ramirez." The bat man shifted his beer to his left hand, extending his right to shake the priest's.

"Are you about ready for another cold one, Mark?" Tim jauntily swung his empty bottle in his hand and offered to take the Jesuit's.

Father Townsend's was not quite half empty. "Not yet," he replied, "but thanks anyway." Connell shrugged and headed back toward the house.

"Your home is beautiful, Luis."

Señor Castillo beamed with pleasure. "*Gracias, Padre*. Rosa and me worked very hard to build up this place. If you had seen what it was before. Only sage and dirt, like up above." He pointed further into the hills, where the land was not yet developed. The contrast was stark. "Someday, maybe I will buy that and plant more grapes. But for now, this is enough."

Father LaBelle ducked his head under the awning and, spotting his host, came forward.

"*Luis, me alegro verte. Ésta es una fiesta muy bonita. Mil gracias por la invitación.*"

"*De nada, Padre. Su presencia aquí es una honor*

para nuestra familia." Bones knew José Ramirez and
greeted him, then turned his attention to Mark Townsend. "So what did you think of the *quinceañera,* Mark?
Quite the celebration, huh? Nothing like that over on the
coast, I'll wager."

"Nothing even close," Mark agreed.

"Makes your liturgies look like a long snooze on a
slow day, huh?"

Mark just grinned at his fellow Jesuit. Bones was
having fun playing the role of country priest. There was
no point in reminding him that he had studied his theology at the Gregorian Pontifical University in Rome for
four years before coming to Yakima. Somehow, that
would not quite fit the image of the bumpkin priest in
cowboy boots that Joe LaBelle had assumed. Rome was
another lifetime and besides, no one at the Castillo's
fiesta would be particularly impressed. They respected
this priest for who he was now, not for what or where
he had once studied.

"I assume you saw the good Brother down below."
Bones was still addressing Mark. Father Townsend saw
Luis Castillo bite down on his lip and he hurried to
answer.

"Yes, he was there when we arrived," he informed
LaBelle.

"I noticed his wife is with him. She doesn't usually
show up at the vigils."

He caught Mark by surprise. No one had said anything about a wife. "I didn't know he was married."

"Sister Elizabeth. She's a tiny little thing, easy to
miss. She has on kind of a brown shift," LaBelle observed. "Looks sort of like a nun."

The description was no help. Mark did not remember
seeing her.

The mariachi band launched into a loud, rousing song
and conversation became next to impossible without
yelling. Their group broke up as the individuals began
drifting to other parts of the yard. Mark replaced his
empty bottle of beer with another and began wandering
through the crowd, nodding pleasantly to strangers who

looked his way, pausing to greet the few who recognized him as a visiting padre. This was not unlike a parish picnic. Mark's role was less clearly defined, but he still knew what was expected of him. The scent of meats sizzling on the open grills began wafting above the crowd, and long tables were filling up with platters of food. Heaping piles of *tamales* wrapped in corn husks were set next to bowls of refritos and rice. There were soft *tortillas* and bowls of salsas, *arroz con pollo*, *ensalada*, *frijoles*, handmade *tacos* and *sopa de verduras*. For the children large glass containers brimmed with *jugos de frutas*.

Few events are as hazardous for priests as parish picnics and potlucks. For any cleric hoping to stay in his parishioners' good graces, these social occasions can be minefields. One false move and your reputation is ruined. Many an aspiring pastor has found himself blackballed and shunned after bungling his way through a meal in the parish hall. Salads, casseroles, and pie can detonate with disastrous results if mishandled. There are no warning labels on any of the stuff, so no way of telling which dishes can be safely handled. Potentially, any one of them can blow up with deadly force.

If Father takes a second helping of Shrimp Surprise without even sampling the Sweet and Sour Turkey, he might as well call the bishop and ask for his transfer. If he compliments Mrs. Klein's crumbcake but fails to mention Mrs. Miller's rumballs, he has just cut himself off from the Altar Society. And might as well call the bishop. God forbid he should ever show any sign of not enjoying every last bite that goes into his mouth! Just try hiding Tuna L'Orange under a slice of bread or spitting Heavenly Prune Whip into your napkin. No need to call the bishop—somebody has already done it for you.

Proper parochial protocol demands the priest sample every dish set on the table, and then to exclaim with equal enthusiasm over every morsel. If, as in the case of extremely large churches, there are too many dishes for the priest to reasonably taste, he is allowed to take helpings from only half. But then he is required, by

Canon Law, to know which dishes, prepared by which cooks, he has neglected to taste. And at the next church function, he is to eat only from those selections, ignoring anything prepared by a cook he sampled at the previous function. Even if that includes Mrs. Harkins's German Chocolate Cheesecake.

If a priest eats everything put in front of him, he will surely die. But if he fails to taste it, he might as well have.

Father Townsend always did his best to observe his sacerdotal duties. He was reaching a point though, where something other than his waistband was going to have to give. His assistant back in Seattle, Father Dan Morrow, was counseling a regimen of regular exercise. But so far, Mark was still in denial. And at the Castillo's fiesta, knowing Dan was not around to disapprove, Father Townsend worked the buffet like a monsignor.

As the sun began setting and the air cooled, the fiesta heated up. The center of the patio was cleared for dancing and the mariachis were replaced by two teenage DJs and a boombox. Chairs were set around the tables for the oldsters, quite content to let Yolanda and her friends take center stage.

Mark was sitting near the back wall, comfortable and relaxed, watching the festivities around him. He smiled when he saw Joe Bones working his way around the tables, greeting his parishioners. If they were on the other side of the Cascades, that would be him. He leaned back in his chair and closed his eyes. Moments later, he felt a nudge at his side. Dennis Grib was pulling up a chair.

"Caught you napping, huh?"

"Just resting my eyes a minute."

"Angelina asked me to find you," Dennis said. "She's in the kitchen, fixing some food to take down to Brother Gabriel. She wants to know if you'd like to go down with us."

As a matter of fact, that was about the last thing Mark wanted to do. He was feeling pleasantly sleepy after eating a full meal and drinking three beers and would have been perfectly content to sit back and let the activity swirl around him.

"Sure," he conceded, "lead the way."

He followed Dennis into the crowded kitchen where Rosa was closely supervising the cleanup as her caterers put away food and washed dishes. Standing at an island counter in the center, Angelina was heaping leftovers onto paper plates, covering them with foil.

"He found you," she said brightly, handing off her plates to Dennis, who began setting them into a cardboard box. "Do you want to walk down with us, Father? Just to visit for a moment?"

Without waiting for a reply, she handed the priest a milk jug, rinsed out and filled with lemonade, and a stack of paper cups. Dennis carried the cardboard box of food and Angelina led the way out the front door. She did not want her uncle Luis to see them taking food down the road, she said. Nor her husband. Mark had a hunch that Connell could care less. He had last seen him at a picnic table in a corner of the garden, empty Corona bottles lined up in front of him like a picket fence.

Pale light still glowed in the western sky and a full moon was already rising. All the lights were burning in the Castillo's house and in the enclosed yard behind, colored lanterns cast shadows against the adobe walls. On the road below them, Mark could still make out several cars parked along the far side, with the white figure of Brother Gabriel standing in the midst of eight or nine other people.

"I heard that Brother Gabriel's wife was here," he said to Angelina.

"Yes? Sister Elizabeth? I did not see her when we came up." She scanned the crowd below them, as if looking for the woman. "But she is easy to miss. So tiny."

"What's their last name, Angelina?"

"Grimes," she answered. "But Gabriel and Elizabeth are not their real names, either. David and Linda Grimes. They are originally from Bakersfield, in California. He

was a Presbyterian minister there until his congregation
let him go.''

"Do you know why?"

"*Sí.* He was having his visions about the world's end
and was starting to preach about them. His sermons were
all about the coming Rapture. He said that he knew they
would not tolerate it, but he felt that he had to be true
to what he was hearing. So that is when he came up
here.''

"And you've looked into his background down
there?''

"Some," she admitted. "But I need to do more before I start writing.''

They were at the bottom of the hill and things were
much darker. The people across the road were watching
their approach.

"*Buenas noches, Hermano!*" she called out. "*Somos
Angelina, y el Padre Mark, y el Hermano Dennis.*"

They crossed the road and Dennis Grib handed the
box of food to one of Gabriel's assistants. Someone took
the lemonade and cups from Mark's hands.

"*You are very kind to us, Angelina.*" Brother Gabriel
smiled his appreciation.

"*I thought you would be hungry. You've been out
here for a long time.*"

"*Yes, but it is important prayer, especially with so
many in one place.*" His accent, to Mark's untrained ear,
sounded very good. The evangelist switched easily to
English when he addressed the priest. "It is nice to see
you again too, Father. Are you enjoying the fiesta?" He
motioned with his head to the bright, colorful lights on
the hill above them.

"It's a nice party," said Mark.

"Luis and Rosa are good and generous people," the
evangelist observed. "Even if the Señor's tolerance isn't
all that it could be.''

The moon was the only light now, and Gabriel's people moved slowly about in the darkness. But the
preacher's white vestments and his hair were still very
visible. He seemed to glow. The distant lights from the

top of the hill reflected in his pale eyes and they burned like two small embers.

"What do you hope to accomplish by keeping vigil?" Mark asked.

"Ah, Father, you already know the answer to that. We must be watchful and alert, for we know not the day nor the hour."

"Do you believe the end is coming soon?"

"When you see the desolating abomination standing where he should not . . ." There was a tremor to Gabriel's high, lisping voice as he quoted the Scripture.

"And do you actually see that?" Mark could barely make out the man's face, but he listened carefully to the voice.

If the question disturbed him, Brother Gabriel offered no sign of it. "What is more surprising, Father, is that you don't."

The same flush of anger that Mark felt toward Paul Stanley that afternoon rose up once again. He could feel a tremor course through his body. He clenched his jaw and stared hard at the short albino in front of him. Brother Gabriel stood calmly, waiting for his reply.

"The Bible also warns about false prophets performing signs and wonders to mislead people," Mark rejoined.

"Yes," Gabriel quickly replied. "I hear that quoted often." His voice sounded light and playful.

The food was distributed and Angelina approached the two men holding a plate and cup.

"This is yours, Brother." She offered him the food and drink.

Gabriel shook his head. "Thank you, Angelina, but no. Give it to one of the others, please."

There was the sound of footsteps coming down the drive behind them. In the dark, a loud, slurred voice called out. "Angie!" Tim Connell stumbled across the road. "What's going on?"

"We are visiting with Brother Gabriel," she replied.

Tim rocked unsteadily on his feet. He was swaying and looked on the verge of falling. Dennis Grib stepped next to the man and held his arm. "Why don't we move over to the back of that pickup so Tim can sit down," he suggested. He helped Connell negotiate the few steps it took to reach the truck's tailgate, then eased him onto it. "There you go, Tim." The others moved closer and Connell watched the dark figures through bleary eyes. Sensing some tension, one of Gabriel's assistants joined them. He was the same bald-headed man Mark had seen at the church that morning. Wherever Gabriel went, this Tony seemed to follow.

"Brother," Angelina's voice broke the silence, "there was something you said you wanted to tell me." Gabriel remained silent. "Remember? Earlier today, across from the church?"

"Not now," he said quickly. "It was nothing. Later." A small, soft-featured woman, dressed in a loose dark dress, moved close to him as he spoke. Her dark hair was cut short. Gabriel laid his hand lightly on her shoulder. "Father, this is Sister Elizabeth." The woman nodded nervously at the priest and looked up at her husband but said nothing.

Angelina seemed perturbed. "Brother Gabriel, what is it? You said there was something you wanted to tell me." Her voice was insistent. She was not going to let it go.

All eyes fixed on the preacher, waiting for his reaction.

"My apologies." He reached a pale arm out and grabbed Angelina's arm, hurriedly pulling her away from the group gathered around them. He was murmuring in her ear even as they moved away, speaking quickly in a soft voice, turning his head so as not to be overheard. Others were closer and might have heard more, but all Mark caught were snatches of a few words: *later* and *alone*, and something that sounded like *river-walk*.

Gabriel spoke hurriedly and their conversation was extremely brief, but there was still time for Tim Connell to react. He jerked upright when the preacher latched onto his wife's arm, escorting her away. It took a few

moments to register, but then he lurched from the tailgate, stumbling into Dennis Grib. "Now just a minute,"
he grumbled, trying to regain his balance. "What the
hell . . . ?" But by the time he was headed toward them,
Angelina and Gabriel were already returning. "What the
hell?" he repeated.

"It is all right, Timeo. Let's go." She reached for her
husband's hand but he angrily jerked it away. He swayed
unsteadily, facing the evangelist's white figure.

"Who the hell do you think you are?" Tim demanded
loudly. "She's my wife, dammit! You watch your step
or you're gonna . . ." Mark saw him begin to reach under his shirt but just as he did, Dennis Grib grabbed his
arm and began pulling him back.

"Tim!" Angelina's voice carried the force of a slap,
spinning the man around to her. "I can handle this,"
she ordered. "Leave him alone."

"I think we'd better be going, Brother." Tony was at
the preacher's side, tugging on his sleeve. Sister Elizabeth moved between her husband and Tim Connell. She
said nothing, but her stance made it clear no one should
lay a hand on Brother Gabriel.

"Father," Angelina said, "can you help Tim?"

"I can do it," Dennis volunteered. He wrapped his
arm around the man's waist, effectively preventing the
drunk from trying to reach whatever he was hiding.
"Come on, Tim, let's go."

The two groups slowly separated. Tim continued his
grumbling as they made their way up the hill, but it was
too indistinct and garbled to make any sense. The rest
of them walked in silence. They could hear the cars starting up behind them, their tires crunching as they rolled
away from the gravel roadside. As they reached the high
adobe walls of the garden, they were met by half a dozen
people coming out of the gate.

"Angelina?" Rosa's voice was worried.

"Everything is all right."

"We heard yelling," Luis said. "What's going on?"

"It's okay, Uncle. Tim was just upset."

". . . bastard grabbed my wife . . ." Connell slurred.

Luis moved past them, as if to head down the drive. His friend, José Ramirez, was right beside him.

"Come back, Uncle. They're gone." Angelina's voice was tired and in the light spilling out from the garden, Mark could see the tension in her face. "Everything is all right."

"What happened?" Rosa asked.

"Brother Gabriel wants to talk to me. Alone." She turned to Tim, making it clear she meant that for him. "He wants to meet with me later tonight, at that park next to the river."

"But surely you will not go?" protested her aunt.

Angelina shrugged. "Why not? What could happen? This is why I am here, to get his story. Whatever it is he has to tell me, it must be important."

"Like hell!" Connell bellowed.

"Oh, Timeo." Angelina's voice was full of disgust. Her husband's drunken posturing was not only annoying but embarrassing. "Why don't you go to bed?"

"Your aunt and your husband are right, Angelina. You must not go." Luis's voice was angry, determined. "It would be foolish to see this man alone. You should not trust him."

"He is not dangerous," she replied. "Nothing will happen to me."

Father Townsend said nothing. The exchange continued for some minutes more; everyone determined to dissuade Angelina from her late night rendezvous with Brother Gabriel, and she, equally determined to follow through with her plans. Mark saw no sense getting embroiled in an argument that was going nowhere. Rosa grew tearful and Luis became angrier. Even José Ramirez entered the fray, backing up his friend. Tim Connell stood swaying to one side, remaining silent but quite obviously very disturbed. He kept waving his hands in front of him, as if to brush away his wife's reasons for wanting to meet the strange preacher. No matter what she said, he waved his hands in angry dismissal. Father Townsend kept an eye open, hoping to get a glimpse of whatever the man had tucked beneath his shirt. He had an uneasy feeling he already knew what was there.

Angelina was losing her temper, and her voice grew loud and strident as she continued to argue with the people surrounding her. She was determined to keep her 1 a.m. appointment and refused to acknowledge any risk or danger. He merely wanted to talk, she insisted. What kind of a writer would she be to turn down this opportunity for an interview, no matter how unusual it seemed? Eventually it became clear to everyone that she was not going to back down. Their arguments and protests weakened, then fell off completely. No one was happy with Angelina's decision, but they knew there was nothing they could say to change her mind. They looked at her with troubled eyes.

She tried to reassure them. "It will be okay. Don't worry. I'll make sure nothing happens." No one looked convinced.

Finally, Luis spoke. "Enough, then. Come back inside. Our guests are waiting and we need to start the fireworks."

"Just what we need," a voice beside Mark whispered. He turned and caught Dennis Grib grinning at him.

Slowly they began moving through the gate and into the garden where the music, laughter, and loud voices had continued unabated. Most of the revelers were unaware of the heated exchange just outside the garden wall. As the patio lights were extinguished, the guests' voices grew more excited. Luis had promised a firework display that the whole valley could see. No sooner were the lights turned off than the first loud boom echoed from a spot beyond the barns outside the garden. The sky exploded in a shower of green fire and there was applause and loud oooohs and aaaaahs.

From somewhere in the middle of the patio, a young child's shrill voice screamed into the night, *"¡Bombas! ¡Papá! ¡Bombas!"*

NINE

There was a time when Father Townsend was among the last to leave a party. But the older he got, the more willing he was to trade good times for good sleep. During his earliest year in the Jesuits, Mark's novice master once told his charges that any Jesuit who needed more than six hours of sleep was probably in serious danger of losing his vocation. Up until a couple of years ago, Mark still believed him. He should have known better. This was from the same novice master who believed buttering your toast was a venial sin. And jelly was mortal.

Father Stanley was the first to fold. He arrived at the fiesta late, after the parish's Saturday night Mass, and by nine-thirty he was demanding that Brother drive him back home. Dennis was only too happy to tuck his charge away for the night and then return for more good times at the Castillo's. Mark managed to hold out until the end of the fireworks, but then he had to surrender, seeking out the younger man and asking for a ride back to the parish house. The good-natured Brother obliged, making yet another run back into town, then returning for more fun. At twenty-four, he was still young enough to get by on the novice master's six hours.

While Tim Connell was planning to stay in Yakima

with his wife, Mark was due back in Seattle by Monday
morning. Reluctantly, he had made a plane reservation
for Sunday afternoon. As much as he hated flying, it
was the only way to get back to his own parish in time
for dinner. As he drifted toward sleep, the priest wondered if Connell might be headed back across the mountains sooner than he planned. Angelina already appeared
fed up with her husband's antics. Ever since arriving,
the man had done little more than swill beer and complain about the work his wife was trying to accomplish.
For whatever reason, Connell had apparently decided
that Brother Gabriel's attentions toward Angelina were
less than honorable. But he seemed incapable of con-
fronting either his wife or Gabriel without fortifying
himself with a six-pack beforehand. His boozy protests
and complaints were having no effect other than to al-
ienate himself further from his wife. And Father Townsend had the uneasy feeling that Connell's most recent
confrontation had been on the verge of turning dangerously violent. He felt sorry for the man. Tim was going
about things all wrong, and his drinking was definitely
getting in the way of reconciling with Angelina. Perhaps,
if they did return to Seattle together, Father Townsend
could raise the issue of Tim's drinking. It would not be
the first time he spoke to a parishioner about the problem. Probably not the last, either. But someone needed
to say something to him. Otherwise, the marriage of Tim
Connell to Angelina Sandoval Ybarra was going to become history. And unless the Jesuit was mistaken, that
would happen fairly soon.

Angelina was a talented and determined young
woman, devoted to and focused on her career as a journalist. She did not strike Mark as the type to have much
patience for any man who found his courage in a bottle.
She claimed she wanted Tim in Yakima because she was
afraid. But she told Mark she wanted him to help her
with advice on how to write about this religious phe-
nomenon. So far, Tim had done nothing to protect her
and Mark had found no way to advise her. The reporter's

behavior gave no evidence that she wanted or needed either man's protection or advice.

Father Townsend rolled uncomfortably in his bed. He felt like he was letting someone down. There is a gene in priests that causes an intense desire to be of help. And when that desire remains unfulfilled, it creates anxiety which, in turn, releases noxious molecules of failure. Mark knew the toxic feeling. And he did not like it one bit.

He rolled once more and opened his eyes. The digital clock next to his bed read 1:20. Somewhere in Yakima's Riverside Park, a Latina writer was meeting an albino evangelist with a secret message. Would he still be wearing his white vestments, or did he dress differently after hours? Gabriel apparently gave no indication about what he wanted to tell her. At least, none that Angelina was willing to share with those who knew of their scheduled interview. What had Brother Gabriel whispered so hurriedly, so convincingly? Mark had heard only a few words and nothing that made sense. But others were standing closer to them and perhaps had caught some of what was said. Whatever it was, Father Townsend hoped that Angelina was getting what she wanted.

TEN

Brother Grib was knocking at the door, his head partway in the bedroom, as the bells at St. Joseph started to peal. Mark was not sure which woke him, the knocking or the bells, but he needed neither.

"What time is it?" he grumped.

"Eight o'clock. Sorry, Mark, but you need to get up. There's a problem." Parishes and problems are practically synonymous, so Father Townsend was not terribly alarmed. Not until Dennis continued. "Brother Gabriel is dead."

"What?" He was sitting up now, wide awake.

"We just got a call. Someone found him at Riverside Park."

The priest was out of bed, hopping on one leg, trying to pull a tangled pair of khakis onto the other. "What about Angelina? Is she okay?"

Grib shrugged his shoulders. "I don't know. That's why I thought you'd want to check."

Bones and Paul Stanley were both over at the church. Paul was taking the eight o'clock Mass and Joe was hanging out in the sacristy, just in case. Father Stanley's lapses during the weekday were one thing, but LaBelle would not allow them at the Sunday liturgies. He insisted Paul stick to the text. The one published this century.

On their way out the kitchen, Mark snatched a quick cup of coffee which he carefully held over the car floor as Dennis Grib raced through Yakima's nearly deserted streets. The kid was no slouch behind the wheel, and not above fudging a few red lights, either. They were sailing down Yakima Avenue in record time.

Mark took a cautious sip of coffee. "How'd you hear about it, Dennis?"

Grib's eyes never left the road. "A parishioner called. He was walking his dog on the greenway and spotted a bunch of police cars at the park and went over to investigate. I guess someone told him who it was."

"Did he know what happened?"

Grib shook his head.

Mark rubbed his eyes. He felt like he was still half-asleep, and probably should have at least taken the time to throw some water on his face. He rubbed his tongue across his teeth. That, too. He was not thinking clearly yet. The late night and festivities had taken their toll and he was having a difficult time wrapping his mind around the news of Gabriel's death. But Townsend's greater concern was for Angelina Sandoval Ybarra. He tried offering a silent prayer.

"How much further?"

"We're almost there," replied Dennis. He gunned his car up the highway's overpass and shot down the other side. A sign pointed them toward Terrace Heights, but Brother Grib hung a sharp right at the Washington's Fruit Place Visitor Center and turned into the drive at Sarg Hubbard Riverside Park. Only then did he begin to slow down. Just in front of them, a line of police cars blocked the way. Dennis pulled off to the side and parked.

They could see people moving across the grassy slope in front of them. Some were uniformed officers, but the majority were in street clothes. More than a couple looked like they might have been roused from their own beds just like Father Townsend. All wore grim expressions. Most of the activity seemed to be taking place off to one side of the roadway. There was a curved marble memorial dedicated to Yakima's citizens who died in wars, and the yellow police tape began there. It was stretched along the pathway nearest to the river, tied around lamp poles to keep it suspended. In the other direction, the tape was draped across a wide expanse of green grass, again wrapped around light poles to hold it in place. The lightest of breezes from off the river riffled against the twisted yellow plastic. Inside the tape's perimeter, almost at exact center, rose a twelve-foot wooden viewing platform. There were enough police standing around it to lift the structure and carry it off to their headquarters, had they wanted.

Outside the police line, about three dozen people stood silently watching the activity inside. There were a number of early morning joggers, judging from their running shorts and strained expressions; as well as some bicyclists; people with dogs; and even a couple who were dressed in their Sunday best, apparently rerouted on their way to church. The two Jesuits left their car and joined the others.

Not that there was much to see. The viewing platform was perched on a rise, high enough to prevent the people below from seeing anything. The breeze occasionally lifted what looked like the corner of a white sheet, but from that distance and angle, it was hard to tell. Two men were standing on top however, one holding a camera and looking over the side and the other writing in a notepad. Father Townsend shuffled his feet impatiently. He needed to get in there and find out about Angelina.

A uninformed policeman hurried along the inside perimeter of the tape, carrying a small brown paper bag. He was passing within three feet of them.

"Excuse me, officer, I need to talk to someone."

"In a minute, bud." The cop pushed by, not bothering to even glance their way.

"Try yelling," suggested Dennis.

The park was unnaturally quiet. Anyone speaking was doing so in quiet whispers. With the exception of an occasional bird's chirp, or an eerie, unattached voice crackling out of some officer's radio, there were no other sounds. Mark was not about to start yelling. Brother Grib, on the other hand, did not share his inhibition.

"Hey, up there!" The young Jesuit's voice rolled over the scene. Heads jerked up immediately, swiveling to stare in their direction. "We need to see somebody!"

Two somebodys were already trotting toward them. One was in uniform, the other in a rumpled gray suit.

"Whata ya' need?" the uniform barked.

"Is that Brother Gabriel?" Dennis motioned with his head toward the platform.

The cop only glared at him. The suit answered.

"What's your name?"

"We need to find out what happened," Dennis replied. Mark was still stunned by his companion's brashness and had yet to find his voice.

"This doesn't concern you," the one in the uniform said firmly. "Now keep your voice down and stay behind that tape."

"It does, too," argued Dennis, "if that's Brother Gabriel."

"You know this Brother Gabriel?" It was the suit this time.

"We were with him last night," Dennis told him.

"Nooooo." Mark finally found his voice, which sounded like a long sigh of displeasure.

Both policemen looked over at him and waited for more. Mark cleared his throat.

"Uhmm, I'm Father Mark Townsend and this is Dennis . . . Brother Dennis Grib. We're over at St. Joe's. Well, actually, Dennis is at St. Joe's. I'm in Seattle . . . at St. Joe . . ." he finished as lamely as he began.

The one wearing the suit asked again, "You know Brother Gabriel?"

"Just slightly," Mark answered.

"This guy says you saw him last night."

"Yes, well, we need to explain . . ."

"You better," the one in uniform ordered.

"Matt." The man in the suit gave his head a slight shake, as if warning the other to ease off.

Several of the onlookers, sensing something was going on, had moved closer. They kept their eyes fixed on the platform straight ahead, but their ears were twitching like rabbits.

"Is there someplace we can talk?" Mark asked. Having gained the attention of the police, Brother Grib seemed content to let Father Townsend take the lead. He stayed beside him, but was letting Mark do all the talking.

The man wearing the gray suit introduced himself as a Yakima police detective. His name was Bill Yoder. After signalling the other policeman that he would take care of them he lifted up the police tape and invited the Jesuits to duck under it. He led them across the grass to a deserted picnic table at the bottom of a small slope.

"Why don't you gentlemen have a seat," he suggested politely. "Then tell me what you know."

The two Jesuits did as they were told.

"We were at a party last night," Mark began. "Brother Gabriel was outside and we talked to him for a while. But there was this woman with us . . ."

"Wait a minute," Yoder interrupted, waving Mark into silence. "Just a minute now." He pulled a notepad from his jacket and opened it. "You were at a party with Brother Gabriel?" Detective Yoder looked as dubious as he sounded.

"No." Mark hunched his shoulders and tried again. "There was a party in Moxee . . . for a *quinceañera* . . ." he hesitated, then asked, "You know what that is?" Yoder nodded so Mark continued. "We were there and Brother Gabriel and some of his people were outside, doing one of their vigils." He stopped again. "Do you know about those?"

Yoder took a deep breath and slowly let it out. "Let's try to find a bottom line here, shall we? Let me ask just a couple of questions, Father . . . What's your name again?"

Mark told him and the detective wrote it down. He did the same with Brother Grib.

"Okay now," Yoder raised his pencil, "next question. Why are you here this morning? And what do you want?"

Two questions, Mark thought. But he gave the policeman one answer for both. "We're looking for Angelina Sandoval Ybarra."

Detective Yoder spent the next hour taking the Jesuits' statements. Between the two of them, they managed to supply enough information to tie him up for the next three days, chasing down the names, facts, and whereabouts of everyone they mentioned. Father Townsend realized that their story was convoluted, filled with starts and stops and a whole host of names. But that was the detective's problem, not theirs. Even as Dennis and he answered the detective's questions, Mark continued to ask questions of his own, pressing for information. Yoder assured Father Townsend there was only one body on top of the viewing platform. He declined the priest's request to see it, explaining that he could not allow anyone to climb up there and taint what little evidence there was. But he did describe the scene for Father Townsend. An albino male with long white hair, dressed in tan slacks, a pale yellow shirt, and wearing brown sandals, was lying face up in the center of the viewing platform's top level. A .40 caliber pistol was lying approximately six feet from the body. And that was it.

Once Mark was satisfied Angelina was not in the park, he was anxious to leave. The detective's description of the murder scene was not that enlightening. The body was not Angelina's. Hopefully, he would find her back at the Castillos' having morning coffee next to her husband while deciding what to wear for church. Brother Gabriel's death meant a dramatic ending for the article she was writing. Mark hoped that was all it meant, but he had an uneasy feeling it was not.

Dennis Grib seemed equally uneasy. He twisted in his

place on the picnic bench and impatiently drummed his feet on the ground. Detective Yoder looked up from his writing.

"I apologize for keeping you so long," he said, "but I want to make sure I have everything. Now as far as you know, Ybarra was meeting the Brother here at one o'clock. Is that correct?"

"That's what she told us," Mark answered.

"And she was coming by herself?"

Exasperated, Grib spoke up. "That's what she said. Can we go now?"

Detective Yoder raised a cautionary finger. He was not going to be rushed. "And neither of you have communicated with her since you left the party. Is that right?"

Both nodded.

"Okay, then. I guess I need to go have a talk with Ms. Ybarra," the detective said. "And I'm going to need the two of you to come in and sign your statements later on. Tomorrow morning is fine."

"I can't," Mark protested. "I'm flying back to Seattle this afternoon."

Yoder cocked his head and studied the priest a moment. "Why don't you come by before you leave, Father. I'll see if I can't have something typed up by then."

Mark felt his stomach heave. It was not just the coffee making him queasy. Nor the thought of flying in a small plane. He bid goodbye to the detective and followed Grib back to their car. Dinner in Seattle was already looking iffy.

"Padre, Angelina is not here." Rosa's pale and worried face looked searchingly up at Mark's. News of Brother Gabriel's death was already on the radio, including the Spanish station Rosa kept tuned in her kitchen. "And Tim is gone, too. Come, look."

She led Mark and Dennis down the hall to the guest bedroom, stepping aside to let them enter first. She was right, there was no sign of either one of them. Their bed was neatly made and Tim's open suitcase lay on top of the dresser. The closet door was pulled open and Angelina's black crepe sheath was hanging in clear view. She had changed into a cotton dress after returning from the church, but there was no sign of that one either. Nor of the clothes Tim wore at the fiesta. Apparently, neither had spent the night in the Castillos' guest bedroom.

"Both cars are gone." Luis's voice came from down the hallway. He had gone outside to look behind the house, where the cars were usually parked.

Father Townsend checked his watch, which showed a quarter to eleven. If Angelina had kept her appointment with Brother Gabriel, that put her out of the house some ten or eleven hours ago. Unless, of course, she had returned. His eyes searched the room once more. There was nothing to indicate when she had left or if she had returned. But Tim's absence was more puzzling in some ways.

Mark turned to Rosa and Luis. "Neither of you know when Tim left? You didn't hear a car or anything?"

The two of them looked at each other, then Rosa slowly shook her head. "No, Padre. I thought he was in here. I was trying to be quiet so they could sleep." In the distance, a chime sounded. Rosa turned to her husband. "Luis, get the door, please."

Father Townsend was pretty sure he knew who it was. He took one last look around the room, then led them back down the hallway. Luis was just leading Bill Yoder toward them. The look on the detective's face, when he spotted Townsend and Grib, was anything but polite.

"What are you doing here?" It was not quite a snarl, but close enough.

Mark decided there was no sense making something up. "We're looking for Angelina."

"And her husband," contributed Dennis. Mark winced visibly.

"Her husband?" The detective's antennae were extended fully. "Where's her husband?"

The five of them were crowded uncomfortably in the narrow hallway between the front of the house and the back bedroom. Rosa motioned to her husband and he politely invited everyone back out to the living room. Once they were settled, Yoder picked up where he left off.

"You're telling me there's two people missing from here? This Angelina and now her husband?"

Luis and Rosa looked scared, too scared to speak. Having a policeman come to their house was terrifying. They sat on the couch, clutching each other's hands, huddled next to each other. Both turned to Father Townsend, wanting him to speak.

Mark cleared his throat. "Apparently both Angelina and Tim are out at the moment." Yoder's notepad was in his hand, pencil poised. "Tim Connell. That's Angelina's husband."

"The guy you rode over from Seattle with." Detective Yoder had listened a lot closer than Mark realized. "So where are they?" The priest hesitated and Bill Yoder looked up expectantly. "Father?"

"We're not quite sure," the Jesuit finally admitted.

ELEVEN

Mark Townsend felt stymied. There was nothing more he could do besides reassure Luis and Rosa that he would keep in touch. When Detective Yoder finished interviewing the two Jesuits a second time he escorted them to their car, firmly ordering them to butt out. He stood outside the Castillos' house with his arms crossed and waited until they reached the bottom of the drive. Yoder was making it clear he wanted them out of the way.

Dennis had clammed up in front of the policeman, but once alone with Mark he let loose with a torrent of questions, observations, and speculations. Who the hell did Yoder think he was, talking to them that way? Did Mark notice how that cop was always watching whenever anyone said anything? Maybe Tim went back to Seattle. Where was Angelina hiding? What did Mark want to do now?

What Mark wanted to do now was pack up and head home. But he realized he could hardly leave Yakima without first knowing what happened to Tim and Angelina. He would call the airline when they got back to the house, cancelling his afternoon reservation and checking on the last flight out that night. Christians live in hope.

The Sunday Masses were over by the time the two of them arrived back at St. Joseph. Paul and Joe were both in the kitchen. The news about Brother Gabriel was already public and both priests wanted to hear what Mark and Dennis knew. Grib fixed ham sandwiches for Mark and himself as they described the scene at the park and their visit to the Castillos' house in Moxee. Father Stanley said he knew Bill Yoder. He was not a Catholic, but nevertheless, he thought he was a good man. There was a gleam of satisfaction in the old man's eyes when he mentioned Brother Gabriel's death. Mark remembered his deprecations about false prophets from the day before and he wondered if the priest actually believed that God's hand was in this tragedy.

Bones was straightforward with his view on things. If you stick your head above the rest of the crowd, he drawled, someone is going to try and lop it off. The fact that the preacher was attacked did not surprise him. What did surprise LaBelle was how long it took before someone tried.

"That man had about as much chance as a twelve-point buck in November," Father LaBelle opined, "and about half the brains. He could have just painted a big bullseye on that cape of his."

While both priests were more than willing to offer their opinions of Gabriel, neither one wanted to speculate much about Angelina or Tim. Father Townsend suspected it was out of respect for his own relationship with the missing couple. No one seemed to have any idea of how to begin looking for them, either. For the time being, waiting was about their only option, other than praying. Father Townsend and Brother Grib went into the house's small chapel to say a quick Mass while Father Stanley headed off for a nap and Bones stretched out in front of the television for some baseball. Sunday afternoons at St. Joe's in Yakima were not that much different from St. Joe's in Seattle.

After their informal liturgy was over, Dennis Grib had a suggestion. Instead of sitting and waiting, maybe they could go take a look around. He had nothing he needed to do, and he would be happy to take Mark for a ride. He offered to drive him by Brother Gabriel's place in Cowiche. Mark never even hesitated. Sitting in the house, waiting for a phone to ring, was not his style.

Grib's car was small, but not as small as Emily. And he had air conditioning. He picked up Highway 12 just past a trailer park and headed west. The road ran parallel along the Naches River, then crossed it beyond Fruit-vale. The riverbed was wide with lots of exposed gravel bars, and bright sunlight glinted off the water. The water, although low, looked clear and cold. Cottonwoods lined both banks. There were high bluffs on either side of them, and some expensive-looking homes built onto the rimrock.

"One of the old Indian trails runs just under that bluff," Dennis informed Mark, pointing as he drove. "And there are caves up there where you can still find arrowheads and stuff. The Yakimas lived all through here. That was before the whites came, of course."

The valley was growing increasingly narrower the further in they drove, and by the time they reached the town of Naches, Mark was feeling slightly claustrophobic. After the vast expanse of the Yakima Valley, the closeness here was startling.

When they were in the center of town, Dennis signaled a left turn off the highway. A large roadside sign advertised APRICOTS, PEARS, PEACHES. A much smaller one pointed the way to Cowiche and Tieton. A minute later they were leaving the valley floor, starting up a steep, winding road. The going was slow, made more so when they pulled behind a long flatbed truck heading for the orchards, piled high with empty wooden fruit bins. There was nowhere to pass, so Dennis slowed to a crawl and kept a safe distance between their car and the truck. Wistfully, Mark looked at his watch. He wondered what time the first flight to Seattle left in the morning.

Apple orchards covered the hilltop. The first row of trees was planted so close to the road's edge that their limbs nearly hung over it. Clusters of fruit ripened among the leaves. The trees were wide, broad-limbed, and close to the ground. None was taller than ten or twelve feet. All of them were heavy with fruit. The truck in front slowed down to make a turn and Dennis executed a quick end run around before the driver even had time to crank his wheels. Once safely past, Grib speeded up. They topped a low rise and the town of Cowiche opened up in front of them. From first appearances, the settlement looked like nothing more than cold storage warehouses surrounded by a few houses. If you were not into apples, it appeared you had no business being up there.

Brother Grib seemed to know where he was going. He steered them through the small community and turned left onto a narrow country lane that led them past more orchards. They topped another rise and were suddenly on top of a bluff overlooking a vast expanse of valley laid out in front of them. After feeling hemmed in by apple trees, the vista's openness caught Mark by surprise. Dennis slowed down, then turned the wheel to the right, nosing his car into the middle of a narrow and dusty drive that led to a house perched at the edge of the rimrock, about a hundred feet from where they were. He stopped and turned off the engine.

"That's his place," he said, pointing.

Brother Gabriel lived in a whitewashed hacienda with a red tiled roof. The house sat off by itself. The dirt drive they were parked on looked to be the only way in. There were no trees anywhere on the property, just the stark white house with two Dodge Ram pickup trucks parked in front. They were big—both V-10's with extended cabs, one midnight black and one cherry red. A garage stood separate from the house, and another white building was built closer to the edge of the bluff. Dennis pointed it out.

"That's what they call the Vigil Room," he informed Mark. "Where those people got raptured."

From that distance, nothing about the property appeared particularly apocalyptic. Nor particularly religious. The house looked expensive and well kept, but was, nevertheless, just a big fancy house on a rocky bluff with a great view. Angelina had already told him that some of Gabriel's wealthy benefactors had set the minister up with a place to live while he carried on his ministry in the Yakima Valley. Mark sadly shook his head. The pity was living in a classy place like this and believing the walls were going to tumble down in a short while. Anticipating the end of the world sort of takes all the fun out of living in a house that nice. Of course, when the end did come, you would have a great view.

The wide front door to the house opened and a tall man in a straw cowboy hat stepped outside. He held his hand above his eyes, squinting at their car in the harsh sunlight. Grib's car, parked in front of the dirt drive, had caught someone's attention. For a moment the man leaned back inside the doorway, as if talking to someone, then stepped out again, closing the door behind him. He came off the porch, headed their way. His cowboy boots caused small explosions of dust wherever he stepped. Without seeming in any hurry he headed directly toward them.

Dennis studied the man approaching them. "What should we do?" he asked. "You want me to drive on?"

"No. No, let's see what he wants." Mark loosened his seatbelt and opened his door. The hot air hit him like a fist. Father Townsend stood next to the car, and raised his own hand to shield his eyes from the bright sun overhead. The man approaching was still about thirty feet away. He was tall and loose-jointed and looked a bit like Joe Bones, although younger. His face beneath his hat was red and weathered. He was wearing a short-sleeved cowboy shirt and blue jeans, but they were both clean and pressed. His dusty boots looked new. When he was about eight feet from Mark, he stopped in his tracks and gave the stranger a curious smile.

"Can I help you with something?" he inquired. The man's voice was not hostile, but cautious.

"I'm sorry if we disturbed you," Father Townsend replied. "We were out for a drive and my friend stopped to show me where Brother Gabriel lived."

Using the past tense caught the cowboy's attention and he jerked his head up. His blue eyes studied Mark. "Did you know Brother?"

"I had only just met him," the priest confessed, "but I was sorry to hear about his death."

"The Lord giveth and the Lord taketh away. Blessed be the name of the Lord."

It was one of those responses that leaves you feeling like the conversation has suddenly veered off the road and abandoned you somewhere two or three sentences behind. And you are never quite sure what to say that will put you back on track. Townsend gaped at the cowboy, trying to come up with anything that would sound even remotely responsive.

Finally the man volunteered, "Sister Elizabeth is devastated, naturally. As are we all."

"Of course," Mark agreed.

"We considered Brother a great prophet, sent to lead us through this vale of tears. Losing him now is like losing our way." With that the tall man bent his head and squeezed his eyes closed. It almost looked like he was trying to force some tears.

"I certainly will keep all of you in my prayers," Father Townsend promised. The cowboy opened his eyes and raised his head, blinking twice.

"We appreciate that," he said. "We can always use prayers." He extended his hand. "I'm Marshall Fairbanks," he said.

"Father Mark Townsend."

"Father?" The man took a step back. "Like a Catholic Father?" For the first time he peered closely at the car, carefully taking notice of Dennis Grib at the wheel. "You're not from Yakima."

"No," replied Mark, "I'm not. I'm from Seattle, just visiting for a couple of days."

Fairbanks nodded, as if reassured. "Is he a priest, too?"

"No, that's Brother Dennis Grib. He works at St. Joseph."

"Oh, yeah," the cowboy said, "I know that church. Brother vigils there. Or did."

"That's where we met," Mark told him. "Just yesterday, in fact."

Marshall Fairbanks looked down at his boots, as if suddenly feeling shy. He kicked at the dust, which rose in a small billowy cloud almost up to his knees before settling back to the ground, some of it falling onto the toes of his boots.

"I guess I'd best get back inside," he said. "We're prayin' with Sister Elizabeth and asking divine guidance for what comes next. I'm sorry I can't invite you inside."

"That's all right," Mark assured him. "We have to get back anyway. We just wanted to pay our respects."

" 'preciate it, then," Fairbanks said. He lifted his hand to the brim of his hat, then turned on his heel and strode quickly back to the house. Father Townsend watched him a few more moments, then climbed back into the car. In the short time the motor was off, the inside had heated considerably. As soon as Mark's door was closed, Dennis started up the car.

"Who was that?" he asked, watching as the man disappeared inside.

"He said his name was Marshall Fairbanks."

Dennis slapped the steering wheel. "So that's Marshall Fairbanks!"

"What about him?"

Brother Grib was backing his car out of the drive onto the road, turning hard on the wheel. His tires spun in some loose gravel as they left the dirt lane. He shifted and started the car back toward Cowiche.

"Marshall Fairbanks is supposed to be one of the richest guys around here," Dennis informed the priest. "His grandfather owned a huge sheep ranch down near Grandview. Then that got sold and they started orchards. Bones says he's so rich he sweats nickels."

"That sounds like something Bones would say."

The young brother grinned. "It does, doesn't it?"

They drove back through Cowiche, following the

winding road past the orchards and down to the valley floor. From the hillside they caught glimpses of the Naches River as it flowed toward the larger Yakima. Once off the hills, Brother Grib followed it home.

There was no reason why a man with Fairbanks's wealth could not consider himself lost and in need of redemption. Especially if he put as much faith as he apparently did in Brother Gabriel and his message. Clearly, Marshall Fairbanks would be considered one of Brother Gabriel's wealthier benefactors. Angelina had never mentioned anyone by name, although she said the evangelist had two rich supporters. There were two matching Ram pickups parked in front of the house. If Fairbanks owned one, then who drove the other? He tried picturing Sister Elizabeth behind the wheel. Tim's Emily was more her style. Gabriel's small wife would fit much easier inside a Volkswagen Beetle than she would in one of the big rigs parked in front of her house.

The Jesuits rode in silence back to the residence, each one lost in his own thoughts. Their drive out to Cowiche had been distracting, but hardly helpful. Angelina Sandoval Ybarra was still missing, as was her husband.

Dennis parked his car in the narrow driveway behind the house and they let themselves in through the kitchen door. There was no cook on Sunday so the kitchen was deserted. But from the other room they could hear the television. Father Stanley had the volume turned up so he could hear and a chair pulled within four feet of the set so he could see. An old nun in a brown habit was interviewing a young priest with a beard. Paul was closely following their conversation, and it was not until Dennis walked around the set that he finally glanced up at them. Mark was the one he addressed.

"Your friend's in jail."

Message delivered, he turned his attention back to the TV.

TWELVE

"There's not much to see, is there?"

Dennis Grib's question surprised Mark. He thought there was actually quite a bit. He could see down the narrow cut to Union Gap and across to the Cascades. Downtown Yakima was right in front of them and to one side, the Sundome's cement hulk. Just below them was a small lake with a floating stage built out into it, and behind them was the Yakima River. From the top of the wooden viewing platform, there was actually quite a lot to see. Father Townsend turned around to answer and saw Brother Grib's eyes fixed on the structure's wooden deck. Repeated scrubbings had failed to wash away the bloody stain entirely. But it was not much and the sun would soon bleach out even that small reminder.

"No," the priest assented, looking down at the spot, "no, there isn't much to see."

They were not alone. Once the police removed their yellow plastic tape, people started crawling all over the structure. About ten individuals had squeezed up the narrow steps and were crowded on top with Dennis and Mark. Most were Hispanics. Townsend wondered how many were Gabriel's followers. Like both the Jesuits, they stood away from the platform's center, as if treading on the dark stain was, in some way, disrespectful.

Mark figured it was something like standing on a grave. The same people who avoided walking over the dead would probably not want to walk where a man died. Father Townsend carefully stepped around the dark stain and headed toward the steps. There was nothing more to see up there.

Dennis followed Mark down the stairs. "How long do you think they're going to hold Tim?" he asked the priest.

Luis Castillo had called the parish as soon as Tim notified him he was at the jail and left a message with Father Stanley. When he got the message, Mark Townsend went immediately from the church to the jail, but was not allowed to see his parishioner. Connell was being interrogated and was unavailable, they told him.

"I don't know," Mark replied as they headed across the grass to their car, "my guess is that they'll release him when they're done questioning him."

Why the police had him in the first place was not entirely clear. Sure, Tim was no fan of Brother Gabriel's, but that hardly made him a suspect. It probably had something to do with his missing wife.

Dennis unlocked the door on Mark's side of the car. "So what now? Where do you want to go next?" The young man seemed to enjoy driving around the valley.

"I'm kind of hungry. How about you?"

They bought a bucket of chicken and a dozen biscuits. Dennis said Father Stanley liked macaroni salad, so they ordered a quart of that, too. If he was back in Seattle, Mark and his associate, Father Dan Morrow, would be ordering a large number twenty-five with extra pepperoni from Olympic Pizza. Morrow would be glued to a Mariners' game in front of the TV and Townsend would be dispatched to pick it up. Carry-out on Sunday night was part of the day's rituals. One of the more relaxed and less public ones.

Paul Stanley was taking Dan Morrow's place, his chair parked in front of the television at the same spot as when they left, the volume turned up just as loud. Bones was finishing a shower, so Mark and Dennis laid out Sunday dinner on the kitchen table, then announced to Paul that he could serve himself. At the end of the inning, the old priest scooted into the kitchen. He poured himself a glass of milk, took one drumstick, a biscuit, and about half the quart of salad. Dennis was right about the macaroni. He was back in front of the television before the next pitch and just as LaBelle wandered downstairs.

"Sunday night chicken!" the pastor chortled in delight. "That's what my mama always cooked. In fact, she used to serve it in a red and white cardboard bucket just like that one."

There was cold beer in the refrigerator and Dennis grabbed three bottles as they settled around the table for their meal. Anyone wanting to follow the game could hear it well enough through the open doorway.

"So there's still no word from your jailbird friend, huh?" Bones asked from behind a breast.

"Not yet," answered Mark. "I thought he would have called by now."

"There's a parishioner who's a cop," LaBelle told him between bites. "I could call her if you want me to, ask if she knows anything."

"That'd be good," Townsend said, lifting his beer. "By the way, how well do you know a guy named Marshall Fairbanks? I met him up in Cowiche this afternoon."

Bones glanced over at Brother Grib. "Dennis drove you up to Brother Gabe's hideaway, huh?" He nodded before biting off another mouthful of chicken. He gulped it down, then continued, "Fairbanks is so rich he sweats . . ."

". . . nickels," Dennis finished for him. Then looking over at Mark, "I told you."

"As a matter of fact, with inflation, I think he's up to quarters now. But the guy can afford it. He's one of the richest men around here."

"And a supporter of Brother Gabriel's?"

Joe LaBelle nodded, his mouth full of salad.

"There's supposed to be another one," Mark told

him. "Angelina told me that there were two Anglos who put up most of the money for Brother's ministry."

"That'd be Len Patowski. They're both in apples. Fairbanks is a grower and Patowski runs a nursery. Len's probably got just as much money as Marshall, but twice the brains. He's done all right for himself. Where Fairbanks inherited most of his loot, Patowski started from scratch. He began with a couple of orchards down by Sunnyside and eventually started a nursery, growing trees. I don't know how much he's got now, but it's plenty."

From the other room came the loud crack of a bat followed by a whoop from Father Stanley.

"I'm not surprised that Fairbanks bought Gabriel's hooey," LaBelle continued, "but I thought old Patowski had more smarts than that. From what I hear, the two of 'em gave matching gifts. And then they donated that little hillside retreat for the Brother and his Mrs. I don't know what Brother Gabe slipped in their coffee, but it sure loosened their wallets. I'd like to use a little on some of the Catholics around here. Benefactors like that don't grow on trees, and that's a fact."

Mark commiserated with his friend. Fund-raising in Yakima did not sound any easier than in Seattle.

"I wonder if Angelina ever interviewed either of them," Father Townsend mused. "It'd be interesting to know if she's talked to them."

"I don't know," Joe rejoined, "but I wouldn't be surprised. She's been calling folks up and down this valley. For a reporter, she's pretty thorough. Anyone who has anything to do with Gabriel, she's probably talked to."

"It's too bad you can't ask her," Dennis said. "But maybe she'll still show up."

He was trying to sound encouraging, but none of the Jesuits at the table believed Angelina Sandoval Ybarra would materialize anytime soon. If at all. An awkward quiet fell over them as they continued eating. Only the sounds of baseball and Father Stanley's querulous armchair coaching broke the silence.

Finally, Joe LaBelle spoke. "So Mark, what are your plans? You gonna stick around here or head back to Gomorrah? You know that you're welcome to stay as long as you'd like. In fact, I'm willing to call the provincial right now and tell him you've decided to trade up." Bones made like he was reaching for the phone. "Just say the word!"

Mark smiled his gratitude. For all of his joking, Joe LaBelle was the type of man who would do anything for you. His offer of hospitality was sincere.

"That's a tempting offer, Joe, but I guess I'd better decline. Although I think I will stick around here for another day—at least until I can talk to Tim and find out what's going on. And maybe Angelina will show up in the meantime. I'll call Dan and let him know I'm staying over."

LaBelle looked across the table at Dennis Grib and then back to Mark.

"You know, Brother Grib is an okay watchdog. I've sicced him onto Paul and he's done all right shepherding the old man around town. He's pretty good to have around."

Hearing the compliment, Dennis blushed with pleasure.

"He also speaks the local dialect," LaBelle continued, "which—no offense, Father—I notice you are a wee deficient in. In fact, if you don't mind me saying, your Spanish sounds like something you picked up in Taco Bell."

Townsend feigned great offense. "Father! How dare you say that! For your information, it was Taco Time, not Taco Bell."

"Please accept my humble apologies, Monsignor. I have made a horrible error in judgement." LaBelle performed a contrite bow over the table. "I deserve to be flogged with a limp burrito."

Townsend waved a hasty and sloppy cross over his fellow priest. "*Te absolvo*," he solemnly intoned, "with an order of fries."

Dennis Grib was leaning back in his chair, enjoying

their private performance. Their banter and quick asides were signals of their respect and affection for each other. A house of celibate men can turn pretty sour without humor. Ignatius Loyola used to push away from the table and dance Basque jigs to get his fellow Jesuits laughing. The comedy of LaBelle and Townsend was in the same vein.

Father LaBelle got back to his point. "Anyway, Mark, while you're here, why don't you let Dennis drive you around? He can do some translation if you get stuck and he knows the area and quite a few of the people. Also, I think he and Paul could use some time away from each other. Whata' you say?"

Mark checked with Dennis, whose eyes were shining bright.

"Sounds fine to me," he agreed, "if Dennis doesn't mind."

"It'd be fun," the young brother said eagerly, "I'd like to."

"All right then. And while you're driving Mark around," Bones winked at the younger man, "see if you can't recruit him. If he stays over on the wet side much longer he's going to lose his immortal soul."

With dinner over, the three men began gathering up the dirty plates, chicken bones, and empty bottles. There were a few pieces of chicken left over, one biscuit, and no macaroni salad. Father Stanley had seen to that. Now the old priest was slumped forward in his chair, gently snoring. Despite Coach Stanley's best efforts, the Mariners gave it away in the ninth.

After helping clean up, Brother Grib excused himself and headed over to lock up the church. Bones retired to his room and Mark headed for the phone to call Dan Morrow. He would take some heat from his associate for not returning when he promised, but he knew the schedule in Seattle was light. In late August the parish all but shut down. Morrow might grouse about his absence, but Mark knew he would not be missed.

The doorbell rang in the middle of Mark's phone conversation with Dan Morrow. He was listening to his associate castigate him for neglecting his priestly duties in Seattle to work on his tan in Yakima. Father Townsend assured him that he was not concerned with tanning and that he would return home as soon as possible. But with Angelina missing and Tim in jail, he could hardly walk away. Grudgingly, Morrow conceded. Most of it was an act they put on for each other's sake anyway.

Mark was saying goodbye when he heard a tap at his bedroom door. He turned to see Father Stanley cautiously pushing it open, poking his head into Mark's room. The old priest, seeing Townsend was on the phone, mouthed the words "Tim Connell" and pointed downstairs before withdrawing his head and easing the door closed.

"Dan, I've got to go." Townsend said quickly. "Tim Connell just showed up."

A dejected Tim Connell was leaning forward in the middle of the living room couch, his arms resting on his knees, his eyes fixed on the carpet at his feet. He lifted them slowly when he heard Mark's footsteps on the stairs but made no other movement. His face was gray and pasty and his clothes were wrinkled. He needed a shave.

"Tim, are you all right?"

"Hi, Father." There was an awkward, embarrassed tone to a voice that sounded raw and tired.

Townsend hurried to his side. "I've been worried about you. Luis called and said you were at the jail. I tried to get in to see you."

Connell's eyes had dropped back to the carpet. Mark was standing over the poor man. He laid a hand on his shoulder.

"Can I get you anything?" he asked quietly.

Tim colored slightly. "Do you have a beer?" he asked. "And maybe a sandwich?"

The Jesuit led him into the kitchen and pulled out a chair at the table for him. Tim docilely sat down, laying his arms on the table in front of him. His eyes followed the priest around the room as Mark collected a plate and silverware. He pulled the leftover chicken from the refrigerator and found the remaining biscuit. Father Townsend hesitated, but then reached in for the beer Connell requested. Setting it in front of him, Mark took the chair across the table from Tim.

"Thanks," Tim mumbled. He was ravenous and devoured everything in quick time. Neither man spoke while he ate. Mark waited until he finished the last of the chicken and pushed his plate away. Tim raised the beer bottle and drained it, placing it next to the plate of bones. Mark did not offer him another one.

"I guess you want to know what happened," Connell began, "although I've got to say that there's not a whole lot to tell you. I don't remember very much."

"Tell me what you know," Mark urged.

His parishioner looked on him with red-rimmed eyes. "I don't know where Angelina is. She's disappeared." His voice caught. "The police think she went to see Brother Gabriel, like he asked her to. But now they can't find her." His voice was jagged and close to breaking.

"Tim," Mark interrupted him, "why did they hold you so long?"

Connell's problem was not remembering. Father Townsend had spent enough time around drunks to know about blackouts.

There were about seven hours he could not remember, and it was those seven hours, he informed Father Townsend, that the police were most anxious to hear about. At least, judging from the questions Detective Bill Yoder had asked him.

Connell was able to remember the Castillos' fiesta. And he remembered seeing Brother Gabriel at the bottom of the hill. He recalled getting angry. But he insisted it was directed more at his wife than it was the preacher. He told Mark the same thing he told the detective—his wife was crazy to go to a 1 a.m. meeting with a weirdo like Gabriel. He remembered trying to convince her not to go—even demanding that she stay there with him.

At that point the young man, overcome by worry, alcohol, and fatigue, broke down and cried. His wife was missing, a man was dead, and he could not remember what happened next. Father Townsend waited impatiently until Connell gained control, then pushed him to finish his story. Tim informed the priest he did not remember leaving the party. Nor did he recall where he went or what he did. But that morning, at about eleven-thirty, he woke up in the car, finding himself stretched across the two front seats, the gearshift poking him in the gut. He was parked behind some apple bins next to a cold storage warehouse across from railroad tracks in Yakima's south end. He sat up, started the car and drove up First, trying to figure out where he was. That part he remembered. Tim drove past a place called the Sweet Apple Tavern just as its OPEN light flickered to life. He said he stopped for coffee. Why he ended up ordering a beer instead was beyond him.

Embarrassed, Tim Connell lifted the empty beer bottle off the kitchen table and began peeling away its label. He described the policeman coming up to him in the tavern. Connell was hunched over a barstool, his hands wrapped around a nearly full bottle of beer. The cop strolled up to him and said someone at police headquarters was interested in talking to him. Then he leaned Connell against the bar, patted him down, and handcuffed him before escorting him out.

Yoder had been waiting at his desk when Connell arrived. Tim was led into an interrogation room and was handed a styrofoam cup of coffee. The detective waited until he had drunk most of it before coming into the room.

Tim set down the beer bottle, sniffled loudly and dabbed at his eyes with a crumpled napkin. "Hell, Father, he asked me so many questions. He said the gun they found next to Gabriel's body was mine."

Father Townsend held himself in check. His immediate impulse was to leap up, lean across the table, and wring Tim Connell's neck. But he forced himself to remain calm.

"You had a gun?" he asked as smoothly as he could.

Connell nodded. As best he could, he recounted the interrogation with Detective Bill Yoder.

"Do you recall if you own a gun?"

"What do you mean?"

"What don't you understand? You know the word *own*? The word *gun*? Now put them together. Do you own a gun?"

He jerked his head slightly.

"Is that a yes, Mr. Connell?"

"Yes," he finally admitted, "a forty caliber Taurus."

The detective had paused, watching Connell's face.

"All right. Now this one's important. Do you remember where you put it?"

Tim told him it was hidden under the seat of his car.

"Why'd you put it there, Mr. Connell?"

"Because I was coming to Yakima and because Angie said she was scared. I didn't know what was over here."

"But you were going to come prepared. Is that it?"

He did not answer.

"Is the gun registered?"

"Yes . . . when I bought it in Seattle."

"When did you last see it?"

"I guess when I put it in the car."

"You never took it out? You never told someone else to take it?"

Tim admitted he had taken it out once.

Mark was pretty sure he knew when.

"It was during the party at the Castillos," Tim told him. "When Angie went down the hill to see that . . . that . . . Brother Gabriel."

"You had the gun with you?" Mark said.

Connell nodded. "I had it under my shirt . . . tucked in my pants."

"Go on," Mark encouraged. "Who else knew about it?"

"I don't think anyone," Connell told him. "I, uh, I . . . didn't want Angie to know I had it. But when we got up to the house she made me put it back in my car.

Then I remember she locked it up and we went back into the party.''

"So she knew about the gun?"

"Yes."

"Did you tell the police that?" Father Townsend asked.

He had. Yoder wanted to know if his wife had handled it before he put it back in his car. Tim told him no.

"Then he wanted to know if I thought you knew I had the gun."

"Me?" exclaimed Mark. "I never knew you had a gun!"

He had a dozen more questions he wanted to ask Tim, beginning with the obvious *why*. He was about to start peppering the man with them when he took another look at Tim's sloping shoulders and downcast eyes. He had already endured a day-long interrogation. He did not need another one.

"So the police think Brother Gabriel was shot with your gun. And your wife is missing after agreeing to meet him in the park." Connell nodded agreement. "And I guess that means her car is missing, too."

Tim shook his head. "No," he replied. "That's another thing. I've got the Blazer. Angelina had Emily— the Volks.''

"Why'd you two switch?" Mark wanted to know.

Tim shrugged. "I'm not sure. The police asked me the same thing. There's a lot I don't remember after the party. I must have had the Blazer keys in my pocket, so when I left I drove away in that. But I'm not sure."

Townsend figured that was possible. Tim Connell had driven the three of them from the church up to the Castillos. He had no recollection of Tim handing the car keys back to his wife. If Angelina kept Emily's keys to prevent Tim from getting his gun out, she could have driven the Volkswagen to her rendezvous with Brother Gabriel.

"Do you think she went back to Seattle?" Mark asked.

"The police already checked," Tim said. "They've

been going by our apartment all day, but there's no sign of her. There's police looking for her all over the state, they told me.'' Raising his arms off the table, he buried his head in his hands.

Mark studied the abject figure across from him: For such a supposedly bright man, Tim Connell was acting pretty dumb.

Father Townsend had listened carefully to his story, twisting and tugging at the ends of his mustache. There were so many gaping holes in what Tim could and could not remember—it was like trying to catch rain in your hands. Mark could feel his frustration increasing. And then he realized it was probably minuscule compared to what was going on inside this man.

"You need to go back to the Castillos and rest," he counseled Tim. "You must be exhausted."

Connell slowly nodded. He pushed himself back from the table, as if to stand up.

"Tim." Mark had one last question for the man. "Before you go . . . do you remember who knew Angelina was meeting Brother Gabriel?"

The Jesuit's question stopped him. This was one the police had never asked and he hesitated before answering, struggling to recall.

"Well . . . let's see," he slowly drew it out. "I guess there was you and Brother Dennis, because you were down there, huh? And I know Luis Castillo knew. I sort of hoped he'd tell Ange she shouldn't go." He thought a long moment. "And that friend of Luis's . . . he was standing there. What's his name? . . . José . . . Ramirez. His son was one of the believers who got raptured or disappeared. And I guess that's everybody. Oh yeah, Rosa was there too, wasn't she? That's all the people I can think of."

Mark remembered the angry exchange between Angelina and her husband. In his mind he searched the faces standing around the two as they argued. As far he remembered, Tim was including everyone who was there. Was there anyone else? Father Townsend thought a moment longer, then pushed his own chair back. No one that he could recall.

THIRTEEN

The *Yakima Herald* gave Brother Gabriel's murder a lot of coverage. It was the top story on the front page, filling the upper half and spilling over to pages six and seven. The text itself contained very little that Father Townsend did not already know, but there were a couple of terrific pictures. Since his arrival in the valley, Gabriel's dramatic image had been photographed repeatedly. There was a picture of him standing behind a microphone, surrounded by people, as he gesticulated toward a mural behind him. If you looked closely, you could see what some might interpret as a hazy image of the Lady of Guadalupe floating in the mist above a cascading river. Indians with long fishing nets were leaning toward her. Another photo showed the preacher inside the Vigil Room at his home in Cowiche. He was in his white robe, seated on a plank bench in a stark white room. The caption under the picture explained that Brother Gabriel was as mystified as everyone else over the alleged disappearance of several people from the room. He was quoted as saying, "If it's not from Satan, then it's from God. This room is a holy place, dedicated to those who choose to await the new times, so I can only assume it is from God."

Father Townsend moved the newspaper closer to his

face, studying the photo closely. As far as he could see, the Vigil Room was pretty much as Angelina described it to him. There were long narrow air vents up near the ceiling, but no windows that he could see. The floor looked like a solid concrete slab, the walls made of cinderblock. The single entrance into the room was out of the frame, probably behind the photographer's back, judging from the way light spilt across the floor. Townsend laid the paper down with a sigh.

Someone once observed that Jesuits do not believe in unanswerable riddles and do not seem too fond of miracles, either. Mark could not presume to speak for the rest of his companions, but that pretty much nailed his own belief. Not that miracles do not occur, but they are nothing you can be comfortable around. The minute you become overly fond of them, you are in danger of passing from the sublime into the weird. And riddles, by their very nature, have to have answers. Otherwise they move dangerously close to miracles and you are back where you started.

Father Townsend snapped the newspaper with his fingers. He wanted to see inside that room.

The news story rehashed Gabriel's earlier career as a Presbyterian minister named David Grimes, living in Bakersfield, California. There was a statement from one of Grimes's former parishioners who remembered the albino minister as strange-looking but fervent and devoted. "Then he went kind of loopy on us," the man was quoted as saying, "and he started with this talk about the end of the world. I think he really believed in it, but that was just too much for us. Then he started in on that Mary stuff and that's when we decided it was time for a change."

Brother Gabriel's early days in the Yakima Valley sounded difficult. According to the *Herald*, David and Linda Grimes lived in the back of their station wagon for several months. The now Sister Elizabeth recalled for the reporter that Brother's custom of preaching outside was more a necessity than a choice. They could not afford to rent a meeting hall or even a covered awning, so Gabriel began going out to wherever there were crowds to preach his message.

"The Lord missioned his apostles to the highways and byways," Sister Elizabeth said, "and told them that the churches would be replaced by the Spirit and truth. Brother Gabriel was fulfilling our heavenly Lord's mandate."

When the minister's message began attracting larger crowds, a few stepped forward with offers to help. The newspaper reported that he turned down all offers to build a church, although he did accept the donation of a house. The idea of a Vigil Room evolved gradually, according to Sister Elizabeth.

"I believe that idea came from personal revelation," she said. "Brother never really explained it completely. To be honest, I think he was a little frightened by the sacred power of that room." She went on to say that he kept vigil only one night every week, and always alone. The other nights it was made available to others.

Sister Elizabeth was uncertain what would happen to the ministry now that her husband was dead. According to the article, she was meeting with Brother Gabriel's advisors. The funeral would be announced as soon as the police released the body, and it was possible that some sort of vigil or wake might be held beforehand. The Sister and advisors had not decided that by the time the newspaper was printed.

Father Townsend had no game plan. Other than supporting Tim Connell and trying to find out what happened to Angelina Sandoval Ybarra, he had no reason for remaining in Yakima. But when he called Rosa Castillo, she told him Tim had already left the house. She did not know where he went or when he would be back.

"No sé, Padre." She caught herself. "I do not know, Father. He slept a long time and when he got up I made him a breakfast. But then he drove away and I have not seen him yet. Maybe he is looking for Angelina?"

Maybe. The Jesuit had a hunch that caring for Tim Connell was going to be difficult. The man had his own support system, although it was based on schooners and pints. As for finding out what happened to Angelina, he was at a loss. The local police were looking for her and, from what Connell told him, they had the Seattle police and state troopers keeping an eye out, too. Frustrated, the priest put in a call to the Yakima police department, asking for Detective Yoder. Whoever answered patched Mark through to Yoder's voice mail. Mark waited for the detective's message to end, then identified himself and said he was still in town. He hesitated but then hung up. There was nothing he could ask that Yoder would answer anyway.

After lunch, Dennis Grib had to drive Paul Stanley to a doctor's appointment. The Jesuit house was empty and Mark roamed through it restlessly. He tried watching television, but the programming was vapid. He tried reading, but his attention wandered. Praying was out of the question. His mind strayed and he was unable to focus on anything for more than a minute or two. He felt like someone wandering through a junkyard, picking up odd pieces of trash and then discarding them. There was nothing he could hang on to.

St. Ignatius once compared the effect of evil spirits to water splashing on stones. "The action of the evil spirit," he warned, "is violent, noisy, and disturbing." There was no doubt in Mark Townsend's mind: the events of the last twenty-four hours were like water falling on stones.

He was sitting at the kitchen table when the two Jesuits returned from the doctor's. Grumbling, Paul Stanley stormed up to his room, ignoring Mark's greeting. Brother Grib strolled through the back door after him, grinning broadly.

"What's up with Paul?" Mark asked.

Dennis pulled a soft drink from the refrigerator. "Looks like Padre's got some plumbing problems," he said. "But the doctor doesn't think it's the prostate."

"That's lucky."

"Yeah, I wouldn't wish that on my worse enemy," Dennis agreed. "I told Father that all that piss and vinegar was finally backing up on him. He didn't think that was too funny." He finished his drink in three gulps and arced the empty can with an overhand pass into the recycle bin. "Have you heard from Tim?"

"Not yet."

"Maybe we ought to go check the Sweet Apple," Brother Grib suggested.

Mark grudgingly admitted he had already thought of that. "But if he's there, I don't want to know about it."

"So what's next?"

Father Townsend shook his head impatiently. "I'm not sure, Dennis. But there's something that doesn't add up for me." He splayed his fingers across the table top in front of him. "If Angelina did go to the park to meet Brother Gabriel, she either got there before or after he was killed." Mark hesitated, glancing up at Dennis. "I guess that's obvious. But if he was still alive when she left, why wouldn't she have gone home? And if he was already dead, why did she run? It doesn't add up."

Brother Grib dropped into the chair opposite him. "There's another possibility, Mark. What if she was killed, too?"

Townsend nodded. "I thought of that. But that doesn't make sense either. Where's her body? Why leave Gabriel's and not hers? And wouldn't there have been some sign of another killing? Blood or something?" Mark folded his hands together. "No, I don't think she was killed. Not there, at least."

"Somewhere else? You think someone took her?"

"Something's happened to her. Unless she's on the run, then she's either dead or someone has her. I can't see any other options."

Brother Grib considered a moment. "It makes sense," he finally agreed, "but which is it? And if she's not involved, doesn't that point to Tim?"

Mark had to agree. "Unfortunately. That's got to be what the police are thinking. I'd love to talk this through with that Detective Yoder, but I'm sure that has to be it. I mean, with it being Connell's gun and everything . . ."

Brother Grib studied the priest across the table. Father

Townsend's hand strayed up to his face and he unconsciously fingered the strands of his mustache, then began pulling and twisting at them. His mouth twitched and puckered as he silently considered the options. "That's got to be it," he muttered.

"And if it's Angelina and not Tim?" questioned Dennis.

Townsend's eyebrows arched. "What are you saying? That she killed Brother Gabriel? For what reason?"

"I'm not sure." Dennis was shaking his head. "Maybe they were involved somehow. Maybe the guy went after her. Maybe . . . maybe she was in cahoots with him . . . I don't know."

"Tim told me this was the biggest story of her career. You think maybe she was making it up with Brother Gabriel's help?"

"It just seems to me that either she's in it all the way or completely out of it. Guilty as sin or totally innocent."

Mark knew he was right. But until they could find the woman, it did not look like any of their questions were going to get answered. Finding Angelina would solve everything. Then Mark Townsend could go home.

FOURTEEN

"Buena's a dump."

Brother Grib was steering with his left hand while pounding his thigh with his right, keeping a steady rhythm with the salsa music he had cranked up on the radio. The car's engine was racing as fast as the music and Father Townsend glanced down at his seatbelt, double-checking. The young brother had driven much slower on their trip to Cowiche. Either he was feeling more comfortable around Mark or loud Latino music got him racing. Mark reached forward and turned down the volume.

"Why a dump?" he asked.

The young man shrugged, his head still keeping rhythm with the music. "It just is. You'll see."

He was taking the priest to meet José Ramirez, the man who accompanied Luis Castillo down the roadway during his confrontation with Brother Gabriel. Father Townsend thought he was worth talking to, if only to get another perspective on Brother Gabriel. The Jesuits waited until after dinner to give Ramirez time to get home from the orchards.

José and Elena Ramirez lost their oldest boy after he began believing Gabriel's warnings of the End Time. He was a simple, impressionable kid, only nineteen years old. He believed the Brother's dire warnings about the end of the world and started keeping vigil. Francisco was one of the first people to disappear from the Vigil Room. The Ramirez family was devastated. Besides being their first born, he was also the family's hardest worker. He was raised in the orchards and could outpick even his father. On his best days he could pick close to two hundred bushels of apples. His absence hurt the family on several levels.

The town of Buena was eighteen miles east of Yakima, just off of Interstate 82. Father LaBelle knew the Ramirez family lived at a place called Buena Vista, which he said was near a church. "Don't worry," he assured them, "you can't miss it." From what the two of them could see, there was not much to miss. They passed a Yakima County sheriff's precinct office and headed toward the center of town which, at first glance, seemed populated entirely by Mexican children and mongrel dogs. They were everywhere. Dennis slowed the car and kept a vigilant watch on both sides of the pot-holed road. Kids were darting across the street in wild abandon while their dogs loped after them. Those with bicycles wobbled uncertainly down the bumpy road, accidents waiting to happen. Steering a car through their midst was like wading through a flock of baby ducks. They had a sort of hysterical, kinetic energy that took on a life of its own. About a dozen youngsters were gathered in front of the Silver Dollar Market and Cafe, a small convenience store doing a booming business in ice cream treats. A sagging homemade banner across the store's front advertised HIELO/ICE. Dennis eased his car over to one side of the building, as far away from the knot of children as he could get. He parked, but left the engine running.

"Wait here. I'll run in and ask about the Buena Vista."

When he opened his door a wave of heat displaced the car's cooler air. Mark had no objection to staying inside as long as the air-conditioner kept humming. There was no reason to get out anyway. Brother Grib

was right: Buena was a dump. The houses looked tired
and worn, dusty and desperately needing paint. Roofs
sagged. Tumbleweeds piled against barbed wire fences
and the few small patches of lawn and garden looked
brown and wilted. Even the trees were decimated with
broken limbs and sparse leaves. Buena was hot, dusty,
and rundown. Broken down cars were parked everywhere, their trunks and hoods raised. They were mostly
big old Chevys, Plymouths, and Chryslers; stripped of
parts, now lying exposed, looking skeletal. A gray, aged
picket fence, sagging badly, was festooned with faded
red Christmas garlands. At one end, an emaciated rooster
perched on top of a picket, keeping cocked eyes on his
surroundings. On a phone booth next to the market,
someone had scrawled in broad strokes with a blue felt
marker: WSP Task Villen.

Dennis emerged from the store clutching two ice
creams. He climbed inside, handing one to Mark.

"Thanks. Did you find the Buena Vista?"

"It's just up the road," Dennis said, pointing with his
ice cream, "about two blocks."

Mark looked but saw only more rundown homes and
a few battered trailers lining both sides of the dusty road.
There was no sign of any church, just a decrepit gas
station. Dennis slowly backed out of the store's parking
lot, then began inching forward. Youngsters parted like
waves before them. He crept slowly up the street as both
of them kept an eye out for the Buena Vista. Mark spotted the church first. The Buena Pentecostal Faith Revival
Worship was in the old gas station. The pumps were
gone, but the concrete island was still in the middle of
the parking lot. Images of doves and a cross were
painted over the station's windows. Just beyond, Dennis
slowed to a stop. There were three wooden signs nailed
to a cottonwood beside a dirt driveway. The first read:
THIS CAMP NO TRESPASSING CLOSED OUTSIDERS. The second and largest read: DON'T PARK IN DRIVEWAY DON'T
WORK ON CARS IN CAMP. The third and smallest read:
BUENA VISTA DEAD END. An understatement, if ever
there was one.

The Buena Vista was seven shacks and two hump-backed trailers arranged in a circle around a dusty drive. In the center was another shack, partitioned down the middle. One end had a door for HOMBRES, at the other there was one for DAMAS. Water spigots emerged from the building's middle. The ground beneath was black mud.

Mark visibly recoiled. "This can't be right."

"What do you mean?"

"This isn't . . . no one . . . the Ramirezes can't live here."

Brother Grib looked at him with a wry smile. For anyone not used to migrant housing, their first closeup view often elicited dismay and rejection. Housing like this was only supposed to exist in other countries, never in the U.S. And the closest most people got to it was on the couch, across from their televisions.

"Wait until you see inside," Dennis warned, "it gets even better."

Ignoring the signs, he turned his car into the drive and parked at the end of a line of vehicles, next to a battered pickup truck. They got out and were immediately assaulted by the heat and the smell of fried onions. If dinner was over, it was only barely.

A stooped, gray-haired woman emerged from one of the shacks with a yellow plastic dishpan in her arms. Dirty plates and glasses were heaped inside. Keeping a wary eye on the two white men she edged her way toward the water spigots. Mark and Dennis watched as she set her dishpan in the mud beneath a spigot and turned on the water. A trickle splashed over the dirty dishes. It sounded like someone urinating. Dennis headed her way.

The woman crouching next to her pan looked terrified as he approached. He quickly held out a hand, palm up, and smiled reassuringly.

"*Buenas tardes,*" he greeted her. "*Soy Hermano Dennis de la iglesia de San José en Yakima. Y esto es Padre Mark. ¿Como esta usted?*

Despite his assurances that they were from the church, the old woman was still wary. Men from immigration were tricky and would tell you anything to catch *los ilegales*. She nodded to him, but only slightly.

Brother Grib smiled again. They should have worn their clerical shirts. The sight of the Roman collar was more convincing than anything he could tell this woman. Suddenly inspired, he reached into the pocket of his jeans, extracting his rosary. He held it out in front of him.

"Ves, soy religioso—un hermano Jesuita," he told her in Spanish. *"El padre y yo estamos buscando la familia de José y Elena Ramirez. ¿Sabes en que casa viven?"*

The rosary seemed to convince her. Still squatting next to her dishes, the old woman pointed toward a shack on the other side of the circle. *"Los Ramirez viven allá,"* she informed him.

Thanking her, Dennis and Mark headed across the lot.

"Is that the only water?" Mark asked in a low, worried voice.

"That's it, Padre. There's probably a sink and a shower in each of the communal bathrooms, but none of these cabins have running water inside them."

"Is this even legal?"

Brother Grib shrugged. Whether it was or not made no difference. No one was going to complain. Least of all, the people living here.

There was no window in the front of the Ramirez's shack, but the battered wooden door was propped wide open with a rock. Pinned next to the doorway was a faded picture of the Lady of Guadalupe. In heavy black type beneath was printed: *Este Hogar es Católico. No acceptamos Propaganda. Viva la Virgen de Guadalupe, Madre de Dios*. They were still several feet away when Mark paused to read and translate the posted message.

"What propaganda? Are they talking about proselytizing?"

"Pentecostals," Dennis informed him, "and guys like Brother Gabriel. Why do you think so many Hispanics are quitting the Catholics? It's because the Pentecostals are willing to come out here and be where they are.

Catholics don't do that. We wait for them to come to us."

"What are you talking about, Dennis? Joe is out visiting all the time."

"Bones is one man," Grib argued. "When Pentecostals visit, the entire church gets involved. There's no contest."

From inside the cabin came the sound of movement, a chair scraping on the floor. They could hear a shrill voice speaking Spanish, followed by canned laughter. And when they reached the door, they could see the glow of a television in a corner of the room.

"*¡Hola!*" Brother Grib called into the room. "José? Elena?"

A small face peered around the corner at them, quickly followed by another, even smaller. There was the sound of more movement from inside and suddenly a young girl, about ten, materialized at the door. She was wearing a blue T-shirt and white jeans cut and frayed just above the knees. She stared at the two men a moment, then spoke.

"*¿Quienen son?*" she asked.

Quickly and loudly, Dennis said their names, making certain to add the titles, Brother and Father. And immediately José Ramirez stepped forward, resting a hand on his daughter's shoulder, beaming at his visitors, inviting them in.

There was one bare light bulb hanging on a cord from the center of the ceiling, but the room was still incredibly dark and Mark's eyes took a few moments to adjust. He was aware of a lot of scurrying taking place in the room, and of furniture being shifted around. He was invited to sit on a kitchen chair a small figure vacated and pushed his way. As he settled and his eyes grew accustomed to the dark, he tried counting the bodies. There was constant movement around the room, but as near as he could tell, there were close to ten people inside a space that measured no more than twelve feet in any direction. The room was stifling hot; nothing more than a dark box with one lightbulb, a battered couch, several kitchen chairs, and a narrow kitchen table. There was also the television. And on top of it sat a *santuario*, a small shrine. Next to a statue of Jesus was a vase of wild flowers and a flickering votive candle. Leaning against the votive's glass was a small color photo of a smiling young man. In a narrow alcove in a back corner, Mark could make out a tiny two-burner stove and a small refrigerator. A partially open door against the back wall revealed a cluttered bedroom about the same size as the kitchen. This was home to José and Elena Ramirez and what looked like about eight children. Or was it nine? They kept moving, climbing over one another and their parents. The oldest seemed about fourteen. But for all their moving around, their eyes and attention were focused entirely on the two white visitors.

Once they were seated, Dennis Grib introduced themselves once again. He was speaking in Spanish, nodding toward Father Townsend as he again mentioned his name. José and Elena smiled nervously at the priest, then turned their attention back to Dennis. He explained why they were there.

"Father Mark is from a church in Seattle, Washington and he is looking for one of his parishioners, a Chicana named Angelina Sandoval Ybarra. She is the writer who was interviewing Brother Gabriel. Also, the niece of Luis and Rosa Castillo."

José nodded solemnly. He knew the woman Dennis was talking about.

"She is missing?" he asked.

"Sí." As quickly as he could, Dennis explained the circumstances. Father Townsend was able to follow most of what the young Jesuit was saying, but he was just as happy to let Dennis do the talking. If they had to rely on his own Spanish skills, they would still be standing outside as he tried explaining who they were.

Dennis was speaking to him. "Señor Ramirez wants to know if Angelina went into the Vigil Room up at Brother's house." José interrupted. Dennis listened, then translated. "He says that's where Paco disappeared."

"Paco?"

"Francisco, his son."

"I don't think Angelina went back up there. But I'm not positive." Mark thought a moment. "Did you tell him her car is missing, too?"

"Ah!" Dennis turned back to José and informed him. The man nodded wisely and Elena reached out and grasped her husband's hand.

"That is different than what happened to my son," she told Dennis in Spanish. *"Paco had no car. He went to that place in Cowiche and never came home. The men told us he was taken up in the rapture. That he will not return to this life."*

"It's nonsense!" José barked.

Dennis started to translate but Mark curtly nodded. Even if he was having difficulty understanding the words, he certainly had no trouble translating José's disagreement.

"There was no rapture," the Mexican man continued, *"that is stupid! Like that preacher himself. All that talk about going up to God. Nothing but lies!"* Roughly, he pulled his hand away from his wife's, gesturing wildly. *"Brother Gabriel was nothing but a coyote, and those animals deserve to be shot. He got what he deserved."*

"¡Niños!" his wife called to their children. *"Vayanse y jueguen."*

Reluctantly the children began shuffling out the door.

Mark waited until the last one slipped out the door, then looked at José. "Please tell me about your son," he asked, leaning forward in his chair.

His angry outburst over, José slumped heavily in his chair. He reached across for his wife's hand, the one he had discarded only moments before. Fondly, he clasped it in his. *"I do not know what Father wants me to tell him,"* he said to Brother Grib. His voice choked. *"He was my very beautiful son, my oldest. And now he is gone."*

"I think Father wants to hear about the rapture," Dennis replied.

"There was no rapture," José told him. *"I can tell you how I know this. Because when my Paco disap-*

*peared, a piece of my soul turned black. And it remains
so even today. That is not from God. I know it as well
as my wife's own name. God does not make raptures or
anything else that turns men's souls black. It is only the
devil who does that.''*

He waited while Dennis translated his words to the
priest. Then José Ramirez looked deep into Father
Townsend's eyes and nodded. "That is true," he spoke
in English, desperately needing the priest to understand.
"El díablo has taken my beautiful son."

Francisco turned nineteen in late March, just three
days after the Ramirez family arrived in Yakima Valley.
Their drive from Toluca, Michoacan, south of Mexico
City, had wiped out the family along with most of their
money. The two youngest children were sick with fever.
For his birthday, Paco received a new pair of cotton
work gloves. This was his third time in the United States
and he knew how birthdays were supposed to be celebrated. He knew about the malls and pizza parlors and
cars full of friends, laughing and having good times. His
mother saw the pained look on his face as he sat in the
middle of their cramped quarters in the Buena Vista, his
younger brothers and sisters clamoring around him, fit-
ting the gloves onto his long, slender hands. She knew
he was happy to be in the United States. It was being
with his family that made him look that way.

Although it was only March, there was plenty of work
in the orchards, getting the trees ready. Laborers were
already pruning. José and his son had no difficulty finding work. Elena made the rounds of the fruit-packing
plants, adding her name to the growing list of women
waiting for jobs. The first harvest was still months away,
but it was important to get your name listed early.

Work in the orchards was hard and tiring, and would
continue to be so until late in the fall, after the last apple
was picked and the empty wooden lugs were piled in
stacks for the winter. The work was exhausting but the
pay was fifteen times what the family could earn back
in Michoacan. For this they could put up with the heat,

the sweat, and the blisters, and even the Buena Vista.

But Francisco was nineteen, and he knew that life in the United States offered more than sweat and blisters and living in dirt and poverty. He saw it on the television. He knew that there were clothes and music and foods made especially for him. And for the gringo kids who sped through Buena in fast cars, forcing the young children to scurry to the edges of the dusty roads and to shield their faces from the flying gravel and dust. Paco knew that there was a life he was intended to have in the United States, and that what he was doing with his family was only a lie. This was not the way it was supposed to be for Paco Ramirez. Everything he saw and heard reinforced that.

When you are young and you have so much of your life still in front of you, the options are endless. You can be anyone, go anywhere, do anything. If you have doubts, pick up a teen magazine or turn on your radio or TV and they will reassure you. If you buy the clothes that give you the right look, then your big truck can conquer any mountain and you can go to the bright, the loud, and the beautiful, where people just like you are already living and owning everything the world has to give them. You are the one, and all of this exists for you.

But if you are nineteen and sleeping on the floor next to your six-year-old brother and across from your twelve-year-old sister and you have to walk across a muddy yard to relieve yourself in a tin trough next to a toothless old man who smells of death, you know you have been cheated. There is nothing here for you. And that is when you begin to look elsewhere.

Francisco first saw Brother Gabriel at a park in Toppenish. He was a strange-looking man, even frightening at first; whiter than anyone he had ever seen before. His skin and his hair glowed and he talked like he was from God. And the things he said were the first true words that the young man from Michoacan heard in the United States. "*Nothing that we have or want to have will last. Before any of us know it, everything will be gone. You*

*are foolish if you value the things of this world. The one
thing you should value is your relationship with the Al-
mighty. He alone has the power to give and to take
away, he is the master of life and of death.''*

Brother Gabriel explained that power, and he pointed
to evidence that God's force was about to come crashing
down to earth. Everything, he said, would be swept
clean. And either God would start it all over again or,
if He was fed up with trying to correct humankind, just
end the world. As proof, Brother Gabriel pointed to a
painting high up on a building behind him. He pointed
out the Virgin standing above the mist of a waterfall.
*''Mary is reminding us that everything will be washed
away.''*

When you are nineteen and you have nothing but cotton work gloves, you yearn for the day when everything
will be swept clean. You pray that the Buena Vista is
washed away, with its ramshackled hovels, its trough for
a toilet, the stupid signs, the old man who smells like
death, and even your own family. Yes, God can take it
all, and the sooner the better. So you begin to hope for
it. And when the gringo kids in the fast cars come tearing down the road, you pray that they will disappear.
Maybe only one hubcap is left rattling in the road. And
the malls, with their clothes and music and food, are
suddenly emptied. And the fruit on the trees can begin
to rot. You pray hard to God to make it so and then you
wait.

That is what happens when you are nineteen with
nothing.

Paco began keeping vigil. First in fear, but then in
growing anticipation. His parents grew more and more
concerned. As soon as the weather was warm enough,
their son began dragging his blanket outside at night,
wrapping it over his shoulders and staring up at the sky.
He told them he was waiting for the Lord. They reminded him that he could find the Lord inside the
church. But Paco said no, he was really waiting and that
the Lord was coming. José tried arguing with him, but
that only drove the young man further away from them.

He began following Brother Gabriel on his vigils around the valley. His work in the fields slowed down. And his mother added another candle to the *santurario* on top of their television. She never said it was for Paco, but the rest of the family knew.

Eventually Francisco decided to spend one night a week at Brother Gabriel's Vigil Room. One of Brother's followers would drive him up to Cowiche and bring him home in the morning. That lasted three weeks. The third time, Paco never came home.

Brother Gabriel came himself, and told the family their Paco was one of the privileged chosen, that their boy was selected to go before the rest. He brought them his shoes as evidence that Paco was truly gone. And he invited the family to join him in waiting for the Rapture.

Elena and one of Brother's assistants had to hold José away from the preacher, who was hurriedly pushed into the big car waiting in the Buena Vista's dusty drive. Only when Brother Gabriel was whisked away did they dare release him. José fought the assistant who was left behind, and bloodied the man's nose before he could escape in his own car. Now with Paco gone, the Ramirez family was barely earning enough to survive.

José Ramirez waited until Dennis was finished translating. His eyes never left Father Townsend's face.

"That is why I know Brother Gabriel was the devil. God does not do such evil, that is only from el díablo. Tell the Father that."

Dennis repeated the Mexican's words in English. Mark listened, nodding slowly.

"Quiero, José, que ... que...." Mark's limited Spanish ground to a halt. In frustration, he turned to Dennis. "I'm trying to ask him what the police said about Paco's disappearance. What do they think happened?"

"¿Que dicen la policía cuando le contó que su hijo estaba perdido? ¿La policía saben que le pasó a él?"

José shook his head vigorously. *"No, we cannot go to the police,"* he said. *"We do not have our legal documents to be here. The ones that we have are counterfeit.*

If we go to the police it will only get worse for us."

Dennis explained to Mark that the Ramirezes were illegal, that they were afraid.

"But this is their son," Mark murmured back to him. "They've got to report it."

"They're afraid to."

Father Townsend looked across the room at the two Mexicans watching him with fear in their eyes. Elena had traded her husband's hand for a hem of her dress, which she twisted nervously. José sat helplessly at her side, his own calloused hands hanging useless between his legs. They waited for the Father to tell them everything would be okay. They waited, believing he had the power to calm their fears and restore their son. About the only thing they could still afford was their belief. And from the expressions on their faces, they were willing to hand even that over to Father Townsend.

Mark leaned back uncomfortably in his chair. The room grew deathly silent. From outside, the voices of the children came through the open doorway. No one spoke and Dennis Grib shifted his legs. Father Townsend's eyes moved to the *santuario* and the photo leaning against the vigil candle. Paco Ramirez was a young, handsome man, but there was a tiredness in his eyes. It was a tiredness that went beyond hard work and restless nights. A nineteen-year-old boy should not look that tired. Mark wondered to himself if Francisco's eyes were open or closed at that moment. Was the young man any place where he could look through an open doorway and see the evening sky? Or had the world finally come to its end for Paco Ramirez?

FIFTEEN

Leaving Buena was a relief. Their visit with the Ramirez family left Mark feeling frustrated and desolate. José and Elena were obviously good people, working hard to provide a life for their children. They had uprooted their family and moved over two thousand miles into another country in search of a better life. But what they found was more poverty and hard work. And now heartache. José Ramirez blamed Brother Gabriel for that.

Dennis Grib was keeping them off the highway. He had turned onto a secondary road after leaving the Buena Vista, following it north. The night was cool and they turned off the air-conditioner, unrolling their windows to let the fresh soft air blow against their faces. Respectful of Mark's quiet mood, Dennis kept the radio off and they rolled along the country road in relative silence, each lost in his own thoughts.

Father Townsend felt he had done nothing to help the Ramirez family. They willingly told him their story and the tragedy of their missing son. Mark was a complete stranger to them, an Anglo to boot, yet they had confided in him. Only because of his title, he knew that. Father. *Padre.* The word carried weight far beyond its length or meaning. But the burden was not so much with the word itself, as with the expectations piled onto it. There were times, such as in Buena, when the Jesuit wished he was just Mark. Just Mark, without any expectations. Just Mark, without the burden of anyone's faith. But there had to be times when Elena and José felt the same way. Just Elena, just José, without the expectations and burdens of being Mother, Father, Parent.

Mark stirred. "It's a crazy world, Dennis."

Brother Grib looked across at him. "How so?"

"It just is," Mark shrugged. He was reluctant to try explaining his thoughts to the young man. "Where are we?"

"We're parallel to the highway," Dennis explained. He pointed over to the right. "Moxee is just over those hills. They're called the Rattlesnake Hills."

The name fit; they were covered with sagebrush and outcroppings of rock. You could almost hear the rattles.

"Is there a way over them?" asked Mark.

"Yeah. There's a road that'll take you right into Moxee." Grib slowed down. "You want to go that way?"

"Maybe we could stop and see Tim and the Castillos, find out if they've heard anything."

About a mile further, Brother Grib turned, heading up a narrow road leading over the Rattlesnake Hills. When they reached the crest, the sun's last light was spilling over the Yakima Valley below them. In every direction they could see orchards. Dense shadows were forming beneath the trees and soon it would be dark. Grib found the road that turned toward the Castillo farm. A few minutes later he was pulling into the drive in front of their house. As they made the turn, Father Townsend gazed across at the side of the road where Brother Gabriel had kept vigil two nights earlier. When they reached the house Mark was hoping to spot Emily parked outside, but there was no sign of the Volkswagen. Nor of the Blazer, either.

"It doesn't look like Tim is here." Brother Grib was reading his mind.

"Let's go in anyway," Mark muttered.

Rosa answered the door, her hands still wet from

washing dishes. She led the Jesuits into the living room where Luis was planted in front of the television. He politely clicked it off when he saw them enter.

"Padre! Brother! Welcome!" he boomed, rising from his chair. "It is nice to see you. Have you eaten?"

They assured him they had and the four of them settled into chairs.

"Tim's not here?" Despite the missing car, Mark was hoping.

Rosa shook her head sadly, but her husband answered. He sounded disgusted. "He's been gone all day. Rosa said he slept until after ten, then ate and left. Yes?"

His wife nodded agreement. "Maybe he's looking for Angelina," she said softly.

Luis snorted. "In a Corona bottle, yes."

"You think he's drinking?" asked Mark.

"When is he not?" Luis retorted.

"What about Angelina," Brother Grib said, "has anyone heard from her?"

"Nada," Luis replied curtly. "The police came by again, but there is no sign of her. She is gone."

"It is like God snatched her away," his wife said timorously. She made an odd fluttering gesture with her hands and Mark smiled in spite of himself.

"We went to Buena and saw José Ramirez," Brother Grib volunteered.

"Ah, sí," Luis said, *"tienen problemas tabién."* Catching Mark's look of uncertainty, he translated. "They have their own problems, no?"

Father Townsend nodded distractedly and the man turned his attention back to Brother Grib. "What Paco has done to his family is a sin. Now they will lose everything because of him."

"What do you mean?" asked Dennis.

"José is a hard worker, and his wife too, but Paco was young and strong and he was the one who earned most of their money. They depended on him. By running away he is spitting on his family."

"You think that's what happened," Dennis leaned forward, "that he ran away?"

"What? Brother, you don't think he was raptured, do you? Do you believe in that craziness? No!"

Brother Grib shook his head. "It's just hard to believe Paco would take off like that."

"And leave his family," Rosa added.

The young Jesuit nodded back.

"There are many people who are not unhappy that Brother Gabriel is dead," claimed Luis. "People like Luis Ramirez have every right to want him dead."

"Luis!" his wife scolded. "*¡Qué terrible decir esto!*"

Her husband raised his chin defiantly. "It is an awful thing to say, but it is true. Not only was that man destroying families, he was destroying our church. He had to be stopped. It is good that he was."

"Shhhssssh!" his wife hissed. "Talk like that will get you in big trouble. You want the police to come back for you? Keep saying those things and they will. There are many more people in this valley who believe Brother Gabriel was a holy man, even if he wasn't Catholic."

"Even if he made Paco disappear?" Luis was arguing back. "Even then you think he is holy? His crazy talk destroys families and he is holy? He makes people disappear, even your own Angelina, and still he is holy? Those others are crazy like him if they believe that!"

Rosa Castillo clamped her mouth shut and glared at her husband.

Father Townsend stirred. He was only half-listening, but something in Luis's last outburst caught his attention.

"These people who disappeared," he said, "do you know how many? *¿Quantas personas?*"

Luis and Rosa exchanged looks. Neither one was exactly sure.

"Maybe a dozen," Rosa guessed, sounding doubtful.

"More," Luis insisted. "Much more. Double, perhaps."

Rosa looked thoughtful but did not dispute her husband. The whole subject of the rapture was talked about in hushed voices within the Hispanic community. Families like the Ramirez, who were there illegally, were not anxious to draw attention to themselves. Others were too ashamed to say much about it. To suggest your son or daughter was taken up by God was not something you spoke about freely. Young people in the valley were always coming and going and most people thought nothing of it. But if a family suddenly announced their son or daughter was raptured up to heaven, that was hard to ignore. Only the most ardent of Brother Gabriel's followers were willing to subject their family to that kind of scrutiny, that kind of gossip and speculation. The result was that most people, like Luis and Rosa, had only the vaguest idea of how many were actually missing.

"Is that something Angelina would have known?" Mark asked. "She was looking into it."

"Perhaps," Rosa said. "I know she talked to families. She was trying to understand."

"But she did not believe it," Luis asserted. "She did not believe in the raptures."

Father Townsend was tugging his mustache. "Then what was it? What did she think?"

Both Luis and Rosa hesitated, each waiting for the other to give some reply to the priest.

Mark waited, but when there was no reply he continued. "If there is no rapture, then where did those people go?"

"If not to God, then to the devil," Luis answered. "Someone should ask that woman—that Sister Elizabeth. I bet she knows."

Rosa· pursed her lips but said nothing. Nonetheless, Mark caught it.

"Rosa?"

"No pienso que . . ." The woman became flustered and began again, this time in English. "I do not think Sister Elizabeth would know. She believes in the Rapture, like her husband did." Luis started to protest but she talked over his noise. "I have watched her when she stands outside the church. She is devout and not like some of the others who always push their way to the front and who make noise when we come out. I think Sister Elizabeth is a good woman."

Luis threw his hands up in the air and rolled his eyes. "My wife!" he exclaimed. "She thinks everyone is good and no one is bad."

"That is not true, Luis," she protested. "Only you! You are the only bad person I know."

But she was smiling as she said it.

Darkness was complete by the time they left the Castillo house. Lights from nearby farmhouses dotted the black space in front of them as Dennis cautiously negotiated his way down the lane. He turned and headed toward the highway through Moxee. Mark was quiet, mulling over the evening's two conversations, first with José and Elena Ramirez, then with Luis and Elena Castillo. Most of what they said somehow seemed to fit together. But like the tumbleweeds scattered over the dry hills above the valley, there was too much blowing around still, and certain parts seemed like they would never come to rest. The priest's intention was to remain in Yakima long enough to find out what happened to Angelina Sandoval Ybarra. Now he realized he was in danger of becoming hung up on these other disappearances as well.

"We have to find out the names of the people who were raptured," he told Dennis on their way back into Yakima. "And how many there were."

Brother Grib glanced over at him. "How do we do that?"

Father Townsend fell silent as he thought. Finally he replied, "We ask Sister Elizabeth. Let's go up to Cowiche tomorrow and talk to her."

"You think that's a good idea?"

"Why not? No matter what she says, we'll find out more than we know now. Rosa thinks she's a good woman and has nothing to hide. Luis thinks she's as crazy as her husband. I think we have to find out for ourselves, and the easiest way to do that is to talk to her. It can't hurt."

Brother Grib was on Yakima Avenue, signalling toward St. Joseph's. Mark, realizing where they were, pointed with his hand to drive forward. "Keep going," he commanded, "a few more blocks."

There was no traffic and Dennis pulled out of the turn lane and proceeded down the road.

"Where are we going now?"

"Drive by the Sweet Apple," Mark directed.

The Blazer was parked across the street from the seedy tavern. Dennis slowed down and both Jesuits took a long look. But other than the lopsided BUD and garish OPEN signs suspended in the window, there was nothing to see.

"You wanna stop?" Dennis asked.

Father Townsend sighed. "No," he said, "let's go home."

SIXTEEN

Saints are not always saints.

There was a time in Ignatius Loyola's life, shortly after he found religion, when he set off on pilgrimage, riding a burro to Montserrat, in northern Spain. He was intending to keep a vigil in front of the Black Madonna of Montserrat, to dedicate the rest of his life to holiness. While on the road he was approached by a Moor riding in the same direction. They greeted one another in a friendly way and, for the sake of each other's company, began to ride together.

Eventually their conversation turned to religion and to what each man believed. There was little disagreement until they approached the subject of Mary. Ignatius believed as the Church taught him, that Mary remained a virgin throughout her life. The Moor held otherwise. She was mortal and a woman like all others and after giving birth could hardly be considered a virgin. No, definitely not after the birth.

They argued over it for some time, neither convincing the other. Eventually the Moor rode on ahead, evidently preferring his own company to that of his ignorant companion.

Ignatius, still fuming, watched the man trot away. The more he thought about it, the angrier he got—first at the

Moor, then at himself. If he was truly his Lady's champion, he would have defended her honor more vigorously. Even to death, if it came to that. The longer he brooded, the madder he became at his own failure to act decisively. He decided to catch up to the Moor and defend the Virgin's honor.

But before he could, he reached a fork in the road. Did the Moor turn right? Or did he ride straight ahead? Ignatius had no clue. Unable to decide, he dropped his donkey's reins and let his animal carry him where it wanted. He decided if it should happen he came upon the Moor, he would kill him.

Ignatius never saw the man again.

On Tuesday afternoon, Dennis Grib drove Father Townsend to Cowiche for the second time. Riding in the backseat, grumbling most of the way, sat Father Paul Stanley, his eyes peeled for Moors.

"You're driving too fast!" he leaned over the seat to complain into Brother Grib's ear. "Just because you're visiting heretics doesn't mean you have to rush to them. Slow down, Brother!" Dennis rolled his eyes at Mark. "I saw that!" Father Stanley clamored. "I'm not completely blind."

"Father," Dennis said with more patience than he was feeling, "you need to sit back and put on your seatbelt. That's the law, you know."

Father Stanley did as the law commanded. They were on the slow climb up the road between Naches and Cowiche and were the last car in a long line behind an orchard truck.

"We'll be a few minutes late," Dennis warned Mark.

Father Townsend glanced at his watch. He had called ahead and spoken directly with Sister Elizabeth, asking if he could visit with her. She did not ask him why and he offered her no explanation. He said he would just like to stop by and talk for awhile. They agreed that two o'clock would be a good time for both of them. He was not sure how she would react when three Jesuits showed up at her door and he was trying to find a way of suggesting Paul and Dennis wait in the car. So far, none of his plans seemed politic enough. He knew if he told Father Stanley to wait for him in the car, the old priest would beat him through Sister Elizabeth's front door. Why he demanded to come along was still a mystery.

"What do you know about this part of the valley, Father?" Mark turned in his seat to address the old man directly. "Do you know the history?"

"Indians," Father Stanley replied, "this whole area was Indian country. There's painted rocks back a ways and kids still find arrowheads around those bluffs. I've heard there's caves up there where they used to hide from the soldiers. But I don't know much about it." He grinned wickedly. "That was before my time."

"And now it's all apple orchards, huh?"

"Mostly," agreed Paul. "Some cherries, I guess."

They were on top and both sides of the road were lined with the cars of field workers. In the orchards themselves they could see people moving about, men climbing the tall, spindly orchard ladders. These were the final days before harvest time and everyone was busy.

"I'm amazed how many people it takes," said Mark, watching out his side window. "It's got to be grueling work."

"Especially in this heat," Dennis agreed. "I've heard that twenty thousand Mexicans come into the valley every year to work the harvests."

"Then they leave," grumped Father Stanley, "taking their money with them."

Dennis Grib immediately bristled. "They earn every penny. That's their right. Besides, if it wasn't for them, these apples would rot right where they fall."

"I beg to disagree, Brother. The orchardists did perfectly fine before the Mexicans came here."

"But that was over fifty years ago!" Grib protested. "Before Bracero you didn't have even half the trees that are here now. If it wasn't for migrant labor, the Yakima Valley would be up to its armpits in rotting fruit."

Mark considered the possibility. Brother Grib's image

was alarming and more than a little revolting. He cut in on their argument. "I don't know what Bracero means."

"The Bracero program," Father Stanley answered before Dennis had a chance, "was an opportunity for Mexican laborers to work in the U.S. during World War Two. During the war there was a shortage of farm workers."

Brother Grib moaned loudly. "Paul, that's bunk and you know it! Sure there was a shortage, especially here in Yakima Valley. But tell him the real reason why. Come on, be honest!"

Paul Stanley's jaw was jutting almost into the front seat. "We were at war. You're too young to know anything about it. Our national security was at risk."

"Hooey!" Grib rejoined. "What was at risk was our nation's integrity." He turned toward Father Townsend, swerving their car into the other lane as he did so. An oncoming pickup loudly sounded its horn and Dennis swerved back, narrowly avoiding a collision. Nevertheless, he continued to rant. "After Pearl Harbor we shipped all the Japanese into concentration camps. 'For national security.' Give me a break!"

There was something Mark was missing. The argument had shifted from apples to Pearl Harbor and in the midst of it, Father Townsend got distracted when his life passed before his eyes. "So what does this have to do with Bracero?" he asked.

"Everything!" Both of Grib's hands left the steering wheel. Seeing Mark's expression, he quickly grabbed it back. "Don't you see, Mark? When they cleaned out the Japanese, they had to get somebody in here to replace the pickers. All they did was substitute one minority for another. Lock up the stable work force and bring on the migrants. As long as the harvest isn't affected, it's okay."

Paul Stanley looked livid, his face glowing like a Red Delicious.

"That's outrageous!" he sputtered. "It's an oversimplification and it's inflammatory."

"It's true," Brother Grib asserted, watching the old

priest in his rearview mirror. "Go look it up. I did my senior research on the Bracero program. Go look in the Yakima library, Paul. You will find books on the history of the Japanese in this valley, but not one volume on the history of Hispanics. Why do you think that is? Because they have no history here?

"In 1942, in one month, over a thousand Japanese were shipped out of Yakima Valley. That was the same year the Bracero program started. Doesn't that seem like quite a coincidence?"

Dennis ended his lecture just as he signaled his turn into the drive leading to Sister Elizabeth's stucco house. Behind him, Father Stanley rode in silence, his angry eyes drilling holes into the back of the Moor's head.

Sister Elizabeth answered the door herself. She was wearing a plain, white cotton shift that effectively disguised her figure. Mark wondered if the dress was meant to emulate the white alb her husband wore. She wore no makeup that he could detect, and there were dark circles under both her eyes. She looked drained.

The inside of the expansive house was light and cool. Whoever had built the place was aware of Yakima summers and remembered to include central air-conditioning. She led the three of them into the living room, a huge affair with wide picture windows looking out over the nearby cliffs and into the valley below. From the entrance they stepped down into a soft, peach-colored carpet. The three Jesuits settled onto a long sectional couch behind a glass coffee table arranged with glasses and a pitcher of iced tea. Sister Elizabeth sat in a straight-back armchair pulled out from the mahogany dining room set, looking like a demure school girl or religious postulant called up in front of a board of inquiring clerics. Father Townsend shifted on the couch, feeling increasingly uncomfortable. Waves of tension were continuing to emanate from both Paul Stanley and Dennis Grib. He should have left them in the car.

"Now, Fathers," said Sister Elizabeth in a soft, reverential voice, "how can I be of help?"

Two Jesuit heads swiveled in Mark's direction. He was the point man on this visit.

"First of all, I want to express our condolences to you. We were very sorry to hear about your husband. We will remember him in our prayers at St. Joseph."

Sister lowered her eyes. Mark heard a soft mutter coming from Paul Stanley's direction, but when he glanced over the old priest was merely glaring.

"This must be a confusing time for you and Brother's followers," Mark continued, "besides feeling the pain of the loss."

The woman tipped her head to one side and looked at him curiously. Then she slowly nodded.

"Yes," she said quietly, "we feel the pain. But I don't know what you mean by confusion."

"Having Brother Gabriel's ministry cut short, especially in that way. It hasn't disrupted things?"

"Oh. I see. Yes, I suppose in that sense. Our vigils are suspended for the time being, that's true. Mr. Fairbanks and Mr. Patowski thought that was best, at least until after the funeral." She paused, thinking. "But there is no real confusion. More disappointment. Brother Gabriel will miss seeing the harvest."

She shifted in her chair, turning so she could look out the picture windows and onto the valley. With her head turned, her words were barely discernible.

"Brother loved this time of the year," she told them. "When we lived in Bakersfield he always wanted to take time off to go work in the fields. He wanted to own a farm." Turning back, she smiled sadly. "But the Lord had other plans."

"In his own way perhaps he was a farmer," Mark suggested. "He was just preparing for a different kind of harvest."

"Yes, he knew that," Sister Elizabeth agreed. "The fruits of his labors. But he wanted a real farm, with cows and chickens and vegetables to plant. He loved to see things grow. That's why we came to Yakima after we left Bakersfield. Brother felt certain he was supposed to be in a place like this. The Lord confirmed that for him."

"How so?" The question was Brother Grib's.

"By the appearances. When the Virgin made her presence known."

Paul Stanley let out a loud, undisguised snort and Sister Elizabeth looked at him for several long seconds, then smiled sweetly but said nothing. She was used to rude noises from unbelievers.

"Sister Elizabeth." Mark waited until she turned her gaze back on him. He was determined not to let Father Stanley derail the conversation. "Now that your husband is dead, what will become of the raptures?"

She thought a moment before replying.

"You understand, sir, that what has taken place so far is not the Rapture? That awesome day is still to come. What has happened so far is merely a foretaste. Whether or not they continue is not up to me."

"But those people were raptured?"

"Presumably," the woman told him. "But whether to someplace permanent or temporary, I don't know."

Her answer surprised him. Father Townsend was expecting something much more definitive, bordering on absolute certitude. He probed further.

"What did your husband believe?"

"That they were gone," she said simply. "He never knew if they would return or not. When it first began to happen, he was as surprised as anyone." Sister Elizabeth hesitated, but then continued. "When the first ones left, he was going to close the Vigil Room."

"Why?" asked Brother Grib.

"He felt it was too dangerous," she replied. "Brother Gabriel was not completely sure if it was from God or from some dark source. He said he had no clear evidence that this was truly God's work."

Even Father Stanley was taken aback. What she was admitting caught all three by surprise. Father Townsend was about to speak, but Dennis beat him. His was the same question, though.

"So why did he let it go on?"

Sister Elizabeth leaned forward in her chair and picked up the tumbler of iced tea. Holding it up, she silently offered to pour some for her visitors. Each man declined. Cautiously, she poured out a glass for herself. When she was finished, she took a tentative sip from the glass, then set it back down.

"After we left California, my husband said he never wanted to be inside another church. He believed the time had come to move out of them and to begin encountering God in the world. His ministry was going to be on the highways and byways." She stopped and smiled. "That was his term," she informed them.

"Brother believed that churches had served their purpose and that the Lord was pretty much finished with them. He thought their work was done, that the message they were sent to proclaim was already heard. Now it is time to assemble those who believe and to bid farewell to those who do not. But the churches were not the places for assembly, he said. That had to be done outside and in public places. He was against buildings for that reason. We are in the time of anticipation, and we know not the day nor the hour. The Lord wants us to be vigilant.

"My husband said that churches hold us in. When you have a church building, you begin worrying about how to keep it going. Who will pay the bills? Who will keep it clean? Who will make repairs? That takes people, and so you begin counting heads. You worry when numbers begin to drop and you begin thinking about ways to increase membership. The more people you have, the more secure your church begins to feel. Brother said this time was not about feeling secure and not about numbers. He believed it was time to begin letting go. Can you understand what he was saying?"

"That's not right!" Father Stanley bellowed loudly. Both Mark and Dennis were startled by the outburst, but Sister Elizabeth calmly turned to the old man.

"Whether right or wrong, sir, can you understand it?" Paul chewed on the side of his tongue, but said nothing more. Sister offered him another patient smile and continued.

"When the idea for a place to keep watch was first raised, he was opposed. He thought it would be too much like a church. But some wanted a place where they could wait. They said it was not for worship, but would only be a place where people could sit and wait."

"Like a bus station," Dennis Grib suggested.

Father Townsend raised his eyebrows. But if he thought Brother Gabriel's widow would be offended by the rude comparison, he was mistaken.

"Exactly!" she said, sounding delighted with his choice of imagery. "That was all it was intended to be— a place where people could wait together." She lifted her iced tea and took another sip.

"My husband finally agreed, but only if it would be so simple that there would be no expense to keep it going. He said that none of us had any time to worry about a building. So when the Vigil Room was built, it was kept very plain and simple. It's just a room with some benches." She smiled at Dennis. "Like a bus station."

Mark reminded her, "But people began leaving."

"Yes," she assented. "The first two left together, about two weeks after it was finished. They were two young women who came for dinner one night. It was late when we finished and they were staying in Sunnyside. Someone offered to drive them back, but they asked Brother if they could stay the night and keep vigil in the new room. No one had stayed in there at night before, and Brother was not sure it was a good idea. But he finally agreed.

"In the morning, when he went to check on them, they were gone. At first we thought they had changed their minds and found a way home. But their shoes were still there and we wondered why they would leave their shoes. Not until the next day did we decide that they actually were gone. Even then, no one was really sure what happened.

"About a week later, it was a young man who left.

He came here because he was unhappy and worried, something was wrong at home; and he asked if he could stay in there for one night a week. My husband said yes. But he told the young man he would lock him inside and that he had to stay the whole night . . .''

''Why?'' Mark interrupted. ''Why did he lock him inside?''

Sister Elizabeth looked doubtful. ''I'm not sure. I think Brother was afraid. He was very upset when the two women disappeared. He told the man that if he stayed, he would have to be locked inside.''

''But what if he needed a bathroom?'' Dennis objected. Paul Stanley was vigorously nodding his head in agreement.

''There is one inside,'' she assured them. Then she laughed. ''Just like a bus station.''

Father Townsend watched as the woman paused to sip her drink. Although her guard was still up, the woman had become much more animated in telling them the story of the Vigil Room. As if relieved somehow. Her brief laugh over the bathroom in the bus station sounded like something she was unaccustomed to doing. Mark wondered if Sister Elizabeth had much joy in her life with Brother Gabriel. He suspected not.

''Would you like to see?'' She moved to the very edge of her chair, as if to stand.

Mark took a moment before he realized she was asking about the room.

''I'd like that very much,'' he told her. ''If it's all right.''

''It's only a room,'' she told him, standing up. ''Although it looks a bit different right now.'' Seeing Mark's puzzled look, she continued. ''We are bringing Brother's body here,'' she informed the Jesuits, ''and will keep a vigil for him. There are already some flowers inside, and the men built a bier for his casket. Ordinarily, the room is empty. Except for the benches, of course. Bus stations always have benches.''

* * *

The Vigil Room was a cinderblock building about fifty feet away from the side of the house and a few feet from the edge of the rimrock overlooking the valley. Sister Elizabeth led the men out the front door and down the walk. A gravel path angled from the driveway to the front of the building. The door was made of solid wood and left unpainted. The knob turned easily; it was unlocked.

The air was hot and stuffy inside, heavy with the aroma of several sprays of cut flowers that were sitting on the floor against one wall, waiting to be arranged. The interior walls, like the exterior, were painted white. The only fresh air came from narrow open slats, covered by screen, between the top of the walls and the ceiling. To Father Townsend, the room looked and felt like a workshop or a garage big enough for three cars. The benches Sister mentioned were in two rows, facing each other. They were simple wooden ones, like park benches. Uncomfortable for spending a long night in vigil, which might have been the point. A bier was set up near the flowers. It was a makeshift affair, and looked like some boards laid across two sawhorses with a couple of white sheets draped over the top. In a back corner, across from the doorway, was a smaller, cinderblock room with another wooden door.

"The bathroom?"

Sister nodded.

The room was built on a pad of poured concrete. Mark looked for any breaks or lines but could see none. As far as he could tell, the floor was solid. There were no windows anywhere in the room, no other way in or out of the building. The ceiling arched to a peak in the center, and the inside framing was exposed. From what he could see, there were no trap doors.

Sister Elizabeth watched the three Jesuits with a wry smile. She was used to people's close examination of the room. They always spent the first few minutes looking for secret entrances. Mark saw the look on her face.

"I'm sorry," he said. "I was looking . . ."

"That's all right," she assured him, "you're not the

first. I've looked myself. As far as I know, this door is the only way in or out.''

Father Stanley was unwilling to take her word for it. He roamed throughout the square room, carefully studying the floor, the walls, the ceiling. When he reached the corner with the bathroom, he yanked open the door and went inside. Moments later, they heard the toilet flush. Then the sound of water running. A few seconds afterwards, the old priest stuck his head out.

"The sink works but not the shower. How come?"

"Mr. Patowski decided we didn't need it. This is not a motel. They never connected it, so the only water is in the sink. And the toilet, of course."

Mark and Dennis wandered around the room. But there was nothing to see. There were no pictures on the walls, no tables or other furnishings. Only the two rows of benches and, at one end, the flowers and makeshift bier. Nothing about the space felt hallowed or particularly miraculous. It was just a room. After hearing the ominous stories about people disappearing, Father Townsend found the reality somewhat disappointing. He made one more slow tour of the room. The bathroom was simply that; a toilet, a sink, and a shower. The shower stall was being used as a makeshift closet. Inside it were a push broom and a dustpan, a mop and bucket, and several rolls of toilet paper.

When Mark emerged he saw Father Stanley occupying one of the benches.

"Can we go now?" the old man asked in a peevish voice. "My feet hurt."

"Keep your shoes on, Paul," warned Brother Grib jokingly. "We don't want you disappearing on us."

His humor seemed out of place and Mark watched for Sister Elizabeth's reaction. But the woman only smiled placidly. Father Townsend was surprised once more by how little she seemed invested in the workings of the Vigil Room.

"Sister Elizabeth?" Townsend waited until she turned toward him. "When the raptures took place, were there any noises or lights or anything? What went on in here?''

She offered a slight shrug. "I don't know. They were always at night and I was asleep. Our bedroom is on the other side of the house and neither of us ever heard or saw a thing. We would let people in for the night, and in the morning they were gone.''

"And always with the door locked?''

"Except for that first time, yes.''

Brother Grib moved next to her. "Their shoes were always here.''

"In front of the benches,'' she replied, pointing to a spot just beyond Paul Stanley's feet. Self-consciously, the old man shuffled his own feet to one side, as if trying to get them out of the line of fire.

"But I gather not everyone who came here was raptured,'' Mark observed. "Only some of the people.''

"That's correct,'' the woman replied. "When Brother Gabriel came to unlock the door in the morning, we never knew if there would be somebody inside or not.''

"Was there ever a time when some were taken and some left behind?''

Sister Elizabeth shook her head. "No.''

"All or nothing,'' Dennis observed. He had seen and heard enough. "Come on, Paul, I'll help you to the car.''

The four of them left together, Sister Elizabeth and Father Townsend following the other two. As they approached the driveway, Mark asked her how many were raptured from the Vigil Room.

"We had thirty-seven leave,'' she said calmly.

Dennis Grib stopped in his tracks and turned around. "Thirty-seven!'' he exclaimed. "Really? That many?''

Mark was just as surprised as Dennis. The numbers they had heard were considerably lower. Rather than a few isolated instances, the raptures were beginning to sound like a mass exodus.

"Is there a list of the names?'' Father Townsend asked.

Sister Elizabeth stopped walking. They were still on the gravel path and she turned to face the priest squarely.

She spoke slowly, patiently. "Sir, I hope you can see that I have nothing here to hide. I have tried to answer all of your questions as best as I can. But I don't know why you're asking me these things. All I know is what I've told you; people came here and they left. I don't know how or why or where." She paused long enough to give Mark time to respond. When she saw he would not, she continued. "I believe there is a list, yes. But I don't have it. If you want to know about those people, you'll need to see Mr. Patowski or Mr. Fairbanks. They know more about this than I do. After the raptures began, they were the ones who worked with my husband to limit the number of people coming here. I'm sure they can tell you much more than I."

She turned on the path and resumed walking. Mark quickly fell in beside her.

"There were limits? I don't understand."

Her eyes were now fixed on the Jesuits' car and she was heading determinedly toward it, as if anxious to see them off. "Once word began to get out, more and more people started showing up. They stood out on the road and kept staring at our house. Most were afraid to come to the door, so they just stood there. Sometimes as many as twenty or thirty people would be standing there. Some would even kneel.

"Neither Brother Gabriel nor I approved of this. After all, this is our home. Finally, my husband spoke with Mr. Patowski and Mr. Fairbanks and expressed his concerns. He was worried that something might happen here. Either someone would try to do something or . . . or, whatever. He was afraid someone would get hurt.

"We decided to limit the number of people allowed in the Vigil Room. Either Mr. Patowski or Mr. Fairbanks would go out to the road and talk with the people and select some to spend the night. Then they asked the others to leave."

"And would they?"

She had reached the car. She turned and waited expectantly for Mark to open his door. When she saw he was waiting for her reply, she said, "Sometimes. But

sometimes they stayed the night, kneeling on the side of
the road, keeping their own vigil. Now do you see, sir?
Why I am happy we are not keeping the vigil? I know
the people meant well, and I know this was part of our
ministry. But I felt like I was being held captive. Even
here in our home, I could never get away. It was not a
pleasant feeling. Sometimes . . . sometimes . . .'' Her
voice faltered. ''. . . nevermind. Good day, sir.''

SEVENTEEN

"I remember one time in the novitiate when they brought Xavier's arm; we stayed up half the night to see that old thing. Pass the potatoes, please." Bones reached across the dining table and took the bowl from Dennis Grib, then continued with his story. "There were all these other people who showed up at the novitiate," he remembered, "wanting to get a look at St. Francis's arm. Probably twenty or thirty of them. They were standing outside in front of the novitiate in the pouring rain. Finally the novice director told them they could wait in the chapel."

Brother Grib could not contain himself. "Excuse me, Joe, but what do you mean?" The youngest Jesuit at the table was not fully versed in the Society's lexicon of the sacred and extravagant. "You mean someone has St. Francis Xavier's arm? His real arm?"

"That's exactly what I mean," Bones replied. "Now don't interrupt."

Mark Townsend and Paul Stanley both were grinning, anticipating young Dennis's reaction. They knew the story well.

"So anyway," Bones speared a bite of ham with his fork, "we're all standing around and waiting for this arm to show up. Those other folks are inside and the chapel is starting to smell like a kennel of wet dogs. And old Father Buzzy decides we need to burn some incense to get rid of the smell. I mean, you can't bring Xavier's arm all the way from Rome and then send it back smelling like a drowned dachshund. So he convinces the rector to light some candles and fire up the incense and set up a little procession with some novices. Charlie thinks this is a great idea, so he gives the go ahead.

"Meanwhile, these folks in the chapel are starting to say the rosary and they're into their prayer and most of us novices are out by the front door waiting for Xavier's arm to show up. Buzzy grabbed five of us and dragged us into the sacristy where he got everything set up for this procession."

Father LaBelle waggled his fork at young Grib, the piece of ham still firmly imbedded on its tines. "You're too young to remember Jerry Taylor, he died before you were around. But the other bandits are still with us, including our provincial, Jack Elliott. Anyways, Buzzy makes us put on long white albs and then hands us these heavy brass candle holders with these honkin' long candles. And he gives the thurible to Jerry Taylor. But he's got about five chunks of charcoal crammed inside the thing and it's hotter than a nun's flannel nightie. Then Father Buzzy makes us parade to the back of the chapel and stand there while we wait for Xavier's arm. And while we're waiting, he takes about a shovelful of incense and dumps it over the coals in Jerry's thurible.

"That thing started popping and hissing and billowing so much smoke we could barely see one another. But it got rid of that wet dog smell." Joe Bones finally bit down on the piece of ham. He chewed thoughtfully while he replayed the scene in his mind. He loved telling this story.

"So the arm still hasn't arrived. I mean, it's about one o'clock in the morning and we're dead on our feet waiting for this thing. And Father Buzzy, God bless his soul, decides to throw on some more charcoal and incense. The thurible is so hot by now that Taylor can barely lift the lid without burning his fingers. But they put more in it and Jerry gives it a few swings to get things started and there's more smoke and people are starting to choke from all the incense. Those folks' rosary finally peters out and they're sitting there, gagging and coughing, waiting for the holy relic.

"All of a sudden, this big Chrysler pulls up in front of the novitiate and out steps this fat Roman monsignor with the arm wrapped up in red silk. Once they get him out of the rain, he unwraps it and gets in line behind the candles and the incense and we all hike down the aisle to the front of the chapel where he holds it over his head like he's just won an Oscar. Only it's so dark and damn smokey that all anyone can really see is this silver box. He could have had his lunch in there and none of us would have known.

"But meanwhile, poor Jerry Taylor is holding that hot thurible too close to his alb and it suddenly bursts into flames. He lets out a yelp and drops the incense and starts whacking at his alb, trying to put it out. Those of us with candles don't have anywhere to put 'em and we're too dumb to blow them out, so we just stand there looking like goons. And the monsignor with Xavier's arm can't do anything. Finally, old Father Buzzy comes running up from the back of the chapel with the holy water font and he throws that on Jerry. Now there's water, hot coals, and steaming incense all over the floor, the room is filled with more smoke, Jerry Taylor is standing there in a wet, steaming alb cussing up a storm, and no one can see a damn thing. Suddenly, from the back of the chapel, a woman stands up and starts crying at the top of her voice, 'A miracle! It's a miracle!'

"Well, that sent that fat monsignor right over the edge. Within two minutes he had Xavier's arm wrapped up and was tearing off in his big Chrysler. None of us ever did get to see it."

Brother Grib's mouth was hanging open. Father Townsend was laughing out loud and even Father Stanley was chortling.

"You forgot about the picture," Mark reminded Father LaBelle.

"Oh, yeah. Three months later that woman sent the novitiate a picture she painted of Xavier's arm rising up through this thick cloud with burning candles all around it. Charlie took one look at it, wrapped it up, and gave it to Father Buzzy on St. Xavier's feast day."

Bones had gotten lost in his story, but remembering the picture put him back on track. "That's the point I was trying to make," he told Dennis Grib. "One man's debacle is another man's miracle. Those people kneeling up in Cowiche believe something supernatural is taking place. Now you may think it's all smoke and mirrors, and maybe it is, but for them it's real."

"Yeah, but at least Xavier's arm was real," Dennis argued.

"And so were all those people who disappeared," Joe reminded him. "What you see depends on how you look at it, Dennis."

Father Stanley, surprisingly, nodded in agreement. "There is such a thing as seeing with the eyes of faith," he knowingly pronounced.

Brother Grib was shaking his head. "I still don't get it," he replied.

He was not the only one having difficulties. That afternoon's visit with Brother Gabriel's widow left Father Townsend feeling more uncertain than ever. He was beginning to realize that some of his early assumptions might be wrong. Sister Elizabeth had told them that her husband was uncomfortable with the Vigil Room. That changed Mark's impression of the man considerably. He had started with the premise that Brother Gabriel was a charlatan, playing off of people's hysteria by warning them about the end of the world. The ones being raptured, he figured, were part of Gabriel's scam. But Mark could not imagine recruiting thirty-seven people and convincing all of them to make themselves disappear. The sheer number made that possibility seem unlikely.

The Jesuit had assumed that Brother Gabriel and everyone associated with him conspired to concoct a hoax about the Rapture. The *why* was still puzzling, as was Angelina Sandoval Ybarra's role in all of it. And then there was her own disappearance. The one thing that had seemed clear to the priest was that the hoax, at some point, turned deadly serious. But now Brother Gabriel's role was a lot less clear. Either he was the innocent victim his wife made him out to be, or his duplicitous scheme had somehow backfired.

Father Townsend had lots of questions and very few answers. Since their return from Cowiche, he had tried sorting things out, first in his room, then with a long walk around the neighborhood. But by dinner time he was no farther in his thinking than when he started. It was like trying to catch a glimpse of Xavier's arm through clouds of smoke.

With a start, Mark realized the other Jesuits around the table were watching him, as if waiting for a reply.

"I'm sorry," he apologized, "my mind was wandering."

"That's all right, Father Townsend," Joe LaBelle said in his most patronizing voice. "It's so seldom we get to see somebody go into ecstasy right here at the table. It was really quite inspiring. I was asking what your plans are for tomorrow."

Mark threw up his hands.

"I'm not sure what to do," he confessed. "That's kind of what I was thinking about. I'm beginning to wonder if I shouldn't just go home. If Angelina hasn't shown up by now, I don't know what I can do to find her. And it's not as if her husband is out looking."

"Not unless she's hiding at the Sweet Apple Tavern," Dennis Grib murmured.

"Don't give up too soon, Mark," LaBelle counseled his friend.

"That's right," Dennis chimed in. "Don't forget that there's still thirty-eight people missing."

"Thirty-seven," Mark corrected him. "Sister Elizabeth said there were thirty-seven."

Father Stanley cleared his throat. "I think he was including your friend, Angelina."

* * *

The evening air had not cooled. Mark attempted another walk through the neighborhood after dinner, but before he went a block his clothes were starting to stick to him. He rerouted his steps and headed for an enclosed shopping mall three blocks away. Window shopping was not quite the same as a meditative walk, but there was air conditioning. And ice cream.

Apparently most of Yakima had the same idea. The mall was packed with hordes of people seeking relief from the heat. Families, teenagers, and elders moved slowly around and around the indoor plaza. The stores were open, although the only ones that seemed to be racking up any sales were the food concessions. Father Townsend took one look at the long line of people in front of the ice cream parlor and continued walking. The mall was not only crowded but noisy with everyone trying to be heard over everybody else. The voices mingled and swelled into a loud buzz. It was the same type of disorienting experience that occurs anytime too many voices are crowded into too small of a space. The more he tried listening, the more Mark realized there was something that made this experience unique. All of the voices he could distinguish were speaking Spanish. At least three-fourths of the people around him were Hispanic. If it were not for the signs above the stores written in English, the priest could easily have imagined himself somewhere in Latin America.

Intrigued, he started circling through the mall again, this time observing the people more closely. He had a difficult time understanding what most around him were saying, but in many instances it was easy to guess. The mother bending over her young daughter, dabbing ice cream off the front of her shirt, was obviously reminding the child to be more careful. And the plans of a young couple holding hands and staring at a display of rings in a jeweler's window were not hard to imagine.

An elderly couple moved off a bench and Mark gratefully dropped down onto the vacated spot. Most of the actual words being spoken were indecipherable to him, but the activities, gestures, and behaviors seemed universal. Leaning back, he relaxed, letting the sea of humanity flow around him.

Thirty-eight people plucked out from the crowded mall would hardly make a difference. There were so many moving about that the space occupied by thirty-eight would disappear in the blink of an eye. Yet if thirty-eight people did suddenly disappear, the lives of just about everyone in the mall would be affected. The world is not that large. Those thirty-eight would have relatives, friends, and acquaintances who would also have other relatives, friends, and acquaintances. Toss a stone into a pond and you'll cause a ripple. Throw in thirty-eight and you'll create a roiling sea as ripples collide and crash against each other. Father Townsend watched as the crowd swirled around him. If he had some way of asking every man, woman, and child if they knew of a relative, friend, or acquaintance who was missing, he wondered how many would answer yes.

Imagining what a mother was saying to her child, or two lovers standing in front of a jewelry store, was not that difficult. But to look any deeper into these people's lives was beyond Mark's capability. And his own inability to understand them made conversation impossible. Other than taking up space on a bench, his presence in their midst meant nothing. Thirty-eight relatives, friends, and acquaintances were missing and there was nothing he could do for any of them. If there was one person who could disappear from the mall without making any splash at all, Father Townsend realized, it would be himself.

EIGHTEEN

"Padre? Hermano?"

Rosa Castillo's dark brown eyes peered quizzically at them through the small crack of the open door. The surprise of finding two Jesuits at the door was evident in her voice and on her face. At seven-thirty in the morning the woman had every right to be surprised. Father Townsend would have had them there even earlier if Dennis had not insisted on eating breakfast first.

"Que pasa?" the woman asked, still peering from behind her door.

"¿Podremos entrar?" Dennis politely asked.

Remembering her manners, the woman opened her door for them. *"Sí, sí,"* she said. "Please do come in." The tile hallway was quiet and cool. She was wearing a simple house dress with a clean white apron. "Luis is working in the vineyards," she told them. "Should I call him?" Her surprise had now turned to worry. Priests do not show up so early and unexpectedly unless there was something wrong.

"No es necesario," Dennis assured her, raising a hand, *"we are only here to visit."*

Not entirely convinced, the woman gave them a slight smile. "May I serve you coffee?" she offered.

They moved through the quiet house into the kitchen

where she poured coffee for the three of them, setting the cups on a tray and escorting them through the back door, onto the patio. In a far corner of the flower garden, a sprinkler was gently arcing sprays of water over a bright patch of dahlias. She placed the tray on the patio table and carefully adjusted the large umbrella to shield them from the sun before inviting the men to sit. The three of them settled into chairs. The day was warming up but the temperature in the garden was cool and the flowers and green grass and the sound of the sprinkler could have lulled them into a tranquil mood if Father Townsend had allowed it. He took an initial sip of his coffee, then set his cup down.

"Rosa, I'm sorry to visit so early," he began, "but Dennis and I have a lot to do today."

He caught the look of surprise on Brother Grib's face but continued speaking.

"Did Angelina leave any notes here? Notebooks or a computer or anything? Because I'd like to see them if she did."

She nodded slightly. "I think that there are, yes. But they are in her bedroom and I have not looked too much, Father. Her husband is still using the room, you see." Her eyes shifted to the far corner of the house where Angelina and Tim's room was located. There was a glass door that opened directly onto the patio, although at the moment it was closed and drapes prevented them from seeing in.

The priest's eyebrows arched. "Is Tim here?"

"I think he is, yes," Rosa answered. "He came in very late though. I think he is probably still asleep."

"You mean hung over." Brother Grib's voice sounded harsh, he was making no effort to disguise what he thought of Tim Connell.

Rosa said nothing but sipped her coffee and watched the two Jesuits.

"Shall I go wake him up?" Dennis offered.

Father Townsend shook his head. "I'll do it."

Instead of going to the door across the patio, Mark went in through the house. He stopped in the kitchen and poured a fresh cup of coffee, then headed down the hallway. The door to the guest bedroom was still closed and he put his ear next to the wood and listened for a moment before rapping.

"Tim! Tim! Wake up!" He waited a few moments and listened for some sound of stirring from inside, then gave another impatient knock, louder this time. "Tim, wake up! It's Mark." The door was locked, but he jiggled the handle and then knocked even louder. "Hey, Connell! Wake up!"

At last there were sounds of stirring. Townsend continued knocking and calling out until a very rumpled and bleary-eyed Tim Connell opened the door. He stood in the doorway, swaying slightly in his boxers and T-shirt, trying to focus his eyes on the priest. Mark took a step back. The man smelled as bad as he looked.

"Here," he said, extending the coffee, "drink this. Then get dressed and come outside. We need to talk." The priest turned on his heel and left the befuddled man standing in the doorway.

Twenty minutes later, Connell emerged through the door onto the patio, the empty coffee cup in his hand. But he was dressed and walking and had made at least a cursory effort to clean his face and comb his hair. He was still steeped in eau de Sweet Apple though, and his eyes looked bloodshot. Rosa stood and took the cup from his hands.

"I'll get you some more," she murmured. "Do you want to eat?"

Tim shook his head miserably. "No, thank you, Rosa. Just coffee." He dropped into the chair she vacated as Dennis Grib glared at him. The young Jesuit could not stand drunks and was taking a particular dislike to this one. He could not understand how a man would go on drinking when his wife was missing. Mark Townsend understood. You do not have to sit in a confessional too many hours before you learn that souls are either strengthened or broken by suffering. For some, it is a constant struggle. For others, not even a contest. Tim

Connell was one of those who had lost before he even started.

"A rough night, huh?"

Connell did not respond but kept his eyes fixed morosely on the table top. Rosa returned with his coffee, set it in front of him, then beat a hasty exit back into the house.

Mark waited until the man showed some sign of life, lifting the cup to his lips and drinking noisily. "Tim," he said, "you need to get a grip. The way you're going isn't helping Angie, and it isn't helping you either. You're going to end up a lot worse off if you don't stop."

Connell glanced over at him, then down at the table again. His only response was a mumbled, "I know."

"You've got to do this for Angelina, if not for yourself."

The young man nodded, then spoke. "I'll try." There was neither strength nor conviction in his voice. But for the moment, Mark let it go.

"We need to look through the notes Angelina kept," he said. "I want to know what she found out about this Vigil Room of Brother Gabriel's. In particular, I want to know how many names of the raptured she had."

"What for?"

Mark decided not to try to describe his walk through the mall. "It seems strange to me that thirty-seven people could disappear without causing much alarm," he offered. "That's a lot of people when you think of it. And yet there doesn't seem to be much concern. Or even interest. As far as I can tell, Angelina was about the only one who thought it was worth looking into."

Tim seemed more concerned about getting the coffee to his lips without spilling than in anything the priest was saying. Brother Grib was listening closely, however.

"But is thirty-seven really that big of a deal? I'm sure there's a lot more than that who have left their families or wandered away. People leave home all the time. Not in the same way as these people, but they're still missing.'' Dennis ended with a shrug. ''It just doesn't seem like it's that significant.''

''To me it does,'' countered Mark. ''If there was a plane crash and thirty-seven people died, people would pay attention. That'd be on the front page.''

''Yeah, but Mark, these people aren't dead. They've just disappeared.''

Father Townsend looked the young Jesuit straight in the eye. ''You're sure of that, Dennis?''

A small desk was set up in a corner of the bedroom. With the drapes open, Angelina could look out at Rosa's garden while she wrote. She had left a laptop computer placed in the center, flanked by pens, writing pads, and a thick stack of note cards. Her computer was plugged into a small printer that sat on the floor, out of the way. In the desk's one drawer, Mark discovered her notes. They filled two reporter's notebooks and most of a third. Angelina's handwriting was not pretty. Her words were shaped with sharp, straight lines and jagged angles. Her notes looked like they were jabbed onto the page rather than written. There were no gentle curves, nothing seemed to flow easily. Father Townsend flipped the pages quickly the first time through. He got the impression she felt passionately about the words she was writing down; someone impatient, in a hurry, perhaps even angry. Nothing looked styled or shaped. These were hard, sharp impressions, written in a hurry, driven with some force. They were the notes of a reporter, not a poet.

On the front cover of each notebook, Angelina had written a number, followed by the date when she started writing in that particular one. Mark gave the first to Tim, the second to Dennis and kept the third for himself.

''Check for anything about the Vigil Room,'' he instructed, ''and especially if you find any names.''

Dennis dropped to the floor and started reading his notebook while Tim perched on the edge of the unmade bed. Mark stayed in the desk chair and began reading. Only a couple of minutes passed before Dennis spoke up.

"I think maybe I found one. Hector Lopez, June sixteen. And she's got it underlined."

"That's all it says?" Mark asked doubtfully.

"Just the name and date," confirmed Dennis. "The stuff right before is a census statistic that says there's forty-five thousand Latinos in the Yakima Valley and right afterwards is a quote or something about Brother Gabriel."

Father Townsend wrote the name down on a yellow legal pad. Underneath he added the name of Francisco Ramirez. Two down, thirty-five to go. "Keep reading," he instructed.

Moments later, Dennis spoke again. "Two more. Nico and Maria Aquino. She's written underneath, 'gone May twenty-third.' That's gotta mean raptured, don't you think?"

Mark thought so, and added their names to the list.

"Missing April five," Tim was reading from his notebook. "Miguel Santos, twenty-six years old. And underneath that she's got written Moxee. So maybe he's from around here."

The three men spent forty minutes reading through the notebooks. By the time they were through, the yellow pad had a list of twenty-two names on it. Some, like Nico and Maria Aquino, seemed definite, but some other names sounded less so. In one of the notebooks, Angelina had jotted the name of a Gustavo Cueves, followed by a dollar sign and a question mark. None of them could guess what she intended, but Mark wrote his name down anyway. There were several others that seemed just as iffy. From the total list, thirteen of the names also included dates. All of the names were Hispanic. Only a few included addresses or the names of towns in the Yakima Valley. There were no phone numbers. Trying to track all of them would be an impossible task, but there were at least half a dozen that seemed likely. Father Townsend circled those names.

"What about her computer?" asked Dennis. "Are we going to check that?"

Father Townsend looked at Tim Connell. He was lying sprawled across the bed and looked half-asleep. When he saw the priest watching, he shrugged his indifference.

"I don't know what's on there," he said, "but you can look if you want."

Mark found the computer's switch and flipped it. Green lights on the console began blinking and he heard the innards start to hum.

"That will take a minute to boot up," he told them, standing up from the desk. "I'm going to ask Rosa something." He picked up the yellow notepad and wandered out to the kitchen. She was sitting at the table, a plastic bowl in front of her, shelling peas. Mark pulled out a chair opposite her.

"We found the name of someone who might live here in Moxee," he told her. "Do you know a man named Miguel Santos?"

She kept her fingers busy as she thought, splitting the pods with her thumb and riffling the green peas into her bowl. Finally she nodded. "I think maybe he is with Carla Santos. She works at the grocery store. I know her from church."

"Miguel is her husband?"

The old woman nodded slightly. "Or he was. There was trouble between them, but I do not know what happened. Earlier in the spring they separated apart. But I know Carla is still here because I see her at the store and in church. But I think Miguel is gone."

"Was he one of the ones who was raptured?"

"I do not know, Padre. No one has said so."

"Was Miguel Catholic?"

Rosa stopped shelling. "Maybe not," she replied, "because he never came to church. Only Carla and her baby would be there. I think Miguel was not Catholic."

"But you don't know if he was a follower of Brother Gabriel's."

"I'm sorry," she said.

Back in the bedroom, Father Townsend sat in front of Angelina's computer, Dennis hovering over his shoulder. Tim Connell remained on his bed, his eyes staring up at the ceiling. Brother Grib's arm snaked over Mark's shoulder and he pointed to one of the icons on the screen.

"Try that one," he urged.

Mark clicked on the icon marked Yakima. There was a burst of energy as the machine clicked and whirred, then the screen flickered and filled with text. Over a dozen files scrolled onto the screen and some of them looked quite large. One was called "Rapture."

The file's text dealt not only with the unusual incidents in Cowiche, but also the theological meaning of the Rapture. Angelina had done her homework. Several texts were cited as resources as well as biblical passages, mostly from Revelation. She had included quotes by Brother Gabriel, too.

" 'I think we have achieved the time when seals are being placed and foreheads are being marked. We are on the verge of the exodus being organized. If I am correct, then the angel's censor of fire will soon be thrown down upon the earth. I believe that the angels entrusted with the earth's destruction are poised and ready.' "

Dennis Grib was reading the screen over Mark's shoulder. "This stuff gives me the creeps," he said. "It sounds like he really believed the end of the world was coming."

"I think he may have," Father Townsend murmured in reply as he scrolled further down. "I think he may have."

Five pages into the text, near the end, they found the names. For the most part, they matched the ones written in Angelina's notes. Hector Lopez, Nico and Maria Aquino, and Miguel Santos were among the names listed. Gustavo Cueves was not. Her list totalled thirty-two, still five names shy of the thirty-seven mentioned by Sister Elizabeth. But her notes in the computer were fleshed out with more details than the notebooks. Many of the names included descriptions, ages, and distinguishing marks like tattoos or scars. Quite a few included the names of hometowns in Mexico, Guatemala, or Honduras. Angelina had also tried to identify where the people were living in the Yakima Valley and the type of work they did. There was a lot of information to assimilate and Mark set down the yellow pad he was writing on.

"Tim, do you care if I print this page out?" asked Father Townsend.

From the bed where he lay, Connell slowly rolled his head back and forth. He did not care much about anything.

"Padre Mark?" Rosa's disembodied voice floated in from the hallway. "Excuse me? Padre?" She appeared in the doorway of the bedroom. Her eyes flitted from Tim Connell lying across the unmade bed to the cluttered floor and his clothes strewn over two chairs and finally came to a stop on Father Townsend's face. "There is a telephone call for you."

Mark followed her back into the kitchen and picked up the phone from the table.

"Hello?"

"Mark, this is Joe."

"What's up, Bones?"

"You haven't been listening to the news, have you?"

"We're reading through Angelina's notes," he told the priest. "Why? What's on the news?"

"Well," Joe Bones drawled, drawing the word out for several seconds, "you might want to get your heinies back up to Cowiche. They're reporting on the radio that your favorite evangelist might be back."

Mark was plainly mystified. "I know that already, Joe. Sister Elizabeth told us they were bringing him back last night. They plan to have a vigil up there before the burial. That's not news."

Father LaBelle was chuckling. "That's not quite what I mean, old buddy. According to the news reports, Bro Gabe has taken a hike."

"What?"

Bones was laughing now. "He's up and gone, Mark. Disappeared! All that's left is an empty casket."

NINETEEN

The road leading to Brother Gabriel's house was clogged and traffic was at a standstill. The dead evangelist's disappearance was already big news. Three television crews had already found their way to Cowiche and their trucks were pulled into the field in front of the house, antennae pointing into heaven. Two Yakima County sheriffs, wearing bright orange vests, tried directing traffic, but they were overwhelmed by the sheer volume of cars and pickup trucks aimed into the narrow road leading past the residence. They wore grim looks of determination as they waved their arms and shouted directions, but despite their strenuous efforts the county road remained gridlocked. Traffic was unable to move forward or backward and there was no space to turn around. Those who were most determined to get closer were simply pulling off the road, parking their cars, and walking.

From where they were stalled in line, Father Townsend guessed the driveway up to the house was at least several hundred yards ahead of them. He squirmed impatiently, trying to see over the cars ahead of them. Brother Grib had put his car in park; it was obvious to him that they were not driving any further down this road.

At the edge of the orchard next to the Jesuits' car, three Hispanic teenage boys pulled ladders close together and climbed up. From the top they could see over the traffic and watch the circus. One of them reached out and plucked an apple from a tree. After giving the fruit a cursory wipe with the front of his T-shirt, he sank his teeth into it. Dennis Grib rolled down his window and poked his head out.

"*¿Amigos, que ven desde arriban?*"

"*Nada,*" one of them called down, "*solamente los locos.*" He was grinning as he said it.

Dennis turned back to Mark. "What do you want to do?" he asked. "I don't think we're going to get any closer than this."

The priest had to agree. They had not moved in over ten minutes. No one had.

"I need to get up there, Dennis, and find out what's going on. Staying back here is useless, we can't see a thing. We might as well go home and watch it on TV."

That sounded good to Dennis, but he knew better than to agree out loud. Father Townsend was clearly getting frustrated. Instead, he suggested, "Why don't you walk up there if you want. I'll stay here with the car. Go see what you can find out and then come back. I've got a hunch I won't be going anywhere for awhile."

Townsend looked doubtful. "You don't mind?"

"Not at all," Grib assured him. "Go ahead."

Once out of the car, Father Townsend made good progress. But by the time he reached the driveway leading to the house he was sweating hard. It was just after noon and the sun was directly overhead. A crowd of forty or fifty people was standing in the road, all facing the house. A single sheriff's deputy was guarding the driveway, his arms folded across his chest. A radio clipped to his belt was emitting static bleats. Across the drive and on either side someone had placed several sawhorses and laid lengths of two-by-four lumber across the top. Red and white signs were stapled onto the makeshift barrier: *NO TRESPASSING. PROHIBIDA LA ENTRADA.* They were the same ones Mark had seen posted at the edge of the orchards.

The television camera crews had muscled their way to the front of the crowd, taking aim at the house, the crowd, the deputy . . . anything that moved. A reporter with a microphone was moving through the crowd, followed by her cameraman, trying to find someone who spoke English. The few in the crowd were turning her down. She started to approach Father Townsend but he waved her off before she could even ask. Mark fixed his attention on the house and the Vigil Room. He spotted two men standing in the shadows on the side of the house, talking earnestly together. There was no sign of Sister Elizabeth and he felt sure she would remain inside, out of sight from the curious onlookers. There were several vehicles in front of the house, including the two Dodge pickups Mark had noticed the first time he was there. As he studied the house, a plan came to mind and he edged his way through the crowd until he was standing directly in front of the deputy's roadblock.

He nodded curtly to the officer and started to lift up the wooden barrier.

"Hold on, sir," the deputy said. "You'll have to remain back."

Mark gave the man an annoyed look. "I'm Father Townsend," he informed him. "Here to see Sister Elizabeth."

The deputy held out a cautionary arm. "Just wait there, please."

Keeping his eyes fixed on Father Townsend, he unclipped the radio from his belt and began talking into it. Mark tried to maintain a look of impatience while he waited. It took several minutes but finally the deputy clipped his radio back on his belt and lifted the barrier himself.

"All right," he said, "you can go ahead now."

Technically there was no lie involved. As a matter of fact, he was there to see Sister Elizabeth. He knew his ruse would never have worked if she was not willing to see him. So with some confidence he strode toward the house, conscious of the reporters and their cameramen calling to him from the crowd. He kept walking and did not turn around.

Marshall Fairbanks opened the front door as Father Townsend stepped onto the porch. His arm gripped the door firmly as he looked the priest up and down.

"We've met before, haven't we?"

"Yes, we have," the priest replied. "I was up here the other day and you came out to the road to talk to me."

"Ah, yes," Fairbanks jerked his head and released his hold on the door. "I remember. There was someone else with you."

"Brother Grib." Mark nodded in the direction of the road. "He's parked down the road. It was impossible to get any closer."

The man glanced over Father Townsend's shoulder at the crowd standing on the road. His lips curled into a thin smile. " 'What did ye go out to the desert to see? A reed swaying in the wind? Tell me, what did ye go out to see?' "

Mark turned and looked back at the crowd of people watching them. Keeping his back turned to Marshall Fairbanks, he added to the man's scriptural quotation, " 'I send my messenger ahead of you, to prepare your way before you.' "

He heard the older man's chuckle. "Amen." Turning back, he caught the tail end of a smile. "Won't you come inside, Father?"

Sister Elizabeth was sitting in the center of the white sofa in the living room, facing the vast view of the valley below them. Three other men were in chairs facing hers. All of them looked up expectantly as Fairbanks led Father Townsend into the room.

"You already know Sister," he said, directing the priest's attention toward the others, "and these are some of Brother Gabriel's counselors: Len Patowski, Eldon Krantz, and Tony Maruca."

All three stood and shook the priest's hand as he worked his way around the circle. When he finished,

Fairbanks motioned him to sit at one end of the couch while he moved to the other. Sister Elizabeth remained seated, clutching a crumpled handkerchief, her eyes fixed on the priest as he greeted the others. She waited until he was seated before speaking.

"It's kind of you to come, Father. But I'm afraid I'm not very good company today." She lifted up the handkerchief for him to see. "These gentlemen must think I'm a big baby."

Len Patowski shifted his considerable bulk in his chair. "Now, Sister," he crooned, leaning forward, "we think nothing of the sort. You've had a terrible shock. We all have. A few tears are perfectly in order."

The others nodded in agreement.

"I'm sorry for intruding," Father Townsend told her, "but when I heard the news I felt I had to come." He turned to the others. "Are the reports true? He really has disappeared?"

Patowski shifted again. He seemed to be having trouble finding a comfortable position. "That is the situation, Reverend. Brother Gabriel is no longer with us." Sister Elizabeth emitted a heavy sob and wrung her handkerchief tighter. "It happened last night."

"During the vigil?"

"Afterwards," Marshall Fairbanks replied, leaning forward to look at Mark from the other side of Sister Elizabeth. "We were finished with our prayers and vigil and we sent everybody home . . ."

"We were going to resume this morning," Len Patowski cut in.

Fairbanks nodded. "But this morning he was gone."

"Everything was just as we left it," Patowski explained, "except Brother's casket was empty. The door was still locked and nothing in the Vigil Room was disturbed."

"But the casket lid was up, Len. And I remember closing it before we left."

"I remember that too, Marshall. Yes, it was definitely closed when we locked the door."

Both fell silent as they pondered the mystifying events

of the previous night. So far, neither Tony Maruca nor Eldon Krantz had contributed to the conversation. Mark glanced over at the two of them. He recognized Maruca as the man who had so closely shadowed Brother Gabriel during Mark's two encounters with the evangelist, first in front of St. Joseph Church, then again at the bottom of the hill during the *quinceañera* fiesta. At both times, Tony Maruca had acted more like a bodyguard than a counselor. Although if he was assigned to protect Gabriel, he had done a lousy job. Mark studied the young man sitting back in his chair. He certainly did not look like a bodyguard. He stood no more than five-six, five-seven at the most, and could not have weighed more than a hundred and forty pounds. He was small-framed and did not look particularly strong. Eldon Krantz was built about the same. Mark could not recall seeing him in the crowd around Brother Gabriel, but he would have been fairly easy to overlook. The only reason he remembered Maruca was from the way the man hovered next to the preacher's elbow. Like a shadow.

"Do the police have any idea what happened?" Father Townsend asked the group.

Heads slowly began to wag.

"I'm afraid they are not much help," Len Patowski informed him. "Other than checking out the place, they are not investigating."

"Why not?"

Sister Elizabeth explained. "They say that unless there is reason to suspect a crime was committed, it's not a police matter."

Mark protested, "But Sister, your husband's body has disappeared."

The woman dropped her eyes down to her lap.

Patowski shifted in his chair. "Father Townsend, that does not necessarily mean something is wrong. There may be several explanations for Brother Gabriel being gone."

"Like the rapture? Is that it?" Without intending it, Mark's voice sounded incredulous.

Len Patowski slowly closed his eyes and leaned back

in his chair. At the same time, Marshall Fairbanks cleared his throat and began quoting Scripture again. " '*Talitha, koum,*' " he said piously. " 'At this the family's astonishment knew no bounds.' "

Townsend's mouth fell open. What the man was proposing was astounding.

"Are you trying to tell me that you think Brother Gabriel is raised from the dead?"

Fairbanks reached out and laid a consoling hand on Sister Elizabeth's quaking shoulders. "We don't know what happened, Father Townsend. But with the Lord, anything is possible. We know from our Scripture that such things are possible. It might have been a rapture, or maybe something more."

"Or something less." Patowski was speaking. "It would certainly be helpful if your lady friend would come forward. I know the police are anxious to speak with her."

"Angelina? You think she's involved?"

Sister Elizabeth was crying again. "I don't know what to think," she sobbed. "But my husband is gone. Gone!" She jumped up and ran out of the room. A moment later, Marshall Fairbanks got up and followed her down the hallway. Tony Maruca and Eldon Krantz did not move a muscle, but Len Patowski was rocking back and forth in his chair. Mark realized the huge man was trying to stand up.

"Forgive us, Father," he wheezed, getting to his feet, "but these are trying times. Our little community is being torn apart by all of this. It's difficult for us to know what we should think or do. We're gonna have to give a lot more prayer and meditation to these events before we can understand what the good Lord is asking us to do." Two sets of pudgy fingers locked themselves together in front of the big man's belly. "Like yourself, we need to listen to the voice of God in our lives. Isn't that true?"

Father Townsend stood up from the couch. He felt a little light-headed by what he had just seen and heard.

"Before I go, could I look inside the Vigil Room?"

Patowski was frowning, pursing his lips. "Sister Elizabeth showed it to me the other day," Mark hurriedly added. "I'd just like to take another look."

Patowski reconsidered. "Well," he said, smiling, "if Sister has already let you inside. Eldon, why don't you go with Father and let him look around a bit. Be sure and lock up afterwards."

Father Townsend bid the men goodbye and asked them to assure Sister Elizabeth of his prayers, then followed Krantz out the front door. As soon as they stepped outside the house, the television cameras were aimed in their direction and reporters began shouting questions at them.

"Ignore 'em," Krantz grumbled from the side of his mouth. "Don't even look at them." He led the priest off the porch and onto the gravel path to the cinderblock building. Stopping in front of the heavy wooden door, he fished in his pocket for the key. Unlocking the door, he stepped aside to let the priest enter first.

The room was just as hot and stuffy as the day before. Everything looked about the same, too. The rows of benches were arranged just the same. A bronze-colored casket sat on top of the cloth-covered bier and there were more flowers than the day before. They were arrayed on the floor around the casket. The casket's lid was up, both the upper and lower halves. Mark went up the aisle between the rows of benches and peered inside. Empty. A satin pillow lay inside, slightly indented from the weight of Brother Gabriel's head. The silk lining inside the casket looked undisturbed. It was just an empty coffin. Townsend turned and looked slowly around the room. Eldon Krantz was leaning against the back wall, watching him.

"Do you spend much time in here?" Mark asked him. His voice echoed slightly in the near empty room.

"Not very much," the man admitted.

"You believe what they say? About people being raptured here?"

Krantz shrugged. "I don't know. I guess. Maybe."

The passion of a committed believer was notably missing.

"Sister Elizabeth told me that Brother Gabriel had some doubts himself," Mark said to the man.

"Yeah, I knew that," Krantz replied. "He was never too keen about this place."

"And yet he let it stay open."

Krantz made no reply. Mark wandered around the room, his eyes searching the floor.

"If you're looking for a trap door," Krantz said, "you won't find one. This floor is solid cement. There ain't a seam in it. I know, because I helped pour it."

"Did you?" Mark said. "When was that?"

"About a year and a half ago. Just after Fairbanks and Patowski moved Brother up here."

"This was Fairbanks's house before?"

"Yes, but he moved down to the valley, closer to his orchards."

"Orchards?"

"Some he owns out by Moxee," Krantz said. "He and Patowski are partners."

Father Townsend was still wandering around the Vigil Room. He poked his head inside the bathroom. The same broom and mop leaned against the sink; the dustpan and bucket were next to them. There were still three rolls of toilet paper stacked on the floor beside the bucket.

"How long have they been partners?" Mark wondered.

There was no response and Father Townsend stuck his head out from the bathroom.

"I don't know," Krantz answered.

He left the bathroom and wandered back over to the empty casket. "I'm from Seattle," he informed the man, "and don't know anything about orchards."

Krantz was watching him closely. "That's about all that's around here," he said. "It's either orchard or sagebrush. Not much else."

"Have you lived here all your life?"

The man shook his head. "Only about five years. I'm from Nevada."

"Lots of sagebrush there, too," Father Townsend observed.

"Better believe it."

There was nothing more for him to see and he was feeling increasingly uncomfortable walking around the room under Eldon Krantz's constant gaze. He was running out of things to say, too, so he thanked the man and they both stepped back outside. Krantz checked to make sure the door locked behind them.

"Tell me, Eldon, what do you think happened to Angelina Sandoval Ybarra?"

They started walking back toward the house. From the roadway both men could hear voices calling in their direction.

"I think she went away," Krantz said. "After Brother got killed."

"Did she do it?"

He stopped in his tracks and gave the priest a hard look. Mark turned and waited, his back to the reporters eagerly calling out to them.

"How would I know?" he finally answered. "I wasn't there." He started to turn away but then hesitated. "If I were you," he said with a sly smile, "I'd go ask her husband."

Father Townsend recalled a Jesuit in Seattle once describing news reporters as sharks in a feeding frenzy. He felt like a bloody piece of meat passing through their midst as he tried to reach the car. Cameras and microphones were thrust in his face, people shouted questions at him, and no matter which way he turned, his forward progress was impeded. The deputy sheriff who lifted the barricade for him looked on with sympathy but did nothing to ease his plight. The priest had to fight his way through on his own, tossing out little bites of information as he struggled through the hungry crowd.

He did tell them his name, and that he was a Catholic priest from Seattle. He came to offer Sister Elizabeth his condolences. No, he did not know Brother Gabriel well, they had only met recently. And no, he definitely was not one of his followers.

"Do you believe in the resurrection, Father?" The question was shouted by an earnest-looking young man with bleached hair and tortoiseshell glasses and it stopped the priest's forward progress. The cameras encircled him, their eyes fixed on him, never blinking.

"Yes, I do." Mark swallowed. "Do I believe in Brother Gabriel's resurrection?" He paused. "Eventually," he said.

As he made his escape he imagined sharp teeth grinding.

Somehow Dennis Grib had managed to get his car turned around. He was parked on the opposite side of the road, facing away from the house. But he spotted Mark in his mirror and started the motor as the Jesuit threaded his way through the traffic. The air conditioning was on high when Townsend slid into the passenger's seat.

"Let's get out of here," Father Townsend urged, looking over his shoulder. There was no sign he was being followed.

Grib slowly angled his car back down the road, past the cars jammed up on either side. The line of traffic now stretched nearly half a mile. Some were still sitting in their cars, waiting for the line to move, but the majority of people had simply abandoned their vehicles and hiked up the road to join the crowd of gawkers. There were at least seventy-five people standing behind the makeshift barricade now, staring across at Brother Gabriel's house.

" 'What did ye go out to the desert to see?' " Mark mumbled to himself.

"Pardon me?" Dennis kept his eyes on the road, still dodging parked cars. "What'd you say?"

"Nothing," Mark told him, "it was nothing."

TWENTY

As they wound their way down to the valley, Mark described his visit for Dennis Grib. While his conversation with Sister Elizabeth and the counselors was pleasant enough, he had to admit that he came away with little, if anything, that was helpful. The body was clearly missing, but the police did not seem that interested in finding out more about it. No crime, according to what the grieving Sister had told him. That sounded as strange to Dennis as it did to Mark. Apparently a rapture was not the same thing as a body snatching. Neither of the Jesuits believed for a moment that Brother Gabriel had risen from the dead. What puzzled Mark was why Marshall Fairbanks would even hint at such a thing. Or was the orchardist that fanatical of a believer?

"What if he wasn't really dead?" proposed Dennis. "But he just made it look like he was."

Mark snorted. "It's pretty hard to fake a bullet hole, Dennis. And I don't think he could have held his breath the whole time the police were investigating." He shook his head at the thought. "Not to mention trying to survive an autopsy."

"That's not what I mean, Mark!" Dennis lifted his hands off the steering wheel and the car started to shimmy. "That's not it."

"All right, all right. Just keep driving. I know what you mean," Mark assured him. "You think they used someone else's body instead of Brother's. They just made it look like it was him."

"Yeah. They dressed someone up to look like Brother Gabriel and killed him instead."

"And their reason for that?" Mark gave his young companion a bemused look. When he saw Dennis was stumped, he continued, "I think it'd be pretty hard to make someone up like an albino. I guess anything's possible, but it sounds pretty lame to me."

Brother Grib fell silent. Realizing he might have overstepped, Mark tried making amends. "But I have to admit that your idea is as good as any I can think of. The problem is, we're always left with the same question. Why? Why is all this happening?"

Mollified a bit, Dennis spoke up. "They didn't give any reasons for it, huh?"

"I didn't ask them straight out why this was happening," Townsend replied. "But one of them thinks Angelina is involved, and before I left, one of the other counselors suggested I should talk to Tim."

They were coming into Yakima and Dennis turned onto First, heading back to the church. "So maybe they are involved," he said. "We know that she was supposed to meet Gabriel at the park, and we know Tim Connell left the Castillos to go look for her. I realize they're your parishioners, Mark, but it's possible that they're involved."

As much as he hated to admit it, Mark knew that Dennis was right.

As they pulled into a parking spot behind St. Joseph Church, the church bells rang three times. Father Townsend glanced at his watch.

"We missed lunch," he said. "Are you hungry?"

"A little," Dennis confessed, "but let's keep going. I'll grab an apple or something inside."

Getting out of the car was like stepping into a furnace. Heat radiated off the rock walls of the church, and they hurried to get inside. The parish offices had air-conditioning and all units were going full blast. Dennis led the way past the receptionist and upstairs. His own office was on the second floor, halfway down the hall. In former days, the offices were the Jesuit residence and Brother Grib's desk was set up in one of the old bedrooms. There was still a sink and mirror in one corner of the narrow room. He flipped on his computer and then headed back out of the room.

"Make yourself comfortable," he instructed. "I'm going to use the can and then look for something to eat. You want anything?"

"Any kind of soft drink would be great."

Father Townsend took the chair angled at the side of Dennis's desk and waited. Unlike his own cluttered office back in Seattle, there was not much to look at. Mark had one large bulletin board completely covered over with the photographs of friends, relations, and parishioners: baby pictures, weddings, baptisms, lots of Christmas photos. This was Grib's first apostolic assignment, and he had not yet started accumulating the iconographic clutter that helps remind a celibate that he's connected and loved. Mark Townsend had seen enough lonely men's rooms, and he believed that barren walls often indicated a bleak existence for whoever lived inside them. He noted with approval that Dennis Grib was beginning to display a few treasured mementoes. On the desk near his computer were two framed photographs. One was of his parents. They flanked each side of their son as the three of them smiled brightly toward the camera. The other was of Dennis and his novice classmates, a row of five young men dressed in black clerics, looking hopeful. Against one wall he had hung a brightly colored Mexican blanket, and on another, a framed print of the Lady of Guadalupe. At least there was enough in the room to indicate Brother Grib was connected with people he cared about and who cared about him. Mark leaned back and waited for his young companion to return.

Once he had, the two of them searched the names of

parishioners on the computer. They wanted a match between the missing Hispanics on Angelina's list and those registered at St. Joseph. They did a search of the thirty-two names they had, but found no one who was listed with the church. Since most of the Catholic Hispanics in the Yakima region attended St. Joseph, that meant that either none of the missing were Catholic or that none of them had lived in Yakima long enough to register at the parish.

"Try one more," Mark suggested. "Rosa mentioned a Carla Santos. Try her."

Finally they found a match. Carla Santos was a registered member and the address listed was in Moxee. But according to the parish records, she was single. There was no mention of a Miguel Santos. There was, however, a child named Juan Miguel Santos.

By the time they drove back to Moxee and found the address listed in the parish registry, it was after five o'clock. Although the sun was clearly beginning its descent, the temperature was still uncomfortably hot. Reluctant to leave their air-conditioned car, the two Jesuits parked at the curb across from the Santos house and gave it the once over. It was small, run down, and desperate for a new coat of paint. The wood siding, exposed to too many scorching summers and frigid winters, was cracked and, in spots, pulling away. What was once white paint had blistered and flaked and aged to a dirty and tired gray. At one end, near the foundation, a large piece of unpainted plywood was nailed over the siding. The front door was wide open and a lopsided screen door sagged on loose hinges. A mangy-looking mutt of some indeterminate ancestry lay in a bundle across the cement sidewalk. The small plot of lawn in front of the house was dried out and had gone mostly to weeds. A child's green plastic wagon lay tipped over in the dry grass. Parked in the dirt driveway next to the house was a battered Chevy truck that looked like vintage scrap and two years past junk. If the thing still ran, its mechanic was a god.

Brother Grib tipped his head at the open door. "Looks like someone's home."

He turned off the motor and reluctantly the Jesuits left their car's cool comfort.

"I don't know how you can live in this heat," Mark murmured to Dennis as they stepped over the panting dog in their path. The mutt never even lifted his head. Grib rapped solidly against the loose screen door and tried to peer in. From somewhere in the darkness a woman's high voice called out, *"Momento, por favor."*

They stood at the screen door for a full two minutes before a young Hispanic woman appeared from out of the gloom, lugging a baby boy against her hip. When she saw the two Anglo men standing in the sunlight outside her door, she stopped in her tracks and raised one hand to her mouth, staring at them in apparent fright.

Seeing her reaction, Dennis Grib quickly tried to re-assure her. *"Señora,"* he called through the screen, *"soy Hermano Dennis de la iglesia de San José. Y éste es el Padre Mark. Somos jesuítas."* Under his breath, he whispered to Townsend, "She thinks we're Immigration." To the woman he said again, *"Los jesuítas de la iglesia de San José."*

Still not completely convinced, the woman hesitantly approached. The child on her hip, sensing her fear, began to squirm in protest. Carla Santos was wearing a light brown cotton dress with a name tag pinned above her left breast. Her black hair was pulled back into a single braid which, by this time of day, was loose and in danger of unraveling completely. A sheen of sweat glistened on her forehead. She was small and thin and looked like she was about twenty-one. An exhausted and very haggard twenty-one.

"¿Qué?" she asked in a small, timid voice.

"Buenos tardes," Dennis said in a friendly voice. "Carla?"

She nodded. "Yes. I am Carla Santos. You are Jesuits?" She spoke English with a heavy Spanish accent, but took care to enunciate her words clearly. She was used to having to make herself understood in a second language, although not entirely confident in her skill.

Brother Grib smiled in appreciation of her effort. He knew his own level of skill in her language was even less. *"Sí,"* he replied. *"Jesuítas."*

"Please, come in," she said, pushing the screen door open.

The air inside the small, cramped house was hot and heavy, thick with smells of hot oil, onions, and soiled clothes. The tiny room they stood in was littered with the child's clothes and toys. The mother shifted her baby from one hip to the other and pointed toward a cluttered, broken couch. "Please sit," she invited. Nervously, she remained standing in the center of the room.

"If this is a bad time . . ." Mark started to say.

Quickly, she shook her head. "No. No. Is okay." She gestured again toward the couch. "Please," she said again.

Both men had to move clothes off of the couch before they could take a seat, and once they had she stood her boy on the floor and took her place in a straight-back chair facing them. Her child, still fearful of the strangers in the house, clung tightly to the hem of his mother's dress, never taking his eyes off the gringos.

Brother Grib was waiting for Father Townsend to speak. Mark realized with a start that the young Jesuit was suddenly feeling unsure of himself. After so many years of working in a parish, Mark had forgotten what it was like to walk into a stranger's house and strike up a conversation. Dennis was able to help with the translation, but Mark would need to lead the conversation from this point on. He smiled pleasantly and leaned forward.

"I'm Father Mark Townsend," he began. "I'm visiting in Yakima from a church in Seattle. Brother Grib is driving me around to meet people here in the valley. I'm sorry if we've come at a bad time."

Again, Carla Santos shook her head in denial. "No. Is okay, Father." She offered a small, timid smile. "This time is okay for me."

"You look like you might have just gotten off work," he observed.

"Yes," she replied, looking down at her dress, "I work at the Safeway. I just am done and came home."

"You have a fine-looking son," Mark told her. "How old is he?"

"*Tres.* Juanito is almost three." At the sound of his mother pronouncing his name, the small child looked up at her and grinned.

"Have you lived in Moxee very long?"

A shadow of uncertainty passed across the woman's face before she answered. "It is three years. I came to here before he was borned." She laid a hand lightly on her son's head.

"So Juanito is a U.S. citizen," Dennis contributed.

"*Sí,*" his mother said quickly. "Yes, he is."

"You and Miguel must be very proud of him," Mark observed.

"*Sí.*"

The priest leaned forward on the couch and extended his arms toward the boy. "Juanito," he called in a soft voice. The baby turned and stared at the strange man. "Juanito," Mark called again, wiggling his fingers.

The child grinned foolishly and looked up at his mother. She smiled down at him and said, "*Es okay. Vaya el Padre. Vaya te.*" Cautiously, the boy took the first of several hesitant steps toward the man on the couch, then turned back to his mother for reassurance. "*Es okay, Juanito.*"

As the boy slowly moved toward Father Townsend, and while keeping his attention fixed on the child, he spoke again. "I imagine he misses his father, yes?"

"*Sí . . .*" The woman stopped short.

But it was too late.

Mark kept his eyes locked on the baby as he edged his way toward him. He continued wiggling his fingers, smiling and encouraging the child. With a final step, Juan was within reach of the priest's arms. Mark lifted him high above his head, eliciting giggles and then laughter from the boy.

"He's a big one," Mark observed, setting him back on the floor in front of him. "He is big for only three."

His diverting conversation no longer worked. In a frightened voice, Carla asked him, "How do you know about my Miguel, Father?"

"One of my parishioners in Seattle is named Angelina Sandoval Ybarra," he explained in a calm voice. "She's the reason I came to Yakima. Angelina is a reporter and she has been working on a story about Brother Gabriel and his work here in the valley. She disappeared when Brother was killed and I am looking for her. I found your husband's name in her notes."

Carla looked confused. The priest had spoken quickly and too long for her to follow but she was understandably embarrassed to tell him she did not understand. Brother Grib sensed her discomfort and quickly translated the priest's explanation into Spanish. When he was done, Mark continued.

"We think that Miguel was one of the people who went to Brother Gabriel's Vigil Room and then disappeared. They say that he was raptured. Is that what you were told?"

Uncertain, Carla looked to Brother Grib, who quickly translated. Then she nodded yes.

"Have you told anyone about this, Carla? Have you gone to the police?"

"No!" she said quickly. The word *police* needed no translation. At the sound of his mother's loud voice, Juanito swiveled around to look at her. Mark lifted the child and settled him on his knee, then began gently bouncing the boy up and down to distract him.

"*¿Por que?*" he asked.

The words left her mouth in a torrent. Father Townsend obviously knew about her husband's situation and was asking sympathetic questions and now she could not get it out fast enough. Carla Santos had kept too much bottled up inside her for too long. She let everything out and it was several minutes before she stopped. While she spoke, Father Townsend kept his eyes fixed on hers, his hands gently holding her son as he continued bounc-

ing him on his knee. But his attention was with Carla.
Brother Grib leaned forward intently, listening to the
woman's story and concentrating hard to remember
everything she was saying. Near the end, Carla was using her hands to try to convey what she was saying in
Spanish. Her concern for her husband's welfare was obvious in her voice and in her gestures. Finally, she
stopped.

Mark turned to Dennis expectantly. The young
Brother caught his look and held up a hand. *"Un momento,"* he told Mark. "Carla, let me see if I understand . . ." Realizing what he was doing, he stopped and
then started over, in Spanish this time. Father Townsend
waited while the two of them carried on their exchange
for several more minutes. Dennis was seeking clarifica-
tions about what the woman had said. He wanted to
make certain he had everything right. Juan, growing
tired of the grownups talking and realizing the gringo's
attention was no longer on him, squirmed until he was
set back down on the floor. Then he raced off to a corner
of the room and his toys.

Dennis finished with his questions and turned away
from Carla and toward Mark.

"Okay, Mark. Are you ready?" Townsend signalled
that he was. "I'll start back a ways so that it makes
sense," Dennis told him. "It's a little out of order from
the way she explained it.

"Carla and Miguel both grew up in the same village
in Jalisco, a place called Queseria, south of Guadalajara.
They were born there and their families are good friends.
When Carla became pregnant, she and Miguel decided
they wanted the baby to be born in the United States."
Dennis paused, then added, "That automatically makes
him a citizen."

"I know that," said Mark impatiently.

"Oh. Okay. So anyway, the families couldn't afford
to get both Carla and Miguel up here because it was too
expensive. But they put together enough to pay for
Carla's trip. I didn't ask her how she got here, but I
presume they paid to have her smuggled across. That's

how it's usually done. But anyway, she made it up here
to Yakima where some distant relative of some sort was
living. I didn't understand what the relationship was.
And then she had her baby.

"Meanwhile, Miguel and the families were trying to
save enough for him to come up. After she had her baby,
Carla found work at a cannery and began sending a little
money back home. Oh yeah, and she got her green card
somehow. So she's legal. That's how she got the job at
Safeway. She said she's worked there a little over a year
now."

"When did Miguel come up?" asked Mark.

"Okay," Dennis said. "The families actually had
enough for Miguel to come up right after Juan was born.
She says that they paid someone to guide him across the
border. They're called *coyotes*. They're smugglers. Anyway, the one they paid was crooked and he got away
with the money and left Miguel and five others stranded
in Nogales, on the Mexican side. Miguel and three of
them decided to try and make it across on their own."
Dennis hesitated, then continued. "They didn't make it,
though. They were caught less than two miles inside the
border and detained, then sent back into Mexico. Carla
said that after that Miguel got scared and went back to
Queseria and his family.

"Meanwhile, she's up here with her baby, trying to
make enough to take care of him and still send some
money home. That went on for several more months
until Miguel made another try. And the second time he
got nailed again and sent back. So now the families have
spent about two thousand bucks for nothing. Miguel is
still in Jalisco, and Carla and the baby are here in Washington. She's getting scared because she doesn't think
she can last on her own and Miguel is worried that she'll
meet someone else.

"The families agree to try it one more time, except
they contract with a *coyote* who agrees to get paid only
when they're safely in the U.S. That's the better way to
do it," Brother Grib observed, "but you have to know
somebody who is willing to trust you."

"Did she say who it was?"

Dennis shook his head. "I didn't ask her. Should I?"

"No," Mark said. "Go on with the story."

"Okay. So this time it works and Miguel gets across. There's a whole system to get these people where they're going. They buy them fake Social Security and resident cards and everything. The smuggler drove Miguel as far as San Francisco, then put him on a plane to Seattle. From there he flew to Yakima. Carla says she handed him his son as soon as he walked into the airport and that Miguel sat down and cried louder than the baby."

She was listening as Dennis retold the story and kept glancing over at Father Townsend to make sure he understood, although she was having difficulty understanding everything herself. But the young Chicana felt that everything was riding on making this priest comprehend. Not only her own future, but her son's as well. When she heard Dennis describe Miguel's arrival in Yakima, she got up from her chair and left the room momentarily, returning with a framed photograph which she silently placed in Father Townsend's hands.

The picture was overexposed and slightly out of focus, but showed a tall and thin Mexican carefully holding a small bundle in his arms, smiling through his tears. He was standing in front of a large window that caught the camera's flash. People with suitcases were moving behind him. The man was standing proudly, holding his son in his arms for the first time. Miguel was wearing black jeans and sneakers and had a denim jacket pulled over his brown T-shirt. He wore a brand new Giants cap on his head. His eyes looked surprisingly small for his long face, although they were lit up with the delight of the moment. He had a long, narrow nose and, beneath it, a sparse mustache. There was a pronounced cleft in his chin. Mark studied the photo as Dennis resumed Carla Santos's story.

"Carla says that Miguel had a hard time getting work at first and that they were barely able to make it. But once the orchards started up, Miguel worked regularly.

They were able to rent this place and were even starting to repay their families.''

"Just a minute," Mark interrupted. "Where did they live before here?"

"Qué?" Carla knew the Father had a question. Dennis translated it for her.

"In Buena." She answered in English. "It was too small and not enough clean. For the baby."

"At the Buena Vista?" asked Father Townsend.

"Sí, la Buena Vista."

Dennis anticipated Mark's next question. *"Senora, did you know José and Elena Ramirez? Did they live there then?"*

"Sí."

The two Jesuits exchanged looks but made no comment. Dennis resumed the story.

"Miguel was raised a Catholic, like Carla, but was never very interested in church. She said that once she had the baby she started going regularly to St. Joe's but that Miguel would stay home. She's not sure exactly when it started, but maybe about four months ago he began telling her about Brother Gabriel and the appearances of Our Lady of Guadalupe. She says at first he just mentioned it, but then started talking more and more about it.''

"Were you living here or in Buena when Miguel first mentioned Brother Gabriel?"

Dennis translated the question for her and she told them it was around the time that they moved. Perhaps they were still in Buena, she said.

"When Brother Gabriel started standing outside of St. Joe's on Sundays, Carla knew immediately who he was. Miguel used to pick her up after Mass and sometimes he'd be across the street talking to some of them when she came out. She didn't like the way Gabriel looked and was scared of him, but Miguel told her he was a good man. She says they had some arguments about it.

"Then, about six weeks ago, Miguel announced he wanted to go to Cowiche and spend a night in the Vigil Room. At the time, she thought he might have a girlfriend and was using this as an excuse to leave for a night. They had a couple of big fights over it and finally, one night, Miguel just left. That's the last she's seen of him. About three days after he took off, a man came by the house and told her that Miguel had joined a chosen few who have gone on ahead. She says he never really explained what that meant and she was too scared and upset to ask questions.

"Only the two families in Queseria know about this, she says. Because Miguel was illegal, Carla's afraid to tell anyone about it. She doesn't know the laws here and she's afraid it'll mean they'll send her back to Mexico. And she's afraid for her baby, too. She doesn't want him to lose his citizenship."

"You told her that won't happen, didn't you?"

"Yeah, I did," Dennis replied. "But you can see she's still pretty scared."

The young Chicana was trembling. Father Townsend smiled sympathetically. He recognized the risk she had taken, disclosing so much to them. He knew that her husband's disappearance was probably the most frightening thing she had ever faced. For the past few weeks the woman had bravely tried to continue her life, suppressing the terror, the worry, and the shame; pretending that nothing was wrong, keeping up appearances at her job, at the church, and with the few acquaintances she knew. Father Townsend tried putting himself in the young Mexican woman's place. Like so many other migrant Mexicans, her faith, while strong, was fairly simple. She would know her prayers and follow her devotions, but the rest of it she left up to the priests and sisters. Carla would know about heaven and God and the saints and the Holy Mother. And she would also be clear about hell and the ones who lurked there. She could not understand what kind of strange powers this Brother Gabriel had, but she feared them. If anyone found out that her husband was gone, Carla had explained, she was afraid that she and her child would be in danger.

She told the Jesuits that at first she had scoffed at

Miguel's stories about the Virgin's appearances. After all, they were only stories he had heard, and neither one of them knew anyone who had actually seen *La Guadalupana*. But the more that Miguel listened to Brother Gabriel and his followers, the more convinced he began to sound. Her husband began to change. Now he was gone. What all this meant was more than the poor young woman could comprehend.

Mark Townsend was turning her story over in his mind, trying to connect as much of it with other information as he could. The fact that Miguel and Carla Santos knew José and Elena Ramirez at the Buena Vista sounded like too much of a coincidence. Especially when both Miguel Santos and Paco Ramirez had disappeared after going to Cowiche.

Mark twisted the ends of his mustache as if that would help sort things out. There were still too many loose ends, too many unanswered questions. He was about to ask some of them when a deep rumble from a car's engine sounded from outside. Upon hearing the sound, Juanito dropped his toy and began running toward the screen door. His mother intercepted him though, scooping the child up in her arms. There was a wild look of alarm on her face. The loud engine stopped and they heard a car door open and close. Juanito wiggled expectantly in his mother's arms, leaning toward the open front door.

Moments later, the screen door screeched as it opened and into the doorway stepped the dark figure of a man. But silhouetted against the light from outside, his features were hard to see. Spotting the two strangers sitting on the couch, he took two more steps inside, quickly moving closer to Carla and the baby.

Mark squinted up at the stranger now standing threateningly in front them and then down at the photograph he was still holding. He heard Dennis Grib's gasp and looked again, first at the man and then at the photo. His guts tightened and he suddenly felt light-headed.

Miguel Santos was home.

TWENTY-ONE

Father Townsend was still busy comparing the man standing in front of them with the image in the photo, refusing to believe what his eyes confirmed. So Dennis saw it first.

"Mark! He has a gun."

The Chicano's hand was under his shirt, reaching into the waistband of his pants. A silvery glint of chrome shone through his fingers as he slowly lowered his arm to his side. Whatever kind of gun he had was small enough to hide in the palm of his hand. He made no other motion toward them, but hovered protectively over the woman and her boy.

"*¿Quienes son?*" he demanded in a cold voice.

Dennis was about to answer when Carla spoke up.

"No," she protested, her head moving quickly from Miguel to them. "Is okay."

Turning back, she began speaking in rapid Spanish, pointing toward them, explaining that they were Jesuits from the church. Her words tumbled rapidly as she tried to calm him. Meanwhile, Townsend and Grib remained fixed on the couch, not daring to move until he understood they meant no harm.

Santos listened carefully, his eyes fixed on the two of them. When Carla finished, he visibly relaxed and tried nonchalantly to slip his hand into his pants pocket as he offered them a sheepish smile of apology.

Mark and Dennis were still too stunned to move. They were staring at him like someone returned from the dead. In an instant, Carla Santos realized that was exactly what the Jesuits were considering.

"Oh, Padre, él no es mi esposo," she said quickly. "This is not my husband. *Esto es Raul, el hermano de mi esposo."*

"His brother?"

"Sí. Brother. *Miguel y Raul son hermanos."*

"Twins," Dennis concluded. "They've got to be twins."

The man she was calling Raul nodded in agreement. *"Somos gemelos."*

Father Townsend tried taking a couple of deep breaths, both to relax and to clear his head. At first, and even second glance, the man standing in the room and the one in the photo looked exactly the same. But with a closer examination, he could see some differences. Raul Santos probably weighed five or ten pounds more, but it was all muscle. And his mustache was slightly thicker than Miguel's. He had the same small eyes, though, and the long, thin nose and the pronounced cleft in his chin. Clearly, Raul and Miguel Santos were twins.

Carla forced her brother-in-law into the chair she had been using, then hurried into the kitchen to drag out another. She set it in the space between Raul and the two Jesuits, nervously shifting her eyes from one man to the next. It was obvious to Mark that she had not anticipated his return, at least not until they were gone from the house. There had been no reason to question or suspect anything the woman had told them, but now her entire tale was covered with a pall of suspicion. Why would she not have told them about Raul? Why try to keep him a secret?

Carla began talking to Raul in Spanish and Dennis, in a low voice, explained to Mark what was being said.

"She's telling him that we know about Miguel," Dennis said, "and that she's told us how Miguel got up here and then disappeared. She's saying we're here to help, that you have a friend who has also disappeared. He's asking how we knew about Miguel and her in the first place.''

Carla spent a few moments explaining to Raul what the Jesuits had told her. She ended by telling him that she had not said anything about him, which was why there was confusion when he walked into the room. At that, the young man chuckled and glanced over at them.

"So you thought I was Miguel, eh? Maybe a ghost?"

Dennis translated and Mark nodded. *"Mas o menos.* More or less.'' With his eyes still fixed on the man in front of him, Mark directed Dennis. "Ask him how long he's been up here. When did he come from Mexico?"

Raul listened attentively, then answered in Spanish. He came as soon as Carla called home and told them Miguel was missing.

"Did you have trouble getting up here?" Mark asked. "Like your brother?"

"No," the man replied with a sly smile, *"I have more friends than Miguel, friends who can help get things up here."*

"You mean people who can smuggle?"

Raul shrugged his shoulders but said nothing.

"They say that if you know the right people, it's not hard to get here," Dennis informed Mark. "But you have to have the right connections. My hunch is that this man does.''

Townsend suspected his hunch was right. There was something about Raul, other than the small pistol in his pocket, that seemed more than a little menacing. "Ask him if he believes that his brother was raptured," Mark instructed.

When he heard the question, Raul snorted and spit out a terse response. *"¡Es mierde!''* He continued in rap- idfire Spanish without pausing to let Dennis catch up.

"He's saying that he doesn't believe any of it, that Miguel was a good guy but not holy enough to get to heaven that quick. God wouldn't want Miguel, not now anyway. So he doesn't think his brother was raptured.

Raul has gone up to Cowiche and tried to see the place where it happened, but there were too many people around and he couldn't get close. But he still doesn't believe it.''

"Tell him we've been up there, too, and that we got inside the Vigil Room."

In response, Raul asked, *"And do you believe in the Rapture, Padre?"*

Townsend hesitated, then shook his head no.

"Entonces, háblame acerca de mi hermano. ¿Donde está?"

"I don't know."

Raul stood up. *"Then you are of no use to me."*

"Raul!" Carla loudly protested, scolding him for being rude to the priests. *"They are trying to help,"* she said.

Mark waited until she was finished before speaking again. "Like you, Raul, I am trying to find somebody. She wasn't raptured either, but I suspect if she is still alive that she is in trouble. That is probably true about your brother also. If he is still alive, he is in trouble."

Santos apologized for his rudeness and sat back down. He explained that he was nervous and worried about Miguel. When he came into the house and saw the two of them there, he thought they were some of Brother Gabriel's men. He said he was grateful the priests wanted to help, but he did not see how they could. He was hearing stories about others who had also gone to Cowiche and never returned, that it was not just his brother who was missing. But the people he had spoken to were afraid.

"We know of at least thirty-two names," Dennis informed him, *"all of them Hispanics."*

"Hiiiiii," Santos exclaimed. *"So many! I had heard of four others. But people are not talking about it with one another, so no one knows there are so many."*

"Why is there so much fear?" Mark asked.

Raul understood his question, he nodded and explained. *"The ones I have spoken to are here to work in the harvests. They are the ones you call illegal be-*

cause they do not have their papers. And if the police know about them, they will be arrested and sent home.''
He paused and pointed with his chin at his sister-in-law, Carla. *''Most are like her, hoping the ones who disappeared will come back on their own. But they are afraid to tell the authorities.''*

Mark listened closely to his explanation. What Raul was saying made sense. "I have wondered why there were no Anglos missing," Mark said. "Why only Chicanos?"

Raul Santos's lips curled. For the first time since coming into the house, he answered in English. "When you are invisible to start with," he sneered, "it is not so hard to disappear."

Their visit with Carla Santos lasted much longer than either Mark or Dennis had anticipated. The two Jesuits were invited to stay for dinner with Raul, Carla, and Juanito. They did not put up much of a fight. There was still much to discuss. So while Carla warmed tortillas, heated *refritos* and sliced *carne asada* to fry with onions, green peppers, and chiles, the three men kept an eye on her baby and shared their discoveries with one another. During their dinner, an alliance was formed inside the small Santos kitchen.

Raul Santos was not at all hesitant to admit he was in the country illegally. He told them he had forged documents and showed Mark and Dennis his counterfeit Social Security and worker's permit. Obtaining such pieces of paper was not very difficult, he explained. Again, it depended upon who you knew. Whether accurate or not, he gave them the impression that he was part of a mysterious organization that cast a shadow large enough to fall across both sides of the Mexican/United States border. He kept his explanations vague, and neither Mark nor Dennis tried to push for much clarity. He was unlikely to have offered any, even if they had asked directly. So they kept their attention and their discussion focused on the issues at hand. Where was Miguel Santos? Where was Angelina Sandoval Ybarra? And were those two missing souls somehow joined by the murder of the evangelist Brother Gabriel?

Mark and Dennis showed him the list of names they had assembled. In addition to Paco Ramirez, Raul was able to pick out only three others that he recognized. They were the names of people whose relatives he had stumbled across in his own search for his brother. Each had told him pretty much the same story. They were in the Yakima Valley to work during the harvest and some-one in the family had disappeared after visiting Brother Gabriel's Vigil Room in Cowiche. Two of the families believed what they had heard, that a rapture had oc-curred. The others had doubts. But because of their own status, none of them wanted to go to the police. One of those was the Ramirez family. José Ramirez had told Raul that he would take care of it himself. Santos did not know what he meant by that, but Mark recalled the man's angry words during his own visit with him. What-ever Ramirez meant, it was not good.

By the time their discussion was winding down, dark-ness had fallen and the sound of crickets and night birds could be heard coming through the kitchen's open win-dow. The baby was fast asleep in his mother's arms, but Carla was too engrossed with the conversation to get up and put her son to bed. Mark had a hunch that this was the first time in weeks that the woman had experienced even a small glimmer of hope. He also had a hunch that Dennis Grib was about to crash. Of all of them, he was forced to be the most attentive, listening carefully to every word in order to translate accurately what was being said. Over the last hour, Mark noticed him making mistakes, speaking Spanish to Father Townsend or En-glish to Raul. Dennis caught himself when he saw Mark's expression and switched back, but Father Town-send could see that his young companion was fading fast.

For the first time since arriving in Yakima, Mark Townsend felt like some parts of this baffling riddle were starting to make sense. There were still huge holes, however. Brother Gabriel was still an enigma. And what part Angelina Sandoval Ybarra played remained a puzzle to him. Her request for Mark's help had seemed sincere. And everything she had told him after he arrived had sounded truthful. But her sudden disappearance after Gabriel's death, followed by her own husband's strange behavior, was hugely suspicious. Angelina was not some illegal immigrant trapped by poverty, ignorance, and religious fervor. She was intelligent, educated, and a disciplined reporter. Somehow, Father Townsend was convinced, her own mysterious absence was inextricably tied in with the other missing persons. But was she a victim like the others, or something more? As his conversation with Raul and Carla drew to a close, the priest realized that he could not leave Yakima in peace without knowing the answer.

TWENTY-TWO

For the first time since Mark arrived in Yakima, this morning started off cooler. A layer of clouds had finally managed to cross the Cascades. When he spotted them out his bedroom window, he began smiling. For the Jesuit, it was like looking up and catching sight of a good friend showing up unexpectedly. Eagerly, he dressed and hurried down to the kitchen for coffee, then let himself out the front door and settled onto the cool porch steps. There was actually a slight chill on his arms and Mark shivered with delight. The day was starting out fine.

He sipped his coffee as he waited for Dennis Grib to wake up. The two of them were meeting Raul Santos in Moxee at eight. Before saying goodnight, they had agreed to team up and work together. Townsend debated whether or not to contact Tim Connell, to ask if he wanted to join them. But on the trip back into Yakima, Dennis had managed to dissuade him. The man had done nothing to help them so far, he argued, and having him along might actually hurt their cause. They were planning to talk with some of the migrant workers and, if surrounded by too many gringo faces, they were likely to clam up. The fact that Mark and he were *religiosos* would make their presence acceptable, but most strangers with white faces were suspect among Hispanic migrants.

Mark was seated on the porch steps when he heard the front door swing open behind him.

"... 'morning. Lousy day, huh?"

Mark looked up at the sound of his friend's voice. "You think so? I kind of like this weather," he said. "It reminds me of Seattle."

"Seattle!" Dennis snorted facetiously. Realizing how he sounded, a look of mock horror crossed his face. "Omigod, I sound like Bones! Less than a year here and I'm ruined!"

"Yes, I'm afraid you are," Mark said solemnly. "In my report to the provincial I'll tell him he might as well assign you here permanently. You've become a Yaki-maniac, just like Joe."

"Please don't," Dennis pleaded. "I'll do anything you ask."

"Good. Drive me to Moxee."

Grib took Yakima Avenue to reach the freeway. The roads were busy with people heading to work, but most of the traffic was coming into town so they were not slowed much. Mark marveled at the difference from Seattle's morning commute. At seven-thirty on a weekday morning in Seattle, traffic was nearly at a standstill. Here the roads were busy, but you could hardly call them congested. The pace in central Washington had some advantages. Mark glanced over at his young driver, then back out the side window. Perhaps a little bit of Bones was rubbing off on him, too.

They made it into Moxee and pulled up in front of the Santos house at two minutes after eight. The front door was closed and the curtains were still drawn.

"You think they're up?" Dennis wondered.

As if in response, the door opened and Carla waved, signalling them to come inside. They got out of the car and greeted her.

"Come in for coffee," she invited. "Raul is getting ready."

"He slept late, huh?" observed Father Townsend as he settled onto the couch.

"*Sí,*" she replied, "but he was out until early this morning." She hurried into the kitchen to pour them coffee. Dennis and Mark exchanged looks. They had not left the Santos's until nearly eleven o'clock and when they had, everyone was yawning and saying goodnight. Apparently Raul had not been so tired after all. But was his late-night excursion business or pleasure? They heard Carla's boy cry out from the bedroom and as the woman brought them their coffee she excused herself and hurried to the back of the small house to check on her child. Moments later, Raul Santos wandered out of the bathroom, a white towel tied loosely around his waist. His black hair was wet and there was still a sheen of moisture on his brown skin. He had a muscular build and his upper arms and chest flexed involuntarily when he spotted the two Jesuits sitting in the living room.

"*¿Qué hora es?*"

Dennis informed him it was after eight. The Chicano apologized and said he would be right with them.

Carla would not let them leave the house without fixing breakfast. Mark and Dennis tried to decline and even Raul protested they were in a hurry, but she refused to listen. She hurriedly scrambled eggs and fried chorizo sausage, cutting it into pieces and mixing it with the eggs. Then folding the mixture inside warm flour tortillas, she wrapped them in paper towels. Pouring the men fresh coffee, she sent them on their way after wishing them success.

Once in the car, Raul directed Dennis to head toward Buena. Mark took the back seat, letting Raul ride shotgun with Grib. They rode in silence for several miles as each man hungrily worked on his breakfast. Dennis found his way onto Konnowac Pass road, the same one he had taken when they had traveled from Buena to the Castillos' home above Moxee. Mark was having second thoughts about leaving Tim Connell behind, but he kept them to himself. Grib seemed convinced the man was useless to them and he did not want to get into that debate again. Not now, anyway.

They turned onto the old Yakima Valley Highway, but before they reached Buena, Raul had them turn north, onto a secondary road that carried them past grape vineyards and orchards lining both sides of the narrow country road. The field laborers had arrived hours earlier, and their battered cars and trucks were already parked on the sides of the road.

"Raul, have you ever worked in the orchards?" Mark asked.

Santos answered in Spanish.

"He did when he was younger," Grib translated, turning his head slightly toward Mark but keeping an eye on the road. "But he says never again, that the work is too hard and the pay too little. He says there's easier ways to make money."

Townsend debated whether or not to ask what those easier ways were, but decided against it. He wondered if the young Chicano's chrome-plated pistol was tucked inside his waistband or in his pocket this morning. He had looked for a telltale bulge when they got into the car, but did not see one. But it was small enough to hide easily and Mark had a hunch it was probably seldom out of reach. He had an uneasy feeling about Raul Santos, but for now he would set it aside. Father Townsend sensed that the man could help them find some much-needed answers, so for the time being they would maintain their alliance, uneasy as it might feel.

"*A la derecha,*" ordered Raul, signalling with his thumb for Dennis to turn right onto a dirt track leading directly into an apple orchard. A row of wooden bins ran next to it. Further along they saw more stacked in among the trees, although there was no sign of anyone in the near vicinity. Planted next to the road on a wooden stake, a red and white sign warned *Peligro*. There was an upraised hand printed below, and the words PROHIBIDA LA ENTRADA. Dennis began to roll to a stop but Raul motioned him to keep moving.

"*Adelante.*" He pointed ahead.

They followed the track through the orchard until the rows of trees ran out. A few feet past the last ones there was nothing but weeds, sagebrush, and rocks.

Santos was already opening his door before Dennis had even come to a full stop. *"Estamos aquí,"* the Mexican said, jumping out of the car. He stood impatiently, waiting for Mark and Dennis to climb out. The sky was still gray with clouds and the air felt moist and heavy. Raul Santos set off at a brisk walk between the last two rows and the Jesuits had to hustle to catch up. The trees they passed were heavy with fruit and the apples visible among the leaves looked nearly ready for harvest. Spoiled fruit lay on the ground around them, the sweet smell of apple heavy in the damp air.

They hiked a couple of hundred feet through the trees before Raul raised his hand to his mouth and called out. Fifty feet in front of them, from behind four lugs tipped onto their sides, three faces rose to peer over the top. The men were squatting behind the wooden apple bins, apparently waiting for them. When they stepped out from behind their cover, Mark recognized José Ramirez. Raul knew him too, walking straight up to him and offering his hand. The two flanking Ramirez were introduced as Victor Chacon and Angel Velasquez.

Chacon was about the same age as the older Ramirez, with a big belly under his white T-shirt and short hair that was as much gray as black. He wore gold wire-rimmed glasses, and when he smiled there were gaps from missing teeth. Valasquez was short and wiry and looked about twenty-five. His hair was cropped close around the sides but was long and combed back over the crown of his head. He was wearing jeans and a scoop necked T-shirt. Both of his upper arms were heavily tattooed. Neither man appeared to speak English. Dennis Grib's assignment as translator was going to keep him busy. He moved closer to Mark's right side and did his best to keep the priest apprised of what was being said. After introductions were complete, they moved back around the apple bins where six smaller boxes were arranged as seats on the dirt ground.

Santos wasted no time. He informed the others that the two Jesuits were looking for a missing Chicana, although she was not a field worker. But she did have ties to Brother Gabriel, he told them. The Jesuits had already been up to Cowiche and had even gone inside the Vigil Room. They were in the house too, and spoke to Señores Fairbanks and Patowski. The men nodded, their interest already piqued. Their eyes kept shifting over to the gringos as Raul continued talking.

Chacon interrupted and Dennis leaned closer to Mark's ear.

"You've had better luck than we have, Padre." Grib spoke quickly, trying to keep up with the man's fast words. "We have not been able to get anywhere near the house or Vigil Room. We put Angel up there, hoping they would select him to keep a vigil one night, but they passed him over. No one knew him, and we think they must only accept ones that they recognize. Angel could not get in."

"They're not still keeping vigils, are they?" Mark asked.

"*No,*" replied the older man. "*This was before. Since the Brother was killed, there have been no vigils.*"

Angel added, "*So no one else has disappeared. That is something, at least.*"

"You're convinced that they aren't really raptures?"

Chacon gave the priest a wide, gap-toothed grin. "*If there are raptures, then Velasquez here is really an angel. And believe me, Padre, I know Angel is no angel.*" He laughed wickedly and the younger man scowled first, then blushed, which only brought chuckles from the rest of them.

"We've been in there twice," Mark told them. He waited for Dennis, then continued. "And both times I looked for some way that people could leave. There is only the one door. If they took people out from there, I think someone would have seen it happening."

"*Then there has to be another way,*" Chacon said. "*Only you have not found it yet. But I know it must be there.*"

José Ramirez spoke up. *"I agree with Victor, there has to be a way in and out. Nobody believes that stuff about the raptures."*

"But his followers do." Grib spoke in their language, forgetting his duty to the priest for a moment. *"They're convinced that some people are being chosen to go ahead of the rest. And what about the appearances of the Virgin? The ones here in the valley. Are those fake, too?"*

All three fell silent, fixing their eyes on the ground. Mark was not entirely sure what he had said, but he was irritated at Grib's interruption. The younger Jesuit had cautioned him about the migrants' mistrust of Anglos. Now they had clammed up. The conversation was headed nowhere fast. He was about to warn Dennis to stick to translating when Raul spoke.

"Even among ourselves there are differences in what we believe. But what does it matter? The important thing is that José, your son, is gone, and my brother. And if what the padre says is true, then many more besides. You said thirty-two, yes?"

"We have that many names," Mark responded, "but Sister Elizabeth told us that a total of thirty-seven were raptured."

"¿Quantos?" asked Victor Chacon. Ramirez repeated the number in Spanish. The older man shook his head and sighed.

"So now we find out what has truly happened," Raul announced. With his right hand he cracked the knuckles of his left. *"We find the answers for ourselves."*

Father Townsend was growing uneasy with the direction their conversation was taking. He was still not sure why they were having this meeting in such a secluded spot. Nor why he and Grib were being included in the plans these four Mexicans were hatching. He shifted uncomfortably on his wooden box and looked at the orchard around them. They were seated in an open space between the rows of trees, an area about fourteen feet across, wide enough to let sunlight fall on both sides and for tractors to pass through without damaging the trunks

and limbs. The straight lines of apple trees stretched for
as far as his eyes could see. The county road they turned
off from was almost half a mile back and the dry waste-
land just beyond the orchard's edge looked barren and
unwelcoming. The Jesuit priest had found himself in isolated places before, where he did not always understand
what was being said. But he had never had the uncomfortable sensations he was having now. Mark Townsend
felt sure that something was being plotted even while
they sat there. Whatever it was made him start to fidget.

As if sensing Mark's discomfort, Raul Santos turned
his full attention toward the priest, speaking directly to
him. His words were loud and passionate.

*"Unless we find out what is happening . . . unless we
find out the truth, more people will disappear. The
Brother's death was not the end of it. Now some are
saying he is alive again and more people are believing
there are big miracles. People are being stupid, thinking
this is the end of the world. There are no virgins and
there are no raptures. Solamente Chicanos locos. And
who cares if a few crazy Chicanos disappear? If they
are illegals, it is no matter. No one is looking for them.
No one cares."*

As Dennis hurried to finish translating, Mark tried to
think of some response. The other three men in the circle
were watching him, waiting.

Finally, he spoke. "What is it that you want us to
do?"

Raul gave a jerk of his head. *"Bueno."*

Their plan was brutal and horrendous. Before Santos
even finished laying it out, Mark was recoiling. There
was no way he could take part in what they had planned.
Brother Grib gulped as he explained what the man was
saying.

The Mexicans wanted the Jesuits' help to kidnap Sister Elizabeth. If Mark and Dennis could arrange to get
into the house when she was alone, without her guard-
ians, they would follow and do the rest. And if the Jesuits wanted, they could tell the police that they were
overpowered, unable to resist. Once they had the woman

in their control, they felt sure they could force her to tell them what really took place in the Vigil Room. And if she would not or could not, they would use her to get answers from the two men who helped set up the ministry for her husband, Fairbanks and Patowski.

Mark was starting to shake his head, but Santos ignored him.

"We know about you Jesuits," he was saying, "from how you are in Mexico. Your brothers are helping down there, too. In Chiapas and elsewhere. And we know the story of Miguel Pro and how he helped in our revolution. You cannot deny these facts. This is not so big a thing we are asking. Just get us into the house. Then you have to do nothing more. We can take care of the rest. We will even find out about your friend, Angelina Sandoval Ybarra."

His voice was insistent, but he was not pleading with the priest. He wanted them to understand their plan completely and he was holding nothing back. Either the Jesuits would agree to help or they would refuse. Father Townsend had a strong hunch that how he answered would determine what happened to them next. This deserted edge of the orchard was looking more and more ominous as the four men across from him leaned forward, waiting for his reply.

Mark coughed, then spoke, keeping his eyes fixed on Raul Santos.

"The plan you are proposing sounds like something Jesuits might try, Raul." Dennis Grib let go of a small gasp but Mark kept his eyes on the Mexican. He waited until Grib translated for the sake of the others. "There are people who think that Jesuits believe the end always justifies the means, and that this lets us do anything we want."

"You don't?" Raul interrupted with a wicked grin.

Townsend tried to smile back. "It only seems that way. But no, the end does not always justify the means. But in this case . . ." He purposely let the phrase hang. The Mexicans waited for him to continue.

"I can see one big problem with your plan. Let's say

that Dennis and I are successful—that we get into the house and do arrange for you to kidnap the woman. You know what happens then? There will be police all over this valley, looking for her and whoever took her.''

Santos was waving an irritated hand before Grib was even finished with his translation. "We are not afraid of the police,'' he barked. "No."

Father Townsend raised his own hand in caution. "Maybe you are not.'' He was trying to sound agreeable. "But think for a moment. How many others are afraid? From what I have heard, the families are not reporting the missing because they are afraid the police will begin investigating. And if they do, a lot of them will be forced to leave. Isn't this true?''

Raul remained silent, but Mark saw the nods from the other men. He continued. "If my hunch is right, every one of those who have disappeared is here illegally. I don't know that for sure because we haven't been able to contact all the families, but I suspect it's true. Thirty-seven people have disappeared and I think every one of them is illegal.'' For the first time since he started speaking, Mark looked directly at José Ramirez. "Would you agree, José? Probably all those families are not legal?''

The older man waited until Dennis was done translating, then slowly nodded.

"Then if that is true,'' Mark looked back at Raul, "your plan puts all of those people at risk of being arrested. How many is that? Maybe a hundred and fifty? Two hundred? If Sister Elizabeth is kidnapped, the police will look for someone with a motive. They will find out about the families of the disappeared and they will go after them.''

"But that has not happened with Brother Gabriel,'' Santos argued. "He's dead and they're not looking for the families.''

"True,'' Father Townsend replied. "Instead, they are looking for my friend, Angelina. And right now they are investigating her husband. But I guarantee you, it is only a matter of time. Unless they can prove Tim Connell or

Angelina killed the Brother, they will expand their investigation.''

"Sí, es verdad," Ramirez said, nodding. He shrugged his shoulders. *"The padre is right. No one is doing anything because they are afraid. If the police go after the families, then everyone will be sent home. That is true. We have to find another way."*

Raul Santos made no attempt to hide his disgust. He spit into the dirt and turned away. Ramirez continued to speak, now addressing Father Townsend. Mark waited for Grib's translation.

"He wants to know what you think they should do," Dennis informed the priest. "What can they do without causing any danger to the families? He says they can't sit by anymore, they have to do something."

"I agree with you, José. You are right to want to find out what happened to your son, Paco. I don't believe he was raptured any more than you do. I don't believe anyone was raptured."

Mark could see it in the Mexican's eyes. His words were giving him hope and he grabbed hold like a man drowning, weak and fearful. He was looking for anything that could keep him afloat.

"Do you believe my son is still alive?" he pleaded.

Townsend hesitated. He knew what Ramirez wanted to hear.

"Sí."

Relief flooded the old man's eyes.

There are times, unfortunately, when the end does seem to justify the means.

TWENTY-THREE

Mark Townsend really did believe that José Ramirez's son was alive. He was fairly certain all thirty-seven were still alive and somewhere on this earth. Where, however, was still a mystery. But about his friend, Angelina Sandoval Ybarra, he was less sure. Her disappearance was as baffling as any, yet the circumstances were much more ominous. Where she was and whether or not she was still alive were both mysteries. Brother Gabriel was dead, that much was certain. But where his body might be was yet another mystery. Who killed him and why? Father Townsend had an orchard full of mysteries. The harvest was plentiful. But as he looked around at the men surrounding him, he knew that the answers were too few.

The four Mexicans and Dennis Grib remained seated on their crates behind the overturned apple bins, far back in the orchard, beneath gray skies, waiting for him to give them some direction. Telling José Ramirez he thought his son was still alive was one thing. Proving it was another. Mark stared up at the clouds through the thick branches overhead. His eyes refocused on the fruit left to ripen further. Apples hung over him like questions.

It was time to start picking.

216

"Do any of you know where to find Marshall Fairbanks or Len Patowski?" he asked. "Do you know where they live?"

Ramirez nodded and told Grib.

"He says Patowski's nursery is outside of Moxee. Fairbanks has orchards all over the valley and moves around them. He could be anywhere, but Patowski is probably at his nursery if he isn't up with Sister Elizabeth."

"I want to go there," he told Dennis. "Ask José if he knows how to get to the nursery."

While Grib got directions, Mark turned his attention to Raul. Standing up, he motioned the young man to follow him. They walked a few yards further down the row before turning to face each other.

"You knew we couldn't get involved in a kidnapping," Mark confronted him. "Why'd you even suggest it?"

Santos tipped his head to one side, looking over Mark's shoulder at the others.

"Because they are willing to do anything to find those people," he said quietly. His accent was heavy, and he made no attempt to hide the edge in his voice. "And I am, too." His eyes shifted to Mark. "Is that true for you, Padre? To do anything to help these people?" Raul began shaking his head. "No, I think not. You priests talk about what is just and about helping the poor. But not if it means taking risks. Your sermons sound so great in the churches. But out here in the orchards, they don't sound so good. But you are right about one thing. If the police catch on, then Immigration will come after all those families. They do not care about who is disappeared. Only about who is legal and who is not. So once again our people are caught. Either we say nothing and people disappear, or we say something and we all disappear back to our own country.

"This is what we are used to up here. You understand how it is, Padre? It is like this all the time. If our wages are not what they should be, we can say nothing. If we do, someone calls Immigration and we get sent back home with nothing. So we take what they choose to give us and keep our mouths shut. In church you can say all you want about justice. But come out to the orchards and try preaching about it. See what happens then.''

"I know there are abuses," Mark told him. "But there's also laws. And not all the growers are bad."

"No, of course not," Santos agreed. "Like anywhere, there are some who are fair and some who are not. But you see, the laws and the good ones do not help if you have no way to protect or defend yourself against the bad. And the people we are talking about have no protection.

"Do you remember a few years ago, what happened in New York? Over fifty Mexicans were forced to sell trinkets in the subways. Some were small children. All of them were deaf. If they tried to get away, they were beaten. The ones who did this to them were other Mexicans. When it finally was found out, Immigration wanted to put all of them in jail. Even though they were being treated like slaves. They were illegal, and that was all that mattered.

"If the people here in Yakima are only paid half of what they should get, so what? In New York we could not hear. Here, we cannot speak. It makes no difference. And if some of us disappear, who is even to care? Over half the ones picking in the orchards are illegal. Send them away and only more will come to take their place. So maybe Padre, if I suggest you do something like a kidnap with us, you will know what it is to feel illegal. And maybe then I will come to your church and hear you talk about justice for the poor, yes?''

His voice was hard like steel. His words were razor sharp. Raul spoke calmly, methodically, driving each point clear through with a dagger's accuracy. All the while, his eyes glittered like black ice and they never strayed from Father Townsend's face.

Mark waited until the young Mexican was finished. He felt two rivulets of sweat running down his back and he was surprised there were only two. He swallowed hard and was about to speak when Santos, with a sudden jolt, strode past him and rejoined the others. Mark followed in his wake.

"Come on, Dennis, let's go," he said curtly.

Grib stood up eagerly. "What about Raul? Are you going with us?"

The Mexican shook his head but said nothing.

"Let's go," Mark said. He strode past Dennis and the others without turning, heading toward the car parked at the row's end. Grib hurriedly said his goodbyes, then hustled to catch up with the priest.

"What happened, Mark?"

Townsend was ignoring his question. Dennis laid a hand on the priest's shoulder, trying unsuccessfully to stop him.

"Tell me what happened."

Mark continued walking. "We need to find those people," he replied. "We need to find them quick."

The Patowski Fruit Nursery was a mile and a half outside of Moxee. From the front, it was not much to look at. A low barn-red shed faced the road, with just enough of a gravel strip in front to accommodate half a dozen cars. Evidently droves of customers were not required to make Patowski's business a success. A high chain-link fence extended off both ends of the building, running out about forty feet before turning toward the back, behind the front office. Behind the fence the Jesuits could see rows of small saplings.

There were no cars in the parking strip in front. Dennis rolled up to the building's door. No lights were on inside, and the few small windows were dark. Stuck into the pane of glass in the door was a large CLOSED sign. Dennis shifted his car into park but left the engine running.

"What do we do now?" he asked Mark.

Father Townsend's fingers were tugging at his mustache and he was staring at the CLOSED sign as if he could will it away. There was no sense getting out of the car to try the door. A large silver padlock was clearly visible. The Patowski Fruit Nursery was not open for business.

"I guess we go home." He made no attempt to hide his disappointment.

Brother Grib put his car in gear and cranked the wheel, pulling back onto the road. He drove about two hundred feet before braking suddenly. Turning the wheel furiously, he made a U-turn and started back.

"A pickup just pulled in," he informed Mark. "It looked like Patowski's."

Sure enough, the large man was just climbing out of his cherry-red Dodge Ram when Grib and Townsend pulled back into the lot. His feet were on the ground and he was leaning back into the cab when he heard them pull in behind him. Len Patowski hefted his bulk back around and eyed the approaching car. When he spotted the priest in the front seat, he offered a wide smile.

He waited until Mark was out of the car. "Well, well. What a surprise! Father Townsend, isn't it? We met at Cowiche?"

Mark shook the man's hand and introduced him to Dennis, adding that the Brother was working at St. Joe. Patowski nodded and offered Brother Grib his fleshy hand.

"A pleasure to meet you, Brother Grib. Welcome." He stood next to his truck, beaming cordially at the two Jesuits. "What can I do for you gentlemen today?"

"I'll be going back to Seattle soon, and wanted to buy something for the Jesuit community before I go. A thank you for their hospitality." Grib's eyes grew large. He had no idea where the priest was going with this. "I was thinking of a tree," Mark continued. He looked pointedly toward the rows of saplings behind the fence. "An apple tree."

Patowski rubbed his hands together. "An apple tree is a fine idea for a gift, Father. Blossoms in the spring, shade in the summer, and fruit in the fall. You can't do much better than all of that. But you're going home without finding your friend? I'm sorry to hear that."

"Yes, well it can't be helped," Father Townsend replied with a shrug. "There's been no sign of her and the police are stumped. I don't think there's anything more I can do here."

"No, I suppose there isn't," Len Patowski agreed. "Still, it seems a shame."

"What about Brother Gabriel? Have they found his body?"

The man's jowls waggled as he shook his head. "Like your friend," he said. "Completely disappeared." He stuck both hands into his pants pockets and rocked back on his heels. "Of course, there's all sorts of rumors in the valley. Some of the believers are saying they've seen him. That would be an interesting development if it was true, don't you think?"

Interesting was not strong enough: incredible, miraculous, momentous, earth-shaking. Coming back from the dead went far beyond interesting.

"Yes," Father Townsend agreed, "that would be interesting."

The nursery owner pulled a large ring of keys out of his pocket. "Well, let's go in and find you that tree you wanted, shall we?" He started toward the building, then stopped and turned back to his truck. "Just let me get something first." He waddled back to the cab and reached inside, pulling out a large brown paper sack. He tried holding onto it with one hand while he fumbled with his keys in the other.

"Can I hold that for you?" Dennis offered.

"No, no. I can manage."

But Patowski's fingers were short and stubby and sorting through the keys with one hand was more than he could handle. Reluctantly, he passed the sack off to Brother Grib. "If you'll just hold that for a minute," he asked. As soon as he had the padlock off, he reached out and lifted the sack from Dennis's hands, leading the way into his building.

Even from the inside, the Fruit Nursery was not much to look at. The floor was bare cement. A few shelves contained a smattering of products, pesticides and fertilizers mainly. A long wooden counter ran through the center of the room and was piled thick with paper and catalogs. A cash register and phone sat at one end. The back of the store was mostly sliding glass doors, and outside of those was where the real business took place. Behind the building there were long rows of pots, each holding the start of a fruit tree. Some were only a foot or so high, some were several feet tall. Each one had a tag attached, identifying what it was. There were two greenhouses at the back of the property, and through the glass Mark could see they were also filled with small potted starts. The area inside the chain link fence covered at least two acres.

Patowski set his sack down on the long counter and turned back to his guests.

"So, Father, what kind of apple tree did you want?"

The question was an obvious one, but Mark had no idea.

"Red ones?" he guessed.

The nursery owner cocked his head and smiled encouragingly.

"I don't know anything about apples," Father Townsend had to admit. "What about it, Dennis? What kind of tree would you want?"

Brother Grib was trying to play along, but he still had no idea what Mark was after. There was no place in their yard for an apple tree anyway.

"Those Red Delicious are good," he volunteered.

"And it's a nice-looking tree in a yard," Patowski said agreeably. "You can't go wrong with Red Delicious. Of course, there's some others that are mighty fine." His smile, like his voice, was condescending.

"I guess you don't get too many customers looking to buy just one tree, do you?" Mark asked.

"Not a whole lot," Patowski admitted. "Mostly all my customers are orchardists, and we're usually talking purchases of anywhere from a hundred to five hundred trees at a whack." He waved his beefy hand toward the potted trees out back. "But this isn't the stock I sell them. I've got another seventy-five acres of nursery trees out in the Columbia Basin, and that's where I plant root stalks and graft my buds.'' His smile grew even broader. ''That doesn't mean I won't sell you one. After all, a buck is buck, huh?''

The man led the two Jesuits over to the counter, lifting a catalog and opening it in front of them.

''All these are apples, gentlemen. You can take your pick of most any of them and I can either pull it out of the back or get you a start darn quick. Help yourself.''

There were over a hundred glossy pages in the book, each one picturing a tree and the fruit it produced, as well as a written description. Mark flipped through a few of the pages. One of Patowski's short, fat fingers halted his progress.

''Now that's a fine, fine apple, Padre. Your Braeburn is probably one of the most popular of the gourmet apples. Leastways in this valley. It came up from New Zealand and caught on real good. It's what we call a bi-colored. Not as pretty as a Gala, but darn close. It's dense and firm with plenty of juice. You can't go wrong with a Braeburn. Or a Gala, for that matter. It's another New Zealand. That one's a little more creamy, and a lot of folks prefer that. But the typing on both is very nice.'' His fingers took over the pages, rapidly flipping through them, stopping on one about halfway through. ''Now if you want something a little jazzier, with some snap, I'd go for the Fuji. You can probably guess where it came from. It's crisp and has a sweet, sweet smell. You put that in your yard and you'll be real pleased. I've got a bunch of those as whips out back. Or if you want, I can sell you one that's pretty well grown. Another year of growth and you can be picking.'' He patted the page with his hand and leaned back against the counter, a smile of genuine contentment on his face. Len Patowski knew his apples.

Mark Townsend knew apple pie, apple sauce, and apples with cheese. There were red ones, yellow ones, and green ones and some a little bit of each. Beyond that, he was lost.

''I think this is a little over my head,'' he confessed. ''I was just thinking of buying a tree for the yard.''

"You can do that," Patowski rejoined, "certainly you can. But you might as well choose something you're going to enjoy."

"You need to be a rocket scientist just to grow apples," Dennis exclaimed.

Len Patowski had a captive audience and was enjoying the attention. "It's not rocket science, son, but it is a science. You go out in the trees and talk to some of them growers and they can tell you more about apples in half a day than you can read in a lifetime. Apples are a big business. Especially around here. A lot of the growers today are calling themselves horticulturists. No one's just an apple farmer anymore. Not when you're managing ranches that are a couple of hundred acres. It's a science alright. You sink twenty, thirty thousand dollars into planting trees, you're gonna think it through pretty much and not leave a whole lot to chance."

"And you can make a good living?" asked Mark. He was sizing up the big man in front of him, watching closely as he got more and more excited.

"Hell, yes! Pardon my language, Father. But my, yes, there's good money if you know what you're doing. Those Galas I was telling you about? Time was, when they first hit here, you could get five hundred dollars a bin for them. That didn't last, of course. But some fellows who got at the head of the line did mighty well."

He shifted his girth, finding a comfortable position against the counter. "There's a thing we call bud wood. It's about the size of a pencil and holds about ten buds each. When Galas first came, there was bud wood being smuggled out of New Zealand inside of licorice boxes. That's how valuable that stuff can get." Patowski's eyes were glittering and he licked his thick lips. "You find me the latest in an apple—one that folks are gonna want to buy—and I'll make us both rich. Don't matter where in the world it comes from, long as we can grow it here."

"And which of us will get the richest, the one with the orchard or the one with the nursery?" Mark asked it with a smile.

But his question caught Len Patowski short and the man sputtered a moment. Then his own smile grew back and he slapped his hand on the counter.

"You're a quick learner, Father. I'll give you that." He turned his back on the priest and began flipping through the catalog again. "Apples are a crazy sort of business. There's all sorts of ways to turn 'em into cash. You can mash them into juice or shine them up and sell them right off the tree. I can't hardly begin naming all the variables."

"You're talking about orchardists."

Patowski nodded. "That I am. Those guys with the ranches have got plenty to figure out. But the money's out there for them."

"But that's true for nurseries, too?" wondered Brother Grib.

"Oh, yes," Patowski admitted. "We do okay for ourselves. But you always want to stay ahead of the rest, and that means you got to have that one piece of fruit no one else has. If a nursery stocks something no one else has, then it's doing fine. But of course, your big, big money is in the patents."

Patowski's eyes had a faraway look to them, and his voice was turning slow and dreamy. He sounded almost like he was putting himself under some kind of spell. As Father Townsend continued listening to the large man, he began fingering the ends of his mustache. This was getting interesting.

"Why patents? You mean for apples?"

"Exactly that. You own the patent for something like the Gala and you'll die a rich and happy man. Once the nurseries start propagating your new fruit, you're going to get paid for every tree they grow."

"So there's money in it for both."

"There's plenty of money. As long as your timing is right."

Mark slid the catalog away from the fat man and began paging through it slowly. To him, the pictures of the trees and the fruit looked all the same. The brightly colored fruit printed on the glossy pages were only apples, but to the man leaning over the counter next to him, they were pages and pictures of money. Fortunes growing on trees. Mark's eyes shifted to the brown bag further down the counter.

"If I wanted to buy the most perfect apple tree you have, what would that be?" He made sure Len Patowski saw where he was looking, then shifted his eyes to the big man's face. "Is there a picture of it in here?" He lifted the catalog from the counter.

Patowski never looked at the catalog in Father Townsend's hands. His eyes stayed fixed on the priest's eyes, first watching as they moved down the counter to the bulging sack, then back to his own face. He knew what the priest was asking and he locked his fingers together and laid them across his paunch and smiled proudly. He knew all right.

"Would you like to sample the most perfect apple of all, Father? Have a little taste?"

He shifted his weight away from the counter and sauntered over to the paper sack. Opening it, he stuck a hand inside and lifted out a round globe of fruit. Carrying it back, he placed it gently in Mark Townsend's outstretched hand.

"There it is."

It looked like an apple. It was round and about the size of a softball and fit comfortably in Mark's hand. Father Townsend lifted it closer to his face. The way that Len Patowski was beaming when he handed it over meant there was something special about this fruit. He examined it carefully.

Even in the room's weak light he could see the shine. The skin felt soft and cool against his palm. The color was dappled, beginning with a rich and deep red and then shifting slowly to a light and almost burnished gold. Mark was reminded of a sunset he had once witnessed on the high prairie in Montana. He lifted the apple to his nose and inhaled. The fruit smelled sweet and spicy.

Dennis Grib was waiting for his turn and Mark passed the apple to him.

"What makes this one so special?"

Patowski grinned and lifted another apple out of the sack, cradling it in his huge hand.

"First off is your coloration. Most orchardists in this state are going to tell you that color is primary. That's why the Red Delicious is so popular here. And you can see there's some of that same deep red." A pudgy finger pointed to the darkest part of the skin. "But now watch how it gently turns. Looks almost like the light is actually changing, don't it? Then it turns this bright gold. I don't know any apple this pretty." He turned the fruit in his hand until it was upside down. "And it's got legs. It's a nice type."

"Legs?"

Patowski fingered the meaty points growing out from the central core. Then reaching into his pants, he pulled out a buck knife, flipped it open and quickly halved the apple. The sound of the blade slicing into the meat was sharp and crisp and the fruit's sweet aroma filled the space around them. With the tip of the knife's blade, the nursery man flicked at the apple's skin.

"See how thin that is? Yet I can tell you that this fruit is hearty. That's what you look for—something that isn't going to bruise too easy. And this one don't. A soft, thin skin that doesn't bruise. You have got yourself one perfect piece of fruit."

Pressing the knife's blade against one side of the apple, he pressed against the other with his thumb. Thin, clear rivulets of juice ran down the blade as he shaved off a slice. Balancing it along the knife's blade, he held it out. Mark accepted the offering and lifted it to his mouth. The apple's sweet smell was overwhelming and when he bit into it, the same spicy sweetness flooded his mouth. The fruit was crisp and cool and was nothing but sweet delight. Father Townsend's lips curled up in happiness. Patowski's apple was one of the finest things he had ever tasted.

"This is delicious," he proclaimed, stuffing the remaining piece into his mouth. "It's wonderful."

Obviously delighted with the priest's response, Len Patowski shaved another slice and passed it to Brother

Grib, whose own mouth broke into a smile similar to Mark's. He nodded his head in happy agreement.

"It's great," he enthused. "What's it called?"

Patowski held up the remaining portion of apple in front of them. "This, gentlemen, will be known as the Millennium Star."

Reaching over, he lifted the other piece of fruit that Dennis was still cradling in his hand.

"There's some other things about this apple that don't mean anything to your mouth, but will prove mighty attractive to the orchardists." He turned the fruit over in his hands as he spoke. "This is a self-pollinating apple." Seeing the blank look on their faces, he explained. "You go in most orchards and look around and you'll find certain trees that are planted as pollenizers. They're usually some sort of crab apple. For instance, Galas use mostly snowdrift crab apples. But this little beauty takes care of that all on its own. That's one more advantage. And it's a long keeper. That means you can put it in storage in September and pull it out four, five, six months later and still have a near perfect piece of fruit. Buyers like that a lot. A whole lot."

Patowski turned his back and carefully placed the uncut piece of fruit back into the sack. Turning back to the Jesuits, he finished dividing the remaining portions of the cut apple into three sections, sharing the pieces with them.

"Enjoy, gentlemen."

And they did. The succulent pieces of the Millennium Star were quickly devoured.

As soon as he was finished swallowing, Mark spoke.

"That's the tree I'd like to get."

The nursery man laughed out loud.

"You and every grower in this valley, Padre! But unfortunately, the Millennium Star isn't on the market. Not yet, anyway."

"How come?"

The answer was marketing. Patowski launched into a long and tedious explanation about marketing. How new varieties of fruit have to be slowly introduced. How both the consumers and the orchardists first need to be sold and how the demand needs to build before the plants are sold for wide distribution. He talked about a buyer's market versus the seller's market and how, as the nursery holding the Millennium Star's patent, he had to make sure there was enough of a demand before he began selling whips of the new variety.

"I don't understand what a whip is," Grib managed to interject.

"Whips are three years of growth," Patowski said irritably. He did not like being interrupted. "That's what you start your orchard with."

He would not let go of any of the Stars until they had their marketing plan in place, he explained. But as soon as the first Millennium Star hit the market, it would knock the Red Delicious right out of the running, he crowed, along with the Braeburns, Galas, and Fujis.

Mark Townsend listened patiently. A lot of what the fat man was telling him went right over his head. The intricacies of raising and marketing apples did not interest him, anyway. What did, though, was Len Patowski's seemingly total devotion to the fruit in the brown paper sack. The Millennium Star.

Dennis Grib was not showing the same patience as Mark Townsend. After listening to Patowski's lecture for ten minutes, he began shifting from one foot to the other. After twelve minutes, his face took on a pained expression. At fifteen, he had heard enough.

"Oof, whoooo!" His groans of protest brought the lecture to a sudden halt. "Boy, I am sorry," Dennis apologized, "but I think that apple's gone right through me. Do you have a bathroom I can use? Please?" As if to emphasize his plight, the young man shifted his legs nervously.

With a look of real consternation, the owner directed Grib to a bathroom in the far left corner of the building. Hearing the Millennium Star blamed for Dennis's gastro discomfort was clearly disturbing to the big man.

Mark waited until Dennis was in the bathroom. "I think a Red Delicious."

"What? What's that, Father?" Patowski's attention

was fixed on the closed bathroom door. "Red Delicious?"

"I think that's the kind of tree I'll buy. That is, if you're sure the Millennium Star is not for sale."

He was still distracted, but the sooner these two left, the better. "A Delicious it is," he said swiftly, turning on his heels. "Whyn't you come pick it out."

He led the way around the counter and through a sliding glass door into the back lot. Mark followed behind the large man as he waddled past rows of potted trees, finally reaching several long rows of small starts with RD tags attached to their spindly trunks.

"Take your pick," the man said. "They're all pretty much the same—good, healthy, and top producers."

Mark took a few minutes to examine the potted trees while Patowski stood by impatiently. He finally bent down and lifted one by the pot.

"Is this one okay?"

"Fine. Fine," Patowski quickly assured him. "That one's just fine." He turned and began hurrying back toward the shed, leaving Mark to carry the potted tree himself. Dennis was just emerging through the glass doorway as they approached.

"You okay now?" the fat man asked worriedly.

Brother Grib wiped his forehead with his arm and gave a sheepish grin. "I'm sorry about that," he said, "but I think it was the combination of an egg and sausage burrito for breakfast and then the apple. It just hit my system wrong."

Patowski was scowling. "Them burritos can do it to you. That's for sure. I doubt it was the apple though. You hardly swallowed more than a couple of bites. Had to be that burrito."

He led them back inside and down the counter to his cash register. While he rang up the sale, Mark showed off his purchase to Dennis.

"I think this will look good in your yard," the priest said, "don't you?"

Brother Grib's eyebrows lifted as he looked doubtfully at the pot in Father Townsend's arms.

"It's just what we always wanted," he answered.

TWENTY-FOUR

The top branches of Mark's Red Delicious were waving in the wind, poking out the back window of Brother Grib's car. He hoped none of them would break.

"How are you feeling?"

"Much better," Dennis assured him. "I didn't think that old guy was ever going to wind down."

"He knows his apples, that's for certain. And he was sure protective of that new one."

"Real, real protective," confirmed Brother Grib.

"So where is it?"

Dennis scooted forward on the seat, keeping one hand on the steering wheel while he reached behind him with the other. When his hand reappeared, it was grasping a piece of fruit that reminded Father Townsend of a vivid sunset he once saw in Montana.

He took it from the younger Jesuit and eyed it critically. "I figured that's what you were doing."

"He sure wasn't going to hand us one."

"Who do you know who knows apples?" Mark asked.

"Not a soul," Dennis answered, "but Bones will."

Joe LaBelle was less than impressed. "Townsend, I don't know why the hell you did that." He kicked at

231

the plastic pot with the toe of his cowboy boot. "We don't have room for a tree."

"So give it to a parishioner," Mark told him. "I don't care what you do with it."

Bones looked down at the Millennium Star he was holding. "You folks in Seattle are a little crazy, you know that? You want an apple, so you go and buy a tree. You can get 'em a lot cheaper in grocery stores." He kicked at the potted tree a second time. "Don't need a whole tree for one apple."

"I already explained that, Joe. We needed a distraction."

"Yeah, right, I heard you," the pastor grumped, eyeing Dennis Grib, standing next to Mark. "A distraction while you turn my assistant into a thief. Stealing apples. A whole bloody valley crammed with orchards and this dimwit steals an apple."

Mark Townsend lifted the fruit from his friend's hand. "This is one of a kind, Bones. And I need someone who can tell me everything about it."

Father LaBelle scratched behind his ear as he cast another glance at the potted tree in front of him. He looked like he was going to kick it again.

"I'll see what I can do," he said, not at all agreeably. "Meanwhile, get rid of this ridiculous-looking stick you're calling a tree." He took the Millennium Star away from Mark and headed back into the house.

While they lugged their potted tree around a corner of the house, Mark laid out the rest of their day to Dennis. After a quick break for lunch, they had two more trips to make. Whether Brother Grib liked it or not, it was time to include Tim Connell. There was work he could do while the two Jesuits made another trip back to Cowiche.

"We still need to figure out what went on in that Vigil Room," Father Townsend told him.

Back in the house, Dennis went to work on some sandwiches while Mark called up the Castillos. Rosa answered and told him that Tim Connell had left about half an hour earlier. He did not tell her where he was headed, but then he never did. Mark thanked the old woman and hung up. He had a pretty good idea where he could find Tim Connell.

Father Paul Stanley had already laid claim to Mark's bologna sandwich and was polishing off the first half. Dennis was at the counter, building a replacement, which Stanley was eyeing with some interest even as he continued chewing. Mark dropped into a chair opposite the old man and nodded a greeting. Paul, still chewing, nodded back.

"What do you know about the Rapture, Father?"

Stanley scowled and kept chewing.

"We're pretending our hearing aid is on the blink," Dennis said over his shoulder, "so we can get someone to drive to the mall. I told him I'm too busy this afternoon."

The old priest bent over his sandwich, refusing to hear.

"We could probably swing by the mall on our way," Mark said agreeably, "don't you think?"

Father Stanley waited until he spotted Brother Grib's reluctant shrug.

"What was that about a Rapture?" he asked Mark.

Father Townsend raised his voice. "I wondered what you know about it."

"Bunk! I know it's bunk. At least the way they talk about it around here. The only raising up will come at the final judgement time, when the angel of God sounds the trumpet and the dead come back to life. Then watch out! God's vengeance is going to come down hard. You wait and see."

It was not like any of them had any choice in the matter.

"How will we be at the end of time?" Father Townsend asked.

"What do you mean?" Paul Stanley sniffed the air for a trap.

"I mean, what will we look like? How will our bodies be?"

"How the hell do I know?" Father Stanley barked.

"What kind of a question is that?" He suspected the younger priest was mocking him. "All we know is our bodies will be brought back from the dust and we'll be judged."

"I wonder if we'll be wearing clothes," mused Father Townsend. "Do you think?"

Dennis was leaning over the kitchen sink, chortling. Paul Stanley slammed the remainder of his sandwich onto his plate and leaned across the table until his face was inches from Mark's.

"This is nothing to mock, Father. You are treading on dangerous ground."

But Mark Townsend was not laughing. His face was solemn. "But I'm being serious, Paul. I wonder how we'll look. Those people who disappeared up at Brother Gabriel's Vigil Room left with everything but their shoes. Why not their shoes?"

Dennis was not finished laughing, so he sputtered as he spoke. "You don't need them if you're walking on clouds."

Father Stanley had heard enough. "Forget the ride!" he bellowed. "I don't want to go anywhere with you two!" He pushed his chair back from the table. "Members of the Society of Jesus used to have some sense of religious decorum. Apparently that was the old Society. I will tell you this, there will be some mighty surprised looks on some Jesuit faces when Judgement Day finally arrives, that's for sure!"

Ignoring Dennis's raucous laughter, the old priest stomped out of the kitchen. Throughout Paul Stanley's angry outburst, Mark remained strangely passive. He was lost in thought, and Grib's joke about walking on clouds seemed to have drifted right over his head.

Tim Connell was sipping at his lunch in the Sweet Apple Tavern when Father Townsend and Brother Grib barged in. They stood in the open doorway, peering into the dark until one of the patrons at the bar shouted in protest. Bright sunlight, like fresh air, were not considered part of the Sweet Apple's ambiance. As the door

squeezed closed and the familiar gloom returned, Mark
caught a glimpse of Tim hunkered into a booth near the
back. He poked Dennis and pointed in that direction.

"Hi, Tim." Father Townsend slipped into the bench
opposite his parishioner, scooting far enough over to allow Dennis some room. Connell looked up from his
glass but said nothing. Mark waited for some sort of
reply but when nothing came, he continued on his own.

"Tim, this has got to stop. You're going to ruin
everything. Can't you see that?"

Connell sniffed and lifted his beer to his lips. "So?"

Brother Grib snorted in disgust.

"So if you want Angelina back," Mark spoke quietly,
"I need your help. Dennis and I are going to Cowiche,
but there's work we need done here in town."

That got his attention. He set his glass back on the
table and searched the priest's face, not quite trusting his
ears.

"You know where she is?"

Mark shook his head. "Not yet. No. But I think I'm
getting closer."

"She's alive?"

Townsend hesitated, then nodded. In quick fashion,
he described what he needed Tim to do. Sometimes the
end does justify the means.

By the time they reached Cowiche, it was late in the
afternoon and a cool breeze was stirring through the orchards on the high bluffs above the valley floor. The
cloud cover had remained over the Yakima Valley all
day, and while neither Mark nor Dennis needed a jacket,
they were able to ride without the air-conditioning
blowing in their faces. The cooler air seemed to carry
the first faint promise of fall and it made Mark ache for
home. As Dennis negotiated the curved road leading to
Cowiche, the priest looked longingly over his shoulder
at the high range of mountains to the west.

Dennis presumed they were headed to Brother Gabriel's house, so he was surprised when Mark asked him
to pull off to the side of the road. He listened carefully

as Townsend explained what he was looking for.

"I don't know this area very well," he admitted to Mark, "so your guess is as good as mine."

They were searching for a back road. One that skirted beyond the house that was perched at the edge of the rocky outcrop looking over the valley. One that would drop them down further below and would double back.

"It's probably not much more than a dirt trail," Mark suggested. He had his eyes fixed on the road ahead, already searching for a turn-off.

If there was such a trail, it was well disguised. The two Jesuits coasted back and forth along the country roads that passed and intersected on both sides of the spacious white house built near the cliff's edge. Father Townsend would not let Dennis drive past it in case someone looked out and spotted their car. So he made Grib circle back around each time they explored one side or the other. There were not that many roads, and they passed up and down them several times, never spotting what Mark wanted so badly to find.

In the end, they pulled off the road beside a barbed wire fence and wire gate that blocked entrance into what looked like an abandoned quarry. There were large piles of hewn basalt and rubble behind the fence. They were about half a mile on the east side of the house, and the expanse between them was mostly sage and scrub pine. There was a slight rise to the ground so they could not see the house from where they stopped. Nor could they be seen. The edge of the bluff was just on the other side of the old quarry.

"This will have to do," Mark told his driver. "We're going to have to get out and walk."

The idea of clamoring through sagebrush was not that enticing to Brother Grib. And it became less so when Mark made it clear they were going to climb down below the cliff's edge. The priest from Seattle might have forgotten it, but Dennis was quick to remind him that this was rattlesnake country. Climbing around on rocky ledges was not a smart idea.

Mark grinned at his companion and shrugged as he

opened his car door. "Then we'll need to be careful."

The gate into the rock piles was secured with a thick chain and padlock, both fairly new, so the Jesuits helped each other through the barbed strands of the fence, pushing one down with a foot while lifting up on the other. When they were both through, they headed across the gravel lot to the edge, where the ground fell away. Once there, they stopped, looking over the valley stretching out below them.

"This would make a great place for a house," Dennis observed.

But Father Townsend's attention was already elsewhere. He pointed directly below them, to a narrow and rocky ledge. Tracing it to the right, they spotted a steep decline leading down from the abandoned quarry. Following its route around to their left, they studied the narrow pathway as it curved out of sight around an outcropping from the cliff.

"I think that's what we were looking for," Mark told Dennis. "Let's get down there and check it out."

They followed the decline down the ledge. It was wide enough for the two of them to walk beside each other, but barely. And not without coming dangerously close to the edge in spots. The ground's surface was covered with sharp rocks. Negotiating their way was slow and difficult and both men trod gingerly, feeling the stones' points pushing against the soles of their shoes. Dennis was trying to keep one eye on where he stepped and the other along both sides of the ledge, watching for snakes. He had both ears tuned for rattles, too. The rocky path was definitely leading them back toward Brother Gabriel's estate. They were now trudging about fifty feet below the top of the rimrock.

"Imagine what this would be like if you were walking through here in the dark," Mark suggested to him. "And then imagine doing it barefoot."

Dennis stopped dead in his tracks.

"You think that's how they did it?"

Father Townsend nodded as he continued walking. There was nothing above them that gave any clue how close they might be getting. The thick basalt cliffs seemed to cut back in from the top and Mark figured they were probably shielded from view, even if someone were to look over from above. But he had no idea where the house might be from down below. He told Dennis to keep his eyes open for some way that would lead them up.

They hiked for forty-five minutes over the rough terrain before they found it, but when they did, both men knew immediately what it was. The cave's entrance was just under five feet high, and barely wide enough for one body to pass through. The light fell only a few feet inside before things turned black.

"Snakes," Dennis hissed. "Don't tell me there aren't snakes in there."

"I suspect not," Mark told him in a quiet voice. "If there ever were, they were probably chased away. Let's check it out." With that, he slipped inside.

The light from the entrance let them see further inside the cave than they could while standing outside. And while the ceiling never raised, the sides of the cave expanded to where Mark had to stretch out both arms to their full extent before he could feel the rock walls. The ground was definitely pointing them up.

"Remember Paul telling us about the Indians hiding out in these cliffs?" Mark whispered back to Dennis. "I suspect this might be one of the places. Probably caused by some sort of fissure or something."

"Probably loaded with snakes," he heard Dennis reply. Mark grinned in the blackness.

At about another twenty feet back, the height of the cave began to drop. Both Townsend and Grib squatted down, leaning back on their haunches while they scuffled forward, using their hands to keep their balance.

"I hope it isn't much further," Dennis complained.

"Shhhh," Mark cautioned. There was a pencil-thin line of light near the cave's roof about ten feet in front of him. "Stay where you are a minute."

He tried moving as quietly as he could. The ground was covered with loose rock and the weight of his feet and hands made them shift and slide against each other. In the dark and quiet, each little slide sounded like an avalanche. Father Townsend inched his way forward, his eyes fixed on the narrow slice of pale light. When he was squatting directly below it, he slowly raised his arms, feeling in the darkness over his head. His hands felt smoothness. With fingers extended, he traced along the flat surface. The area was square, about two feet on all sides. Along two sides, his fingers found twin sets of parallel tracks. There were small sliding locks that, when bolted, kept the panel in place until someone from below released it. Cautiously, Mark released and slid back both bolts. Carefully, as quietly as he could, he inched the panel aside.

The light that fell into the cave from above was pale and weak and was coming from the high vents near the building's ceiling. As near as he could tell, no electrical lights were burning inside the Vigil Room. As the gap in the floor widened, Mark looked directly up at a spigot.

He turned back toward Dennis and muttered, ''It's the shower. We're underneath the shower.''

The shower stall in the bathroom was the one part of the floor that was not solid concrete. It was the one part of the floor that he had not inspected for telltale cracks. Mark recalled someone mentioning that water to the shower was never hooked up. Now he knew why. There was nothing supernatural about people disappearing from the Vigil Room. It was subterranean. He carefully slid the panel back in place and resecured the bolts. Turning around in the low and confining tunnel was a bit difficult, but once he assured Dennis they were leaving, the young brother eagerly led the way. In short order, both men were standing back outside on the stony ledge. With a jerk of his head, Mark indicated that Dennis should lead the way back toward the quarry. He did not want to risk speaking until they were further away from the house that he now knew was directly overhead.

Dennis, on the other hand, could barely contain himself. And as they picked their way along the rocky shelf, he continuously kept turning to Father Townsend, hissing exclamations of surprise and outrage. Their discovery inside the cave seemed to energize the young man, as if he had received a jolt of adrenaline. His arms and legs were twitching nervously, and his eyes were wide with excitement. If he did not calm down, Mark was sure he was going to cause a small rock slide that would bring out everyone overhead to peer down onto their ledge.

"Take it easy, Dennis."

Instead of excited, Father Townsend felt drained. He would have liked nothing more than to curl up and fall into a deep and dreamless sleep. His mind, like his body, was eager to shut down, and he was having difficulty sorting through the troubling images in his head. As they picked their way along the ledge toward their car, Mark was imagining the terrified Mexicans who had stumbled over these same rocks in the dark, step by painful step on bare feet, the cold, sharp rocks cutting into tender flesh. No one raptured out of the Vigil Room was walking on clouds, that was for sure.

As if reading his thoughts, Dennis turned on the track and exclaimed excitedly, "I figured out why their shoes were left in the room!" They were far enough away now, and Mark let him continue. "It was so they wouldn't run." He looked down at the narrow ledge in front of them. "This is hard enough to walk on with shoes in daylight. It'd be impossible at night."

With thick-soled boots, it would not be hard for two men to herd three or four barefoot Mexicans at night, no matter how young or strong they might be. Your entire attention would be fixed on trying to protect yourself from the sharpest of rocks. The last thing you would think about was trying to escape by running along the narrow rock ledge in total blackness. The trip to the quarry would take well over an hour under such conditions, but time was probably not a factor at that point.

Father Townsend and Brother Grib made it back to their car in a little over half an hour, but that was with shoes and in daylight. Dennis was still wired and moved quickly toward the car. It was all Mark could do to drag himself forward and fall into the front seat. He was exhausted. What drained him of all energy was not the exploration and discovery just completed. Rather, it was the awful realization that, for the thirty-seven men and women dragged barefoot over the rough rocks, the worse and most dangerous part of their journey was still to come. Mark Townsend felt weakened by the sheer brutality of it.

TWENTY-FIVE

The right and sensible thing would have been to go straight to the police. And although they did discuss it winding down the drive from Cowiche into Naches, neither one of the Jesuits was ready to insist that they do what both knew was right and sensible. A nasty French saying claims that whenever two Jesuits are together, the devil makes three. Perhaps it was that third who kept them on the road to Moxee.

By the time Dennis pulled in front of Luis and Rosa's house, it was after six o'clock. The sky was dark with clouds and it appeared night would fall earlier than usual. The Castillos were just sitting for dinner when their doorbell rang. Luis led two very dirty and tired-looking Jesuits into the kitchen while Rosa scurried for extra plates. Mark and Dennis took turns telling the couple what they had discovered. While one talked, the other hungrily ate, nodding at crucial points. Luis's mouth stretched thin and angry as he listened, and his wife's eyes filled with tears. When their story was finally ended, each one at the table sat silently, as if waiting for one of the others to say something that would make sense out of the horror they were imagining.

Finally, in a voice surprisingly strong, Rosa spoke. "It

must end," she pronounced. "Do what you must, but make it stop."

Dennis returned to what was right and sensible. "Maybe the police . . ."

"No!" Luis barked. "No police!"

"We'll need others," Mark said. "And we still have to wait for Tim. Unless he finds . . ."

"I will get others," Luis interrupted again. "José Ramirez will want to come. And he can get Chacon and Velasquez. Brother, you can find Raul Santos, yes?"

Dennis was finishing the last bites of his meal, but he nodded assent.

"*Bueno,*" Castillo said. "We will meet back here. By then, Tim Connell should be home." He stood, then added cruelly, "If he is not already drunk."

Inwardly, Mark winced. But he knew the man was right. Involving Connell—asking him to be responsible for anything—was risky. Grib had tried to dissuade him, but Mark was determined. If there was to be any redemption for Tim Connell in this life, it had to be now. Castillo and Brother Grib left in their separate cars to fetch the others. Mark stayed behind to help Rosa clean up. And to wait hopefully for the return of Angelina's husband.

They were just finishing in the kitchen when they heard a car drive up. The engine stopped and a car door opened and closed. Rosa squeezed her eyes shut then opened them, looking directly into Father Townsend's face.

"*Es Timeo,*" she said quietly.

Mark met him at the front door and moved next to him, closer than he needed to. He was looking intently into the young man's eyes.

"Whoa! Father!" Tim protested. "You're worse than Angie." He shook his head and offered the priest a crooked smile. "I'm sober, all right? I haven't touched a drop since you left me this morning." He held up a thick sheaf of papers. "I haven't had time. Do you know how hard this stuff is to get? After today, I can appreciate the kind of digging Angie does. It's hard work.''

''But you got them?'' Mark asked impatiently. He was forgetting that Connell knew none of the day's other events, so focused was he on the pages in Tim's hands. ''You found what we need?''

Connell smiled happily. ''I think I might have. At least it should be in here somewhere.''

Mark was already paging through the papers when Rosa came up behind him.

''You are hungry, no? Come into the kitchen and eat. Padre, you too. Come. Before the others get here.''

''What others?''

Mark remained intent on rifling through the documents. He was either ignoring Tim's question or he failed to hear it.

''Come,'' Rosa urged again, pulling on his hand. ''Come eat.''

Once they were seated and Father Townsend had a chance to scan through the materials Tim handed him, the story was finally retold. Mark laid the pages down and described the trip to Cowiche. Although he kept shoveling the food into his mouth, Connell tasted nothing and had no idea what he was eating. All of his attention was on Mark's recounting of their discovery beneath the basalt cliffs overlooking the Yakima valley.

''So they brought them out at night,'' Connell said, laying down his fork. He thought a moment, then asked, ''But why down below? Why not just take them out the front door and load them up? Why risk getting someone hurt on the rocks?''

''Because there were others outside, up by the road,'' Mark told him. ''Sister Elizabeth told us that when they held the vigils, people gathered along the road, hoping they'd get chosen. Some of them hung around afterward. They couldn't take people out the door because someone would have seen it.''

Connell closed his eyes and leaned back in his chair, as if trying to imagine the scene Mark was describing. It was not difficult. Straightening back up, he laid his hands on the papers next to the priest.

"And with these you think we can figure out where they are?"

Father Townsend shrugged. "We should be able to narrow it down quite a bit. Where can you hide nearly forty people? There can't be that many possibilities."

He picked up the sheaf of papers from the table. There were building permits, property tax assessments, land use declarations, and permits for water rights. Connell had scoured Yakima's county offices for every possible shred of information he could extract on Leonard Patowski and Marshall Fairbanks.

Brother Gabriel's two richest benefactors had not only funded his ministry, they graciously provided the Cowiche residence for the evangelist and his wife. They had also built the Vigil Room. Joe Bones said that benefactors like them did not grow on trees. But Father Townsend was beginning to wonder.

Somewhere in the pile of legalese Tim had managed to collect, Mark was hoping to pick up the thin, fragile trail that began in the narrow dark cave beneath Brother Gabriel's Vigil Room. He thought he had enough loose threads to begin tying some of them together. If his hunch was right and he could connect enough of the threads, they might lead him to the missing persons. And hopefully, to whoever killed Brother Gabriel.

Dennis returned with Raul Santos a full hour before Luis arrived back. By then they had Tim's copies of county records spread across the tabletop in the Castillo kitchen. Rosa was serving coffee and trying to convince anyone that he was hungry. She could offer no help with the documents they studied, but as long as they were in her kitchen she would keep control—at least over their stomachs.

They had finished sorting the records into four piles by the time Luis strode in with Ramirez, Chacon, and Velasquez. Up to that point, the conversation around the table had been conducted mostly in English, with Dennis needing to provide only occasional translations for Raul. But with the arrival of the others, the balance shifted and all conversation was conducted in Spanish. Mark listened helplessly as the men's intense voices rose around him. Other than catching occasional words and short phrases, he was lost. Suddenly, and quite uncomfortably, he was one of the outsiders. Dennis, seeing the priest's confusion, scooted his chair next to Mark's left side and leaned close to his ear. From then on, he did his best to keep Mark and Tim aware of what was being said.

The Hispanics seemed to have a clear idea of what they were looking for. They were much more familiar with orchards and their operation than any of the Anglos. They shuffled and reshuffled the documents, arguing over their significance and eventually began winnowing through the stacks. The first pages to go were any documents related to buildings owned or managed by either of the two men in downtown Yakima. That was the easy part, as were the papers pertaining to the house in Cowiche and the Patowski Fruit Nursery. But what they were left with was still a significantly large sheaf of documents referring to orchards or properties owned either singly or in partnership by the two. At this point, they turned back to Father Townsend and Brother Grib.

"We would like you to tell us again about your meeting with Mr. Patowski," Luis Castillo said. "Especially that new apple he showed you."

While Mark recounted their visit, Dennis provided the translation. The process was frustrating because it meant everything needed to be repeated, slowing the conversation considerably. More than one of the men glanced impatiently at his watch. It was after midnight.

There were two details of Mark's story the men found significant. Patowski's primary concern seemed to be creating a market that would garner huge interest in the patent sale for the Millennium Star. The initial harvests of a new variety, if it became popular among consumers—especially overseas—could reap huge profits. But as the nursery man himself admitted, the big money was in the sale of the patent.

"It is true what he said about smuggling bud sticks,"

Castillo confirmed. "I have heard those stories myself. And something similar happens with vineyards, especially if a new grape looks very good. If there is money to be made, people will figure out a way to steal it. So the secrecy does not surprise me. I am surprised he even let you see the apple."

"We're just dumb religious," Dennis said with a cocky grin. "What do we know about apples?"

"I suspect Dennis is right," said Mark. "He was very proud of that bag of apples and I think he wanted to show them off. He figured a couple of Jesuits were safe subjects for a taste test. He didn't see any risk in showing it to us."

All of them agreed on the significance of the second detail; the fruit Len Patowski showed them was fully grown and ripe. Which meant the Millennium Star was ready for harvest. Somewhere in the region around Yakima was a new variety of apple tree, ready for picking. Len Patowski's nursery in the Columbia Basin was for new starts. Trees that produced apples were fully mature.

"I need to check back with Father LaBelle," Mark told the others. "He was going to try and find out what he could about that apple." He looked woefully at his watch. "But it's pretty late to be calling now." The time was now past one o'clock.

Their attention shifted back to the papers laid out in front of them, and the seven men around the table returned to their examination of the holdings of Marshall Fairbanks and Len Patowski. Their energy was beginning to fade, even with the constant infusions of Rosa's coffee. The strain was showing in their eyes.

Between the four Mexicans most familiar with the Yakima Valley, they were able to identify five of the orchards included in the titles and other documents. Either they had worked on the trees themselves, or they knew of others who had. Three of the five were older, smaller orchards of twenty to thirty acres. Hiding new trees in any of them would be difficult. The other two, however, were high density orchards, meaning a maximum number of trees compacted onto each acre. Rodriguez knew both sites, and he estimated each one to be over a hundred and twenty acres. With upwards of fifteen hundred or more trees per acre, that meant orchards that were probably somewhere in excess of one hundred and eighty thousand trees. Dennis whistled appreciatively.

"*¡Entonces, estamos predidos!*" Raul Santos snarled in dismay. "*No hay ninguna manera que podemos examinar tantos arboles.*" Wearily, Dennis began his translation but Mark waved him off. He might not understand the words, but the sentiment was clear.

It was now two-thirty and none of them were thinking too clearly. But something about Raul's last remarks caught Father Townsend short. He tugged hard at his mustache, as if that would reawaken his slumbering brain cells.

"*Plus there are at least four more properties here.*" From the tone of his voice, Victor Chacon was sharing in Santos's despair. "*And two of those are huge. Finding the right place could take us days.*"

The others began to weigh in with their own opinions and the conversation quickly deteriorated. Nerves were frayed and short fuses began to ignite. The night's work was starting to unravel. All of the arguing was in Spanish and Dennis Grib was too tired to translate. With his lips pressed tightly together and his eyes half-closed, he wearily shook his head at Mark. If Townsend wanted to know what they were saying, let him get a dictionary. He leaned forward and lay his head down on his arms. This was going nowhere. As the arguing continued, Father Townsend pushed himself away from the table and wandered out through the back door onto the patio. After the warm closeness of the kitchen, the outside air felt cold. Leaning his head back, the priest gazed at the night sky.

The thick clouds that hung over Yakima throughout the day were finally breaking apart, and through the open spaces Mark could see stars. The sky was full of them. He hugged his arms against his body and stared into the night. Among the thousands and thousands, where was the Millennium Star?

Fatigue was turning his brain to mush. He was unable
to focus on trees. Instead, he found himself back inside
the mall in downtown Yakima, wandering up and down
the corridors, listening to the voices of the crowd bustling around him. The priest was wondering once again
how many had relations or friends among the missing.
The same odd sensation he had experienced in the mall
came over him in the Castillos' backyard. If there was
one person who could disappear among all the others
without being missed, it would be himself. Under the
grandeur of the night sky, his own insignificance felt
very real. He turned to look at the men in the kitchen.
Dennis remained slumped over the table and the arguing
was slowly dying down. No one had energy for it. A
depressing weariness was replacing determination, confidence, and righteous anger. The men's fatigue was
clearly palpable. The Jesuit lifted his arm away from his
body and tilted the watch on his wrist to catch the
kitchen light.

"It's four o'clock," Father Townsend intoned to himself in a tired voice. "Do you know where your children
are?"

TWENTY-SIX

If you focus too long and too hard on one project, you can reach a point where the work becomes counterproductive. For the men gathered in the Castillo kitchen, their focus slipped past that point sometime around four in the morning. Their bleary eyes were red-rimmed, first with worry, then with fatigue. They argued in circles, unable to gather their thoughts or think creatively. Angel Velasquez started getting silly, cracking lewd cornball jokes that finally drove an embarrassed Rosa to her bedroom and angered her husband. José Ramirez was also mad and he made it known to the others. His son, Paco, was one of the missing. How could they just sit there and do nothing? Ramirez wanted a plan of action and he wanted it immediately. But what he really wanted was an outlet for his pent-up rage, for everything he proposed involved physical harm to either some person or some place. Without trying to appear blatant about it, Raul Santos did what he could to urge him on. But eventually, even Ramirez ran out of steam. Through it all, Dennis Grib slumbered on.

At some point in the middle of it, Tim Connell hopped up and yanked a bottle of beer from the refrigerator. Glaring defiantly at Father Townsend, he tilted the bottle and drained nearly half in the first swallow. That was when Mark decided it was time to quit. They were not much more than an hour away from dawn anyway.

He pushed his chair back and, stretching his arms their full length, yawned mightily. "We need to get some rest," he announced, "and come back to it fresh. We're not getting anywhere with this now."

"*¿Que?*" Victor Chacon looked around the table for someone to translate. Dennis was still out, so Luis obliged.

"*Estoy de acuerdo con el padre.*" Chacon was voting his agreement by stumbling to his feet. "*Dormimos, y entonces regresamos.*"

Mark stood, and with Tim already standing up next to the refrigerator, that made three. Brother Grib cast his vote with a small snore and that made a majority. The other three nodded their agreement. Luis disappeared down the hallway and returned with an armload of blankets. There was an unspoken understanding that no one was leaving until their work was accomplished. The men started shuffling off to various corners of the house. Mark woke Dennis Grib and explained they were spending the night, then Luis led the young man to the living room couch. Returning for the priest, he directed him down the hallway and a second guest bedroom. Mark was not only given his own bed, but privacy to boot. If he was not so tired, the priest would have spent a restless twenty or thirty minutes guiltily wrestling his conscience over accepting this token of clerical privilege. But as it was, he started snoring thirty seconds after his head hit the soft pillow.

His sleep was marred by disturbing dreams, though. There were crowds of people trying to swim through a dense sea of apples. Flailing their arms, some were pulled beneath the surface. Mark was in their midst, searching for someone—he could not remember who, while overhead, millions of stars twinkled. Once, he caught a glimpse of Angelina's face and he recognized her as the one he had to reach. But the horde of people was too thick and, despite his struggles, they prevented him from reaching her. He watched in dismay as she slowly sank out of sight. But then, in her place, up bobbed Brother Gabriel's pale face, laughing soundlessly at the look on Mark's own face.

He awoke with a start. The room was light enough that he could read his watch. It was nearly seven-thirty. Three hours of sleep left him groggy and disoriented, but he could hear the low murmur of men's voices coming from down the hall and he knew the others were already moving about. Reluctantly, Father Townsend got up.

No one looked his best. Unshaved, with wrinkled clothes, Victor Chacon, Angel Velasquez, and Raul Santos had fallen back into the same chairs they had vacated three hours earlier. Luis was helping his wife as she bustled about the kitchen, preparing breakfast. Tim Connell was not up, and through the doorway Mark could see Dennis just beginning to stir on the couch.

"Buenos, Padre." Without slowing her steps, Rosa swept past, shoving a mug of coffee into the priest's hands. "Sit down, *por favor."* When he realized she was not just being polite but trying to keep floor space cleared of numb-faced men, Mark fell into a chair, the same one he had occupied before.

The piles of documents were moved to the center of the table to make room for the plates and silverware that Luis was awkwardly trying to arrange in front of them. Mark leaned across and plucked up the top pages. They were the two deeds for large tracts of land no one knew anything about. Both were considerable distances outside of Yakima. The first was actually closer to Richland, seventy-six miles southeast of Yakima. And the second, as near as anyone could tell, lay due east, about forty miles away from Moxee. As he sipped his coffee and inhaled the exhilarating smells of eggs and sausage cooking, Mark studied the deeds.

The first one, near Richland, was owned by Marshall Fairbanks and covered an area of four hundred acres. The second was owned jointly by Fairbanks and Patowski and was for an area a little under three hundred acres. Other than the precise locations of each, the deeds revealed nothing more that was helpful. Luis was still bustling around the kitchen, trying to keep up with Rosa's brusque orders, so Father Townsend moved out to the living room.

"Good morning," he greeted Dennis. "How'd you sleep?"

Grib was sitting up, but barely. "Short." He held his head in his hands and squeezed his eyes shut. "I feel like I've been out all night with your friend, Connell."

Mark clucked his tongue, making a noise he hoped sounded sympathetic. "Do you know if there's a map in the car?"

Dennis thought there might be one in the glove compartment. The car was unlocked, Mark was free to check. With coffee in one hand and the deeds in the other, the priest went out to do precisely that. The clouds were gone and the air smelled clean and bracing. There was still moisture in the air and its coolness felt good on his skin, although Mark knew that by noon the bright sun would leach it away, leaving only the dry, hot emptiness of late summer.

He settled into the passenger's seat after fishing a worn and smudged Washington state road map from the detritus in the glove compartment. Balancing his mug of coffee on the dashboard, Townsend spread the map across his knees. It was good for showing the routes of Washington's highways and byways, but as a locator for particular parcels of land, the map was pretty useless. As near as he could figure, the site to the southeast lay somewhere outside of a small town called Kiona, in a region enticingly described as the Horse Heaven Hills. The property east of Moxee looked as if it might be tucked into a narrow pocket of land nestled between the military training center and the Hanford nuclear site. The back end of the pocket was cut off by the Columbia river. The map gave no clue what the terrain at either place might look like, but Mark was guessing high rolling hills of sage and brush. One thing was sure. Either location was big enough. Folding the map so that both sections were still showing, he carried it back inside the house.

Breakfast was being served, and whether it was from the food or just plain tiredness, the only sounds made came from silverware clinking against plates and coffee indelicately slurped. Father Townsend found his empty chair and did his best to add to the clatter. There would be time enough for talking when the eating was done. Somewhere in the middle of things, Tim Connell wandered in from his bedroom. With the table now complete, Rosa Castillo, her hands finally at rest in her apron pockets, beamed.

"It has to be one or the other," Mark was insisting.

They were meeting in the living room, with papers and map littering the coffee table and surrounding floor. Once breakfast was finished, Rosa had reclaimed territorial rights to her kitchen. Gaping at the dirty dishes and surrounding clutter, the men readily gave ground. Luis gallantly offered to stay behind and help but was delighted when she banished him with the rest.

"We've eliminated everywhere else. They're either too small or there's too many other people around." He waited for Dennis to translate. Despite the small amount of sleep, the kid was back in top form and he quickly and adeptly recast the priest's words in the language the rest understood. Although not entirely convinced, the others remained silent, waiting for Mark to finish.

"I don't think we're looking for just one tree, or even a few," Mark continued. "I think we're looking for a whole orchard. And I think it's a big one. What do you call them? High density?"

Victor Chacon was nodding before Dennis finished. *"Sí.* High density. *Esto es."*

Father Townsend reached out and lifted the sorted pile of deeds. "These other places are already planted. You know about them. Even these other two big ones—José has already seen what's in them. It doesn't make sense that they'd rip out trees that are already producing."

"No, no tiene sentido," Luis Castillo agreed. *"Yo pienso que el padre tiene razón."*

The others leaned back and considered. These were men accustomed to hard physical labor, scuffling in dirt, wrestling against rough limbs, and shouldering heavy loads. The thin, nearly transparent pages in front of them, filled with letters and figures they did not understand, were foreign and uncomfortable to be around. They were indecipherable symbols for the realities these men knew with their skin, their muscles, and their blood. Put them in an orchard and they knew immediately what to do. But seated on a soft carpet, surrounded by deeds and permits, they were confused.

Finally, Santos spoke for the rest. *"If you are wrong, Padre, then we will have wasted another day."*

Even after Dennis was finished translating, Mark waited to speak. The eyes of the others remained fixed on him, demanding and unwavering.

"I know," he finally murmured. "I'm aware of that."

"Darrell, I'd like you to meet Father Mark Townsend. He's the mossyback I was telling you about. Mark, this is Darrell Porter. He's with WSU's Agricultural Extension Service. He can talk apples all the way back to the Garden of Eden."

Bones stood between the two men as they shook hands, then pointed them both toward chairs. "If you two don't mind, I'd like to sit in on this little pow-wow—maybe learn a thing or two." The three settled into the living room of the Jesuit residence.

Mark rubbed his hand over his unshaved chin and glanced down at his wrinkled clothing. He started to apologize for his appearance, then decided against it. Life was too short. "I didn't know Washington State had a campus here in Yakima," he offered instead.

"Technically, we don't," Porter replied. He was a small barrel of a man, with a bright pink face and thin, wispy hair that he wore swept back along both sides of an otherwise bald head. "But the university has extensions all over the state that are cooperatives with individual counties. Mostly agricultural, of course.''

"Joe . . . Father LaBelle . . . showed you the apple?''

"No, I thought I'd keep it a big surprise,'' Joe cut in. "Of course I did.'' As if by magic, a plastic bag with half an apple appeared in LaBelle's hand. With a quick flick of his wrist he tossed it toward Darrell Porter, who adroitly plucked it from the air. The agent rotated the bag in his hand. The apple's meaty core was browned by exposure.

"This is quite a specimen, Father. Can I ask where you found it?''

LaBelle's eyes remained noncommittal. Apparently he had said nothing to Porter about the apple's origins.

"I'd rather you not, at least for the moment.'' Mark tried his most winning smile, "Let's just say it fell off a tree.''

Porter examined the fruit a few more moments, then carefully balanced the bag on the arm of his chair. "Then let me tell you that it's one hell of a tree,'' he said earnestly. "I've never seen anything like this.''

"So it's good?'' Mark asked.

Darrell Porter was shaking his head. "No, not good,'' he told the priest. "Nearly perfect. This apple has all the makings for success.'' He proceeded to describe the fruit's winning attributes, using much of the same terminology that Len Patowski did. He concluded, "From its coloration to its ethylene content, this one's going to be a winner. Now will you tell me where it's from?''

"Right here,'' Mark replied, "in Yakima.''

The extension agent lifted the bag once more and examined its contents. "Then someone is keeping secrets. Big, big secrets. As far as I'm aware, no one has a clue this is coming.''

"Is that good or bad?''

"For whoever owns this apple, very good,'' Porter told him. "For the rest of the orchardists, not at all good. In fact, for many of them it may spell disaster.''

Mark leaned forward, his fingers automatically moving up to his mustache. "Why?''

"Do you know much about the apple industry, Father?"

LaBelle snorted. "About as much as you know of theology, Darrell."

Joe's right," Father Townsend confirmed, "you'd better start at the beginning."

Porter leaned back in his chair and crossed his legs. "Well, let me start by saying that the industry has changed dramatically over the last ten, fifteen years. Apples are still Washington's number-one cash fruit crop, but the value is way down. And it's going to get worse. In another five years, China is going to be producing almost half of the world's apples. They've already about cornered the market on juice concentrate. So the culled fruit our farmers sell to the juice companies has dropped from sixty to twenty bucks a ton. There's lots who can't survive those kinds of hits."

"Meaning?"

Darrell clasped his hands together and rested his chin on top. "Twenty years ago we had over fifty-five hundred growers in Washington. Since then, about eighteen hundred have called it quits. Most of them were smaller family farms."

"So once again," LaBelle drawled, "it's the little guy who takes it in the shorts."

Porter nodded. "The number of growers has dropped, but our orchards have grown by fifty-seven thousand acres."

"Blessed are the conglomerates," Joe solemnly intoned, "for they shall inherit the earth."

The extension agent had been around Father LaBelle long enough to become accustomed to his wry humor, but every once in awhile he was still caught unprepared. It sounded faintly biblical, but Porter was not sure. He gave the priest an odd look and then a weak smile.

For once, Mark Townsend was growing impatient with his friend's joking. He gave the Jesuit an irritated scowl and then leaned toward Porter.

"I get what you're saying so far." His words tumbled out quickly. "But you still haven't told us why this particular apple is a problem. It seems to me it might even help the industry.''

Darrell Porter gave the tall priest a smile that was plainly telling him to keep his pants on. They wanted him to start at the beginning and he was. And he would get to the point in his own sweet time.

''The problem is, Father, that the market isn't ready for something like this. Exports are down twenty-two percent, even though production is higher than it's ever been. And your profit margin on the lower-priced popular apples—like your Red Delicious—is down to about two percent.'' Porter uncrossed his legs and, like Mark, leaned forward intently. ''The size of your ranch doesn't make much of a difference if you're surviving on that slim of a margin. You're barely hanging on.'' He plucked the plastic bag off the chair and held it out in front of him, then let it fall to the floor. ''Now drop a new apple like this one into the mix—one that looks better, tastes better, and is going to keep longer. And if you're sitting out there with two thousand acres of something you can't even sell for juice . . .'' Porter was fumbling for a way to finish.

LaBelle jumped in, ''. . . you can kiss your rosy red apple goodbye!''

Darrell Porter nodded his agreement.

Father Townsend leaned back in his chair. He was beginning to get the picture, but he needed time to mull things over. When Len Patowski first showed him the Millennium Star he said that marketing was their biggest concern. A demand needed to be created, first among consumers, then among the growers themselves. Only afterward would the patent go up for sale. Which, according to the fat nursery man, was where the big money lay.

''Mr. Porter, what if this apple was already in production,'' Mark wondered, ''and was ready for the market?''

''That's what I was saying earlier. Someone has been real good about keeping secrets.''

Mark pointed to the bag resting on the floor in front

of Darrell Porter's feet. "If that was your apple, what would you be doing with it? Right now, I mean?"

Porter looked down at the browned apple inside the plastic sack, then back up at the priest. What began as a look of doubt changed into one of comprehension as he realized what Father Townsend was asking.

"You mean how would I spring this on everyone? I get it." He pushed his fingers through the wispy strands of his hair. "Well, let me see. First off, I'd want enough of these to make an impact. That means a lot of trees with a lot of apples . . ."

"You're talking a high-density orchard."

Porter nodded appreciatively and even LaBelle looked impressed. "You know about those," the agent said. "Yeah, I'd want as big an orchard as I could manage. I'd probably plant upwards of two thousand trees on each acre."

"You can do that?" LaBelle blurted.

The agent tipped his head. "It's not great over the long haul, but in this case you'll benefit more by an early and precocious harvest." He paused a few moments to think. "And I think I'd want my own CA's, cuz I'm going to release everything all at once." He saw the question on both men's faces. "Controlled atmosphere storage," he explained. "Most storage is CA these days. You put the fruit in an airtight warehouse and then flush out the oxygen, replacing it with nitrogen. Keeps your fruit from spoiling. It's going to take you several weeks to harvest and you're not going to want your early pickings to spoil while you wait for the last one."

He crossed his arms over his chest. The agent was taking great delight imagining the kind of campaign he would mount to introduce the Millennium Star. "Once I've got everything picked and packed, then I'd ship them out to my best markets."

"Which would be . . . ?" Mark prompted.

Porter ticked them off on his fingers. "Japan. Mexico. Maybe a few to western Europe. The rest, here in the states: New York definitely, and Florida. New Jersey. Oh, and Canada. And of course, here. I'd flood Seattle."

"And you'd have enough apples to do all that?" Mark asked.

"I'd have enough to pique their interest, that's for sure. I'd certainly get everybody's attention."

"And after that?"

The agent leaned back into his chair and smiled contentedly. "Then I'd sit back and wait by the phone. Because when the word gets around, someone is going to call and make me an offer I don't want to refuse. I'll be smiling all the way to the bank."

The picture was nearly complete. Father Townsend had just about everything he needed. As usual, Bones had come through with the right person at just the right time. He nodded appreciatively at his fellow priest.

"Joe was right," Mark acknowledged, "you do know your business. But I have one more thing I need to know. That's production costs. Where am I going to take my greatest hit?"

"Where do you think?" Porter answered.

"Labor," Mark quickly replied.

The agent nodded in reply. "We figure it's costing the orchardists about forty-four hundred dollars to grow and harvest an acre of apples. And twenty-eight percent of that is labor."

"So if I've got a hundred acres . . ."

"Just shy half a million." Bones finished for him.

The agent spoke up. "Probably more. I was giving an overall average. But here we're talking premium grade apples, which means some extra care in picking. Given what you're going for, I think you're looking at considerably more." He shrugged. "It's just the cost of doing business," he concluded.

Father Townsend looked down at his watch and was surprised to see it was already after noon. The meeting at the Castillos had not broken up until nearly ten, when the seven of them finally hammered out their plans. José Ramirez, Victor Chacon, and Angel Velasquez were headed toward Richland, hopefully to find and eyeball the property owned by Marshall Fairbanks. Meanwhile a second car was headed east, searching for the other piece of land described in the deeds. Tim Connell, Luis Castillo, and Dennis Grib were riding together. Mark had wanted to keep Dennis with him, but Brother Grib had looked so forlorn about missing out on the adventure that Mark relented. Raul Santos said he had other business to attend to, so he was the one who dropped Mark back at St. Joseph's where, for the last hour and a half, he had picked the brain of the WSU's extension agent.

Although Porter continued to press, Father Townsend refused to divulge where he had gotten the apple. "Sorry," he said with a shrug, "but I just can't say."

"That's okay," Porter assured him. "You priests are just like orchardists—good at keeping secrets."

They had already said their goodbyes and Father LaBelle was escorting Darrell Porter down the sidewalk toward his car when Father Townsend bolted out the front door. Dashing across the grass, he halted in front of the two men.

"I'm sorry, but I thought of one more question," he said.

"Shoot."

"Say you've got a high-density orchard," Mark began, "of anywhere from a hundred to two hundred acres. Somewhere in there. How many people is it going to take to pick the apples?" He leaned forward inquisitively.

Porter considered for a moment. "It all depends. How many trees per acre?"

"Let's say two thousand."

"I'd need to know about my pickers," the agent told him, "and how good they are. You've got some that are . . ."

"The best," Mark interrupted. "They're the best you can find."

Darrell Porter scratched the side of his head a few moments, buying time before answering. Finally though, he dropped his hand and looked up at the tall man waiting in front of him.

"There's a lot of difference between one and two hundred acres, you understand, Father. And a lot of other variables—everything from the weather to the spacing and height of the trees. But for the sake of argument, let's split the difference. I'd say for about a hundred and fifty acres you'd probably need . . . I don't know . . . maybe thirty . . . maybe forty pickers. Somewhere in there.''

The priest's reaction surprised Darrell Porter. Although Father Townsend sounded quite sincere as he expressed his gratitude, his face was drained of all color. If the extension agent did not know better, he would say this Jesuit had just seen a ghost.

TWENTY-SEVEN

"Hold up! Wait! Just a minute, I'm stuck," Tim Connell sputtered.

Crawling through barbed wire is treacherous, especially at night.

Brother Grib patiently kept his foot on the bottom strand and pulled even tighter on the top while Luis Castillo and José Ramirez felt along Connell's back until they found the pointed barbs hooked into his sweatshirt. Deftly they released him and nudged him past the fence.

"Okay, Padre," Luis whispered loudly, "you're next." Mark crouched low and slipped through without incident.

"He has moves like a coyote," Raul Santos joked. *"Maybe I can get him a job on the border."*

The Mexicans chuckled among themselves at the idea of a priest smuggler.

They had waited until after midnight before leaving the Castillos'. Rosa stood nervously in the drive, her hands tightly clutching her rosary, wishing them good luck. Mark Townsend rode with Tim Connell in the Bronco while Dennis Grib and Raul Santos drove their own cars. The rest—Luis, José, Angel, and Victor— each drove a pickup.

The caravan stayed close together as they raced east along the dark highway. There were no road lights this far out and, with the exception of a very few pinpoints coming from distant ranches, no other lights but the moon and stars overhead. They pushed hard and in less than forty-five minutes had reached their destination. There was no place to hide seven vehicles, so once they turned onto the dirt track leading back into the hills, the men drove directly up to the padlocked gate barring their way before turning off their engines. Once their head-lights were off, the cars and trucks were nothing more than a long dark shadow in the night, but they effectively blocked the entrance onto the property jointly owned by Marshall Fairbanks and Len Patowski. There would be no possible way any other vehicle could enter or leave the property.

After everyone was on the other side of the fence, they quickly set off up the road. According to Luis, Tim, and Dennis, who had scouted the ranch that afternoon, they had about a mile and a half hike ahead of them. On the other side of the hills stretching out in front of them was a large and hidden orchard. During the after-noon the three men had to sneak through the sagebrush, hunching over and squatting low to keep out of sight. Grib worried constantly about the threat of rattlesnakes. But now in the dark, the eight men could walk upright along the dusty road, not worrying about either snakes or lookouts. Their only objective was to reach the or-chard as quickly as possible.

Mark found his companion Jesuit in the dark. "We'll need to stay together," he urged Grib. "I won't have a clue what's going on most of the time."

"I'll do my best," Dennis replied nervously.

Earlier in the day, after saying goodbye to the others in Moxee, Luis and Tim had ridden with Brother Grib to search for the second site. After spotting the dirt road leaving the highway, they drove beyond it for another third of a mile before pulling off onto the shoulder. The three of them quickly scrambled away from the highway, staying low to the ground as they threaded their way through the sage to the hills. The going was slow, over rough terrain, and it had taken them three hours to cautiously make their way past the first set of hills and up onto the next. But once there, they knew they had found what they were searching for.

Spread out in a long, narrow valley in front of them was a huge apple orchard. Luis Castillo estimated there were at least a hundred and twenty-five acres planted. From their hidden perch in the rocks above, they spotted just the one road winding down the side of a hill to their left. At the bottom, the road disappeared among the trees. But toward the center of the ranch they could make out several roof lines in a clearing, so the road probably led at least that far into the tract. As they studied the layout of the ranch, Luis pointed to its perimeter. A screened mesh was erected as a windbreak, and as far as they could tell, it seemed to encircle the entire circumference. The dark fabric was stretched about eight feet high, effectively preventing anyone down below from looking through.

"That does not make sense to me," Luis had told the other two as he pointed. "See how it goes all around? It's too much. They only need protection at both ends of the ranch. These hills are just as good for stopping wind," he explained.

Dennis could see the screen at the edge of the orchard directly below them. Luis was right, there was no need for a windbreak so close to the natural shelter of the hills.

None of them had thought to bring binoculars, and without them it was difficult to see much detail. But a couple of the buildings in the orchard's center stood taller than the rest and Luis guessed they were for storage. There were two longer buildings with lower roofs and three or four others that looked smaller in size. But what they were used for was impossible to tell from so far away. The men stayed on top of the hill for about half an hour, studying the scene below them. They occasionally caught sight of figures moving through trees, but they were too far away to see anything clearly. Frustrated, they finally headed back to their car, still crouching low to the ground. Brother Grib was constantly on the alert for snakes.

Traveling along the road leading into the orchard was definitely faster, even in the dark. Not having to stumble in a half crouch helped, too. The dirt track stretched in a straight line from the highway into the hills, and within twenty minutes the eight men were moving upwards. The road began to turn slightly as it climbed the hill.

"How much further?" Mark asked Dennis.

"I'm not sure, but I think there's maybe another small hill after this one. We were further east this afternoon."

The two of them lapsed back into silence as they continued climbing.

By the time all eight men had arrived back at the Castillo house earlier that evening, it was nearly seven o'clock. The car that was sent to investigate the other piece of property near Richmond was the last to return. The glum expression on their faces when they walked into the house was a clear indication that they had found nothing. José Rodriguez seemed particularly upset. His anxiety about his son seemed to grow hourly, and he looked as if he was about to explode.

"Fue un otro día perdido." He started complaining as soon as he entered the house, before Dennis, Tim, or Luis could tell them anything about their own discoveries. José's fists were clenched tightly and from the expression on his tight, red face, it was apparent the man was barely controlling his rage. *"Estoy cansado de espera. ¡Es tiempo hacer algo!"*

When the others were finally able to describe the orchard they found behind the hills, he relaxed a little. But it took some persuasion before he agreed to wait until dark. José Rodriguez was ready for battle.

Now that they were there he seemed calmer, although just as determined. He said very little as they trudged along the road, but Mark noticed José was usually in front of the rest, as if impatient with the pace they were keeping.

When they reached the crest of the hill the road angled right, and in the moonlight they could see that it continued along the crest for a couple of hundred feet before dropping down. For the first time they crouched low to the ground as they stopped to study their route. There was another ridge in front of them, and it looked about a quarter of a mile away. But what lay below and between the two rises was covered in impenetrable darkness. They watched for any small flicker of light, but saw nothing.

"Yo pienso que no debemos quedarnos en el camino," Luis murmured in a low voice. *"Si alguien está abajo de nosotros, ellos podrían a ver. Yo pienso que nosotros deberíamos caminar más abajo, donde esta más obscuro."*

"He wants us to walk below the road," Dennis was whispering directly into Mark's right ear, "so if someone is watching the hilltop they won't see our silhouettes. But what if there's snakes?"

Luis overheard the young Jesuit's translation. "Amigo, don't worry about the snakes. They are more scared of us. And besides, it is too cold tonight. They are down their holes, sound asleep."

With that, he sidestepped his way twenty feet down the hill, until he could safely stand upright against the blackness of the hill. The others followed after him and they cautiously crept along the sage-covered hillside until they again encountered the road as it wound its way down. They were quieter now, and when anyone spoke, it was in a whisper. They continued walking in single file, José still leading the way.

There had been a moment while they were still making their plans back at the house, when Mark came very close to bowing out. Trying to sneak into the orchard at night was dangerous. The proper thing was to go to the police and let them investigate. He knew they were putting their lives at risk this way. But he also knew that the five Mexicans were unwilling to involve the police and would flatly resist him if he suggested it. Because they had more at stake, the Jesuit decided to follow their lead. Besides, Raul Santos's harsh words still buzzed in his ears. "You priests talk about what is just and about helping the poor. But not if it means taking risks."

The age when "Father Knows Best" was long past. The rallying cry was "collaboration." Jesuits, no matter what work they were involved in, were urged to work cooperatively with others, which sometimes meant not taking charge. For an organization of talented men used to automatically assuming command, this was not without some challenges. Following directions instead of giving them did not always come easy. But they were gradually learning. And as they did, the Jesuits' schools, churches, and other works began to benefit. But somehow, in all their talk of collaborative ministries, Father Townsend had never imagined it might include two Jesuits stumbling along a dirt road in the black of night, following an alcoholic husband and five pissed-off Mexicans looking for a fight.

They were nearing the top of the second rise and José Rodriguez raised a cautionary hand. As one body, they froze in place. Mark could feel his heart speed up. Whatever was going to happen was about to start. His lips moved in silent prayer.

José and Luis took the lead and stood together as the others gathered around them. They huddled in the roadway, ears straining as directions were given in hurried whispers.

"You will wait here while two of us go on ahead," José instructed. *"Raul, you and me will go down below and check things out."*

They were already closer than the afternoon's scouting party had gotten to the orchard. But still not knowing what was waiting for them over the rise sent a chill through the men's bodies. José and Raul crept over the top of the rise while the rest waited in the shadows on the other side. They would soon know if this was, in fact, the place they were seeking.

Tim Connell sidled next to the priest and cleared his throat. "Man, I could use a beer," he murmured.

Which is the last thing you need right now, Mark thought. But instead, he replied, "We'll know in a few minutes, I guess."

"Do you think she's here?"

Father Townsend was not sure. And even if Angelina Sandoval Ybarra was down there, he was not sure she was still alive. But he said none of it to her husband. He left Tim's question unanswered. The two fell silent, each with his own thoughts, as they waited for José and Raul.

Thirty minutes after they left, the two men returned, hurrying quietly along the dirt track. The others gathered about them. José did the talking. He told them the entrance to the orchard was blocked by a tall eight-foot chain-link gate. There was a watchman on the other side and he was carrying a rifle. But the guard appeared pretty relaxed. He left the road regularly to patrol both sides. They had heard his footsteps as he walked along the other side of the mesh windbreak. José had new information about that, too. From what they could tell, the mesh was hiding a chain-link fence on the other side. They were guessing that the entire orchard was surrounded by a high fence, hidden behind the mesh. Raul suspected it might be electrified, but they did not get close enough to check. And there was one other thing they discovered.

"On this side of the windbreak there is broken glass," José informed them. *"Raul stepped on a piece that went almost all the way through his shoe. There is glass all over the place, so be careful where you walk."*

"Por que?" asked Luis. And for Father Townsend's benefit, he added in English, "Why would they have broken glass on the ground outside?"

When Mark understood what he was saying, he started nodding. But in the darkness none of them noticed. Then he spoke up in a firm voice, "They're inside." There was no doubt in his voice. "That's why there's glass. They're still barefoot."

"*Ahhhh, sí,*" Luis acknowledged.

Father Townsend was now convinced that the men and women spirited away from the Vigil Room were behind the fenced orchard. The glass, the mesh screen, and the high fence—even the armed watchman—might be there to help hide the Millennium Star, but the elaborate security was in place to keep people in as much as to keep others out. He was sure of it. There were enough precautions to prevent anyone from getting in or out except through the guarded gate blocking the road. He fingered the edges of his mustache as he contemplated the challenge ahead of them.

Meanwhile, the others began to argue among themselves. José and Raul wanted to return to the trucks and drive them in to burst through the gate. But Luis cautioned that a direct attack might endanger the ones inside. Tim sided with Luis. His thoughts were on Angelina, and if she was inside he wanted to do nothing that would expose her to any more danger. And Victor Chacon had his own ideas about digging under the fence.

Brother Grib was doing his best to translate the argument for Mark, but the priest waved him off. Father Townsend was considering another plan and the others were distracting him. He turned and walked away until their voices were nothing more than murmurings in the darkness behind him.

José and Raul had seen just the one guard. Father Townsend was guessing there would be others, but not many. He was sure the people inside the orchard were carefully watched and more than likely locked up at night. They would have to be watched closely during the daytime, when they worked in the orchard, but at night they probably would pose little threat. At night the real danger lay beyond the fence. Whoever was standing guard, the Jesuit reasoned, was more concerned with what was outside the fence. In the morning that would change. But the remote and hidden location, plus the secured perimeter, probably meant there were only a few sentries keeping watch. Father Townsend started back toward the group still arguing at the side of the road, his own plan of attack now in place. He only needed to convince the others.

When Ignatius Loyola lived in Rome, his Jesuits were considered the young upstarts of the Church. And they were looked on with more than suspicion by some of the Vatican's old guard. Over the years, Ignatius let go of his skills in soldiering and adopted the gentle art of diplomacy. Frontal attacks by force seldom did any good, he learned, especially in Rome. He used to remind his companions that it did not necessarily mean you were giving up if you entered through a door opened by others. Once you get inside, the Basque saint told them, you can lead them back out your own way.

TWENTY-EIGHT

The gate into the orchard was illuminated by two lights attached to poles, one on either side. They threw down bright yellow pools of light; one inside the fence, and one spilling across the road in front of the gate. The guard had a clear view of the last twenty-five feet of roadway leading to the gate, but beyond that everything was black. And the brightness of the lights only made the surrounding darkness all the more complete. If it was his decision to make, he would have shot the two lights out and stood in the dark. His eyes would adjust and he could see further. Besides, he felt like a sitting duck. Anyone out there had a clean shot at him. So as much as possible, the man stayed back and tried to blend into the surrounding shadows. Not that there was much to worry about anyway. Not in this godforsaken place.

Because of those damn lights, he heard the man before he saw him. And he had his rifle pointed outside, held at the ready when the Mexican stumbled out of the darkness from the road in front of the gate. His dirty T-shirt was torn in several spots and his dusty jeans had tears, too. He was limping badly, and when the guard looked he could see the man's feet were a bloody mess. He kept his hands raised above his head as he cautiously approached the guard.

"Señor," he called in a weak, frightened voice. *"Señor, don't shoot. I give up. Please don't hurt me."*

The guard's Spanish was not that good, but he could tell the kid was scared and surrendering. How the hell he got over the fence in the first place . . . Whoever was guarding the sheds was going to get his butt kicked. With his rifle pointed at the young man's chest, he motioned him closer to the gate. His escape could not have been easy. The kid was a mess. His clothes were shredded by the fence's barbed wire and the broken glass had done a number on his feet. They were red with blood. He saw the frightened look on the youth's face and the guard waved his rifle menacingly as he motioned him closer. For once, he has happy to have some light. He could imagine how frightening it was for the kid, stumbling around in the dark through the sage and over the glass and sharp rocks, not knowing where he was or which way to go. The lights must have drawn the Mexican back to the gate just like the dumb insects fluttering under the lamps' bright arcs. The stupid kid had no idea where he was, but he was smart enough not to stray too far. Not with his feet cut up like that. Satisfied he was not going to try anything dumb, the guard lowered his rifle and unlatched the gate. Motioning to the young Mexican, he waved him inside.

The kid was shaking like a madman as he stumbled through the gate. When he stepped inside, he crumpled to the ground. Alarmed, the guard bent over to help him. There was a heavy *thwunk* and he sprawled unconscious in the dust beside the kid.

Angel Velasquez sat up and began wiping the blood off his feet. Enough had dripped out of José's bloodied nose to look convincing. He jumped up from the ground with a huge grin on his face, looking like he had just won an Oscar. Raul tossed aside his rock and, with Tim Connell's assistance, started dragging the guard out of the light. The rest slipped through the gate and Luis carefully reset the latch.

"Are you okay?" Luis asked Velasquez.

"Sí," Angel replied with a shrug. *"No problema."*

Walking up to the armed guard at the gate was one of the most frightening things he had ever done. There had been no way of guessing how the guard would react when he saw Angel coming toward him with his hands in the air. When the posted guard figured one of the Mexicans was loose, there was no telling what he would do. Angel's frightened look and shaking hands were not an act. But it had worked just as Padre Mark predicted that it would, and now they were inside. He was still grinning.

Safely away from the light, the eight men regrouped. From here on, things would get much more dangerous.

They knew the road would lead them to the buildings that were spotted earlier in the day. But if there were other guards, the road was the most likely place to encounter them. Moving through the trees was next to impossible. The limbs hung so low that they would almost have to crawl beneath them. Instead, they decided to walk in single file on either side of the dirt road, trying to stay as close to the trees as possible. The lead man on either side would keep a sharp eye out for anyone or anything moving on the road in front of them. The further they could get undetected, the better.

José Ramirez had the guard's rifle slung over his shoulder and he led the way along the left side. Luis and Angel followed behind him. The Anglos—Mark, Dennis, and Tim—followed Raul along the right side. They moved as quickly and quietly as they could.

The air around them was heavy with the sweet, spicy scent of ripening apples. It was the same succulent odor Father Townsend had smelled at Patowski's nursery. Even without examining the fruit in the trees, Mark knew they were moving through an entire orchard of Millennium Stars, ready for harvest. He could almost taste the sharp, crisp sweetness.

Until they reached the outer perimeter of the buildings, they saw no one. And even then, there were only two. They were sitting on an apple lug next to one of the sheds, smoking cigarettes. The murmur of their voices caught the attention of the men creeping toward them. But sneaking up on them was out of the question. The two guards were in an open area that was well lit. One of them had a holster strapped to his side, and there was a rifle leaning next to the other. Horrified, Mark spotted Raul Santos raising his pistol and pointing it at one of the guards. He reached out quickly and pulled it down.

"No," he hissed. "No shooting." He could not see Raul's face in the dark, but he could feel his anger and hear the man's exasperated breath. "No shooting," he repeated firmly.

The men remained crouched in the shadows of the trees near the edge of the clearing, watching the two guards, waiting for something to happen. Angel's trick at the gate would not work again. Something else was needed.

Father Townsend's eyes swept over the circular clearing, looking for some way they could get closer. There were five buildings. The wide doors into the nearest one were open and he could see the outlines of tractors and farm machinery inside. The next one had stove pipes rising above the roof; then a smaller building, more of an enclosed hut. The guards were in front of the largest, which looked like a long barrack. There were two doors along the side facing the other buildings and several small windows that were barred. Completing the circle was a small wooden farmhouse, sadly in need of repair. A large dark pickup was parked in front. In back of the last two buildings the priest could see the squared, flat roofs of two tall storage units rising into the night sky. They looked just like all the other fruit warehouses he had seen in the valley. The priest was guessing there would be no guards next to the warehouses, so some of them could sneak around behind. But if bars covered the windows in front of the barrack, the same would be true in the back.

He began to turn toward Dennis, to whisper his frustration in his ear, when something caught his eye. There was movement to their right, just under the first row of trees, about fifteen feet away. He heard Grib's breath stop short. He saw it, too. Raul squirmed in his place—sensing something was wrong. Panicked, Mark looked behind them. Tim Connell was gone.

The Millennium Star fell out of the night sky, landing at the guards' feet with a dull thud. Both men leapt up, dropping their cigarettes and grabbing their weapons. The one with the rifle swept the clearing in quick, jerky arcs. The man with the pistol cautiously crouched down beside the apple bin. Another apple landed on the ground in front of them.

"What the hell!" the one with the rifle exclaimed loudly. "Who's out there?"

There was only silence.

Raul had his gun raised, pointed at the guards. Mark was trying to spot Tim through the trees, but the man had moved again and was out of sight.

From the left side came a brittle snap. Both guards swiveled, pointing their guns. Moments later, a third Millennium Star splattered hard against the apple bin. But it was thrown from the right and the two men swung back around and started cautiously moving in that direction. The next apple landed heavily against the barrack and its wooden wall reverberated with the sound. From inside came a startled cry of surprise. The one with the pistol suddenly lunged forward, sighted, and fired. The retort was sudden and loud and from inside the building came several more fearful shouts. With their attention fixed on the trees in front of them, the guards never saw the three shadows rushing behind them from out of the dark.

Angel's body left the ground as he leapt forward and his shoulder smashed into the lower back of one. The rifle fell from his hands as the man collapsed in pain. The guard with the pistol started to turn, but not in time. Victor Chacon plowed heavily into the man, knocking him to the ground. José rushed behind with the rifle. The others dashed forward, Raul shouting and waving his pistol. There were more voices beginning to call out from inside the barrack. As Dennis and Raul joined the fray, Mark veered right, heading into the orchard.

"Tim," he cried out. "Tim! Are you okay?" He listened for a response, then yelled again, "Tim Connell!"

Ducking below the tree limbs, he stumbled into the orchard's darkness, hunting for the man, calling his name. There was no answer and the priest's eyes searched around the trees, desperately trying to see through the blackness. "Tim," he shouted. "Tim! Answer me!" He heard a groan and dodged to his right. A black tree limb slapped the side of his face and Mark felt a sharp pain on his cheek. Another small sound pulled him further to the right and then he made out the crumpled shape behind a tree. He fell on his knees in front of Connell, his hands brushing against the man's side.

"Tim, can you hear me? Are you okay?"

Connell moaned softly.

Father Townsend carefully rolled him onto his back. In the dark he could see nothing, and he let his hands move cautiously over the man's body. His fingers found wetness on Tim's chest, near his left shoulder. Connell groaned in pain. Mark could still hear the sounds of struggling and angry voices behind him. There was nothing he could do for Tim alone, in the dark. He needed help. Rising to his feet, he stood over the wounded man.

"Tim, I'll be right back," he promised. "Lie still and try not to move. I'm going to get help, I'll be right back." He had no choice. He started dodging through the trees, back toward the others. Mark had no idea how badly Connell was wounded, but he knew he had to get help to move him.

When Father Townsend emerged from the orchard he was behind the small farmhouse. He could see the glow from lights and could hear loud voices. It sounded like the fighting was over. He started to jog toward the front of the house and was about to call out for help when suddenly a bright light hit him square in the face. Like a deer blinded by headlights, he froze.

"Father Townsend?" The voice was filled with surprise.

Mark squinted but could see nothing past the bright beam shining in his eyes.

"Father Townsend? Is that you?"

He nodded.

The voice chuckled as the light began moving closer.

"I never would have imagined . . ." The voice stopped but the light kept coming.

"There's a man hurt back there," Mark began, pointing over his back. "He's bleeding and . . ."

"Yes, I heard the shot. By the way, I know you can't see it, but there is a gun pointed at you. Please don't make any sudden moves."

The Jesuit had already figured that out. "What are you going to do, Mr. Fairbanks? There's no way you're going to make it out to your truck. Why don't you give up now, before someone else gets hurt? Let me go get some help for Tim Connell."

The light stopped. Marshall Fairbanks was standing about eight feet in front of the priest, too far for Mark to try and lunge forward. He could just make out the man's silhouette behind the flashlight.

"Let me go get help," Father Townsend pleaded.

"Turn around," Fairbanks harshly ordered. "Now move!"

He felt a hand in his back as Fairbanks pushed him forward. He was hurrying him toward the storage units in back of the other buildings. Mark was hoping someone would notice the flashlight's beam bobbing in the dark near the edge of the orchard, but no voices called out. He heard the others talking loudly in front of the buildings and considered yelling for help, but then remembered the gun.

"Where are we going?" he asked.

"Just keep walking, Father," the man instructed. "I'll tell you when we're there."

They were moving behind the barrack. Loud, excited voices were coming from inside. People were beginning to move about and Father Townsend figured the circular clearing would soon be crowded with Mexicans. There was no way Marshall Fairbanks could reach his pickup truck without being spotted. And unless the man had an alternate means of escape, that was his only way out. But he obviously had something planned—he was pushing Mark forward, directly toward one of the apple storage units.

The massive metal door to the unit was closed but Fairbanks, still standing behind the priest, told him how to unlock it. Mark fumbled with the catch but managed to get it open. There was a sigh as the door's seal broke and it rolled back. From over his shoulder, Fairbanks suddenly reached forward and flicked a switch. The inside of the cavernous room was flooded with light.

Angelina Sandoval Ybarra, suddenly awakened, sat up on her cot. After long hours in total darkness, she was blinded by the bright light. She strained to try to see who was at the door. She looked pale and tired. Her hair was matted and her clothes badly soiled and wrinkled. Her eyes filled with fright as she spotted the two figures in the doorway.

"Angelina?" Mark's voice bounced crazily inside the empty room.

"Father Townsend?" Confused, she stood up, stumbling slightly. "Is that you?"

Mark began to move forward but Fairbanks's voice stopped him.

"You stay," he commanded. "Angelina, get over here." Still dazed, the woman stood in place. "Now!" he growled.

Fairbanks had them walk in front of him, side by side, as he directed their steps back toward the clearing. He stood close behind them, the gun trained on their backs. As they drew near the lighted area, he tossed his flashlight aside.

"Walk slowly toward the truck," he instructed, "and don't make any sudden moves. If I have to shoot either one of you, I will. But if we do this right, no one gets hurt."

Mark could hear the desperation in his voice now. Fairbanks was just as scared as they were. Angelina was still having trouble walking and Mark reached out a hand to steady her.

"That's right," Fairbanks urged, "stay close together."

The clearing was filled with Mexicans released from their barracks. There was lots of movement and everyone seemed to be talking at once. Father Townsend searched the crowd for Dennis Grib, but there were too many people moving around. At first no one seemed to notice the three of them edging their way toward the truck. Fairbanks was doing his best to keep low, crouching behind the two of them. But then José Ramirez stepped forward. Reaching behind him, he grabbed Luis Castillo's arm and pulled him back around, pointing toward Father Townsend and the dazed-looking woman beside him. Luis's face lit up when he recognized Angelina and he began walking toward them.

Marshall Fairbanks stood upright, raising his gun until it was pointed directly at Angelina's head.

"Don't come any closer," he warned.

His words were unnecessary. As soon as he saw Marshall Fairbanks, Castillo froze in his tracks. As the gunman continued herding his hostages toward his truck, others in the clearing began to notice. Their voices and their movements stopped cold. Now over three dozen people were silently watching as the three of them slowly neared the truck.

"Todos quédense no se muven." Fairbanks's Spanish held a nasal twang, but his words were clear and everyone understood. No one moved. From near the back of the crowd, Mark spotted Raul Santos. He knew the man was probably still carrying his pistol, but there were too many people in front of him and Marshall Fairbanks was effectively using their two bodies to shield himself. They were only a few feet away from the truck now, and Mark could hear Fairbanks's raspy breath as he urged them closer.

They reached the passenger side and Fairbanks ordered Father Townsend to open the door and climb in. "Scoot over. You're going to drive." With his gun still carefully trained on Angelina's head, he shoved the woman inside, quickly climbing in after her. He kept the door open though, allowing the people a close look at the pistol in his hand. Pulling the keys from his pocket, he tossed them to the Jesuit. "Get us out of here," he brusquely ordered.

The big pickup rumbled to life and Mark began to pull forward. The crowd of Mexicans started to inch forward, forming a large half circle around the truck. They looked as if they were going to block the way. Fairbanks waved his pistol menacingly and they slowly parted. Mark continued nudging the truck forward and they left the clearing. The headlights lit up the narrow dirt road and apple trees on both sides.

"Where are you taking us?" Angelina asked in a thick, dull voice.

"Just as far as I need you," Fairbanks replied. "Don't try doing anything dumb and you'll be all right."

"It would be better for you if you gave yourself up," Mark told him, keeping his eyes on the dirt track in front of them. "You won't get away."

"Just keep driving."

"Why don't you at least let Angelina go," Townsend suggested, "and take me. I won't try anything."

"She's my insurance. If anyone is going to be left behind, it'll be you, Father."

Mark was about to speak, but caught himself. Marshall Fairbanks knew what he was doing. He was a ruthless business man, used to calculating the odds and taking his risks. Trying to cajole him would do no good.

"Please let me go." Angelina's body seemed to fall in on itself as she began to whimper. Her exhaustion and shock were taking over.

"I can't do that." He sounded almost regretful. "You know I can't."

The gate would be coming up soon. Mark's eyes were trying to see through the darkness. If he could not cajole, maybe reasoning would work.

"I know you're not a murderer, Mr. Fairbanks. So if you end this right now, the worst you'll face are the charges for taking those people back there. Probably something like kidnapping.''

Marshall Fairbanks snorted. ''It's a little worse than that, I think, Father. Let's be real.'' He stopped and leaned forward to look directly at the priest behind the wheel. ''But how can you be sure I didn't kill Gabriel?''

Father Townsend glanced to his side. ''Because I know Angelina did.'' The woman moaned softly and buried her head in her hands. Mark rested his right hand on the woman's shoulder.

''How did you figure that?'' Fairbanks wanted to know.

The Jesuit looked over the woman's slumped shoulders into Fairbanks's eyes. ''She's alive,'' he said. ''If you had killed Brother Gabriel, you would have killed her, too. You're not a murderer. I figure if she was just a witness, she'd be dead. Keeping her alive means she's more than a witness.''

They were at the gate and Mark stopped the truck.

''But that doesn't mean I won't kill if I have to. Now turn off the motor and bring the keys,'' Fairbanks instructed. ''We're both getting out—slowly and at the same time. Angelina, you stay inside and don't try anything stupid. Father, this gun is going to be on you the whole time, so don't you do anything either. Let's go!''

The two men slowly opened their doors and stepped out. As soon as he was clear, Marshall Fairbanks swung out in front and trained the sights of the gun onto Father Townsend. Nervously, the priest raised his hands and began walking forward.

''I want you to very carefully open the gate,'' Fairbanks commanded, coming up behind him. ''Very carefully.''

Father Townsend could feel the gun in his back as he approached the gate. Fairbanks was taking no chances. But with Angelina still inside the truck, Mark would not have tried escaping anyway. He fumbled with the gate's latch. ''Hurry up!''

It clicked open. Just as Mark grabbed hold to swing it back, there was a sudden and noisy crash in the thick trees near the roadside. Impulsively, Fairbanks swung around, taking aim. From out of the orchard stumbled the guard Raul and Tim had dragged in there earlier. The Jesuit took advantage of the brief moment Fairbanks was distracted. Quickly, he yanked on the gate, swinging it into Fairbanks's body, smashing it hard against his right side. The gun fired and the guard let out a yelp, diving into the dirt. Father Townsend pulled the heavy gate back and swung it once again, knocking it with all his strength against the man. Fairbanks dropped his gun as he tried blocking the blow. He quickly stooped over to find it and Mark threw himself forward, crashing into him, pushing him over and onto the ground. He threw himself on top and they started to wrestle. Although he was younger, Father Townsend was no match for the brawny orchardist. Marshall Fairbanks squirmed out from under him and gained the upper hand, straddling the priest's body. He landed a solid blow against the side of Mark's head and pulled his arm far back to deliver another.

"Stop it! Stop!" Angelina's broken voice was loud and fierce. "I'll shoot you!" She was holding Fairbanks's pistol in both hands, standing over them. She kept the barrel aimed steadily at his head. The man hesitated, his arm still raised.

In a cold, determined voice she warned him, "Don't. You know that I will do it."

TWENTY-NINE

"So you think she really would have shot him?"

Joe Bones leaned across the table and filled Mark's coffee cup, ignoring his attempts to wave him off. During the last twelve hours the priest guessed he had drank about five gallons of the stuff. He would never sleep again.

"Oh yeah, I think she would have." Automatically he lifted the brimming cup to his lips, but then stopped to explain. "By that time Angelina would have done anything. She thought it was over anyway."

"The poor woman," Bones commiserated. "She's got to be going through hell right now."

The Yakima police had Angelina Sandoval Ybarra in custody. Her husband, Tim Connell, was under police guard at the hospital, being treated for his gunshot wound. Mark knew that Bill Yoder, the detective on the case, wanted desperately to charge one or the other for the murder of Brother Gabriel—he made that quite clear. But whether or not the district attorney's office was going to go along was still a question. Father Townsend had tried his best to persuade them otherwise. But Yoder was looking on the Jesuit's own participation in the affair with suspicion and he warned Father Townsend he was not off the hook yet. If he could find any charges that would stick . . . He let the threat hang and reluctantly released the priest along with Brother Grib. By then it was after noon and both Jesuits were exhausted.

Bones and Father Stanley were waiting impatiently, and as soon as their fellow Jesuits were released they hustled them past the pack of reporters and back to their own residence. A determined-looking Paul Stanley was left scowling on the front porch, doing his best to turn away inquisitive reporters. Dennis had stumbled off to bed shortly after they arrived at the house. Both of them had gone through grueling interrogations and Grib could no longer keep awake. But as exhausted as he felt, Mark Townsend thought that sleep would be impossible. With half a coffee plantation sloshing inside him, mixing with the adrenaline rush from last night's fight, any sleep felt a long way off. So he sat wearily at the table while his friend kept him company. Besides, there was still someone Mark needed to hear from before he could rest.

When Angelina repeated her threat to shoot, Father Townsend could feel Fairbanks's grip loosen. It was as if the orchardist finally realized it was over. He carefully climbed off Father Townsend and sat heavily in the road. Angelina kept the pistol trained on him as he slowly placed his hands on top of his head.

The next two hours were a blur of rushed activity. None of the eight men involved had really considered what they were going to do if they actually succeeded in releasing the imprisoned Mexicans. All along it had been their hope, but the actual accomplishment of it was unexpected.

A very nervous Father Townsend sat in the back of the truck with Fairbanks's pistol turned on the orchardist and the still-dazed guard as Angelina hurriedly drove the pickup back through the orchard. The crowd was still in the center of the compound when they arrived. Most of them were still looking stunned as they waited for someone to give them directions. Luis Castillo, José Ramirez, and Raul Santos were doing their best to keep order. They had Victor Chacon and Angel Velasquez keeping watch over the captured guards while they plotted what to do next. But Fairbanks's escape, using Angelina and Father Townsend as hostages, had left them confused and uncertain.

Brother Grib searched the orchard for Tim Connell and, with the help of several of the Mexicans, carried him out of the orchard and into the farmhouse. Connell was still bleeding from the gunshot wound in his shoulder, but he was conscious and his injury was not life-threatening. When Brother Grib told him Fairbanks had left with Angelina, he started to cry. Then, when his wife came rushing in to find him, Tim cried all the harder.

They put off calling for help until they knew it was safe. By the time the first sheriff's car pulled into the orchard, followed closely behind by an aid car, most of the people had disappeared. There were only a handful left. Marshall Fairbanks and his three henchmen were locked inside the deserted barrack. Angelina was in the small house with her husband, and the two Jesuits were standing in the center of the clearing with Luis Castillo. The only vehicles left were the Dodge Ram owned by Fairbanks and Dennis Grib's dusty beater, still parked at the first gate leading into the property.

When the questions started, none of them made any effort to hide the fact that forty people had already fled into the night. The scores of footprints and numerous tire tracks in the dirt made it evident there had been a recent mass exodus, so why deny it?

Father Townsend patiently explained it three times to the young deputy questioning him, and every time the poor man shook his head in disbelief. Forty people simply do not walk away from a major crime scene, he tried to argue.

"You don't understand," Mark said with a smile. "The ones who left are illegals. They were scared. And if they had stayed here, right now Immigration would be herding them into buses and carting them away, isn't that so? Which means they would have escaped from one confinement only to step into another. None of them wanted that, so they left."

"But that's against the law," the young deputy tried to insist.

Father Townsend continued smiling. The guy would get it eventually.

And enough of them would reappear to make certain the charges against Fairbanks and Patowski would stick. José Ramirez and Raul Santos would make sure of that. Ramirez had already volunteered the testimony of his son, Paco. The reuniting of the father with his son was a loud and emotional affair, carried on in front of all the others standing about. But no one minded their tears and shouts of joy—they were not the only ones crying.

"You're dozing off, partner. Why don't you go to bed?"

"Huh . . . ?" Mark's eyes shot open and his hand jerked, spilling coffee. Joe LaBelle was grinning across the table from him.

"Go to bed, Mark."

"I can't," he told his friend, "not until Raul calls. He said he'd phone as soon as they have everyone back where they belong."

Raul, José, Victor, and Angel took charge of loading the pickups and spiriting the people out of the orchard. Those who remained behind waited an hour before calling for the sheriff, giving the others plenty of time to reach Yakima. By then it was too late for the police to mount an effective search for the disappeared. They were back among their own people. Thirty-seven anonymous campesinos, impossible to pick out of the forty-five thousand Hispanics in the valley.

"If you're not gonna sleep, then keep talking," Bones demanded. "Tell me about Angelina and Bro Gabe. What actually happened out there at the park?"

Mark shrugged. "I'm not really sure," he admitted. "Angie was still pretty confused and was having a hard time talking about it. From what I gathered, she went to the park early that morning, just like Brother Gabriel asked her."

"With her husband's gun?" Joe interrupted.

Mark gave a slight nod. Angelina was a brave woman, but not dumb. Meeting a strange man like Brother Gabriel in a secluded spot in the middle of the night was not something she would do without taking precautions. After Connell had threatened to shoot the evangelist, she had insisted on locking the gun in his car. Father Townsend could only guess the rest.

"When she left, she took Tim's car because she had the keys and knew the gun was inside it," he explained to Father LaBelle. "So when she got to the park, she had it with her. I'm sure she was nervous. Who wouldn't be? Anyway, she got to the viewing platform where Brother said he would meet her." Mark stopped talking. He was tracing his finger through the spilled coffee on the kitchen table, arranging the liquid in thin brown lines across the surface. He was trying to picture what must have happened when the woman, nervous and probably frightened, was confronted by the men on the platform.

"Gabriel wasn't alone," Mark said in a quiet voice.

"He wasn't?"

Townsend nodded. "He never was. Angelina told me that whenever he went out, he had someone with him—usually that Tony guy. And enough people had overheard Brother Gabriel asking to meet her. So they knew something was up." He hesitated, then continued. "I suspect Brother Gabriel had finally figured out what was happening."

"Which was . . . ?"

"About the Vigil Room. His wife told Dennis and me that he was never quite comfortable with the idea that people were being raptured. I think he finally figured out what was going on, Joe. And I think he was going to tell Angelina. He was going to blow the whistle on Patowski and Fairbanks."

Father LaBelle was scowling. "You mean to tell me he wasn't in on the scam? Not from the beginning?"

Mark shook his head. "I don't think so, Joe. I think the guy really believed something spiritual was taking place. The way that Sister Elizabeth described his ministry in California . . . it didn't sound fake. He really believed he was doing the Lord's work. A guy like that just doesn't start kidnapping people."

"So Patowski and Fairbanks took advantage of the naive preacher?"

"They set him up. They found themselves an evangelist who could draw in Mexicans—exactly the ones they were looking for. Simple laborers, young and strong, not well-educated. Just who they wanted."

LaBelle snorted. "To be slaves!"

"That's exactly what they were doing; using slave labor to work in their orchard. They would go out to the roadside and handpick the people they wanted, then lock them in the Vigil Room. Later that night, they came back through the tunnel and took them out."

"They had to be nuts," protested LaBelle. "Both those yokels have enough money to hire half of Yakima if they want."

"But half of Yakima wouldn't keep their secret. They were getting ready to spring a huge surprise on the valley by introducing the Millennium Star. When Dennis and I saw Patowski, he told us that it was going to take over the apple business. So they needed people in their orchard who they could control and keep quiet. And besides, they were making even more money by not having to pay wages."

"I've always said that money's a lot like grace," Bones drawled, "you can never have too much of either. Although I think those goons have proved me wrong. But then why kill the golden goose?"

"Gabriel, you mean?" Mark went back to drawing with the spilt coffee. About this, he felt less sure. "I don't think that's what they intended. I think they were hoping to find a way to shut him up. I think they actually intended to kill Angelina. And maybe make it look like Gabriel did it. I'm not exactly sure what happened in the park, but what they didn't figure on was Angelina showing up with a gun and trying to defend herself. Whatever happened out there . . . in the darkness and confusion . . . she ended up shooting the wrong man."

"You're sure of that, Mark? She told you?"

"Pretty much. She told me that she never intended to shoot Brother Gabriel—that it was an accident."

"But then they made it look like a murder."

"It wasn't very hard," Mark said. "The gun already had her prints on it. All they had to do was make her and her car disappear and the next day the police were combing the state for her. Once Patowski and Fairbanks had her locked away, they could keep going as planned. They might not have gotten all the laborers they wanted, but they had enough for the harvest."

Father LaBelle suddenly snapped his fingers. "That's why they took Gabe's body!" he crowed. Seeing the puzzled expression on Mark's face, he explained, "If you still need more workers, what better way to keep them coming than to fake a miracle? As long as the Mexicans figured Brother Gabriel was still going, they'd keep hanging around. If Patowski and Fairbanks needed any more slaves they could keep picking 'em like fleas off a hound."

Mark had to admit that, in a perverse way, it made sense. When someone is finally able to deaden his own moral affront and give in to darker forces, anything must seem possible. Then there is nothing you can do that does not seem acceptable.

But in reality, of course, the end very seldom justifies the means.

The phone on the wall rang only once before LaBelle grabbed it.

"Hello!" he barked, then automatically added, "St. Joseph's." He scowled at himself, realizing he was at home, not at the church. *"¿Hola? ¿Quien es?"* Bones listened, nodding, then said into the phone, "Okay. *Bueno. Hasta.*"

Mark waited anxiously until he hung up. "Well?"

Bones leaned back in his chair and gave his friend a satisfied smile. "That was Raul. You can relax, he said everyone is safe and it's okay if you want to go home. He said to tell you that he wants to hear you preach sometime. You were good out in the orchard so you're probably okay in the church. He said to go home and tell your own people what you saw.''

Blame it on the lack of sleep or the stress he was under, but Father Townsend's eyes began to mist over. He swallowed hard. ''Thanks, Joe. I think I will.''

Mysteries with a touch
of the mystical
by

JAMES D. DOSS

THE SHAMAN LAUGHS
72690-4/$5.99 US/$7.99 Can

THE SHAMAN SINGS
72496-0/$5.99 US/$7.99 Can

THE SHAMAN'S BONES
79029-7/$5.99 US/$7.99 Can

THE SHAMAN'S GAME
79030-0/$5.99 US/$7.99 Can

AN ARCHEOLOGIST DIGS UP MURDER IN THE ALAN GRAHAM MYSTERIES BY

MALCOLM SHUMAN

THE MERIWETHER MURDER
79424-1/$5.99 US/$7.99 Can

BURIAL GROUND
79423-3/$5.50 US/$7.50 Can

ASSASSIN'S BLOOD
80485-9/$5.99 US/$7.99 Can